THE
WARMASTERS

DAVID WEBER
ERIC FLINT
DAVID DRAKE

THE WARMASTERS

EDITED BY
BILL FAWCETT

THE WARMASTERS

Copyright © 2002 by Bill Fawcett & Associates.
"Ms. Midshipwoman Harrington" copyright © 2001 by David Weber. "Islands" copyright © 2002 by Eric Flint. "Choosing Sides" copyright © 2002 by David Drake.

A Baen Books Original

Baen Publishing Enterprises
P.O. Box 1403
Riverdale, NY 10471
www.baen.com

ISBN: 0-7434-3534-6

Cover art by David Mattingly

First printing, May 2002

Library of Congress Cataloging-in-Publication Data

The warmasters / by David Weber, Eric Flint, David Drake.
    p. cm.
    "A Baen Books original"—T.p. verso.
    Contents: Ms. Midshipwoman Harrington / by David Weber — Island / by Eric
    Flint — Choosing sides / by David Drake.
    ISBN 0-7434-3534-6
    1. Science fiction, American. 2. War stories, American. I. Weber, David, 1952–
    Ms. Midshipwoman Harrington. II. Flint, Eric. Island. III. Drake, David.
    Choosing sides.

PS648.S3 W377 2002
813'0876208358—dc21   2001058997

Distributed by Simon & Schuster
1230 Avenue of the Americas
New York, NY 10020

Production by Windhaven Press, Auburn, NH
Printed in the United States of America

10   9   8   7   6   5   4   3   2   1

Contents

Ms. Midshipwoman Harrington

David Weber

"That looks like your snotty, Senior Chief."

The Marine sentry's low-pitched voice exuded an oddly gleeful sympathy. It was the sort of voice in which a Marine traditionally informed one of the Navy's "vacuum-suckers" that his trousers had just caught fire or something equally exhilarating, and Senior Chief Petty Officer Roland Shelton ignored the jarhead's tone with the lofty disdain of any superior life form for an evolutionary inferior. Yet it was a bit harder than usual this time as his eyes followed the corporal's almost invisible nod and picked the indicated target out of the crowded space dock gallery. She was certainly *someone's* snotty, he acknowledged without apparently so much as looking in her direction. Her midshipwoman's uniform was immaculate, but both it and the tethered counter-grav locker towing behind her were so new he expected to hear her squeak. There was something odd about that locker, too, as if something else half its size had been piggybacked onto it, although he paid that little attention. Midshipmen were always turning up with oddball bits and pieces of personalized gear that they hoped didn't quite violate Regs. Half the time they were wrong, but there would be time enough to straighten that out later if this particular snotty came aboard Shelton's ship. And, he conceded, she seemed to be headed for *War Maiden*'s docking tube, although that might simply be a mistake on her part.

He hoped.

She was a tall young woman, taller than Shelton himself, with dark brown, fuzz-cut hair, and a severe, triangular face which seemed to have been assembled solely from a nose which might charitably be called "strong" and huge, almond-shaped eyes. At the moment the face as a whole showed no expression at all, but the light in those eyes was bright enough to make an experienced petty officer groan in resignation.

She also looked to be about thirteen years old. That probably meant she was a third-generation prolong recipient, but recognizing the cause didn't do a thing to make her look any more mature. Still, she moved well, he admitted almost grudgingly. There was an athletic grace to her carriage and an apparent assurance at odds with her youth, and she avoided collisions with ease as she made her way through the people filling the gallery, almost as if she were performing some sort of free-form dance.

Had that been all Shelton had been able to discern about her, he would probably have put her down (provisionally and a bit hopefully) as somewhat above the average of the young gentlemen and ladies senior Navy noncoms were expected to transform from pigs' ears into silk purses. Unfortunately, it was not all that he could discern, and it took most of his thirty-four T-years of experience not to let his dismay show as he observed the prick-eared, wide-whiskered, six-limbed, silky-pelted Sphinx treecat riding on her shoulder.

A treecat. A treecat in *his* ship. And in the midshipmen's

compartment, at that. The thought was enough to give a man who believed in orderly procedures and Navy traditions hives, and Shelton felt a strong urge to reach out and throttle the expressionlessly smirking Marine at his shoulder.

For a few more seconds he allowed himself to hope that she might walk right past *War Maiden* to the ship she actually sought, or that she might be lost. But any possibility of dodging the pulser dart faded as she walked straight over to the heavy cruiser's tube.

Shelton and the Marine saluted, and she returned the courtesy with a crispness which managed to be both brand new and excited yet curiously mature. She gave Shelton a brief, measuring glance, almost more imagined than seen, but addressed herself solely to the sentry.

"Midshipwoman Harrington to join the ship's company, Corporal," she said in a crisp Sphinx accent, and drew a record chip in an official Navy cover slip from her tunic pocket and extended it. Her soprano was surprisingly soft and sweet for someone her height, Shelton noted as the Marine took the chip and slotted it into his memo board, although her tone was neither hesitant nor shy. Still, he had to wonder if someone who sounded as young as she looked would ever be able to generate a proper snap of command. He allowed no sign of his thoughts to cross his face, but the 'cat on her shoulder cocked its head, gazing at him with bright, grass-green eyes while its whiskers twitched.

"Yes, Ma'am," the Marine said as the chip's data matched that in his memo board and confirmed Ms. Midshipwoman Harrington's orders and legal right to come aboard *War Maiden*. He popped the chip free and handed it back to her, then nodded to Shelton. "Senior Chief Shelton's been expecting you, I believe," he said, still with that irritating edge of imperfectly concealed glee, and Harrington turned to the senior chief and arched one eyebrow.

That surprised Shelton just a bit. However composed she might appear, he'd seen thirty-plus T-years of new-penny snotties reporting for their midshipman cruises, and the light in her eyes was proof enough that she was just as excited and eager as any of the others had been. Yet that arched eyebrow held a cool authority, or perhaps assurance. It wasn't the sort of deliberately projected superiority some snotties used to hide their own anxiety or lack of confidence. It was too natural for that. But that calm, silent question, delivered with neither condescension nor defensiveness, woke a sudden glimmer of hope. There might be some solid metal in this one, the senior chief told himself, but then the 'cat wiggled its whiskers at him, and he gave himself a mental shake.

"Senior Chief Petty Officer Shelton, Ma'am," he heard himself say. "If you'll just follow me, I'll escort you to the Exec."

"Thank you, Senior Chief," she said and followed him into the tube.

With the 'cat.

Honor Harrington tried conscientiously to keep her excitement from showing as she swam the boarding tube behind Senior Chief Shelton, but it was hard. She'd known she was headed for this moment for almost half her life, and she'd sweated and worked for over three-and-a-half endless T-years at Saganami Island to reach it. Now she had, and the butterflies in her midsection propagated like particularly energetic yeast as they reached the inboard end of the tube and she caught the grab bar and swung herself through into the heavy cruiser's internal gravity behind Shelton. In her own mind, that was the symbolic moment when she left His Majesty's Space Station *Hephaestus* to enter the domain of HMS *War Maiden*, and her heart beat harder and stronger as the sights and sounds and distinctive smell of a King's starship closed about her. They were subtly different somehow from those in the space station she'd left behind. No doubt that was her imagination—one artificial environment in space was very like another, after all—but the impression of differentness, of something special waiting just for her, quivered at her core.

The treecat on her shoulder made a soft scolding sound, and her mouth quirked ever so slightly. Nimitz understood her excited joy, as well as the unavoidable trepidation that went with it, but the empathic 'cats were pragmatic souls, and he recognized the signs of Honor Harrington in exhilarated mode. More to the point, he knew the importance of getting off on the right foot aboard *War Maiden*, and she felt his claws dig just a bit deeper into her uniform tunic's specially padded shoulder in a gentle reminder to keep herself focused.

She reached up and brushed his ears in acknowledgment even as her feet found the deck of *War Maiden*'s boat bay, just outside the painted line which indicated the official separation between ship and space station. At least she hadn't embarrassed herself like one of her classmates, who had landed on the wrong side of the line during one of their short, near-space training missions! A part of her wanted to giggle in memory of the absolutely scathing look the training ship's boat bay officer of the deck had bestowed upon her fellow middy, but she suppressed the temptation and came quickly to attention and saluted the OD of *this* boat bay.

"Permission to come aboard to join the ship's company, Ma'am!" she said, and the sandy-haired ensign gave her a cool, considering look, then acknowledged the salute. She brought her hand down from her beret's brim and extended it wordlessly, and Honor produced the chip of her orders once more. The BOD performed the same ritual as the Marine sentry, then nodded, popped the chip from her board, and handed it back.

"Permission granted, Ms. Harrington," she said, much less crisply than Honor but with a certain world-weary maturity. She was, after all, at least a T-year older than Honor, with her own middy cruise safely behind her. The ensign glanced at Shelton, and Honor noticed the way the other young woman's shoulders came back ever so slightly and the way her voice crisped up as she nodded to the SCPO. "Carry on, Senior Chief," she said.

"Aye, aye, Ma'am," Shelton replied, and beckoned respectfully for Honor to follow him once more as he led her towards the lifts.

Lieutenant Commander Abner Layson sat in the chair behind his desk and made an obviously careful study of his newest potential headache's orders. Midshipwoman Harrington sat very upright in her own chair, hands folded in her lap, feet positioned at precisely the right angle, and watched the bulkhead fifteen centimeters above his head with apparent composure. She'd seemed on the edge of flustered when he'd directed her to sit rather than remain at stand-easy while he perused her paperwork, but there was little sign of that in her present demeanor. Unless, of course, the steady flicking of the very tip of her treecat's tail indicated more uneasiness in the 'cat's adopted person than she cared to admit. Interesting that she could conceal the outward signs so readily, though, if that were the case.

He let his eyes return to his reader's display, scanning the official, tersely worded contents of her personnel jacket, while he wondered what had possessed Captain Bachfisch to specifically request such an . . . unlikely prize when the snotty cruise assignments were being handed out.

A bit young, he thought. Although her third-gen prolong made her look even younger than her calendar age, she was only twenty. The Academy was flexible about admission ages, but most midshipmen entered at around eighteen or nineteen T-years of age; Harrington had been barely seventeen when she was admitted. Which was all the more surprising given what seemed to be a total lack of aristocratic connections, patronage, or interest from on high to account for it. On the other hand, her overall grades at Saganami Island had been excellent—aside from some abysmal math scores, at least—and she'd received an unbroken string of "Excellent" and "Superior" ratings from her tactical and command simulation instructors. That was worth noting. Still, he reminded himself, many an Academy overachiever had proven a sad disappointment in actual Fleet service. Scored remarkably high on the kinesthesia tests, too, although that particular requirement was becoming less and less relevant these days. Very high marks in the flight training curriculum as well, including—his eyebrows rose ever so slightly—a new Academy sailplane record. But she might be a bit on the headstrong side, maybe even the careless one, given the official reprimand noted on her Form 107FT for ignoring her flight instruments. And that stack of black marks for lack of air discipline didn't look very promising. On the other hand, they all seemed to come from a single instance. . . .

He accessed the relevant portion of her record, and something suspiciously like a snort escaped before he could throttle it. He turned it into a reasonably convincing coughing fit, but his mouth quivered as he scanned the appended note. Buzzed the Commandant's boat during the Regatta, had she? No wonder Hartley had lowered the boom on her! Still, he must have thought well of her to stop there, although the identity of her partner in crime might also have had a bit to do with it. Couldn't exactly go tossing the King's niece out, now could they? Well, not for anything short of premeditated murder, at any rate. . . .

He sighed and tipped back his chair, pinching the bridge of his nose, and glanced at her under cover of his hand. The treecat worried him. He knew it wasn't supposed to, for regulations were uncompromising on that particular subject and had been ever since the reign of Queen Adrienne. She could not legally be separated from the creature, and she'd obviously gotten through the Academy with it without creating any major waves. But a starship was a much smaller world than Saganami Island, and she wasn't the only middy aboard.

Small jealousies and envies could get out of hand on a long deployment, and she would be the only person on board authorized to take a pet with her. Oh, Layson knew the 'cats weren't really pets. It wasn't a subject he'd ever taken much personal interest in, but the creatures' sentience was well-established, as was the fact that once they empathically bonded to a human, they literally could not be separated without serious consequences for both partners. But they *looked* like pets, and most of the Star Kingdom's citizens knew even less about them than Layson did, which offered fertile ground for misunderstandings and resentment. And the fact that the Bureau of Personnel had seen fit to assign *War Maiden* a brand new assistant tac officer, and that the ATO in any ship was traditionally assigned responsibility for the training and discipline of any midshipmen assigned to her, only deepened his worries about the possible repercussions of the 'cat's presence. The exec hadn't yet had time to learn much about the ATO, but what he had learned so far did not inspire him with a lively confidence in the man's ability.

Yet even the presence of the 'cat was secondary to Layson's true concern. There had to be some reason the Captain had requested Harrington, and try though he might, the exec simply couldn't figure out what that reason might be. Such requests usually represented tokens in the patronage game the Navy's senior officers played so assiduously. They were either a way to gain the support of some well-placed potential patron by standing sponsor to a son or daughter or younger relative, or else a way to pay back a similar favor. But Harrington was a yeoman's daughter, whose only apparent aristocratic association was the highly tenuous one of having roomed with the Earl of Gold Peak's younger offspring for a bit over two T-years. That was a fairly lofty connection, or would have been if it actually existed, but Layson couldn't see any way the Captain could have capitalized on it even if it had. So what could the reason be? Layson didn't know, and that bothered him, because it was a good executive officer's job to keep himself informed of anything which might affect the smooth functioning of the ship he ran for his captain.

"Everything seems to be in order, Ms. Harrington," he told her after a moment, lowering his hand and letting his chair come back upright. "Lieutenant Santino is our assistant tac officer, which makes him your OCT officer, as well. I'll have Senior Chief Shelton deliver you to Snotty Row when we're done here, and you can report to him once you've stowed your gear. In the meantime, however, I make it a policy to spend a few minutes with new middies when they first come aboard. It gives me a chance to get to know them and to get a feel for how they'll fit in here in *War Maiden*."

He paused, and she nodded respectfully.

"Perhaps you can start off then by telling me—briefly, of course—just why you joined the Service," he invited.

"For several reasons, Sir," she said after only the briefest of pauses. "My father was a Navy doctor before he retired and went into private practice, so I was a 'Navy brat' until I was about eleven. And I've always been interested in naval history, clear back to pre-Diaspora Earth. But I suppose the most important reason was the People's Republic, Sir."

"Indeed?" Layson couldn't quite keep the surprise out of his tone.

"Yes, Sir." Her voice was both respectful and thoughtful, but it was also very serious. "I believe war with Haven is inevitable, Sir. Not immediately, but in time."

"And you want to be along for the glory and the adventure, do you?"

"No, Sir." Her expression didn't alter, despite the bite in his question. "I want to help defend the Star Kingdom. And I *don't* want to live under the Peeps."

"I see," he said, and studied her for several more seconds. That was a viewpoint he was more accustomed to hearing from far more senior—and older—officers, not from twenty-year-old midshipwomen. It was also the reason the Royal Manticoran Navy was currently involved in the biggest buildup in its history, and the main reason Harrington's graduating class was ten percent larger than the one before it. But as Harrington had just pointed out, the looming war still lurked in the uncertain future.

And her answer *still* didn't give him a clue as to why Captain Bachfisch wanted her aboard *War Maiden*.

"Well, Ms. Harrington," he said at last, "if you want to help defend the Star Kingdom, you've certainly come to the right place. And you may have an opportunity to start doing it a bit sooner than you anticipated, as well, because we've been ordered to Silesia for antipiracy duties." The young woman sat even straighter in her chair at that, and the 'cat's tail stopped twitching and froze in the curl of a question mark. "But if you truly don't harbor dreams of glory, make it a point not to start harboring them anytime soon. As you're no doubt tired of hearing, this cruise is your true final exam."

He paused, regarding her steadily, and she nodded soberly. A midshipwoman was neither fish nor fowl in many respects. Officially, she remained an officer candidate, holding a midshipwoman's warrant but not yet an officer's commission. Her warrant gave her a temporary place in the chain of command aboard *War Maiden*; it did not guarantee that she would ever hold any authority anywhere *after* this cruise, however. Her actual graduation from the Academy was assured, given her grades and academic performance, but a muffed midshipman's cruise could very well cost her any chance at one of the career tracks which led to eventual command. The Navy always needed non-line staff officers whose duties kept them safely out of the chain of command, after all, and someone who blew his or her first opportunity to shoulder responsibility outside a classroom wasn't the person one wanted commanding a King's ship. And if she screwed up too massively on this cruise, she might receive both an Academy diploma and formal notice that the Crown did not after all require her services in *any* capacity.

"You're here to learn, and the Captain and I will evaluate your performance very carefully. If you have any hope of achieving command in your own right someday, I advise you to see to it that our evaluations are positive ones. Is that understood?"

"Yes, Sir!"

"Good." He gave her a long, steady look, then produced a small smile. "It's a tradition in the Fleet that by the time a middy has survived Saganami Island, he's like a 'cat. Fling him into the Service any way you like, and he'll land on his feet. That, at least, is the type of midshipman the Academy *tries* to turn out, and it's what will be expected of you as a member of *War Maiden*'s company. In your own case, however, there is a rather special complicating factor. One, I'm certain, of which you must be fully aware. Specifically," he pointed with his chin to the treecat stretched across the top of her chair's back, "your . . . companion."

He paused, waiting to see if she would respond. But she simply met his eyes steadily, and he made a mental note that this one had composure by the bucketful.

"No doubt you're more intimately familiar with the Regs where 'cats aboard ship are concerned than I am," he went on after a moment in a tone which said she'd damned well *better* be familiar with them. "I expect you to observe them to the letter. The fact that the two of you managed to survive Saganami Island gives me some reason to hope you'll also manage to survive *War Maiden*. But I expect you to be aware that this is a much smaller environment than the Academy, and the right to be together aboard ship carries with it the responsibility to avoid any situation which might have a negative impact on the smooth and efficient functioning of this ship's company. I trust that, also, is clearly understood. By you both."

"Yes, Sir," she said once more, and he nodded.

"I am delighted to hear it. In that case, Senior Chief Shelton will see you to your quarters, such as they are. Good luck, Ms. Harrington."

"Thank you, Sir."

"Dismissed," he said, and turned back to his data terminal as the middy braced to attention once more and then followed SCPO Shelton from the compartment.

❖   ❖   ❖

Honor finished making up her bunk (with regulation "Saganami Island" corners on the sheets and a blanket taut enough to bounce a five-dollar coin), then detached the special piggyback unit from her locker and lifted the locker itself into the waiting bulkhead brackets. She grinned, remembering one of her classmates—from a dirt-grubber Gryphon family with no Navy connections at all—who had revealed his abysmal ignorance the day their first lockers were issued by wondering aloud why every one of them had to have exactly the same dimensions. That particular question had been answered on their first training cruise, and now Honor settled hers in place, opened the door, flipped off the counter-grav, and toggled the locking magnets once its weight had fully settled.

She gave it a precautionary shake, despite the glowing telltales which purported to show a solid seal. Others had trusted the same telltales when they shouldn't have, but this time they held, and she closed the door and attached the piggyback to the frame of her bunk. She took rather more care with it than she had with the locker, and Nimitz watched alertly from atop her pillow as she did so. Unlike the locker, which was standard Navy issue, she—or rather, her father, who had provided it as a graduation gift—had paid the better part of seventeen thousand Manticoran dollars for that unit. Which was money well spent in her opinion, since it was the life support module which would keep Nimitz alive if the compartment lost pressure. She made very certain that it was securely anchored, then hit the self-test key and nodded in satisfaction as the control panel blinked alive and the diagnostic program confirmed full functionality. Nimitz returned her nod with a satisfied bleek of his own, and she turned away to survey the rest of the berthing compartment known rather unromantically as "Snotty Row" while she awaited Senior Chief Shelton's return.

It was a largish compartment for a ship as small—and as old—as *War Maiden*. In fact, it was about twice the size of her Saganami Island dorm room. Of course, that dorm room had held only two people, her and her friend Michelle Henke, while this compartment was designed to house six. At the moment, only four of the bunks had sheets and blankets on them, though, so it looked as if *War Maiden* was sailing light in the middy department.

That could be good or bad, she reflected, settling into one of the spartan, unpowered chairs at the berthing compartment's well worn table. The good news was that it meant she and her three fellows would have a bit more space, but it would also mean there were only four of them to carry the load. Everyone knew that a lot of what any midshipwoman did on her snotty cruise always constituted little more than makework, duties concocted by the ship's officer candidate training officer and assigned only as learning exercises rather than out of any critical need on her ship's part. But a lot more of those duties were anything *but* makework. Middies were King's officers—the lowest of the low, perhaps, and only temporarily and by virtue of warrant, but still officers—and they were expected to pull their weight aboard ship.

She lifted Nimitz into her lap and ran her fingers slowly over his soft, fluffy pelt, smiling at the crackle of static electricity which followed her touch. He bleeked softly and pressed his head against her, luxuriating in her caresses, and she drew a long, slow breath. It was the first time she'd truly relaxed since packing the last of her meager shipboard belongings into her locker that morning on Saganami Island, and the respite was going to be brief.

She closed her eyes and let mental muscles unkink ever so slightly while she replayed her interview with Commander Layson. The exec of any King's ship was a being of at least demigod status, standing at the right hand of the Captain. As such, Layson's actions and attitudes were not to be questioned by a mere midshipwoman. But there'd been something, an edge she hadn't been able to pin down or define, to his questions. She tried once more to tell herself it was only first-day-aboard-ship nerves. He *was* the

Exec, and it was an executive officer's job to know everything she could about the officers serving under her, even if the officers in question were mere middies. Yet that curious certainty which came to Honor seldom but was never wrong told her there was more to it than that in this case. And whether there was or not, there was no question at all that he regarded Nimitz's presence aboard *War Maiden* as an at least potential problem. For that matter, Senior Chief Shelton seemed to feel the same way, and Honor sighed.

It wasn't the first time, or the second, or even the twentieth time she'd faced that attitude. As Commander Layson had suggested, she was indeed fully conversant with what Navy regulations had to say about treecats and their adoptees in Fleet service. Most Navy personnel were not, because the situation arose so infrequently. 'Cat-human bonds were vanishingly rare even on Honor's native Sphinx. The six-limbed arboreals were almost never seen off-planet, and they were even more uncommon in the Navy than in civilian life. Honor had done a little discreet research, and as far as she could determine, no more than a dozen or so current active-duty personnel of all ranks, including herself, had been adopted. That number was minute compared to the total number of people in the Navy, so it was hardly surprising that the 'cats created a stir whenever they did turn up.

Understanding the reason for the situation didn't change it, however, and Honor had been made almost painfully well aware that Nimitz's presence was regarded as a potentially disruptive influence by the vast majority of people who were unfamiliar with his species. Even those who knew better intellectually had a tendency to regard 'cats as little more than extremely clever pets, and an unfortunate percentage of humans never bothered to learn differently even when the opportunity presented itself. The fact that 'cats were unable to form anything like the sounds of human speech only exacerbated that particular aspect of the situation, and the fact that they were so cute and cuddly helped hone the occasional case of jealous resentment over their presence.

Of course, no one who had ever seen a treecat roused to fury could possibly confuse "cute and cuddly" with "harmless." Indeed, their formidable natural armament was another reason some people worried about their presence, even though Nimitz would never harm a human being except in direct self-defense. Or in Honor's defense, which he regarded as precisely the same thing. But people who'd never seen their lethality demonstrated had a pronounced tendency to coo over the 'cats and wish that *they* could have such an adorable pet.

From there, it was a short step to resenting someone else who did have one. Honor and Nimitz had been forced to deal with that attitude more than once at the Academy, and only the fact that the Regs were on their side and that Nimitz was a natural (and unscrupulous) diplomat had gotten them past some of the worse incidents.

Well, if they'd done it on Saganami Island they could do it here, as well, she told herself, and—

The compartment hatch opened with no warning, and Honor came quickly to her feet, Nimitz in her arms as she turned to face the unexpected opening. She knew the occupied light above the hatch had been lit, and opening an occupied compartment's hatch without at least sounding the admittance chime first was a gross infraction of shipboard etiquette. It was also at least technically a privacy violation which was prohibited by Regs except in cases of emergency. The sheer unexpectedness of it created an unaccustomed confusion in Honor, and she stood frozen as a beefy senior-grade lieutenant, perhaps seven or eight T-years older than her, loomed in the doorway. He was two or three centimeters shorter than Honor, with a certain florid handsomeness, but something about his eyes woke an instinctive dislike in her. Or perhaps it was his posture, for he planted both hands on his hips and rocked forward on the balls of his feet to glower at her.

"Don't even snotties know to stand to attention in the

presence of a superior officer, Snotty?" he demanded disdainfully, and a flush of anger lit Honor's high cheekbones. His eyes gleamed at the sight, and she felt the sub-audible rumble of Nimitz's snarl through her arms. She tightened her grip in warning, but the 'cat knew better than to openly display his occasional dislike for those senior to his person. He clearly thought it was one of the sillier restrictions inherent in Honor's chosen career, but he was willing to humor her in something so important to her.

She held him just a heartbeat longer, concentrating hard for the benefit of his empathic sense on how important it was for him to behave himself this time, then set him quickly on the table and came to attention.

"That's better," the lieutenant growled, and stalked into the compartment. "I'm Lieutenant Santino, the assistant tac officer," he informed her, hands still on hips while she stood rigidly at attention. "Which means that, for my sins, I'm also in charge of Snotty Row this deployment. So tell me, Ms. Harrington, just what the hell are you doing *here* instead of reporting to me?"

"Sir, I was instructed to stow my gear and get settled in here. My understanding was that Senior Chief Shelton was—"

"And what makes you think a petty officer is more important than a *commissioned* officer, Ms. Harrington?" he broke in on her.

"Sir, I didn't say he was," she replied, making her voice come out calm and even despite her mounting anger.

"You certainly implied it if you meant to say his instructions were more important than mine!"

Honor clamped her jaw tight and made no response. He was only going to twist anything she said to suit his own ends, and she refused to play his stupid game.

"*Didn't* you imply that, Ms. Harrington?" he demanded after the silence had lingered a few seconds, and she looked him squarely in the eye.

"No, Sir. I did not." The words were perfectly correct, the tone calm and unchallenging, but the expression in her dark brown eyes was unyielding. Something flickered in his own gaze, and his lips tightened, but she simply stood there.

"Then what did you mean to imply?" he asked very softly.

"Sir, I meant to imply nothing. I was merely attempting to answer your question."

"Then answer it!" he snapped.

"Sir, I was told by Commander Layson—" she delivered the Exec's name with absolutely no emphasis and watched his eyes narrow and his mouth tighten once more "—that I was to remain here until the Senior Chief returned, at which time he would take me to formally report in to you."

Santino glared at her, but the invocation of Layson's name had at least temporarily stymied him. Which was only going to make things worse in the long run, Honor decided.

"Well here I am, Ms. Harrington," he growled after a long, silent moment. "So suppose you just get started reporting in to me."

"Sir! Midshipwoman Honor Harrington reports for duty, Sir!" she barked with the sort of parade ground formality no one but an idiot or an utter newbie would use aboard ship. Anger glittered in his eyes, but she only met his gaze expressionlessly.

It's really, really *stupid to antagonize him this way, girl!* a voice which sounded remarkably like Michelle Henke's chided in her head. *Surely you put up with enough crap at the Academy to realize* that *much!*

But she couldn't help herself. And it probably wouldn't matter that much in the long term, anyway.

"Very well, Ms. Harrington," he said icily. "Now that you've condescended to join us, suppose you accompany me to the chart room. I believe I have just the thing for you to occupy yourself with until dinner."

Honor felt far more nervous than she hoped anyone could guess as she joined the party assembling outside the hatch to Captain Bachfisch's dining cabin. *War Maiden* was only three days out of Manticore orbit, and she and her fellow midshipmen had been surprised, to say the least, to discover that the Captain habitually invited his officers to dine with him. It was particularly surprising because *War Maiden* was almost thirty-five standard years old, and small for her rate. Although the captain's quarters were indisputably larger and far more splendid than Snotty Row, they were cramped and plain compared to those aboard newer, larger ships, which made his dining cabin a tight fit for even half a dozen guests. With space at such a premium, he could hardly invite all of his officers to every dinner, but he apparently rotated the guest list regularly to ensure that all of them dined with him in turn.

It was unheard of, or almost so. But Captain Courvoisier, Honor's favorite instructor at the Academy, had once suggested to her that a wise CO got to know her officers—and see to it that they knew her—as well as possible, and she wondered if this was Captain Bachfisch's way of doing just that. But whatever the Captain thought he was up to, finding herself on the guest list was enough to make any snotty nervous, especially this early in the cruise.

She looked around as unobtrusively as possible as the Captain's steward opened the hatch and she followed her seniors through it. As the most junior person present, she brought up the rear, of course, which was only marginally better than being required to lead the way. At least she didn't have to be the very first person through the hatch! But that only meant everyone else could arrive, take their seats, and turn to watch her enter the compartment last of all. She felt the weight of all those senior eyes upon her and wondered if she'd really been wise to bring Nimitz. It was entirely proper for her to do so, according to Regs, unless the invitation specifically excluded him, yet she felt suddenly uncertain and ill at ease, afraid that her seniors might find her decision presumptuous. The uncertainty made her feel physically awkward as well, as if she had somehow reverted to the gawky, oversized horse she'd always thought herself before Chief MacDougal got her seriously interested in *coup de vitesse*. Her face tried to flush, but she ordered her uneasiness sternly back into its box. This evening promised to be stressful enough without borrowing reasons to crank her adrenaline, but she could at least be grateful that Elvis Santino wasn't present. Midshipman Makira had already endured this particular ordeal, and he *had* had to put up with Santino's presence.

At least her lowly status precluded any confusion over which seat might be hers, and she scarcely needed the steward's small gesture directing her to the very foot of the table. She settled herself into the chair as unobtrusively as she could, and Nimitz, as aware as she of the need to be on his best behavior, parked himself very neatly along the top of her seat back.

The steward circled the table, moving through the dining cabin's cramped confines with the grace of long practice as he poured coffee. Honor had always despised that particular beverage, and she covered her cup with her hand as the steward approached her. The man gave her a quizzical glance, but moved on without comment.

"Don't care for coffee, huh?"

The question came from the senior-grade lieutenant seated to her left, and Honor looked at him quickly. The brown-haired, snub-nosed officer was about Santino's age, or within a year or two either way. Unlike Santino, however, his expression was friendly and his tone was pleasant, without the hectoring sneer the OCTO seemed to achieve so effortlessly.

"I'm afraid not, Sir," she admitted.

"That could be a liability in a Navy career," the lieutenant said cheerfully. He looked across the table at a round-faced, dark-complexioned lieutenant commander and grinned. "Some of us," he observed, "seem to be of the opinion that His Majesty's starships actually run on caffeine, not reactor mass. In fact, *some* of us seem to feel that it's our responsibility to rebunker regularly by taking that caffeine on internally."

The lieutenant commander looked down her nose at him

and sipped from her own cup, then set it precisely back on the saucer.

"I trust, Lieutenant, that it was not your intention to cast aspersions on the quantities of coffee which certain of your hard-working seniors consume on the bridge," she remarked.

"Certainly not! I'm shocked by the very suggestion that you might think I intended anything of the sort, Ma'am!"

"Of course you are," Commander Layson agreed, then looked down the length of the table at Honor from his place to the right of the Captain's as yet unoccupied chair. "Ms. Harrington, allow me to introduce you. To your left, we have Lieutenant Saunders, our assistant astrogator. To his left, Lieutenant Commander LaVacher, our chief engineer, and to your right, Lieutenant Commander Hirake, our tac officer." LaVacher, a petite, startlingly pretty blonde, faced Layson, who sat at Hirake's right, across the table. She and the Exec completed the group of dinner guests, and Layson gave a small wave in Honor's direction. "Ladies and gentlemen, Ms. Midshipwoman Harrington."

Heads had nodded at her as the Exec named each officer in turn, and now Honor nodded respectfully back to them. Not a one of them, she noticed, seemed to exude the towering sense of superiority which was so much a part of Elvis Santino.

Saunders had just opened his mouth to say something more when the hatch leading to the captain's day cabin opened and a tall, spare man in the uniform of a senior-grade captain stepped through it. All of the other officers around the table stood, and Honor quickly followed suit. They remained standing until Captain Bachfisch had taken his own chair and made a small gesture with his right hand.

"Be seated, ladies and gentlemen," he invited.

Chairs scraped gently on the decksole as his juniors obeyed the instruction, and Honor observed Bachfisch covertly as she unfolded her snowy linen napkin and draped it across her lap. It was the first time she'd set eyes upon the man who was master after God aboard *War Maiden*, and her first impression was one of vague dissatisfaction. Captain Bachfisch had a thin, lined face and dark eyes which seemed to hold a hint of perpetual frown. In fact, he looked more like an accountant whose figures hadn't come out even than like Honor's mental image of the captain of a King's ship bound to suppress bloody piracy. Nor did his slightly nasal tenor seem the proper voice for such an exalted personage, and she felt an undeniable pang of disappointment.

But then the steward reappeared and began to serve the meal proper, which banished such mundane concerns quite handily. The quality of the food was several notches higher than anything which normally came in the way of a lowly snotty, and Honor dug in with a will. There was little conversation while they ate, and she was just as glad, for it gave her the opportunity to enjoy the food without having to worry about whether a mere midship–woman was expected to contribute to the table talk. Not that there *was* much table talk. Captain Bachfisch, in particular, applied himself to his dinner in silence. He seemed almost unaware of his guests, and despite the gratitude Honor felt at being allowed to enjoy her meal in relative peace, she wondered why he had bothered to invite them in the first place if he only intended to ignore them. It all seemed very peculiar.

The dinner progressed from salad and an excellent potato soup through glazed chicken with sliced almonds, fluffy rice, stir-fried vegetables and sauteed mushrooms, fresh green peas, and crusty, butter-drenched rolls to a choice of three different desserts. Every time Honor glanced up, the steward seemed to be at her elbow, offering another helping, and she accepted with gusto. Captain Bachfisch might not match her mental image of a dashing and dis-tinguished starship commander, but he set an excellent table. She hadn't tasted food this good since her last visit home.

The apple pie à la mode was even better than the glazed chicken, and Honor needed no prompting when the steward offered her a second helping. The man gave her a small, conspiratorial wink as he slid the second dessert plate in front of her, and she heard something which sounded suspiciously like a chuckle from Lieutenant Saunders' direction. She glanced at the assistant astrogator from the corner of her eye, but his expression was laudably composed. There might have been a hint of a twinkle in his own eyes, but Honor scarcely minded that. She was a direct descendant of the Meyerdahl First Wave, and she was well accustomed to the reactions her genetically modified metabolism's appetite—especially for sweets—drew from unprepared table mates.

But in the end, she was reduced to chasing the last of the melted ice cream around the plate with her spoon, and she sat back with an unobtrusive sigh of repletion as the silent, efficient steward reappeared to collect the empty dishes and make them magically vanish into some private black hole. Wineglasses replaced them, and the steward presented an old-fashioned wax-sealed glass bottle for Captain Bachfisch's inspection. Honor watched the Captain more attentively at that, for her own father was a notable wine snob in his own modest way, and she recognized another as the steward cracked the wax, drew the cork, and handed it to the Captain. Bachfisch sniffed it delicately while the steward poured a small quantity of ruby liquid into his glass, then set the cork aside and sipped the wine itself. He considered for just a moment, then nodded approval, and the steward filled his glass and then circled the table to pour for each of the guests in turn.

A fresh butterfly fluttered its wings ever so gently in Honor's middle as the steward filled her own glass. She was the junior officer present, and she knew what that required of her. She waited until the steward had finished pouring and stepped back, then reached for her glass and stood.

"Ladies and gentlemen, the King!" She was pleased her voice came out sounding so close to normal. It certainly didn't *feel* as if it ought to have, but she appeared to be the only one aware of how nervous she felt.

"The King!" The response sounded almost too loud in the cramped dining cabin, and Honor sank back into her chair quickly, vastly relieved to have gotten through without mischance.

There was a sudden shift of atmosphere around the table, almost as if the loyalty toast were a signal the diners had awaited. It was more of a shift in attitude than anything else, Honor thought, trying to put a mental finger on what had changed. The Captain's guests sat back in their chairs, wineglasses in hand, and Lieutenant Commander Hirake actually crossed her legs.

"May I assume you got those charts properly straightened out, Joseph?" Captain Bachfisch said.

"Yes, Sir," Lieutenant Saunders replied. "You were right, Captain. They were just mislabeled, although Commander Dobrescu and I *are* still a little puzzled over why someone thought we needed updated charts on the People's Republic when we're headed in exactly the opposite direction."

"Oh, that's an easy one, Joseph," Lieutenant Commander Hirake told him. "I imagine *War Maiden*'s original astrogator probably requested them for her maiden voyage. I mean, it's only been thirty-six standard years. That's about average for turnaround on LogCom requests."

Several people around the table chuckled, and Honor managed not to let her surprise show as Captain Bachfisch's lined, disapproving face creased in a smile of its own. The Captain waved a finger at the tac officer and shook his head.

"We can't have you talking that way about LogCom, Janice," he told her severely. "If nothing else, you'll raise future expectations which are doomed to be disappointed."

"I don't know about that, Sir," Commander Layson said. "Seems to me it took about that long to get the emitter head on Graser Four replaced, didn't it?"

"Yes, but that wasn't LogCom alone," Lieutenant Commander LaVacher put in. "The yard dogs on *Hephaestus* actually found it for us in the end, remember? I almost had to demand it at pulser point, but they *did* find it. Of course, they'd probably had it in stores for five or six years while some other poor cruiser waited for it, and we just shortstopped it."

That drew fresh chuckles, and Honor's amazement grew. The men and women in the compartment with her were suddenly very different from those who had shared the almost silent, formal dinner, and Captain Bachfisch was the most different of all. As she watched, he cocked his head at Commander Layson, and his expression was almost playful.

"And I trust that while Joseph was straightening out his charts you and Janice managed to come up with an exercise schedule which is going to make everyone onboard hate us, Abner?"

"Well, we tried, Sir." Layson sighed and shook his head. "We did our best, but I think there are probably three or four ratings in Engineering who are only going to take us in intense dislike instead."

"Hmm." Captain Bachfisch frowned. "I'm a bit disappointed to hear that. When a ship's company has as many grass-green hands as this one, a good exec shouldn't have any trouble at all coming up with a training program guaranteed to get on their bad side."

"Oh, we've managed *that*, Sir. It's just that Irma managed to hang on to most of her original watch crews, and they already know all our tricks."

"Ah? Well, I suppose that is a circumstance beyond your control," Captain Bachfisch allowed, and looked at Lieutenant Commander LaVacher. "I see it's your fault, Irma," he said.

"Guilty as charged, Sir," LaVacher admitted. "Wasn't easy, either, with BuPers hanging over my shoulder and trying to poach my most experienced people the whole time."

"I know it wasn't," the Captain said, and this time there was no teasing note in his approving voice. "I reviewed some of your correspondence with Captain Allerton. I thought right up to the last minute that we were going to lose Chief Heisman, but you finessed Allerton beautifully. I hope this isn't going to cost the Chief that extra rocker, though. We need him, but I don't want him shortchanged out of the deal."

"He won't be, Sir," Layson replied for LaVacher. "Irma and I discussed it before she ever resorted to the 'essential to efficient functioning' argument to hang onto him. We're two senior chiefs light in Engineering alone . . . and we're also going to be in Silesia more than long enough for you to exercise your own discretion in promoting Heisman to fill one of those slots."

"Good," Bachfisch said. "That's what I like to see! Intelligent ship's officers effortlessly outsmarting their natural enemies at BuPers."

It was all Honor could do not to gawk at the changeling who had replaced the dour and unsmiling man in the chair at the head of the table. Then he turned from Layson and LaVacher and looked directly down the table at her, and this time there was a definite twinkle in his deep set eyes.

"I notice your companion has spent the entire meal on the back of your chair, Ms. Harrington," he observed. "I was under the impression that 'cats usually ate at the same time their people did."

"Uh, yes, Sir," Honor said. She felt a warmth along her cheekbones and drew a deep breath. At least his bantering with the more senior officers present had given her some opportunity to adjust before he turned his guns on her, and she took herself firmly in hand. "Yes, Sir," she said much more composedly. "Nimitz normally eats at the same time I do, but he doesn't do very well with vegetables, and we weren't sure what arrangements your steward might have made, so he ate in the berthing compartment before we came to dinner."

"I see." The Captain gazed at her for a moment, then nodded at his steward. "Chief Stennis is a capable sort, Ms. Harrington. If you'll be good enough to provide him with a list of foods suitable for your companion, I feel confident he can arrange an appropriate menu for his next dinner engagement."

"Yes, Sir," Honor said, trying unsuccessfully to hide her relief at the evidence that Nimitz's presence was welcome, and not merely something to be tolerated. "Thank you, Sir."

"You're welcome," Bachfisch replied, then smiled. "In the meantime, is there at least something we can offer him as an after dinner snack while we enjoy our wine?"

"If Chief Stennis has a little celery left over from the salad, that would be perfect, Sir. 'Cats may not do well with most vegetables, but they *all* love celery!"

"Jackson?" The Captain glanced at the steward who smiled and nodded.

"I believe I can handle that, Sir."

Chief Stennis disappeared into his pantry, and Captain Bachfisch returned his attention to Commander Layson and Lieutenant Commander Hirake. Honor settled back in her chair, and the pleased buzz of Nimitz's purr vibrated against the back of her neck. If she'd been a 'cat herself, her own purr would have been even more pleased and considerably louder. She watched *War Maiden*'s captain chatting with his officers and felt a sense of ungrudging admiration. This Captain Bachfisch was a very different proposition from the formal, almost cold CO who had presided over the meal itself. She still didn't understand why he'd seemed so distant then, but she readily appreciated the skill with which he drew each of his officers in turn into the discussion now. And, she admitted, how effortlessly he had made a mere midshipwoman feel at ease in their company. His questions might be humorously phrased, and he might display an almost dangerously pointed wit, yet he had all of them involved in discussing serious issues, and he managed it as a leader, not merely as a captain. She remembered once more what Captain Courvosier had said about the need for a captain to know her officers, and realized that

Bachfisch had just given her an object lesson in how a captain might go about that.

It was a lesson worth learning, and she filed it away carefully as she smiled and reached up to take the plate of celery Chief Stennis brought her.

" . . . and as you can see, we have the Alpha Three upgrade to the emergency local control positions for our energy mounts," Chief MacArthur droned. The sturdy, plain-faced woman bore the hash marks of over twenty-five T-years' service on her sleeve, and the combat ribbons on her chest proved she'd paid cash to learn her weapons skills. It was unfortunate that she'd never mastered the skills of the lecture hall to go with them. Even though Honor was deeply interested in what MacArthur had to tell her, she found it difficult to keep from yawning as the dust-dry instruction continued.

She and Audrey Bradlaugh, *War Maiden*'s other female middy, stood in the number four inboard wing passage, peering over MacArthur's shoulder into the small, heavily armored compartment. It didn't offer a lot of space for the men and women who would man it when the ship cleared for action, and every square centimeter of room it did have was crammed with monitors, readouts, keypads, and access panels. In between those more important bits and pieces were sandwiched the shock-mounted couches and umbilical attachment points for the mere humans of the weapon crew.

"When the buzzer goes, the crew has a maximum of fifteen minutes to don skinsuits and man stations," MacArthur informed them, and Honor and Bradlaugh nodded as if no one had ever told them so before. "Actually, of course, fifteen minutes should give time to spare, although we sometimes run a bit over on shakedown cruises. On the other hand," the petty officer glanced back at her audience, "the Captain isn't what I'd call a patient man with people who screw up his training profiles, so I wouldn't recommend dawdling."

One eyelid flickered in what might have been called a wink on a less expressionless face, and despite herself, Honor grinned at the petty officer. Not that on-mount crew duties were the most humorous subject imaginable. Honor knew that, for she'd logged scores of hours in simulators which recreated every detail of the local control command position in front of her, and her grin faded as she envisioned it in her mind. Her excellent imagination pictured every moment of the shriek of the general quarters alarm, the flashing lights of battle stations, and the sudden claustrophobic tension as the crew plugged in their skinsuit umbilicals and the hatch slammed shut behind them while powerful pumps sucked the air from the passages and compartments around them. The vacuum about their armored capsule would actually help protect it—and them—from atmosphere-transmitted shock and concussion, not to mention fires, yet she doubted anyone could ever embrace it without an atavistic shudder.

Nimitz shifted uneasily on her shoulder as he caught the sudden edge of darkness in her emotions, and she reached up to rest one hand lightly on his head. He pressed back against her palm, and she made a soft crooning sound.

"If Chief MacArthur is *boring* you, Ms. Harrington," an unpleasant voice grated unexpectedly, "I'm sure we can find some extra duty to keep you occupied."

Honor turned quickly, shoulders tightening in automatic response, and her expression was suddenly a better mask than Chief MacArthur's as she faced Elvis Santino. It was obvious the OCTO had come quietly around the bend in the passage while she and Bradlaugh were listening to MacArthur, and she castigated herself for letting him sneak up on her. Now he stood glaring at her, hands once more on hips and lip curled, and she gazed back at him in silence.

Anything she said or did would be wrong, so she said nothing. Which, of course, was *also* the wrong thing to do.

"Well, Ms. Harrington? If you're bored, just say so. I'm

sure Chief MacArthur has better things to do with her time as well. *Are* you bored?"

"No, Sir." She gave the only possible answer as neutrally as possible, and Santino smiled nastily.

"Indeed? I would've thought otherwise, given the way you're humming and playing with your little pet."

Once again, there was no possible response that would not give him another opening. She felt Bradlaugh's unhappiness beside her, but Audrey said nothing, either. There wasn't anything she could say, and she'd experienced sufficient of Santino's nastiness herself. But MacArthur shifted her weight, and turned to face the lieutenant. Her non-expression was more pronounced than ever, and she cleared her throat.

"With all due respect, Sir," she said, "the young ladies have been very attentive this afternoon."

Santino turned his scowl on her.

"I don't recall asking your opinion of their attentiveness, Chief MacArthur." His voice was harsh, but MacArthur never turned a hair.

"I realize that, Sir. But again with all due respect, you just came around the corner. I've been working with Ms. Harrington and Ms. Bradlaugh for the last hour and a half. I just felt that I should make you aware of the fact that they've paid very close attention during that time."

"I see." For a moment, Honor thought the lieutenant was going to chew MacArthur out as well for having the audacity to interfere. But it seemed even Elvis Santino wasn't quite stupid enough to risk making this sort of dispute with a noncom of MacArthur's seniority and in his own shipboard department part of the official record. He rocked up and down on the balls of his feet for several seconds then returned his glare to Honor.

"No matter how much attention you've been paying, there's no excuse for slacking off," he told her. "I realize Regs permit you to carry that creature with you on duty, but I warn you not to abuse that privilege. And stop playing with it when you ought to be concentrating on what you're here to learn! I trust I've made myself sufficiently clear?"

"Yes, Sir," Honor said woodenly. "Perfectly clear."

"Good!" Santino snapped, and strode briskly away.

"Lord! What *is* his problem?" Nassios Makira groaned.

The stocky midshipman heaved himself up to sit on the edge of his upper-tier bunk, legs dangling over the side. Honor couldn't imagine why he liked perching up there so much. He was shorter than she was, true, but the deckhead was too low to let even Nassios sit fully upright on his bunk. Maybe it was *because* she was taller than he was? As a matter of fact, Nassios was one of the shortest people aboard *War Maiden*. So did he spend so much time climbing around like a 'cat or an Old Earth monkey because it was the only way he could get above eye level on everyone else?

"I don't know," Audrey Bradlaugh replied without looking up from the boot in her lap. No names had been mentioned, but she seemed in no doubt about the object of Nassios' plaint. "But I do know that complaining about him is only going to make it worse if it gets back to him," the red-haired midshipwoman added pointedly, reaching for the polish on the berthing compartment table.

"Hey, let the man talk," Basanta Lakhia put in. The dark-skinned young midshipman with the startlingly blond hair lay comfortably stretched out on his own bunk. "No one's gonna be tattling to Santino on him, and even if anyone did, it's not against Regs to discuss a senior officer."

"Not as long as the discussion isn't prejudicial to discipline," Honor corrected.

Somewhat to her surprise, she'd found herself the senior of *War Maiden*'s midshipmen on the basis of their comparative class standings. That, unfortunately, only seemed to make matters worse where Santino was concerned, since her seniority—such as it was—pushed him into somewhat closer proximity with her than with the other middies. It also gave her a greater degree of responsibility to provide a voice of reason in snotty bull sessions, and now she looked up to give Makira a rather pointed glance from where she sat beside Bradlaugh at the table, running a brush over Nimitz's pelt. It was unusual for all four of them to be off-duty at once, but middies tended to be assigned to rotating watch schedules, and this time their off-watch periods happened to overlap. In fact, they had almost two more hours before Audrey and Basanta had to report for duty.

"Honor, you know I'd never, ever want to prejudice discipline," Nassios said piously. "Or that anything *I* did could possibly prejudice it as much as *he* does," he added *sotto voce*.

"Basanta's right that no one is going to be carrying tales, Nassios," Audrey said, looking up at last. "But that's exactly the kind of crack that's going to bring him—and the Exec—down on you like a shuttle with dead countergrav if it gets back to them."

"I know. I know," Nassios sighed. "But you've got to admit he's going awful far out of his way to make himself a royal pain, Audrey! And the way he keeps picking on Honor over Nimitz . . . "

"Maybe he thinks it's part of his job as our training officer," Honor suggested. She finished brushing Nimitz and carefully gathered up the loose fluff for disposal someplace other than in the compartment's air filters.

"Huh! Sure he does!" Basanta snorted.

"I didn't say I agreed with him if he did," Honor said serenely. "But you know as well as I do that there's still the old 'stomp on them hard enough to make them tough' school of snotty-training."

"Yeah, but it's dying out," Nassios argued. "Most of the people you run into who still think that way are old farts from the old school. You know, the ones who think starships should run on steam plants or reaction thrusters . . . or maybe oars! Santino's too young for that kind of crap. Besides, it still doesn't explain the wild hair he's got up his ass over Nimitz!"

"Maybe, and maybe not," Basanta said thoughtfully. "You may have a point, Honor—about the reason he's such a hard ass in the first place, anyway. He's not all that much older than we are, but if his OCTO worked that way, he could just be following in the same tradition."

"And the reason he keeps picking on Nimitz?" Nassios challenged.

"Maybe he's just one of those people who can't get past the image of treecats as dumb animals," Bradlaugh suggested. "Lord knows *I* wasn't ready for how smart the little devil is. And I wouldn't have believed Honor if she'd just told me about it either."

"That could be it," Honor agreed. "Most people can figure out the difference between a treecat and a pet once they come face-to-face with the real thing, but that's hardly universally true. I think it depends on how much imagination they have."

"And imagination isn't something he's exactly brimming over with," Basanta pointed out. "Which goes back to what Honor said in the first place. If he doesn't have much imagination—" his tone suggested that he'd had a rather more pointed noun in mind "—of his own, he probably is treating us the same way his OCTO treated him. Once he got pointed that way, he couldn't figure out another way to go."

"I don't think he needed anyone to point him in that direction," Nassios muttered, and although she was the one who'd put the suggestion forward, Honor agreed with him. For that matter, she felt morally certain that Santino's behavior was a natural product of his disposition which owed nothing to anyone else's example. Not that she doubted for a moment that his defense, if anyone senior to him called him on it, would be that he was only doing it "for their own good."

"If he ever needed a pointer, he doesn't need one anymore, that's for sure," Basanta agreed, then shook himself. "Say, has anybody seen any of the sims Commander Hirake is setting up for us?"

"No, but PO Wallace warned me they were going to be toughies," Audrey chimed in, supporting the change of subject, and Honor sat back down and gathered Nimitz into her arms while the comfortable shop talk flowed around her.

She ought, she reflected, to be happier than she'd ever been in her life, and in many ways she was. But Elvis Santino was doing his best to keep her happiness from being complete, and he was succeeding. Despite anything she might say to the others, she was morally certain the abusive, sarcastic, belittling behavior he directed at all of them, and especially at her and Nimitz, sprang from a pronounced bullying streak. Worse, she suspected that streak was aggravated by natural stupidity.

And he *was* stupid. She only had to watch him performing as *War Maiden*'s assistant tac officer to know that much.

She sighed mentally and pressed her lips together, warning herself once more of the dangers inherent in allowing herself to feel contempt for anyone senior to her. Even if she never let a sign of it show outwardly, it would affect the way she responded to his orders and endless lectures on an officer's proper duties, which could only make things even worse in the end. But she couldn't help it. Her favorite subjects at the Academy had been tactics and ship handling, and she knew she had a natural gift in both areas. Santino did not. He was unimaginative and mentally lazy— at best a plodder, whose poor performance was shielded by Lieutenant Commander Hirake's sheer competence as his boss and carried by Senior Chief Del Conte's matching competence from below. She'd only had a chance to see him in the simulator once or twice, but her fingers had itched with the need to shove him aside and take over the tac console herself.

Which might be another reason he gave her so much grief, she sometimes thought. She'd done her level best not to let her contempt show, but he had access to her Academy records. That meant he knew exactly how high she'd placed in the Tactical Department, and unless he was even stupider than she thought (possible but not likely; he seemed able to zip his own shoes), he had to know she was absolutely convinced that she could have done his job at least twice as well as he could.

And that's only because I'm too naturally modest to think I could do it even better than that, she thought mordantly.

She sighed again, this time physically, pressing her face into Nimitz's coat, and admitted, if only to herself, the real reason she detested Elvis Santino. He reminded her inescapably of Mr. Midshipman Lord Pavel Young, the conceited, vicious, small-minded, oh-so-nobly born cretin who had done his level best to destroy her and her career at Saganami Island.

Her lips tightened, and Nimitz made a scolding sound and reached out to touch her cheek with one long-fingered true-hand. She closed her eyes, fighting against replaying the memory of that dreadful night in the showers yet again, then drew a deep breath, smoothed her expression, and lowered him to her lap once more.

"You okay, Honor?" Audrey asked quietly, her soft voice hidden under a strenuous argument between Nassios and Basanta over the merits of the Academy's new soccer coach.

"Hmm? Oh, sure." She smiled at the redhead. "Just thinking about something else."

"Homesickness, huh?" Audrey smiled back. "I get hit by it every so often, too, you know. Of course," her smile grew into a grin, "I don't have a treecat to keep me company when it does!"

Her infectious chuckle robbed the last sentence of any implied bitterness, and she rummaged in her belt purse for a bedraggled, rather wilted stalk of celery. All of the midshipmen who shared Snotty Row with Honor had taken to hoarding celery almost from the moment they discovered Nimitz's passion for it, and now Audrey smiled fondly as the 'cat seized it avidly and began to devour it.

"Gee, thanks a whole bunch, Audrey!" Honor growled. "You just wrecked his appetite for dinner completely!"

"Sure I did," Audrey replied. "Or I would have, if he didn't carry his own itty-bitty black hole around inside him somewhere."

"As any informed person would know, that's his stomach, not a black hole," Honor told her sternly.

"Sure. It just *works* like a black hole," Basanta put in.

"I've seen you at the mess table, too, boy-oh," Audrey told him, "and if I were you, I wouldn't be throwing any rocks around my glass foyer!"

"I'm just a growing boy," Basanta said with artful innocence, and Honor joined in the laughter.

At least if I have to be stuck with Santino, I got a pretty good bunch to share the misery with, she thought.

HMS *War Maiden* moved steadily through hyperspace. The Gregor Binary System and its terminus of the Manticore Wormhole Junction lay almost a week behind; the Silesian Confederacy lay almost a month ahead, and the heavy cruiser's company had begun to shake down. It was not a painless process. As Captain Bachfisch's after-dinner conversation with Commander Layson had suggested, much of *War Maiden*'s crew was new to the ship, for the cruiser had just emerged from an extensive overhaul period, and the Bureau of Personnel had raided her pre-overhaul crew ruthlessly while she was laid up in space dock. That always happened during a refit, of course, but the situation was worse in the RMN these days due to the Navy's expansion. Every Regular, officer and enlisted alike, knew the expansion process was actually just beginning to hit its stride . . . and that the situation was going to get nothing but worse if King Roger and his ministers stood by their obvious intention to build a fleet capable of resisting the Peeps. The Government and Admiralty faced the unenviable task of balancing the financial costs of new hardware—and especially of yard infrastructure—against the personnel-related costs of providing the manpower to crew and use that hardware, and they were determined to squeeze the last penny out of

every begrudged dollar they could finagle out of Parlia-
ment. Which meant, down here at the sharp end of the
stick, that *War Maiden*'s crew contained a high percentage
of new recruits, with a higher percentage of newly promoted noncoms to ride herd on them than her officers
would have liked, while the personnel retention problems
of the Navy in general left her with several holes among
her senior petty officer slots. Almost a third of her total
crew were on their first long deployment, and there was
a certain inevitable friction between some members of her
company, without the solid core of senior noncommissioned officers who would normally have jumped on it
as soon as it surfaced.

Honor was as aware of the background tension as anyone
else. She and her fellow middies could scarcely have helped
being aware of it under any circumstances, but she had
the added advantage of Nimitz, and she only had to watch
his body language to read his reaction to the crew's
edginess.

The ship was scarcely a hotbed of mutiny, of course,
but there was a sense of rough edges and routines just
out of joint that produced a general air of unsettlement,
and she occasionally wondered if that hovering feeling that
things were somehow out of adjustment helped explain
some of Santino's irascibility. She suspected, even as she
wondered, that the notion was nonsense, nothing more than
an effort to supply some sort of excuse for the way the
OCTO goaded and baited the midshipmen under his nominal
care. Still, she had to admit that it left *her* feeling unsettled.
None of her relatively short training deployments from the
Academy had produced anything quite like it. Of course,
none of the ships involved in those deployments had been
fresh from refit with crews composed largely of replace-
ments, either. Could this sense of connections still waiting to be made be the norm and not the exception? She'd
always known the Academy was a sheltered environment,
one where corners were rounded, sharp edges were
smoothed, and tables of organization were neatly adhered

to, no matter how hard the instructors ran the middies. No doubt that same "classroom-perfect" organization had extended to the training ships homeported at Saganami Island, while *War Maiden* was the real Navy at last. When she thought of it that way, it was almost exciting, like a challenge to earn her adulthood by proving she could deal with the less than perfect reality of a grownup's universe.

Of course, Elvis Santino all by himself was more than enough to make any universe imperfect, she told herself as she hurried down the passage. The OCTO was in an even worse mood than usual today, and all of the middies knew it was going to be impossible to do anything well enough to satisfy him. Not that they had any choice but to try, which was how Honor came to find herself bound all the way forward to Magazine Two just so she could personally count the laser heads to confirm the computer inventory. It was pure makework, an order concocted solely to keep her occupied and let Santino once more demonstrate his petty-tyrant authority. Not that she objected all that strenuously to anything that got her out of his immediate vicinity!

She rounded a corner and turned left along Axial One, the large central passage running directly down the cruiser's long axis. *War Maiden* was old enough that her lift system left much to be desired by modern standards. Honor could have made almost the entire trip from bridge to magazine in one of the lift cars, but its circuitous routing meant the journey would actually have taken longer that way. Besides, she *liked* Axial One. *War Maiden's* internal grav field was reduced to just under .2 G in the out-sized passage, and she fell into the long, bounding, semi-swimming gait that permitted.

More modern warships had abandoned such passages in favor of better designed and laid out lift systems, although most merchantmen retained them. Convenient though they were in many ways, they represented what BuShips had decided was a dangerous weakness in a military starship which was expected to sustain and survive damage from enemy fire. Unlike the smaller shafts lift cars required, passages like Axial One posed severe challenges when it came to things like designing in blast doors and emergency air locks, and the large empty space at the very core of the ship represented at least a marginal sacrifice in structural strength. Or so BuShips had decided. Honor wasn't certain she agreed, but no flag officers or naval architects had shown any interest in seeking her opinion on the matter, so she simply chose to enjoy the opportunity when it presented itself.

Nimitz clung to her shoulder, chittering with delight of his own as the two of them sailed down the passageway with impeccable grace. It was almost as much fun as Honor's hang glider back home on Sphinx, and his fluffy tail streamed behind them. They were far from the only people making use of Axial One, and Honor knew she was technically in violation of the speed limits imposed here under nonemergency conditions, but she didn't much care. She doubted anyone was likely to take her to task for it, and if anyone did, she could always point out that Santino had ordered her to "get down there double-quick, Snotty!"

She was almost to her destination when it happened. She didn't see the events actually leading up to the collision, but the consequences were painfully obvious. A three-man work party from Engineering, towing a countergrav pallet of crated electronic components, had collided head-on with a missile tech using a push-pull to maneuver five linked missile main drive units down the same passage. It was a near-miracle no one had suffered serious physical injury, but there'd obviously been a fair number of bruises, and it was clear that the participants' emotions were even more bruised than their hides.

"—and get your goddamn, worthless pile of frigging junk out of my fucking way!" the missile tech snarled.

"Fuck you and the horse you rode in on!" the senior rating from the Engineering party snapped back. "Nobody ever tell you forward traffic to starboard, sternward traffic to port? Or are you just naturally stupid? You were all over the goddamn place with that piece of shit! It's a damn miracle you didn't kill one of us!"

She gave the linked drive units a furious kick to emphasize her point. Unfortunately, she failed to allow for the low grav conditions, and the result was more prat fall than intimidating. She sent herself flailing through the air towards the center of the passage, where she landed flat on her posterior on the decksole, without even budging the drive units, none of which did a thing for her temper. It did, however, have the effect of infuriating the missile tech even further, and he unbuckled from his push-pull and shoved himself off the saddle with obviously homicidal intent. One of the male Engineering ratings moved to intercept him, and things were headed rapidly downhill when Honor reached out for one of the bulkhead handrails and brought herself to a semi-floating stop.

"Belay that!"

Her soprano was very little louder than normal, yet it cracked like a whip, and the disputants' heads snapped around in sheer surprise. Their surprise only grew when they saw the fuzz-haired midshipwoman who had produced the order.

"I don't know who did what to whom," she told them crisply while they gawked at her in astonishment, "and I don't really care. What matters is getting this mess sorted out and getting you people to wherever it is you're supposed to be." She glared at them for a moment, and then jabbed a finger at the senior Engineering rating. "You," she told the woman. "Chase down those loose crates, get them back on the pallet, and this time get them properly secured! You and you—" she jabbed an index finger at the other two members of the work party "—get over there and give her a hand. And *you*," she wheeled on the missile tech who had just begun to gloat at his rivals' stunned expressions, "get that push-pull back under control, tighten the grav-collars on those missile drives before they fall right out of them, and see to it that you stay in the right heavy tow lane the rest of the way to wherever you're going!"

"Uh, yes, Ma'am!" The missile tech recognized command voice when he heard it, even if it did come from a mid-shipwoman who looked like someone's preteen kid sister, and he knew better than to irritate the person who had produced it. He actually braced to attention before he scurried back over to the bundle of drive units and began adjusting the offending counter-grav collars, and the Engineering working party, which had already come to the same conclusion, spread out, quickly corralling their scattered crates and stacking them oh-so-neatly on their pallet. Honor stood waiting, one toe tapping gently on the decksole while Nimitz watched with interest from her shoulder and the errant ratings—the youngest of them at least six standard years older than she—gave an excellent imitation of small children under the eye of an irritated governess.

It took a remarkably short time for the confusion to be reduced to order, and all four ratings turned carefully expressionless faces back to Honor.

"That's better," she told them in more approving tones. "Now I suggest that all of you get back to doing what you're supposed to be doing just a little more carefully than you were."

"Aye, aye, Ma'am," they chorused, and she nodded. They moved off—far more sedately than before, she suspected—and she resumed her own interrupted trip.

That went fairly well, she told herself, and continued her progress along Axial One, unaware of the grinning senior chief who had arrived behind her just in time to witness the entire episode.

"So, Shellhead," Senior Master Chief Flanagan said comfortably, "what d'you think of this helpless bunch of Momma's dirtside darlings now?"

"Who, me?" Senior Chief Shelton leaned back in his own chair, heels propped on the table in the senior petty officers' mess, and grinned as he nursed a beer stein. Not many were permitted to use that nickname to his face, but Flanagan had known him for over twenty standard years.

More importantly than that, perhaps, Flanagan was also *War Maid*'s Bosun, the senior noncommissioned member of her company.

"Yeah, you," Flanagan told him. "You ever see such a hapless bunch in your entire life? I swear, I think one or two of them aren't real clear on which hatch to open first on the air lock!"

"Oh, they're not as bad as all that," Shelton said. "They've got a few rough edges—hell, let's be honest, they've got a *lot* of rough edges—but we're getting them filed down. By the time we hit Silesia, they'll be ready. And some of them aren't half bad already."

"You think so?" Flanagan's eyebrows rose ever so slightly at Shelton's tone, and the senior chief nodded. "And just who, if you don't mind my asking, brought that particular bit of praise to the surface?"

"Young Harrington, as a matter of fact," Shelton said. "I came across her in Axial One this afternoon tearing a strip off a couple of work parties who'd managed to run smack into each other. 'Tronics crates all over the deck, counter-grav pallet cocked up on its side, push-pull all twisted against the bulkhead, and half a dozen missile drives ready to slip right out of their collars, not to mention a couple of ratings ready to start thumping hell out of each other over whose fault it was. And there she stood, reading them the riot act. Got their sorry asses sorted out in record time, too."

Flanagan found it a little difficult to hide his surprise at the obvious approval in Shelton's voice.

"I wouldn't've thought she had the decibels for reading riot acts," he observed, watching his friend's expression carefully. "Sweet-voiced thing like that, I'd think she'd sound sort of silly shouting at a hairy bunch of spacers."

"Nah," Shelton said with a grin. "That was the beauty of it—never cussed or even raised her voice once. Didn't have to. She may only be a snotty, but that young lady could burn the finish off a battle steel bulkhead with just her tone alone. Haven't seen anything like it in years."

"Sounds like that shithead Santino could learn a little something from his snotties, then," Flanagan observed sourly, and it was Shelton's turn to feel surprise. In all the years he'd known Flanagan, he could count the number of times he'd heard his friend use that tone of voice about a commissioned officer on the fingers of one hand. Well, maybe one and half. Not that the senior chief disagreed with the bosun.

"Actually, I think he could learn a hell of a lot from Harrington," he said after a moment. "For that matter, he could probably learn a lot from all of them. If he could keep his own mouth shut long enough to listen to them, anyway."

"And how likely is *that* to happen?" Flanagan snorted.

"Not very," Shelton conceded. "The man does like to hear himself talk."

"I wouldn't mind that so much, if he weren't such a bastard," Flanagan said, still with such an edge of bitter condemnation that Shelton looked across at him with the first beginnings of true alarm.

"Is there something going on that I should be hearing about, Ian?"

"Probably not anything you don't already know about," Flanagan told him moodily. "It's just that he's such a total asshole. Hell, you're in a better spot to see the way he treats the snotties like dirt than I am, and he's not a lot better with his own tac people. Even he knows better than to piss off a senior noncom, but he came down like a five-grav field on his yeoman yesterday, for a screw-up that was entirely his own fault. You know I've got no use for any officer who beats up on his people when *he's* the one who screwed the pooch. Man's the most worthless piece of crap I've seen in an officer's uniform in years, Shellhead."

"I don't know that I'd go quite that far myself," Shelton said in a considering tone. "I've seen some pretty piss-poor officers, you know. Some of them could at least give him a run for his money. On the other hand, I don't think any of them were *worse* than he is." He paused for a moment, and looked quizzically at his friend. "You know, I think it's probably against Regs for two senior petty officers to sit around and badmouth a commissioned officer over their beer this way."

"And you don't see me doing it with anyone else, do you?" Flanagan returned, then grimaced. "Ah, hell, Shellhead, you know as well as I do that Santino is the worst frigging officer in this ship. Come on, be honest. You're worried about the way he treats the snotties, aren't you?"

"Well, yeah," Shelton admitted. "I see a kid like Harrington—any of them, really, but especially Harrington— with all that promise, and there's Santino, doing his level best to crush it all out of them. I mean, it's one thing to be tough on them. It's something else entirely to ride them twenty-two hours a day out of sheer poison mean- ness because you know there's nothing in the world they can do to fight back."

"You can say that again," Flanagan said. "Not bad enough he's got the chain of command on his side, but they know he can flush their careers any time he damned well pleases if they don't kiss ass enough to make him happy."

"Maybe. But I've got to tell you, Ian, I don't know how much longer Harrington's going to put up with it." Shelton shook his head soberly. "I had my doubts when she turned up with that treecat of hers. First time I'd ever seen one onboard ship. I figured it was bound to make trouble in Snotty Row if nowhere else, and that Harrington might be full of herself for having it in the first place, but I was wrong on both counts. And the girl's got bottom, too. She's going to be a good one someday . . . unless Santino pushes her too hard. She's got a temper in there, however hard she tries to hide it, and Santino sticks in her craw side- ways. One of these days, she's gonna lose it with him, and when she does . . ."

The two noncoms gazed at one another across the table, and neither of them any longer felt like smiling at all.

✧   ✧   ✧

"Tell me, Ms. Harrington," Elvis Santino said, "is it possible that by some vast stretch of the imagination you actually consider this a competently done job?"

The lieutenant stood in the weapon's bay for Graser Three, the second energy mount in *War Maiden*'s port broadside. He and Honor both wore skinsuits as Regs required, since the bay was sealed only by a single hatch, not a proper air lock. When the ship cleared for action, the bay would be opened to space, the emitter assembly would train outboard, and the powered ram would move the entire weapon outward until the emitter head cleared the hull and could bring up its gravity lenses safely. Honor had always been privately amused by the fact that modern energy weapons were "run out" like some echo of the muzzleloading cannon of Old Earth's sailing navies, but at the moment all she felt was a dull, seething resentment for her training officer.

Santino was in his favorite pose, hands propped on hips and feet spread wide. All he needed to complete the handsome HD star image was a bright sun to squint into, Honor thought derisively, and wondered yet again how he could possibly be unaware of the effect that sort of posturing was bound to have on the men and women under his orders. It was more than a merely rhetorical consideration at the moment, since six of those men and women—including SCPO Shelton—stood at her back in silent witness.

"Yes, Sir, I do," she made herself say levelly, and his lips drew back to bare his teeth.

"Then I can only say your judgment is suspect, Ms. Harrington," he told her. "Even from here I can see that the access panel is still open on Ram One!"

"Yes, Sir, it is," Honor agreed. "When we got it open, we—"

"I don't recall inviting excuses, Ms. Harrington!" he snapped. "Is or is not that access panel still open?"

Honor clamped her teeth and decided it was a good thing Nimitz wasn't present. The 'cat had no vac suit. As such, he was thankfully barred from this compartment and so unable to bristle and snarl in response to Santino's attitude.

"Yes, Sir, it is," she said again after a moment, exactly as if she hadn't already agreed it was.

"And you are, perhaps, aware of the standing orders and operating procedures which require all access panels to be closed after inspection and routine maintenance?" he pressed.

"Yes, Sir, I am." Honor's voice was clearer and crisper than usual, and a small tic quivered at the corner of her mouth. Something seemed to gleam for just an instant in Santino's eyes as he observed it, and he leaned towards her.

"Then just how the hell can even *you* stand there and call this a 'competent' job?" he demanded harshly.

"Because, Sir, Ram One has a major engineering casualty," she told him. "The main actuator must have developed a short since its last routine maintenance. There are actual scorch marks inside the casing, and stages one and five both show red on the diagnostic. As per standing orders, I immediately informed Commander LaVacher in Engineering, and she instructed me to open the main breaker, red-tag the actuator, and leave the access panel open until she could get a repair crew up here to deal with it. All of which, Sir, is in my report."

Her dark eyes locked unflinchingly with his, but even as they did, she kicked herself mentally for losing her temper, for she saw the sudden rage flashing in the depths of his glare. She'd kept her voice level and even, but the entire tone of her answer—and especially that last jab about her report—had been well over the line. No one would ever be able to prove it, but she and Santino both knew she'd done it to get some of her own back, and his florid complexion darkened angrily.

"I assume you know the penalty for insubordination," he grated. She said nothing, and his color darkened further. "I asked you a question, Snotty!" he barked.

"I'm sorry, Sir. I was unaware that it was meant as a question. It sounded like a statement."

She could hardly believe it even as she heard her own voice say it, and she sensed Senior Chief Shelton and his work party behind her, watching it all. What was *wrong* with her? Why in heaven's name was she goading him back this way?

"Well it wasn't one!" Santino snapped. "So answer me!"

"Yes, Sir," she said. "I am aware of the penalty for insubordination."

"That's good, Snotty, because you just bought yourself a locker full of it! Now get out of my sight. Go directly to your quarters and remain there until I personally tell you differently!"

"Yes, Sir." She came to attention, saluted crisply, turned on her heel, and marched off with her head high while the man with the power to destroy her career before it even began glared after her.

The hatch signal chimed, and Commander Layson looked up from his display and pressed the admittance button. The hatch slid open, and Lieutenant Santino stepped through it.

"You wanted to see me, Sir?" the lieutenant said.

Layson nodded, but he said nothing, simply gazed at his assistant tactical officer with cool, thoughtful eyes. His face was expressionless, but Santino shifted slightly under that dispassionate gaze. It wasn't quite a fidget, but it was headed in that direction, and still the silence stretched out. At last, after at least three full minutes, Santino could stand it no more and cleared his throat.

"Uh, may I ask why you wanted to see me, Sir?"

"You may." Layson leaned back in his chair and folded his hands across his midsection. He sat that way for several seconds, eyes never leaving Santino's face, stretching the lieutenant's nerves a bit tighter, then went on in a neutral tone. "I understand there was some . . . difficulty with Midshipwoman Harrington this afternoon, Lieutenant," he said at last, his tone very cool. "Suppose you tell me what that was all about."

Santino blinked, then darkened. He hadn't yet gotten around to reporting Harrington's gross insubordination, but obviously the girl had gone crying to the Exec over it already. Just a sort of thing she *would* do. He'd known even before the troublemaking, spoiled brat reported aboard what he'd have to deal with there, and he'd been grateful for the forewarning, even if it wasn't considered quite "proper" for an OCTO to have private, pre-cruise briefings on the snotties who would be in his care. She and her wretched pet and the special treatment they both got had certainly justified the warnings he'd been given about her. He could see the arrogance in her eyes, of course, the way she was not so secretly convinced of her superiority to all about her. That was one of the things he'd been determined to knock out of her, in the faint hope that he might somehow salvage a worthwhile officer out of her. Yet even though today's episode had dealt a death blow to that hope, he was still vaguely surprised that even she'd had the sheer nerve to go whining to the Exec after he'd confined her to quarters, which she knew perfectly well meant no com time, either. Well, he'd just add that to the list when he wrote her fitness report.

He blinked again as he realized the Exec was still waiting, then shook himself.

"Of course, Sir," he said. "She was assigned to a routine maintenance inspection of Graser Three. When I arrived to check her progress, she'd instructed her inspection party to fall out and prepared to sign off on the inspection sheet. I observed, however, that the access panel for one of the power rams was still open in violation of SOP. When I pointed this out to her, she was both insolent in attitude and insubordinate in her language, so I ordered her to her quarters."

"I see." Layson frowned ever so slightly. "And how, precisely, was she insolent and insubordinate, Lieutenant?"

"Well, Sir," Santino said just a bit cautiously, "I asked her if she thought she'd completed her assignment, and she said she did. Then I pointed out the open access panel and asked her if she was familiar with standard procedures and the requirement to keep such panels closed when not actually being used for inspection or repair. Her tone and manner were both insolent when she replied that she was aware of proper procedure. Only when I pressed her for a fuller explanation did she inform me that she had discovered a fault in the ram and reported it to Engineering. Obviously, I had no way to know that before she explained it to me, but once again her manner was extremely insolent, and both her tone and her choice of words were, in my opinion, intended to express contempt for a superior officer. Under the circumstances, I saw no option but to relieve her of duty pending disciplinary action."

"I see," Layson repeated, then let his chair come upright. "Unfortunately, Lieutenant, I've already heard another account of the discussion which doesn't exactly tally with yours."

"Sir?" Santino drew himself up and squared his shoulders. "Sir, if Harrington has been trying to—"

"I didn't say I'd heard it from Midshipwoman Harrington," Layson said frostily, and Santino shut his mouth with a click. "Nor did I say I'd heard it from only one person," the Exec went on with cold dispassion. "In fact, I have six eyewitnesses, and none of them—not one, Lieutenant Santino—describes events as you just did. Would you perhaps care to comment on this minor discrepancy?"

Santino licked his lips and felt sweat prickle under the band of his beret as the ice in the Exec's voice registered.

"Sir, I can only report my own impressions," he said. "And with all due respect, Sir, I've had ample opportunity to watch Harrington's behavior and attitude over the last eight weeks. Perhaps that gives me, as her training officer, somewhat more insight into her character than a petty officer and working party who haven't had the advantage of that perspective."

"The *senior chief* petty officer in question," Layson said quietly, "has been in the King's Navy for seven years longer than you've been *alive*, Lieutenant Santino. In that time, he's had the opportunity to see more midshipmen and midshipwomen than you've seen dinners. I am not prepared to entertain any suggestion that he is too inexperienced to form a reasonable and reliable opinion of Ms. Harrington's character. Do I make myself clear?"

"Yes, Sir!"

Santino was perspiring freely now, and Layson stood behind his desk.

"As a matter of fact, Mr. Santino, I asked Senior Chief Shelton to share the insight of his many years of experience with me some days ago when I began to hear a few disturbing reports about our officer candidates. As such, he was acting under my direct instructions when he gave me his version of your . . . discussion with Ms. Harrington. Frankly, I'm happy he was there, because this episode simply confirms something I'd already come to suspect. Which is, Mr. Santino, that you are clearly too stupid to pour piss out of a boot without printed instructions!"

The Exec's voice cracked like a whip on the last sentence, and Santino flinched. Then his face darkened and his lips thinned.

"Sir, I resent your implications and strongly protest your language! Nothing in the Articles of War requires me to submit to personal insults and abuse!"

"But the Articles *do* require Ms. Harrington and her fellow middies to submit to *your* personal insults and abuse?" Layson's voice was suddenly like silk wrapped around a dagger's blade. "Is that what you're saying, Mr. Santino?"

"I—" Santino began, then cut himself off and licked his lips again as he realized the Exec had set him up.

"Sir, the situations aren't parallel," he said finally. "Harrington and the other snotties are fresh out of the Academy. They're still learning that the world isn't going to stand around and wipe their noses for them. If I seemed—or if Senior Chief Shelton thought I seemed— abusive, I was simply trying to help toughen them up and turn them into proper King's officers!"

He met Layson's cold eyes defiantly, and the Exec's lip curled.

"Somehow I knew you were going to say that, Lieutenant," he observed. "And, of course, no one can prove you're lying. If I *could* prove it, I would have you up on charges so fast your head would spin. Since I can't, I will explain this to you once. I will explain it *only* once, however, and you had better by God be listening."

The Exec didn't raise his voice, but Santino swallowed hard as Layson walked around the desk, hitched a hip up to rest on it, folded his arms across his chest, and looked him straight in the eye.

"For your information, Mr. Santino, those young men and women are already King's officers. They are also in their final form at the Academy, true, and they're here for evaluation as well as training. But while they are here aboard this ship, they are just as much members of her company and King's officers as *you* are. This means they are to be treated with respect, especially by their seniors. A midshipman cruise is supposed to be stressful. It is supposed to put sufficient pressure on a midshipman—or woman—to allow us to evaluate his ability to function under it and to teach *him* that he can hack tough assignments. It is *not* supposed to expose any of them to abuse, to bullying, or to the unearned contempt of a superior officer too stupid to know what his own duties and responsibilities are."

"Sir, I have never abused or bullied—"

"Lieutenant, you've never *stopped* bullying them!" Layson snapped. "As just one example, the term 'snotty,' while universally accepted as a slang label for a midshipman on his training cruise, is not an epithet to be hurled contemptuously at them by their own training officer! You have hectored and hounded them from the outset, and I strongly suspect that it's because you are a coward as well as stupid. After all, who expects a mere midshipwoman to stand up to a superior officer? Especially when she knows that superior officer can flush her career right out the air lock with a bad efficiency report?"

Santino stood rigid, his jaws locked, and Layson regarded him with cold contempt.

"You are relieved as officer candidate training officer for cause, effective immediately, Lieutenant Santino. I will report that fact to the Captain, and he will undoubtedly select another officer to fill that slot. In the meantime, you will prepare all records on the midshipmen formerly under your supervision for immediate transfer to that officer. Further, you will take *no* action against Midshipwoman Harrington, any other midshipman aboard this ship, Senior Chief Shelton, or any member of Ms. Harrington's work party which I or the Captain could conceivably construe as retaliation. Should you choose to do so, I assure you, you will regret it. Is that clearly understood?"

Santino nodded convulsively, and Layson gave him a thin smile.

"I'm afraid I didn't hear you, Mr. Santino. I asked if that was clearly understood."

"Yes, Sir." It came out strangled, and Layson smiled again.

"Very good, Lieutenant," he said softly. "Dismissed."

Honor never knew exactly what Commander Layson had to say to Santino that afternoon, but the vicious hatred which looked at her out of Santino's eyes told her that it had not been pleasant. She and her fellow middies did their best—by and large successfully—to restrain their rejoicing when Commander Layson announced that Lieutenant Saunders would replace him, but it was impossible to fool anyone in a world as small as a single starship.

Conditions on Snotty Row improved both drastically and immediately. There was a tough, professional-minded officer behind Saunders' cheerful face, but Santino's mocking contempt was utterly foreign to the assistant astrogator. No one but a fool—which none of *War Maiden*'s middies were—would write Saunders off as an easy touch, but he obviously felt no temptation to hammer the midshipmen in his care simply because he could, and that was more than enough to endear him to them.

Unfortunately, it was impossible for the middies to completely avoid Santino even after Saunders replaced him.

Tactics were one of the areas in which their training was most intense, which was why the assistant head of that department was traditionally the OCTO aboard any ship. The fact that Santino had been relieved of those duties—obviously for cause—was going to be a serious black mark on his record, which no doubt helped explain some of the hatred which so plainly burned within him. But it also made the change in assignments awkward for everyone involved. He might have been relieved as their training officer, but whatever the Exec and the Captain might have had to say to him in private, he had not been relieved of any other duties. Honor quickly noticed that Lieutenant Commander Hirake seemed to hand out a much higher percentage of their training assignments than had previously been the case, but it was impossible for any of them to report to Hirake without at least entering Santino's proximity. At least half the time, Santino was still the tac officer who actually oversaw their training sims, and none of them enjoyed it a bit when that happened. Nor did he, for that matter. He was careful to restrict himself to formalities, but the glitter in his eyes was ample proof of how difficult he found that. In some ways, it was almost hard not to sympathize with him. Given the circumstances of his relief, his contact with them as simply one more assistant department head was guaranteed to grind his nose into his disgrace. But however well Honor understood what he must be feeling, she, for one, was never tempted to feel sorry for him in the least. Besides, being Elvis Santino, it never occurred to him to blame anyone but Honor Harrington for what had happened to him, and despite anything the Exec had said to him, he was constitutionally incapable of hiding his hatred for her. Since he was going to feel that way whatever she did, she refused to strain herself trying to feel sympathy for someone who so amply merited his disgrace.

In some ways, it was almost worse now that he'd been relieved. Just as he was forced to stifle his fury at Honor on the occasions when their duties brought them into contact, she was required to act as if nothing had ever happened between them. Honor knew that there wasn't a great deal Layson could have done to decrease their contacts without far greater official provocation than Santino had given. Without stripping the man completely of his duties, there was no way to take him out of the queue. Certainly not without completing the lieutenant's public humiliation by absolutely confirming the reason he'd been relieved as OCTO in the first place. And there were times Honor wondered if perhaps Layson didn't have another reason for leaving Santino where he was. It was certainly one way to determine how she and her fellow middies would react under conditions of social strain!

For the most part though, she found herself blossoming and expanding as she was finally freed to throw herself into the learning experience a middy cruise was supposed to be. The fact that *War Maiden* arrived in Silesian space shortly after Santino's relief contributed its own weight to her happiness, although she supposed some people might have found it difficult to understand. After all, the Silesian Confederacy was a snake pit of warring factions, revolutionary governments, and corrupt system governors whose central government, such as it was, maintained its tenuous claim of rule solely on sufferance and the fact that the various unruly factions could never seem to combine effectively against it any more than they could combine effectively against one another. The casual observer, and especially the casual civilian observer, might have been excused for finding such an environment less than desirable. But Honor didn't see it that way, for the unending unrest was what had brought her ship here in the first place, and she was eager to test herself in the real world.

In a perverse sort of way, Silesia's very instability helped explain the enormous opportunities which the Confederacy offered Manticoran merchants. There was quite literally no reliable local supplier for most of the Confederacy's citizens' needs, which opened all sorts of possibilities for outside suppliers. Unfortunately, that same instability

provided all manner of havens and sponsors for the privateers and pirates for whom the Star Kingdom's commerce
offered what were often irresistible targets. The Royal
Manticoran Navy had made its draconian policy concern-
ing pirates (the enforcement of which was *War Maiden*'s
reason for being here) uncompromisingly clear over the
years. The demonstration of that policy had involved quite
a few pirate fatalities, but the capture of a single seven-
or eight-million-ton merchantman could earn a pirate crew
millions upon millions of dollars, and greed was a powerful motivator. Especially since even the stupidest pirate
knew that the Star Kingdom's navy couldn't possibly cover
the trade routes in depth and that no one else—with the
possible exception of the Andermani—would even make the
attempt.

That background explained why the Silesian Confederacy
had been the RMN's main training ground for decades. It
was a place to blood fledgling crews and starship commanders, gain tactical experience in small-scale engage-
ments, and expose Navy personnel to the realities of
labyrinthine political murkiness, all while doing something
useful in its own right—protecting the Star Kingdom's
commerce.

Still, the antipiracy effort was perpetually undersupplied
with warships. That had always been true to some extent,
but the steadily accelerating buildup of the battle fleet had
made it worse in recent years. The increased emphasis on
capital units and the Junction forts, and especially on
manning such crew-intensive propositions, had reduced the
availability of light units for such operational areas as
Silesia.

And there was a corollary to that, one which was bound
to affect HMS *War Maiden* and one Ms. Midshipwoman
Harrington. For if there were fewer units available, then those
which did reach Silesia could expect to be worked hard.

Honor stepped through the wardroom hatch with Nimitz
on her shoulder. It had been late by *War Maiden*'s onboard

clock when she went off duty, and she was tired, but she wasn't yet ready for bed. The heavy cruiser had made her alpha translation into normal space in the Melchor System of the Saginaw Sector shortly before the end of Honor's watch, and she'd had an excellent vantage from which to watch the process, for she was assigned to Astrogation this month. That was a mixed blessing in her opinion. It had its exciting moments, like the ones she'd spent backing up Lieutenant Commander Dobrescu during the approach to the alpha wall. Dobrescu, *War Maiden*'s astrogator, was Lieutenant Saunders' boss, and very good at his job, so there'd never been much chance that he was going to require Honor's assistance in a maneuver he'd performed hundreds of times before, but it had still been . . . not so much exciting as *satisfying* to sit in the backup chair at his side and watch the hyper log spin down to the translation locus. She still preferred Tactical to Astrogation—when Santino was absent, at least—but there *was* something about being the person who guided the ship among the stars.

Now if only she'd been any good at it . . .

Actually, she knew there was very little wrong with her astrogation in and of itself. She understood the *theory* perfectly, and as long as people would just leave her alone with the computers, she felt confident of her ability to find her way about the galaxy. Unfortunately, she was a midshipwoman. That meant she was a trainee, and to the Navy—including Dobrescu and Lieutenant Saunders (however satisfactory he might otherwise have been as an OCTO)—"trainee" meant "student," and students were expected to demonstrate their ability to do the basic calculations with no more than a hand comp and a stylus. And that was pure, sweat-popping, torment for Honor. However well she understood astrogation theory and multi-dimension math, her actual mathematical proficiency was something else altogether. She'd never been any good at math, which was all the more irritating because her aptitude scores indicated that she ought to excel at it. And, if people would just leave her alone and not stand around waiting for her to produce the right answer, she usually did come up with the correct solution in the end. For that matter, if she didn't have time to think about it and remember she was no good at math, she usually got the right answer fairly quickly. But that wasn't the way it worked during snotty-training, and she'd found herself sweating blood every time Dobrescu gave her a problem. Which was both grossly unfair—in her opinion—and stupid.

It wasn't as if Dobrescu or the astrogator of any other starship did his calculations by hand. The entire idea was ridiculous! That was what computers were for in the first place, and if a ship suffered such a massive computer failure as to take Astrogation off-line, figuring out where it was was going to be the *least* of its problems. She'd just *love* to see anyone try to manage a hyper generator, an inertial compensator, or the grav pinch of a fusion plant without computer support! But the Powers That Were weren't particularly interested in the opinions of one Ms. Midshipwoman Harrington, and so she sweated her way through the entire old-fashioned, labor-intensive, frustrating, *stupid* quill-pen-and-parchment business like the obedient little snotty she was.

At least Lieutenant Commander Dobrescu had a sense of humor.

And at least they were now safely back into normal space, with only three dinky little dimensions to worry about.

It would have been nice if Melchor had been a more exciting star to visit, given how hard Honor and her hand comp had worked to overcome the dreadful deficiencies of her ship's computers and get *War Maiden* here safely. Unfortunately, it wasn't. True, the G4 primary boasted three very large gas giants whose orbital spacing had created no less than four asteroid belts, but of its total of seven planets, only one was of any particular interest to humans. That was Arianna, the sole habitable planet of the system, which orbited Melchor at nine light-minutes, over eleven light-minutes inside the star's hyper limit. Arianna was a dry, mountainous world, with narrow, shallow seas, minimal icecaps, and a local flora which tended to the drought-hardy and low-growing. It had been settled over two hundred standard years before, but the hardscrabble colony had never moved much above the subsistence level until about fifty years ago, when an Andermani mining consortium had decided to take advantage of the resource extraction possibilities of all those asteroids. The outside investment and subsequent discovery of an unusual abundance of rare metals had brought an unexpected boom economy to the star system and attracted more immigrants in less time than the Melchor system government could ever have expected. Unfortunately for the Andermani, the local sector governor had seen that boom primarily as an opportunity to fill his own pockets. That wasn't an uncommon occurrence in Silesia, and however angry the Andermani consortium's financial backers might have been, they could not really have been very surprised when the governor began muscling in on their investment. Bribery and kickbacks were a way of life in the Confederacy, and people like the Saginaw sector governor knew how to extract them when they were not offered spontaneously. Within ten years, he and his family had owned over thirty percent of the total consortium, and the original Andermani backers had begun selling off their stock to other Silesians. Within another ten, the entire mining operation had been in Silesian hands and, like so much else in Silesian hands, running very, very poorly.

But this time around, the majority of the stockholders seemed willing to at least make an attempt to restore their fortunes, and the Star Kingdom's Dillingham Cartel had been brought onboard as a minority stockholder, with all sorts of performance incentives, to attempt to turn things back around once more. Which, in no small part, explained *War Maiden*'s presence in Melchor.

Dillingham had moved in Manticoran mining experts and begun a systematic upgrade of the extraction machinery which had been allowed to disintegrate under purely Silesian management. Honor suspected the cartel had been forced to pay high risk bonuses to any Manticorans who had agreed to relocate here, and she knew from the general background brief Captain Bachfisch had shared with *War Maiden*'s company that Dillingham had seen fit to install some truly impressive defensive systems to protect their extraction complexes and Arianna itself. They would not have been very effective against a regular naval force, but they were more than enough to give any piratical riffraff serious pause. Unfortunately, the Confederacy's central government refused to countenance privately flagged warships in its territorial space, so Dillingham had been forced to restrict itself to orbital systems. The ban on private warships was one of the (many) stupid policies of the Confederacy, in Honor's opinion. No doubt it was an attempt to at least put a crimp in the supply of armed vessels which seemed to find a way into pirate hands with dismal regularity, but it was a singularly ineffective one. All it really did in this case was to prevent someone who might have been able to provide the entire star system with a degree of safety which was unhappily rare in Silesia from doing so. The cartel's fixed defenses created zones within the Melchor System into which no raider was likely to stray, but they couldn't possibly protect merchant ships approaching or leaving the star.

Not that the Confederacy government was likely to regard that concern as any skin off its nose. The ships coming and going to Melchor these days were almost all Manticoran—aside from the handful of Andermani who still called there—and if the foreigners couldn't take the heat, then they should get out of the kitchen. Or, as in *War Maiden*'s case, call in their own governments to look after their interests. Of course, the Confederacy scarcely liked to admit that it needed foreign navies to police its own domestic space, but it had learned long ago that Manticore would send its naval units to protect its commerce whatever the Silesians wanted, so it might as well let Manticore pick up the tab for Melchor. And if the Star

Kingdom lost a few merchant ships and their crews in the process, well, it served the pushy foreigners right.

Honor was scarcely so innocent as to be surprised by the situation. That didn't mean she liked it, but like anyone else who aspired to command a King's ship, she recognized the protection of the merchant trade which was the heart, blood, and sinews of the Star Kingdom's economic might as one of the Navy's most important tasks. She didn't begrudge being here to protect Manticoran lives and property, whatever she might think of the so-called local government that made her presence a necessity.

Despite all that, it was highly unlikely *War Maiden* would find anything exciting to do here. As Captain Courvosier had often warned, a warship's life was ten percent hard work, eighty-nine percent boredom, and one percent sheer, howling terror. The percentages might shift a bit in a place like Silesia, but the odds in favor of boredom remained overwhelming. Honor knew that, too, but she was still just a bit on edge and not quite ready to turn in, which explained her detour by the wardroom. Besides, she was hungry. Again.

Her eyes swept the compartment with a hint of wariness as she stepped through the hatch, but then she relaxed. A middy in the wardroom was rather like a junior probationary member of an exclusive club, only less so. He or she had a right to be there, but the tradition was that they were to be seen and not heard unless one of the more senior members of the club invited them to open their mouths. In addition, they had better be prepared to run any errands any of their seniors needed run, because none of those seniors were likely to give up any of their hard-earned rest by getting up and walking across the wardroom when there were younger and more junior legs they could send instead. In fact, the tradition of sending snotties to do the scut work was one of the Navy's longer-standing traditions, part of the semi-hazing which was part and parcel of initiating midshipmen into the tribal wisdom, and Honor didn't really mind it particularly. For the most part, at least.

But this time she was lucky. Santino was off duty, of course, or she wouldn't have been here in the first place, but Lieutenant Commander LaVacher, who, while an otherwise reasonably pleasant human being, had a pronounced talent for and took an unabashed delight in finding things for middies to do, was also absent. Lieutenant Saunders looked up from his contemplation of a book reader and nodded a casual welcome, while Commander Layson and Lieutenant Jeffers, the ship's logistics officer, concentrated on the chessboard between them and Lieutenant Livanos and Lieutenant Tergesen, LaVacher's first and second engineers, respectively, were immersed in some sort of card game with Ensign Baumann. Aside from Saunders' off-handed greeting, no one seemed to notice her at all, and she made a beeline across the compartment towards the waiting mid-rats table. The food in the wardroom was considerably inferior to that served in the officers' mess at normal mealtimes, but rated several more stars than the off-watch rations available to the denizens of Snotty Row. And perhaps even more important, from Honor's perspective, there was more of it.

Nimitz perked up on her shoulder as she spotted the cheese-stuffed celery sticks and passed one up to him, then snuck an olive out of the slightly limp looking bowl of tossed salad and popped it into her own mouth to stave off starvation while she constructed a proper sandwich for more serious attention. Mayonnaise, cold cuts, mustard, Swiss cheese, sliced onion, another layer of cold cuts, dill pickle slices, another slice of Swiss cheese, some lettuce from the salad bowl, and a tomato ring, and she was done. She added a satisfying but not overly greedy heap of potato chips to her plate to keep it company, and poured herself a large glass of cold milk and snagged two cupcakes to keep *it* company, then gathered up a few extra celery sticks for Nimitz and found a seat at one of the unoccupied wardroom tables.

"How in God's name did you put that thing together without counter-grav?"

She turned her head and smiled in response to Commander Layson's question. The Exec gazed at her sandwich for a moment longer, then shook his head in bemusement, and Lieutenant Jeffers chuckled.

"I'm beginning to understand why we seem to be running a little short on commissary supplies," he observed. "I always knew midshipmen were bottomless pits, but—"

It was his turn to shake his head, and Layson laughed out loud.

"What I don't understand," Lieutenant Tergesen said just a bit plaintively, looking up from her cards at the sound of the Exec's laughter, "is how you can stuff all that in and never gain a kilo." The dark-haired engineering officer was in her early thirties, and while she certainly wasn't obese, she *was* a shade on the plump side. "I'd be as broad across the beam as a trash hauler if I gorged on half that many calories!"

"Well, I work out a lot, Ma'am," Honor replied, which was accurate enough, if also a little evasive. People were no longer as prejudiced against "genies" as they once had been, but those like Honor who were descended from genetically engineered ancestors still tended to be cautious about admitting it to anyone they did not know well.

"I'll say she does," Ensign Baumann put in wryly. "I saw her and Sergeant Tausig sparring yesterday evening." The ensign looked around at the wardroom's occupants in general and wrinkled her nose. "She was working out full contact . . . with Tausig."

"With *Tausig*?" Layson half-turned in his own chair to look more fully at Honor. "Tell me, Ms. Harrington. How well do you know Surgeon Lieutenant Chiem?"

"Lieutenant Chiem?" Honor frowned. "I checked in with him when I joined the ship, of course, Sir. And he was present one night when the Captain was kind enough to include me in his dinner party, but I don't really *know* the doctor. Why? Should I, Sir?"

This time the laughter was general, and Honor blushed in perplexity as Nimitz bleeked his own amusement from the back of her chair. Her seniors' mirth held none of the sneering putdown or condescension she might have expected from someone like a Santino, but she was honestly at a loss to account for it. Lieutenant Saunders recognized her confusion, and smiled at her.

"From your reaction, I gather that you weren't aware that the good sergeant was the second runner-up in last year's Fleet unarmed combat competition, Ms. Harrington," he said.

"That he was—" Honor stopped, gawking at the lieutenant, then closed her mouth and shook her head. "No, Sir, I didn't. He never—I mean, the subject never came up. Second runner-up in the *Fleet* matches? Really?"

"Really," Layson replied for the lieutenant, his tone dry. "And everyone knows Sergeant Tausig's theory of instruction normally involves thumping on his students until they either wake up in sick bay or get good enough to thump him back. So if you and Doctor Chiem haven't become close personal acquaintances, you must be pretty good yourself."

"Well, I try, Sir. And I was on the *coup de vitesse* demo team at the Academy, but—" She paused again. "But I'm not in the sergeant's league by a longshot. I only get a few pops in because he lets me."

"I beg to differ," Layson said more dryly than ever. "I hold a black belt myself, Ms. Harrington, and Sergeant Tausig has been known to spend the odd moment kicking my commissioned butt around the salle. And he has never 'let' me get a hit in. I think it's against his religion, and I very much doubt that he would decide to make an exception in your case. So if you 'get a few pops in,' you're doing better than ninety-five percent of the people who step onto the mat with him."

Honor blinked at him, still holding her sandwich for another bite. She'd known Tausig was one of the best she'd ever worked out with, and she knew he was light-years better at the *coup* than she was, but she would never have had the gall to ask to spar with him if she'd known he'd placed that high in the Fleet competition. He must have thought she was out of her mind! Why in the world had he agreed to let her? And if he was going to do that, why go so easy on her? Whatever Commander Layson might think, Honor couldn't believe that—

A high, shrill, atonal shriek cut her thought off like an ax of sound, and her sandwich thumped messily onto her plate as spinal reflex yanked her from her chair. She snatched Nimitz up and was out of the wardroom with the 'cat cradled in her arms before the plate slid off the table and the disintegrating sandwich's stuffing hit the decksole.

Lieutenant Saunders looked up from his displays and glanced at Honor over his shoulder as she arrived on the bridge, then flicked a look at the bulkhead chrono. It was only a brief glance, and then he gave her a quick, smiling nod as she crossed the command deck to him. Regs allowed her an extra five minutes to get to action stations, in order to give her time to secure Nimitz safely in his life-support module in her berthing compartment, but she'd made it in only thirteen minutes. It helped that Snotty Row was relatively close to the bridge, but it helped even more that she'd spent so many extra hours on suit drill at Saganami Island expressly because she'd known she'd have to find time to get her and Nimitz both cleared for action.

Not that even the amount of practice she'd put in could make it any less uncomfortable to make her skinsuit's plumbing connections that rapidly, she thought wryly as she settled gingerly into the assistant astrogation officer's chair. At the moment, Saunders occupied first chair in Astrogation, because Commander Dobrescu was with Commander Layson in Auxiliary Control. In fact, there was an entire backup command crew in AuxCon. Few modern heavy cruisers had auxiliary command decks, since more recent design theory regarded the provision of such a facility in so small a unit as a misuse of mass which could otherwise have been assigned to weapons or defensive systems. In newer ships of *War Maiden*'s type, an additional fire control position was provided at one end of the core hull instead, with just enough extra room for the ship's executive officer to squeeze into alongside the Tac Department personnel who manned it. But since *War Maiden* was an old enough design to provide an AuxCon, Captain Bachfisch had been able to create an entirely separate command crew to back up Commander Layson if something unpleasant should happen to the bridge.

Honor was delighted to be on the bridge itself, but because she was currently assigned to astro training duties, she'd drawn the assistant astrogator's duty here, while Basanta Lakhia filled the same duty for Dobrescu in AuxCon. The person Honor passionately envied at this moment was Audrey Bradlaugh, who sat beside Lieutenant Commander Hirake at Tactical. Honor would have given her left arm—well, a finger or two off her left hand, anyway—to sit in Audrey's chair, but at least she was luckier than Nassios. Captain Bachfisch had given Commander Layson the more experienced astrogator, but he'd kept the senior tac officer for himself, which meant Layson was stuck with Elvis Santino . . . and that Nassios had found himself stuck as Santino's assistant.

There were, Honor conceded, even worse fates than astrogation training duty.

She pushed the thought aside as she brought her own console rapidly online, and her amusement vanished and her stomach tightened when her astro plot came up and steadied. It lacked the detail of the tactical displays available to Hirake and Captain Bachfisch, but it showed enough for her to realize that this was no drill, for *War Maiden*'s arrival had interrupted a grim drama. The icon of a merchantman showed in her plot with the transponder code of a Manticoran vessel, but there was another vessel as well, the angry red bead of an unknown, presumably hostile ship less than four hundred kilometers from the merchie. The unknown vessel had her wedge up; the merchantman did not, and a jagged crimson ring strobed about its alphanumeric transponder code.

"Positive ID on the merchie, Skipper," Lieutenant Commander Hirake reported crisply. "I have her on my shipping list—RMMS *Gryphon's Pride*. She's a Dillingham Cartel ship, all right. Five-point-five million tons, a pure bulk hauler with no passenger accommodations, and she's squawking a Code Seventeen."

An invisible breeze blew across the bridge, cold on the nape of Honor's neck as the tac officer's announcement confirmed what all of them had already known. Code Seventeen was the emergency transponder code which meant "I am being boarded by pirates."

"Range to target?" Captain Bachfisch's tenor was no longer nasal. It was clipped, cool, and clear, and Honor darted a glance over her shoulder. The Captain sat in his command chair, shoulders square yet relaxed, right leg crossed over left while he gazed intently into the tactical display deployed from the chair, and the dark eyes in his thin face no longer frowned. They were the bright, fierce eyes of a predator, and Honor turned back to her own display with a tiny shiver.

"Nine-point-three-one million klicks," Hirake said, and if the Captain's voice was crisp, hers was flat. "We don't have the angle on them, either," she went on in that same disappointed tone. "The bogey's already gotten underway, and we'll never be able to pull enough vector change to run him down."

"Do you concur, Astro?"

"Aye, Sir," Saunders said with equal unhappiness. "Our base vector is away from the merchie at almost eleven thousand KPS, Captain. It'll take us forty-five minutes just to decelerate to relative rest to them, and according to my plot, the bogey is turning well over five hundred gravities."

"They're up to just over five-thirty," Hirake confirmed from Tactical.

"Even at maximum military power, we're twenty gravities slower than that, Sir," Saunders said. "At normal max, they've got over one-point-two KPS squared on us, and they're accelerating on a direct reciprocal of our heading."

"I see." Bachfisch said, and Honor understood the disappointment in his tone perfectly. The pirate ship had to be smaller than *War Maiden* to pull that sort of acceleration, which meant it was certainly more lightly armed, as well, but it didn't matter. Their relative positions and base vectors had given the pirates the opportunity to run, and their higher acceleration curve meant the heavy cruiser could never bring them into even extreme missile range.

"Very well," the Captain said after a moment. "Astro, put us on a course to intercept the merchie. And keep trying to raise them, Com."

"Aye, aye, Sir." Saunders' quiet acknowledgment sounded much too loud against the bitter background silence of the bridge.

There was no response to Lieutenant Sauchuk's repeated hails as *War Maiden* closed on the merchantship, and the taut silence on the heavy cruiser's bridge grew darker and more bitter with each silent minute. It took over two hours for the warship to decelerate to zero relative to the merchantman and then overtake her. *Gryphon's Pride* coasted onward at her base velocity, silent and uncaring, and the cruiser was less than a minnow as she swam toward a rendezvous with her, for the whale-like freighter out-massed *War Maiden* by a factor of almost thirty. But unlike the whale, the minnow was armed, and a platoon of her Marines climbed into their skinsuits and checked their weapons in her boat bay as Captain Bachfisch's helmsman edged his ship into position with finicky precision.

Honor was no longer on the bridge to watch. Bachfisch's eyes had passed over her with incurious impersonality while he punched up Major McKinley, the commander of *War Maiden*'s embarked Marine company, on the internal com and instructed her to prepare a boarding party. But then those eyes had tracked back to his assistant astrogator's assistant.

"I'll be attaching a couple of naval officers, as well," he told McKinley, still looking at Honor.

"Yes, Sir," the Marine's reply came back, and Bachfisch released the com stud.

"Commander Hirake," he said, "please lay below to the boat bay to join the boarding party. And take Ms. Harrington with you."

"Aye, aye, Sir," the tac officer acknowledged and stood. "You have Tactical, Ms. Bradlaugh."

"Aye, aye, Ma'am," Audrey acknowledged, and darted a quick, envious glance at her cabin mate.

"Come along, Ms. Harrington," Hirake said, and Honor stood quickly.

"Sir, I request relief," she said to Saunders, and the lieutenant nodded.

"You stand relieved, Ms. Harrington," he said with equal formality.

"Thank you, Sir." Honor turned to follow Hirake through the bridge hatch, but Captain Bachfisch raised one hand in an admonishing gesture and halted them.

"Don't forget your sidearm this time," he told Hirake rather pointedly, and she nodded. "Good," he said. "In that case, people, let's be about it," he added, and waved them off his bridge.

Hirake said nothing in the lift car. Despite *War Maiden*'s age and the idiosyncratic layout of her lift shafts, the trip from the bridge to the boat bay was relatively brief, but it lasted more than long enough for conflicting waves of anticipation and dread to wash through Honor. She had no idea why the Captain had picked her for this duty, but she'd heard more than enough grizzly stories from instructors and noncoms at the Academy to produce a stomach-clenching apprehension. Yet hunting down pirates—and cleaning up the wreckage in their wake—was part of the duty she'd signed on to perform, and not even the queasiness in her midsection could quench her sense of excitement finally confronting its reality.

Lieutenant Blackburn's Second Platoon was waiting in the boat bay, but Honor was a bit surprised to see that

Captain McKinley and Sergeant-Major Kutkin were also present. She'd assumed McKinley would send one of her junior officers, but she and Kutkin obviously intended to come along in person, for both of them were skinsuited, and the sergeant-major had a pulse rifle slung over his shoulder. Major McKinley didn't carry a rifle, but the pulser holstered at her hip looked almost like a part of her, and its grip was well worn.

The Marine officer's blue eyes examined the newcomers with clinical dispassion and just a hint of disapproval, and Hirake sighed.

"All right, Katingo," she said resignedly. "The Skipper already peeled a strip off me, so give me a damned gun."

"It's nice to know *someone* aboard the ship knows Regs," McKinley observed, and nodded to a noncom standing to one side. Honor hadn't seen him at first, but she recognized Sergeant Tausig as he stepped forward and silently passed a regulation gun belt and pulser to the tac officer. Lieutenant Commander Hirake took them a bit gingerly and buckled the belt around her waist. It was obvious to Honor that the Navy officer felt uncomfortable with the sidearm, but Hirake drew the pulser and made a brief but thorough inspection of its safety and magazine indicators before she returned it to its holster.

"Here, Ma'am," Tausig said, and Honor held out her hand for a matching belt. She felt both the major and the sergeant-major watching her, but she allowed herself to show no sign of her awareness as she buckled the belt and adjusted it comfortably. Then she turned slightly away, drew the pulser—keeping its muzzle pointed carefully away from anyone else—visually checked the safety and both magazine indicators and the power cell readout, then ejected the magazine and cleared the chamber to be certain it was unloaded. She replaced the magazine and reholstered the weapon. The military issue flapped holster was clumsy and bulky compared to the semi-custom civilian rig Honor had always carried in the Sphinx bush, but the pulser's weight felt comfortingly familiar at her hip, and Sergeant Tausig's eyes met hers with a brief flash of approval as she looked up once more.

"All right, people," Major McKinley said, raising her voice as she turned to address Blackburn's platoon. "You all know the drill. Remember, we do this by The Book, and I will personally have the ass of anyone who fucks up."

She didn't ask if her audience understood. She didn't have to, Honor thought. Not when she'd made herself clear in that tone of voice. Of course, it would have been nice if someone had told *Honor* what "the drill" was, but it was an imperfect universe. She'd just have to keep her eyes on everyone else and take her cues from them. And at least, given the Captain's parting injunction to Hirake and McKinley's response to it, she might not be the only one who needed a keeper.

The pinnace was just like dozens of other pinnaces Honor had boarded during Academy training exercises, but it didn't feel that way. Not with forty-six grim, hard-faced, armed-to-the-teeth Marines and their weapons packed into it. She sat next to Lieutenant Commander Hirake at the rear of the passenger compartment, and watched through the view port beside her as the pinnace crossed the last few hundred kilometers between *War Maiden* and *Gryphon's Pride.* The big freighter grew rapidly as they came up on it from astern, and the pinnace's pilot cut his wedge and went to reaction thrusters, then angled his flight to spiral up and around the huge hull.

Honor and Hirake were tied into the Marines' com net. There was no chatter, and Honor sensed the intensity with which the Marines fortunate enough to have view port seats, veterans all, stared out at the freighter. Then the pilot spoke over the net.

"I have debris, Major," he said in a flat, professional voice. "At your ten o'clock high position." There were a few seconds of silence, then, "Looks like bodies, Ma'am."

"I see them, Coxswain," McKinley said tonelessly. Honor was on the wrong side of the pinnace to lean closer to her port and peer forward. For a moment she felt frustrated, but then that changed into gratitude for the accident of seating that had kept her from doing just that. She would have felt ashamed and somehow unclean if Hirake and the Marines had seen her craning her neck while she gawked at the bodies like some sort of sick disaster-watcher or a news service ghoul.

"Coming up on her main starboard midships hatch, Ma'am," the pilot reported a few minutes later. "Looks like the cargo bays are still sealed, but the forward personnel hatch is open. Want me to go for a hard docking?"

"No, we'll stick to The Book," McKinley said. "Hold position at two hundred meters."

"Aye, aye, Ma'am."

The pilot nudged the pinnace into a stationary position relative to the freighter with the pinnace's swept wing tip almost exactly two hundred meters from the hull, and Sergeant-Major Kutkin shoved all two meters of his height up out of his seat. Lieutenant Blackburn was no more than a second behind the sergeant-major, and Kutkin watched with an approving proprietary air as the lieutenant addressed his platoon.

"All right, Marines, let's do it. Carras, you've got point. Janssen, you've got the backdoor. The rest of you in standard, just like we trained for it." He waited a moment, watching as two or three of his troopers adjusted position slightly, then grunted in approval. "Helmet up and let's go," he said.

Honor unclipped her own helmet from the carry point on her chest and put it on. She gave it a little extra twist to be sure it was seated properly and raised her left arm to press the proper key on the sleeve keypad. Her helmet HUD lit immediately, and she automatically checked the telltale which confirmed a good seal and the digital readout on her oxygen supply. Both were nominal, and she took her place—as befitted her lowly status—at the very rear of the queue to the pinnace's port hatch. With so many personnel to unload, the flight crew made no effort to cycle them through the air lock. Instead, they cracked the outer hatch and vented the compartment's air to space. Honor felt the pressure tug at her for several seconds as the air bled outward, but then the sensation of unseen hands plucking at her limbs faded and her skinsuit audio pick-ups brought her the absolute silence of vacuum.

Corporal Carras—the same corporal, Honor realized suddenly, who had been *War Maiden*'s tube sentry when she first joined the ship—pushed himself away from the pinnace. He drifted outward for four or five meters, and then engaged his skinsuit thrusters once he was sure he had cleared their safety perimeter. He accelerated smoothly towards the freighter, riding his thrusters with the practiced grace of some huge bird of prey, and the rest of his section followed.

Even with their obvious practice it took time for all of the Marines to clear the hatch for Hirake and Honor, but at last it was their turn, and despite her best effort to mirror the cool professionalism of Blackburn's Marines, Honor felt a fresh flutter of excited anxiety as she followed Hirake into the open hatch. The lieutenant commander launched herself with a gracefulness which fully matched that of the Marines, yet was somehow subtly different. She sailed away from the pinnace, and Honor pushed herself out into emptiness in the tac officer's wake.

This far out, the system primary was a feeble excuse for a star, and even that was on the far side of the freighter. The pinnace and its erstwhile passengers floated in an ink-black lee of shadow, and hull-mounted spotlights and the smaller helmet lights of skinsuits pierced the ebon dark. The pinnace's powerful spots threw unmoving circles of brilliance on the freighter's hull, picking out the sealed cargo hatch and the smaller personnel hatch which gaped open ahead of it, yet their beams were invisible, for there was no air to diffuse them. Smaller circles curtsied and danced across the illuminated area and into the darkness beyond as the helmet lights of individual Marines swept over the hull. Honor brought up her own helmet lamp as her thrusters propelled her towards the ship, and her eyes were bright. She cherished no illusion that she was a holo-drama heroine about to set forth on grand adventure, yet her pulse was faster than usual, and it was all she could do not to rest her right hand on the butt of her holstered pulser.

Then something moved in the darkness. It was more sensed than seen, an uncertain shape noticed only because it briefly occluded the circle on the hull cast by someone else's light as it rotated slowly, keeping station on the ship. She rotated her own body slightly, bringing her light to bear upon it, and suddenly any temptation she might still have nursed to see this as an adventure vanished.

The crewwoman could not have been more than a very few standard years older than Honor . . . and she would never grow any older. She wore no suit. Indeed, even the standard shipboard coverall she once had worn had been half-ripped from her body and drifted with her in the blackness, tangled about her arms and shoulders like some ungainly, rucked up shroud. An expression of pure horror was visible even through the froth of frozen blood caked about her mouth and nose, and the hideousness of her death had relaxed her sphincters. It was not simply death. It was desecration, and it was ugly, and Honor Harrington swallowed hard as she came face-to-face with it. She remembered all the times she and Academy friends had teased one another, humorously threatening to "space" someone for some real or imagined misdeed, and it was no longer funny.

She didn't know how long she floated there, holding her light on the corpse which had once been a young woman until someone jettisoned her like so much garbage. It seemed later like a century, but in reality it could not have been more than a very few seconds before she tore her eyes away. She had drifted off course, she noted mechanically, and Lieutenant Commander Hirake was twenty or thirty meters ahead of her and to the right. She checked her HUD, and tapped a correction on her thruster controls.

She felt a sort of surprise when her fingers moved the skinsuit gloves' finger servos with rocklike steadiness, and she accelerated smoothly to follow the tac officer through the blackness.

It was interesting, a detached corner of her brain noted almost clinically. Despite her horror, she truly was collected and almost calm—or something which counterfeited those qualities surprisingly well.

But she was very, very careful what else she let her helmet light show her.

"... so that's about it, Sir." Commander Layson sighed, and let the memo board drop onto the corner of Captain Bachfisch's desk. "No survivors. No indications that they even tried to keep any of the poor bastards alive long enough to find out what *Gryphon's Pride* might've had in her secure cargo spaces." He leaned back in his chair and rubbed his eyes wearily. "They just came aboard, amused themselves, and butchered her entire company. Eleven men and five women. The lucky ones were killed out of hand. The others . . ." His voice trailed off, and he shook his head.

"Not exactly what our briefing told us to expect," Bachfisch said quietly. He tipped back in his own chair and gazed at the deckhead.

"No, but this is Silesia," Layson pointed out. "The only thing anyone can count on here is that the lunatics running the asylum will be even crazier than you expected," he added bitterly. "Sometimes I wish we could just go ahead and hand the damned place over to the Andies and be done with it. Let these sick bastards deal with the Andy Navy for a while with no holds barred."

"Now, Abner," Bachfisch said mildly. "You shouldn't go around suggesting things you know would give the Government mass coronaries. Not to mention the way the cartels would react to the very notion of letting someone else control one of their major market areas! Besides, would you really like encouraging someone like the Andermani to bite off that big an expansion in one chunk?"

"All joking aside, Sir, it might not be that bad a thing from our perspective. The Andies have always been into slow and steady expansion, biting off small pieces one at a time and taking time to digest between mouthfuls. If they jumped into a snake pit like Silesia, it would be like grabbing a hexapuma by the tail. They might be able to hang onto the tail, but those six feet full of claws would make it a lively exercise. Could even turn out to be a big enough headache to take them out of the expansion business permanently."

"Wishful thinking, Abner. Wishful thinking." Bachfisch pushed himself up out of his chair and paced moodily across his cramped day cabin. "I told the Admiralty we needed more ships out here," he said, then snorted. "Not that they needed to hear it from me! Unfortunately, more ships are exactly what we don't have, and with the Peeps sharpening their knives for Trevor's Star, Their Lordships aren't going to have any more to spare out this way for the foreseeable future. And the damned Silesians know it."

"I wish you were wrong, Sir. Unfortunately, you're not."

"I only wish I could decide which were worse," Bachfisch half-muttered. "The usual sick, sadistic, murdering scum like the animals that hit *Gryphon's Pride*, or the goddamn 'patriots' and their so-called privateers!"

"I think I prefer the privateers," Layson said. "There aren't as many of them, and at least some of them pretend to play by some sort of rules. And there's at least a sense of semi-accountability to the government or revolutionary committee or whoever the hell issued their letter of marque in the first place."

"I know the logic." Bachfisch chopped at the air with his right hand. "And I know we can at least sometimes lean on whoever chartered them to make them behave— or at least to turn them over to us if they *mis*behave badly enough—but that assumes we know who they are and where they came from in the first place. And anything we gain from that limited sort of accountability on their part, we lose on the capability side."

Layson nodded. It didn't take much of a warship to make a successful pirate cruiser. Aside from a few specialized designs, like the Hauptman Cartel's armed passenger liners, merchantmen were big, slow, lumbering and unarmored targets, helpless before even the lightest shipboard armament. By the same token, no sane pirate—and however sociopathic all too many of them might be, pirates as a group tended to be very sane where matters of survival were concerned—wanted to take on any warship in combat. Even here in Silesia, regular navy crews tended to be better trained and more highly motivated. Besides, a pirate's ship was his principal capital investment. He was in business to make money, not spend it patching the holes in his hull . . . assuming he was fortunate enough to escape from a regular man-of-war in the first place.

But privateers were different. Or they could be, at least. Like pirates, the financial backers who invested in a privateer expected it to be a money-making concern. But privateers also possessed a certain quasi-respectability, for interstellar law continued to recognize privateering as a legal means of making war, despite the strong opposition of nations like the Star Kingdom of Manticore, whose massive merchant marine made it the natural enemy of any legal theory which legitimized private enterprise commerce raiding. As far as Bachfisch and Layson were concerned, there was little if any practical difference between privateers and pirates, but smaller nations which could not afford to raise and maintain large and powerful navies adamantly resisted all efforts to outlaw privateering by interstellar treaty. Oh, they attended the conferences Manticore and other naval powers convened periodically to discuss the issue, but the bottom line was that they saw privateers as a cost-effective means by which even a weak nation could attack the life's blood of a major commercial power like the Star Kingdom and at least tie down major portions of its navy in defensive operations.

Bachfisch and Layson could follow the logic of that argument, however much they might detest it, but privateering as practiced in the Silesian Confederacy was a far cry from the neat theories propounded by the practice's defenders at the interstellar conferences. Breakaway system governments and an incredible variety of "people's movements" proliferated across the Confederacy like weeds in a particularly well-rotted compost heap, and at least half of them issued—sold, really—letters of marque to license privateering in the names of their revolutions. At least two-thirds of those letters went to out and out pirates, who regarded them as get-out-of-jail-free cards. Whereas piracy was a capital offense under interstellar law, privateers were legally regarded as a sort of militia, semi-civilian volunteers in the service of whatever nation had issued their letter of marque in the first place. That meant that their ships could be seized, but that they themselves were protected. The worst that could happen to them (officially, at least) was incarceration along with other prisoners of war, unless they had been so careless as to be captured in the act of murdering, torturing, raping, or otherwise treating the crews of their prizes in traditional piratical fashion.

That was bad enough, but in some ways the genuine patriots were even worse. They were far less likely to indulge themselves in atrocities, but their ships tended to be larger and better armed, and they actually did regard themselves as auxiliary naval units. That made them willing to accept risks no true for-profit pirate would consider running for a moment, up to and including an occasional willingness to engage light warships of whoever they were rebelling against that week. Which wouldn't have bothered the Royal Manticoran Navy excessively, if not for the fact that even the best privateers were still amateurs who sometimes suffered from less than perfect target identification.

The fact that some privateers invariably seemed to believe that attacks on the commerce of major powers like Manticore would somehow tempt those major powers into intervening in their own squabbles in an effort to impose an outside solution to protect their commercial interests was another factor altogether. The Star Kingdom had made it abundantly clear over the years that it would come down like the wrath of God on any revolutionary movement stupid enough to deliberately send its privateers after Manticoran merchant shipping, yet there always seemed to be a new group of lunatics who thought *they* could somehow manipulate the Star Kingdom where everyone else had failed. The Navy eventually got around to teaching them the same lesson it had taught their countless predecessors, but it was ultimately a losing proposition. That particular bunch of crazies would not offend again once the RMN crushed them, but a lot of Manticoran merchant spacers tended to get hurt first, and someone else would always be along in a year or two who would have to learn the lesson all over again.

And at the moment, the Saginaw Sector of the Confederacy (which just happened to contain the Melchor System) was in an even greater than usual state of unrest. At least two of its systems—Krieger's Star and Prism—were in open rebellion against the central government, and there were half a dozen shadow governments and liberation movements all boiling away just beneath the surface. ONI estimated that several of those insurrectionary factions had managed to open communications and establish a degree of coordination which had—yet again—taken the Confederacy's excuse for a government by surprise. Worse, The Honorable Janko Wegener, the Saginaw sector governor, was even more venal than most, and it seemed obvious to ONI that he saw the turmoil in his command area as one more opportunity to line his pockets. At the same time that Wegener fought valiantly to suppress the rebellions in his sector, he was raking off protection money in return for tacitly ignoring at least three liberation movements, and there was compelling evidence to suggest that he was actually permitting privateers to auction their prizes publicly in return for a percentage of their profits. Under the ironclad laws of cronyism which governed the Confederacy, the fact that he was a close relative of the current government's interior minister and an in-law of the premier meant Wegener could get away with it forever (or at least until the Confederacy's political parties' game of musical chairs made someone else premier), and the odds were that he would retire a very wealthy man indeed.

In the meantime, it was up to HMS *War Maiden* and her company to do what they could to keep some sort of lid on the pot he was busily stirring.

"If only we could free up a division or two of the wall and drop them in on Saginaw to pay Governor Wegener a little visit, we might actually be able to do some genuine good," Bachfisch observed after a moment. "As it is, all we're going to manage is to run around pissing on forest fires." He stared off into the distance for several seconds, then shook himself and smiled. "Which is the usual state of affairs in Silesia, after all, isn't it?"

"I'm afraid you're right there, Sir," Layson agreed ruefully. "I just wish we could have started pissing on them by getting into missile range of the bastards who killed *Gryphon's Pride*."

"You and me both," Bachfisch snorted. "But let's face it, Abner, we were luckier than we had any right to count on just to recover the ship herself. If they hadn't wasted time . . . amusing themselves with her crew and gotten her underway sooner instead—or even just killed her transponder to keep us from realizing she'd been taken—they'd have gotten away clean. The fact that we got the hull back may not be much, but it's better than nothing."

"The insurers will be pleased, anyway," Layson sighed, then made a face and shook his head quickly. "Sorry, Sir. I know that wasn't what you meant. And I know the insurers would be just as happy as we would if we'd managed to save the crew as well. It's just—"

"I know," Bachfisch said, waving away his apology. The captain took one more turn around the cabin, then parked himself in the chair behind the desk once more. He picked up Layson's memo board and punched up the display to in the terse report himself. "At least McKinley and her people cleared the ship on the bounce," he observed. "And I notice that even Janice remembered to take a gun this time!"

"With a little prodding," Layson agreed, and they grinned at one another. "I think the problem is that she regards anything smaller than a missile or a broadside energy mount as being beneath a tac officer's dignity," the exec added.

"It's worse than that," Bachfisch said with a small headshake. "She's from downtown Landing, and I don't think she and her family spent more than a day or two all told in the bush when she was a kid." He shrugged. "She never learned to handle a gun before the Academy, and she's never actually needed one in the line of duty since. That's what Marines are for."

"Sergeant Tausig mentioned to me that Ms. Harrington seemed quite competent in that regard," Layson observed in a carefully uninflected tone.

"Good," Bachfisch said. "Of course, her family has a nice little freeholding in the Copper Wall Mountains. That's hexapuma country, and I imagine she grew up packing a gun whenever she went for a hike. Actually, I think she did quite well. At least she kept her lunch down while they recovered and bagged the bodies."

Layson managed to keep his eyebrows from rising. He'd known Harrington was from Sphinx, of course, but he hadn't known she was from the Copper Walls, so how did the Captain know? He looked at Bachfisch for a moment, then drew a deep breath.

"Excuse me, Sir. I realize it's not really any of my business, but I know you must have had a reason for specifically requesting that Ms. Harrington be assigned to us for her snotty cruise."

The sentence was a statement that was also a question, and Bachfisch leaned back in his chair and gazed steadily at his executive officer.

"You're right, I did," he said after a thoughtful pause. "Are you by any chance familiar with Captain Raoul Courvosier, Abner?"

"Captain Courvosier?" Layson's brow furrowed. "Oh, of course. He's the head of the Saganami Tactical Department, isn't he?"

"At the moment," Bachfisch said. "The grapevine says he's up for rear admiral on the current list. They're going to jump him right past commodore, and they'll probably drag him over to head the War College as soon as they do."

"I knew he had a good rep, Sir, but is he really that good?" Layson asked in considerable surprise. It was unusual, to say the least, for the RMN to jump an officer two grades in a single promotion, despite its current rate of expansion.

"He's better than that," Bachfisch said flatly. "In fact, he's probably the finest tactician and one of the three best strategists I've ever had the honor to serve under."

Abner Layson was more than simply surprised by that, particularly since that was precisely the way *he* would have described Captain Thomas Bachfisch.

"If Raoul had been born into a better family—or been even a little more willing to play the suck-up game—he would have had his commodore's star years ago," Bachfisch went on, unaware of his exec's thoughts. "On the other hand, I imagine he's done more good than a dozen commodores at the Academy. But when Raoul Courvosier tells me privately that one of his students has demonstrated in his opinion the potential to be the most outstanding officer of her generation and asks me to put her in my Snotty Row, I'm not about to turn him down. Besides, she's about due for a little offsetting career boost."

"I beg your pardon, Sir?" The question came out almost automatically, for Layson was still grappling with the completely unexpected endorsement of Honor Harrington's capabilities. Of course, he'd been very favorably impressed by her himself, but *the* outstanding officer of her generation?

I said she's due for a career boost," Bachfisch repeated,

and snorted at the confused look Layson gave him. "What? You think *I* was stupid enough to ask for Elvis Santino for my OCTO? Give me a break, Abner!"

"But—" Layson began, then stopped and looked at Bachfisch narrowly. "I'd assumed," he said very slowly, "that Santino was just a particularly obnoxious example of BuPers' ability to pound square pegs into round holes. Are you saying he wasn't, Sir?"

"I can't prove it, but I wouldn't bet against it. Oh, it could be innocent enough. That's why I didn't say anything about it to you ahead of time . . . and why I was so happy that he gave you ample grounds to bring the hammer down on him. The creep had it coming, whatever his motives may have been, but nobody who sees your report and the endorsements from Shelton and Flanagan could possibly question the fact that he was relieved for cause."

"But why would anyone want to question it in the first place?"

"Did you ever happen to encounter Dimitri Young?"

This time, despite all he could do, Layson blinked in surprise at the complete *non sequitur.*

"Uh, no, Sir. I don't believe I can place the name."

"I'm not surprised, and you didn't miss a thing," Bachfisch said dryly. "He was considerably before your time, and he resigned about the time he made commander in order to pursue a political career when he inherited the title from his father."

"Title?" Layson repeated cautiously.

"These days he's the Earl of North Hollow, and from all I hear he's just as big a loss as a human being as he ever was. What's worse, he's reproduced, and his oldest son, Pavel, was a class ahead of Harrington at Saganami."

"Why do I think I'm not going to like this, Sir?"

"Because you have good instincts. It seems that Mr. Midshipman Young and Ms. Midshipwoman Harrington had a small . . . disagreement in the showers one night."

"In the show—" Layson began sharply, then broke off.

"My God," he went on a moment later in a very different tone, "she must have kicked his ass up one side and down the other!"

"As a matter of fact, she did," Bachfisch said, gazing speculatively at his exec.

"Damned straight she did," Layson said with an evil chuckle. "Ms. Harrington works out full contact with Sergeant Tausig, Sir. And she gets through his guard upon occasion."

"Does she?" Bachfisch smiled slowly. "Well, now. I suppose that *does* explain a few things, doesn't it?" He gazed sightlessly at the bulkhead, smiling at something Layson could not see, for several seconds, then shook himself back to the present.

"At any rate," he said more briskly, "Harrington sent him to the infirmary for some fairly serious repairs, and he never did manage to explain just what he was doing in the showers alone with her after hours that inspired her to kick the crap out of him. But neither did she, unfortunately, press charges against him. No," he said, shaking his head before Layson could ask the question, "I don't know why she didn't, and I don't know why Hartley couldn't get her to do it. But she didn't, and the little prick graduated with the rest of his class and went straight into the old-boy patronage system."

"And cranked the same system around to wreck Harrington's career." There was no amusement in Layson's voice this time, and Bachfisch nodded.

"That's Raoul's belief, anyway," the captain said, "and I respect his instincts. Besides, unlike you *I* did know Young's father, and I doubt very much that he's improved with age. That's one reason I have to wonder how we wound up saddled with Santino. North Hollow may not be Navy anymore, but he's got one hell of a lot of clout in the House of Lords, and he sits on the Naval Affairs Committee. So if he does want to punish her for 'humiliating' his precious son, he's in the perfect spot to do it."

"I see, Sir." Layson sat back in his chair, and his mind

worked busily. There was even more going on here than he'd suspected might be the case, and he felt a brief uneasiness at the weight and caliber of the enemies his Captain appeared to be courting. But knowing Bachfisch as well as he did, he also understood perfectly. In many ways, there were actually two Royal Manticoran Navies: the one to which well-connected officers like Pavel Young and Elvis Santino belonged, where all that truly mattered was who was related to whom; and the one which produced officers like Thomas Bachfisch and—he hoped—Abner Layson, whose only claim to their rank was the fact that they put duty and responsibility before life itself. And just as the Navy of patronage and string-pullers looked after their own, so did the Navy of dedication and ability protect and nurture *its* own.

"Does Harrington know?" he asked. "I mean, know that Young and his family are out to get her?"

"I don't know. If she's as observant as I think she is—or even a quarter as good at analyzing interpersonal relationships as she is in the tactical simulator—then it's a pretty sure bet that she does. On the other hand, she didn't press charges against him in the first place, and that raises a question mark, doesn't it? In any case, I don't think a snotty cruise in the middle of Silesia is the best possible place and time for us to be explaining it to her, now is it?"

"You do have a gift for understatement, Sir."

"A modest talent, but one which has its uses," Bachfisch admitted. Then he picked up the memo board and handed it back to Layson. "But that's enough about Ms. Harrington for the moment," he said. "Right now, you and I need to give some thought to where we go from here. I've been thinking that it might be worthwhile to hang around here in Melchor for a while and use the system as a pirate lure, since this is the main magnet for our shipping at the moment. But if we do that too obviously, the local pirates—and probably Wegener—are going to get hinky. So what I was thinking was—"

✧   ✧   ✧

Commodore Anders Dunecki replayed the brief message and clenched his jaw against the urge to swear vilely.

"Is this confirmed?" he asked the messenger without looking up from the display.

"Yes, Sir. The SN made the official announcement last week. According to their communique they picked off *Lydia* a couple of weeks before that, and Commander Presley is almost a month overdue." The nondescript man in civilian clothing shrugged unhappily. "According to the SN they took him out in Hera, and that was where he'd said he was planning to cruise with *Lydia*. We don't have absolute confirmation that it was him, of course, but all the pieces match too well for it to have been anyone else."

"But according to this—" Dunecki jabbed his chin at the holographic screen where the message footer was still displayed "—it was a heavy cruiser that nailed him." He paused, looking at the messenger expectantly, and the other man nodded. "In that case," Dunecki said, "what I want to know is how the hell the SN managed to run a ship that powerful into the area without our hearing about it. There's no way John Presley would have been careless enough to let a heavy cruiser sneak up on him if he'd known she was there to begin with. And he damned well ought to have known!"

The rage Dunecki had struggled to conceal broke through his control with the last sentence, and the messenger sat very still. Anders Dunecki was not a good man to anger, and the messenger had to remind himself that he was only the bearer of the news, and not the one responsible for its content.

"I didn't know Commander Presley as well as you did, Sir," he said carefully after a long moment of silence. "Or for as long. But I'm familiar with his record in the Council's service, and on the basis of that, I'd have to agree that he certainly would have exercised all due prudence if he'd been aware of the escalation in threat levels. Actually, as early as we can tell, at least two heavy cruisers, and possibly as many as three have been transferred into Saginaw in the last month and a half, and there are some indications that more will be following. Apparently—" he allowed himself a predatory smile despite the tension in Dunecki's cabin "—losses in the sector have gotten severe enough for the Navy to reinforce its presence here."

"Which is probably a good thing. Or at least an indication that we're really beginning to hurt them," Dunecki agreed, but his glass-green eyes were frosty, and the messenger's smile seemed to congeal. "At the same time," the commodore went on in the same chill tone, "if they're increasing their strength in-sector, it means the risks are going up for all of us . . . just like they did for Commander Presley. Which, in turn, makes timely intelligence on their movements more important than it ever was before. And that consideration is the reason I'm particularly concerned about Wegener's failure to warn us about this in time for *Lydia* to know she had to watch her back more carefully."

"He may not have known himself," the messenger suggested, and Dunecki snorted harshly.

"The man is Interior Minister Wegener's *nephew,* for God's sake! And he's Premier Stolar's brother-in-law, to boot—not to mention the civilian head of government and military commander-in-chief of the sector." The commodore grimaced. "Do you really think they'd send so many heavy units into his command area without even mentioning them to him?"

"Put that way, it does sound unlikely," the messenger agreed. "But if he knew about them, why didn't he warn us? Sure, we've lost *Lydia,* and a good chunk of our combat power with her, but by the same token we've also lost an equally good-sized chunk of our raiding ability. And that translates into a direct loss of income for Governor Wegener."

"If you were talking about someone placed lower in the chain of command, I'd be tempted to agree that he didn't know ahead of time," Dunecki said. "As you say, losing *Lydia* is going to cut into his revenue stream, and we've always known he was only in it for the money. But the fact is that no one in the Confed navy or government would dare send what sounds like a couple of divisions of heavy cruisers into his bailiwick without telling him they were coming. Not with his family connections to the Cabinet itself, they wouldn't! The only possible conclusion Stolar or Wegener's uncle could draw from that would be that whoever was responsible for withholding information distrusted the good governor, and that would be a fatal move career-wise for whoever made it. No, he knew about it and decided not to tell us."

"But why?" The messenger's tone was that of a man speaking almost to himself, but it was also thoughtful, as if his own mind were questing down the path it was apparent Dunecki had already explored.

"Because he's decided the time's come to pull the plug on us," Dunecki said grimly. The messenger looked up quickly in surprise, and the commodore chuckled. It was a grating sound, with absolutely no humor in it, and the expression which bared his teeth could scarcely have been called a smile.

"Think about it," he invited. "We've just agreed that we've always known Wegener was only in for the money. He certainly never shared our agenda or our ambition to achieve an independent Prism. For that matter, he has to know that we regard Prism as only the first step in liberating the entire sector, and if we manage that—or even look like we might come close to it—not even his connections to the Cabinet could save his job. Hell, they might actually go as far as throwing him to the wolves in a big, fancy inquiry or criminal trial just to prove how lily-white and innocent they themselves were! And greedy as he is, Wegener's also not stupid enough not to know that. Which means that he's always had some point in mind at which he'd cut off his relationship with us and do his damnedest to wipe out the Council and retake control of the system. From what happened to *Lydia* and what you're saying about additional reinforcements, it sounds to me as if we've been successful enough that he's finally decided the time is now."

"If you're right, this is terrible," the messenger muttered. His hands wrapped together in his lap, and he stared down at them, his eyes worried. "Losing the intelligence he's provided would be bad enough by itself, but he knows an awful lot about the Council's future plans, as well. If he acts on the basis of that knowledge . . ."

He let his voice trail off and looked back up at Dunecki.

"He doesn't know as much as he thinks he does." Dunecki's tone surprised the messenger, and his surprise grew as the commodore gave him a grim smile. "Of course he doesn't," Dunecki told him. "The Council has always known he'd turn on us the instant he decided it was no longer in his perceived interest to support us. That's why we've used him solely as an intelligence source rather than try to involve him in our strategic thinking or operational planning, and we've been very careful to use false identities or anonymous contacts whenever we dealt with him. Oh, he knows the identities of the public Council members from the independence government back in Prism, but so does everyone else in the star system. What he *doesn't* know is the identity of anyone else. And the only regular warships he knows we have are the ones he himself managed to 'lose' in our favor, like *Lydia*."

The messenger nodded slowly. The Council for an Independent Prism had been around for decades, and he'd been one of its adherents almost from its inception. But unlike Dunecki, he'd never been a member of the inner circle. He was confident that the Council trusted his loyalty, or they would never have assigned him to the duties he'd carried out for the movement, but he was also a realist. He'd known that another reason he'd been chosen for his various assignments was that the Council was willing to risk him because, in the final analysis, he was expendable. And because he was expendable—and might end up expended and in enemy hands—his superiors had always been careful to limit the information they shared with him, but he'd been active in the movement long enough to know that it was only in the last four or five years that the CIP had become a serious player even by the somewhat elastic standards of Silesia. What he didn't know were the ins and outs of how the organization had made the transition from an ineffectual fringe group to one which had managed to seize effective control of half a star system, but he knew Anders Dunecki and his brother Henryk had played a major role in that accomplishment. And although his commitment to the CIP's ultimate goal was as strong as it had ever been, he was no more a stranger to ambition than anyone else who had committed twenty years of his life to the forcible creation of a new political order.

Now he watched Commodore Dunecki with a carefully blank expression, hoping the time had come for him to learn more. Not merely out of simple curiosity (though he certainly was curious) but because the decision to share that information with him might be an indication that his longtime loyal services were finally about to earn him promotion to a higher and more sensitive level of the movement.

Dunecki gazed back at him impassively. He knew precisely what was going on in the other man's mind, and he rather wished that he could avoid taking the messenger any further into his confidence. Not that he actively distrusted the man, and certainly not because he faulted the messenger's obvious hope that he might finally be about to move beyond the thankless and dangerous role of courier. It was simply a matter of habit. After so many years of not letting the left hand know what the right hand was doing as a survival tactic it went against the grain to admit anyone any deeper into his confidence than he absolutely had to.

Unfortunately, like Anders, Henryk was out of the Prism System on operations. Dunecki knew he could have relied upon his brother to convince the Council that Governor Wegener's apparent change of attitude meant it was time to move to the next planned phase of operations. But in

Henryk's absence, Dunecki was going to require another spokesman to make his case, and the messenger was all that was available.

"Wegener knows about the light cruisers and the frigates," the commodore said after a moment, "mostly because he and Commodore Nielsen were the ones who sold them to us in the first place." He watched the messenger's eyes widen slightly and chuckled. "Oh, I suspect that Nielsen thought he was simply disposing of them to regular pirates, but Wegener knew he was dealing with the CIP from the outset. After all, he was already taking a payoff from us to look the other way while we got ourselves organized in Prism, so there was no reason he shouldn't make a little more money off us by letting us buy a bunch of 'obsolescent' warships if Nielsen was willing to sign off on them for disposal. Of course, Nielsen told his Navy superiors that the ships had gone to the breakers, but I doubt any of them believed that any more than he did. Still, it's going to be at least a little embarrassing for Nielsen if any of his 'scrapped' ships wind up being taken by regular Confed naval units, although I have no doubt he has splendid paperwork to prove that he sold them to ostensibly genuine scrap dealers who have since disappeared after undoubtedly selling the hulls to us nasty rebels.

"But we're pretty sure neither Wegener nor Nielsen knows about the destroyers, and we *know* that they don't know about *Annika, Astrid,* and *Margit.* We bought the destroyers in the Tumult Sector, and *Annika, Astrid,* and *Margit* came from . . . somewhere else entirely."

He paused once more, watching the messenger's face. The odds were that the other man had already known everything Dunecki had just told him—except, perhaps, for the fact that the newly created Prism Space Navy's destroyers had come from Tumult—but his expression indicated that he was beginning to see previously unnoted implications in the information.

"The point," Dunecki went on after a moment, "is that

Wegener and Nielsen have probably based their estimates of our strength on the units that they sold us. They may have made some allowance for one or two additional light units, but we've been very careful in our discussions with our 'trusted ally' the Governor to make it plain that our only ships came from them. We've even passed up two or three nice prizes that Wegener had pointed us at because we didn't have a vessel available to take them."

"Uh, excuse me, Sir," the messenger said, "but I know that you and your brother have both taken prizes. Doesn't that mean that they have to know about *Annika* and *Astrid*, at least?"

"No," Dunecki said. "Henryk and I have taken special precautions. Neither of us has disposed of any of our prizes here in the Confederacy. We have some . . . friends and associates in the People's Republic of Haven who've agreed to help out their fellow revolutionaries." The messenger's eyes narrowed, and the commodore chuckled once more. "Don't worry about it. The Legislaturalists are about as revolutionary as a hunk of nickel iron, but if it suits their purpose to pretend to support 'the People's struggle' as long as it's safely outside their own borders and they can make money on it, it suits our purpose just as well to have some place legitimate privateers can dispose of their prizes and repatriate their crews without questions being asked. It's just a pity that the Peeps aren't willing to help us out with additional ships and weapons, as well."

"So Wegener, Nielsen, and the Confed Navy all think that our naval strength is less than half as great as it really is," the messenger said slowly.

"More like a third," Dunecki corrected. "The ships they know about are all ex-Confed crap, just like their own units. Of course, they don't know about the system upgrades or the . . . technical assistance we've had in improving our missile seekers and EW capability, so even the ships they expect us to have are considerably more effective than they could possibly predict."

"I can see that," the messenger replied. "But does it really matter in the long run? I mean, with all due respect, Sir, even if we're in a position to inflict serious losses on Nielsen because they underestimate our strength, he's got the entire Silesian Navy behind him. You're probably right when you call them 'crap,' but they have an awful lot more ships than we do."

"Yes, they do. But that's where the other point you weren't cleared to hear about comes in." Dunecki leaned back in his chair and regarded the messenger coolly. "Haven't you wondered just how we managed to get our hands on like-new destroyers and heavy cruisers? *Andermani* destroyers and heavy cruisers?"

"Occasionally," the messenger admitted. "I always assumed we must have found someone like Nielsen in the Empire. I mean, you and your brother both have contacts in the Andy Navy, so—"

"In the IAN? You think there's someone in the *IAN* who'd sell first-line warships on the black market?" Almost despite himself, Dunecki laughed uproariously. It took several seconds for him to get his amusement back under control, and he wiped tears of laughter from his eyes as he shook his head at the messenger. "I may have made it clear to captain in the IAN, and Henryk may have been a full commander, but trust me, the Imperial Navy isn't at all like the Confeds! Even if there were someone interested in stealing ships, there are way too many checkpoints and inspectorates. No," he shook his head. "Henryk and I did use contacts in the Empire to set it up, but they weren't with the Navy. Or not directly, anyway."

"Then who did you work with?" the messenger asked.

"Let's just say there are a few people, some of them from rather prominent Andie families, who were able to stomach having their investment stolen by Wegener and his family, but only until Wegener decided to bring in another set of foreigners to take it over and run it. That was a bit too much for them, and one or two of them spoke to their prominent relatives after Henryk and I spoke to *them*, just before he and I came home to Prism. Which brings me to the point I need you to stress to the Council when you get home."

"Yes, Sir." The messenger straightened in his chair, his expression intent, and Dunecki looked straight into his eyes.

"The Andermani money people who made our ships available in the first place have just gotten word to me that the Imperial government is finally ready to act. If we can inflict sufficient losses on the local naval forces to provide the Emperor with a pretext, the Empire will declare that the instability in this region of the Confederacy has become great enough in its opinion to threaten a general destabilization of the area. And to prevent that destabilization, the Imperial Navy will move into Saginaw and impose a cease-fire, under the terms of which the Empire will recognize the Council as the de facto legitimate government of Prism."

"Are you serious?" the messenger stared at Dunecki in disbelief. "Everyone knows the Andies have wanted to move into the Confederacy for years, but the Manties have always said no."

"True, but the Manties are focused on Haven right now. They won't have the resources or the will to take on the Empire over something as unimportant to them as Saginaw."

"But what do the Andies get out of it?"

"The Empire gets the precedent of having successfully intervened to restore order to a sector of the Confederacy, which it can use as an opening wedge for additional interventions. It won't demand any outright territorial concessions—this time. But the next time may be a slightly different story, and the time after that, and the time after that, and the time after that . . ." Dunecki let his voice trail off and smiled evilly. "As for our sponsors, the one thing the Emperor's negotiators will insist upon is that Wegener, or whoever Stolar replaces him with, revoke the trade concessions Wegener made to the Manties in Melchor and regrant them to the original Andy investors. So everybody gets what they want . . . except for the Confeds and the Manties, that is."

"My God." The messenger shook his head. "My God, it might just work."

"It damned well *will* work," Dunecki said flatly, "and it's what the Council has been working towards for the last three years. But we didn't expect such sudden confirmation that the groundwork had finally been completed in the Empire, so no one back home is ready to move. But coupling the word from my Imperial contacts with what happened to *Lydia*, I think we've just run out of time. If Wegener and Nielsen are ready to begin moving against us rather than working with us, we need to act quickly. So what I need you to do is to go back to the Council and tell them that they have to get couriers to Henryk and to Captain Traynor in the *Margit* with instructions to begin all-out operations against the Confed Navy."

"I understand, Sir, but I'm not sure they'll listen to me." The messenger smiled wryly. "I realize you're using me because you don't have anyone else available, but I'm hardly part of the inner circle, and this will be coming at them cold. So what if they refuse?"

"Oh, they won't do that," Dunecki said with cold assurance. "If it looks like they might, just tell them this." He looked levelly at the messenger across his desk, and his expression was grim. "Whatever they may want to decide, *Annika* will commence active operations against the SN one standard week from today."

"I still say there has to be a better way to do this." Midshipman Makira sounded unusually grumpy, and Honor glanced across the table and shook her head at him.

"You have got to be one of the most contrary people that I've ever met, Nassios," she told him severely.

"And just what do you mean by that?" Makira demanded.

"I mean that I don't think there's anything the Captain could do that you couldn't decide was the wrong way to go about it. Not to say that you're a nit-picker—although, now that I think about it, someone whose disposition was less naturally sunny and equable than my own probably would—but you do have an absolute gift for picking up on the potential weaknesses of an idea without paying any attention to its advantages."

"Actually," Makira said in an unusually serious tone, "I think you might have a point there. I really do have a tendency to look for problems first. Maybe that's because I've discovered that that way any of my surprises are pleasant ones. Remember, Captain Courvoisier always said that no plan survives contact with the enemy anyway. The way I see it, that makes a pessimist the ideal commander in a lot of ways."

"Maybe—as long as your pessimism doesn't prevent you from having enough confidence to take the initiative away from the bad guys and hang on to it for yourself," Honor countered. Nimitz looked up from his perch on the end of the Snotty Row table and cocked his head in truly magisterial style as he listened to his person's discussion, and Makira chuckled.

"Not fair," he protested, reaching out to stroke the 'cat's ears. "You and Nimitz are ganging up on me again!"

"Only because you're wrong," Honor informed him with a certain smugness.

"Oh, no, I'm not! Look, all I'm saying is that the way we're going about it now, this is the only star system in our entire patrol area that we're giving any cover at all to. Now," he leaned back and folded his arms, "explain to me where that statement is in error."

"It's not in error at all," she conceded. "The problem is that there isn't an ideal solution to the problem of too many star systems and not enough cruisers. We can only be in one place at a time whatever we do, and if we try to spread ourselves between too many systems, we'll just spend all of our time running around between them in hyper and never accomplish anything at all in n-space." She shrugged. "Under the circumstances, and given the fact that the Star Kingdom's presence here in Melchor is pretty much nailed down, I think it makes a lot of sense to troll for pirates right here."

"And while we're doing that," Makira pointed out, "we can be pretty sure that somewhere else in our patrol area a merchantship we ought to be protecting is about to get its ass into a world of hurt with no one there to look out for her."

"You're probably right. But without detailed advance knowledge of the schedules and orders of every merchie in the entire Saginaw Sector, it's simply impossible for anyone to predict where our shipping is going to be at any given moment, anyway. For that matter, even if we'd had detailed schedules on every civilian ship planning on moving in our area at the time we left Manticore, they'd be hopelessly out of date by now, and you know it. And there aren't any such detailed schedules in the first place, which means every single Manticoran ship in Silesia is basically its own needle inside one huge haystack. So even if we were cruising around from system to system, the odds are that we'd almost certainly be out of position to help out the merchantship you're talking about. If we *were* in position to help, it could only be a case of sheer dumb luck, and you know that as well as I do."

"But at least we'd have a chance for dumb luck to put us there!" he shot back stubbornly. "As it is, we don't even have that!"

"No, we don't—we've got something much better than that: bait. We *know* that every pirate in the sector knows about the Dillingham Cartel's installations here in Melchor. They can be pretty much certain that there are going to be Manticoran ships in and out of this system on a semiregular basis, not to mention the possibility that they might get lucky and actually manage to pull off a successful raid on the installations themselves, despite their defenses. That's the whole point of the Captain's strategy! Instead of chasing off from star system to star system with no assurance that he'll catch up with any pirates, much less pirates in the act of raiding our shipping, he's opted to sit here and set an ambush for anybody who's tempted to hit Dillingham's people. I'd say the odds are much better that we'll actually manage to pick off a few pirates by lying in wait for them than there'd be any other way."

"But we're not even showing the flag in any other system," Makira complained. "There's no sense of presence to deter operations anywhere else in the sector."

"That's probably the single most valid criticism of our approach," Honor agreed. "Unfortunately, the Captain only has one ship and there's no way in the world to cover enough space with a single ship to actually deter anyone who can do simple math. What are the odds that *War Maiden* is going to turn up to intercept any given pirate at any given moment?" She shook her head. "No, unless the Admiralty is prepared to give the Captain at least a complete cruiser division to work with, I don't see how he can possibly be expected to create a broad enough sense of presence to actually deter anybody who's inclined to turn pirate in the first place."

"Then why bother to send us at all?" For the first time, there was a note of true bitterness in Makira's voice. "If all we're doing is trying to hold air in the lock with a screen door, then what's the damned point?"

"The same as it's always been, I suppose," Honor said. "One ship can't deter piracy throughout an entire patrol area the size of the Saginaw Sector—not in any specific sense, at least. But if we can pick off two or three of the scum, then the word will get around among the ones we don't get a shot at. At least we can make a few people who are considering the 'great adventure' as a career choice think about whether or not they really want to run the risk of being one of the unlucky ones. More to the point, the word will also get around that we're paying particular attention to Melchor, which may just remind them that the Star Kingdom takes a dim view of attacks on our nationals. I hate to say it, but in a lot of ways what we're really doing out here is encouraging the local vermin to go pick on someone else's shipping and leave ours alone."

"That's not what they told us back at the Academy,"

Makira said. "They told us our job was to suppress piracy, not just encourage it to go after merchies unlucky enough to belong to some poor sucker of a star nation that doesn't have a decent navy of its own!"

"Of course that's what they told us, and in an absolute sense they were right. But we live in an imperfect galaxy, Nassios, and it's been getting steadily less perfect for years now. Look," she leaned forward across the table, propping her elbows on it while her expression turned very serious, "the Navy only has so many ships and so many people, and important as Silesia is—and as important as the lives of Manticoran spacers are—we can only put so many ships in so many places. Back before the Peeps started conquering everything in sight, we could actually send a big enough chunk of the Navy off to Silesia every year to make a real hole in pirate operations here. But with so much of our available strength diverted to keeping an eye on the Peeps at places like Trevor's Star and Basilisk, we can't do that any more. We simply don't have enough hulls for that kind of deployment. So I'm sure that everyone at the Admiralty understands perfectly well that there's no way we can possibly 'suppress' piracy in our patrol areas. For that matter, I'd bet that any pirate who's not a complete imbecile knows that just as well as *we* do, and you can be absolutely sure that the Andies do!"

Nassios Makira tipped back in his chair, and his expression had gone from one that showed more than a little outrage to one of surprise. He knew that he and the other middies in *War Maiden*'s company all had exactly the same access to information, but it was suddenly apparent to him that Honor had put that information together into a far more complete and coherent picture than he ever had.

"Then why bother to send us?" he repeated, but his tone had gone from one of challenge to one that verged on the plaintive. "If we can't do any good, and everyone knows it, then why are we here?"

"I didn't say we couldn't do any good," Honor told him almost gently. "I said that we couldn't realistically expect to *suppress* piracy. The fact that we can't stamp it out or even drive a significant number of the raiders out of any given area doesn't relieve us of a moral responsibility to do whatever we *can* do. And one of the responsibilities that we have is to protect our own nationals to the greatest possible extent, however limited that extent may be compared to what we'd like to do. We can't afford for the pirates—or the Andies—to decide that we'll simply write off our commitments in Silesia, however strapped for ships we may be. And when I said that what we're really trying to do is to convince pirates to go pick on someone else's merchant shipping, I didn't mean that we had any specific victims in mind. I just meant that our objective is to convince the locals that it's more unsafe to attack our shipping than it is to attack anyone else's. I know there are some people back home who would argue that it's in our true strategic interest to point the pirates here at anybody who competes with our own merchant marine, but they're idiots. Oh, I'm sure we could show some short-term gain if the pirate threat scared everybody looking for freight carriers in Silesia into using our merchies, but the long-term price would be stiff. Besides, once everybody was using Manticoran bottoms, the pirates would have no choice but to come after us again because there wouldn't be any other targets for them!

"Actually," she said after a moment, her tone and expression thoughtful, "there may *be* an additional advantage in pointing pirates at someone else. Everyone has relied on us to play police out here for the better part of a century and a half, but we're scarcely the only ones with an interest in what happens in Silesia. I'm sure that there have been times when the government and the Admiralty both did their very best to make sure that everyone else regarded us as the logical police force for Silesia, if only to depress Andy pretentions in the area. But now that we're having to concentrate on our own forces on the Peeps' frontiers, we need someone else to take up the slack out here. And I'm afraid the only people available are the Andies. The

Confeds certainly aren't going to be able to do anything about it! So maybe there's an advantage I hadn't considered in persuading pirates to pick on Andy merchies instead of ours, if that's going to get the Andy navy involved in going after them more aggressively while we're busy somewhere else."

"Um." Makira rubbed his eyebrow while he pondered everything she'd just said. It made sense. In fact, it made a *lot* of sense, and now that she'd laid it all out, he couldn't quite understand why the same conclusions hadn't suggested themselves to him long since. But still . . .

"All right," he said. "I can see your point, and I don't guess I can really argue with it. But I still think that we could do more to convince pirates to go after someone else's shipping if we put in an appearance in more than one star system. I mean, if Melchor is the only place we ever pop a single pirate—not that we've managed to do even that much so far—then our impact is going to be very limited and localized."

"It's going to be 'limited' whatever we do. That's the inevitable consequence of only having one ship," Honor pointed out with a glimmer of amusement. "But like I said, I'm sure the word will get around. One thing that's always been true is that the 'pirate community,' for lack of a better term, has a very efficient grapevine. Captain Courvoisier says that the word always gets around when someplace turns out to be particularly hazardous to their health, so we can at least push them temporarily out of Melchor. On the other hand, what makes you think that Melchor is going to be the *only* place the Captain stakes out during our deployment? It's the place he's staking out *at the moment*, but there's no reason not to move his operations elsewhere after he feels reasonably confident that he's made an impression on the local lowlife's minds. I think the presence of the Dillingham operation here makes this the best hunting grounds we're likely to find, and it looks to me like the Captain thinks the same. But the same tactics will work just as well anyplace else there are actually pirates operating, and I'd be very surprised if we don't spend some time trolling in other systems, as well."

"Then why didn't you say so in the first place?" Makira demanded with the heat of exasperation. "You've been letting me bitch and carry on about the Captain's obsession with this system for days! Now you're going to sit there and tell me that the whole time you've actually been expecting him to eventually do what I *wanted?*"

"Well," Honor chuckled, "it's not *my* fault if what you've been letting yourself hear wasn't exactly what I've been saying, now is it? Besides, you shouldn't criticize the Captain quite so energetically unless you've really thought through what you're talking about!"

"You," Makira said darkly, "are an evil person who will undoubtedly come to an unhappy end, and if there is any justice in the universe, I'll be there to see it happen."

Honor grinned, and Nimitz bleeked a lazy laugh from the table between them.

"You may laugh . . . for now," he told them both ominously, "but There Will Come a Day when you will remember this conversation and regret it bitterly." He raised his nose with an audible sniff, and Nimitz turned his head to look up at his person. Their eyes met in complete agreement, and then Nassios Makira's arms windmilled wildly as a gray blur of treecat bounded off the table and wrapped itself firmly around his neck. The midshipman began a muffled protest that turned suddenly into a most unmilitary— and high-pitched—sound as Nimitz's long, agile fingers found his armpits and tickled unmercifully. Chair and midshipman alike went over backwards with a high, wailing laugh, and Honor leaned back in her own chair and watched with folded arms as the appropriate penalty for his ominous threat was rigorously applied.

"Well, here we are," Commander Obrad Bajkusa observed. One might have concluded from his tone that he was less than delighted with his own pronouncement, and one would have been correct. Bajkusa had an enormous amount of respect for Commodore Dunecki as both a tactical commander and a military strategist, but he'd disliked the entire concept of this operation from the moment the commodore first briefed him on it over six T-months before. It wasn't so much that he distrusted the motives of the commodore's Andermani . . . associates (although he *did* distrust them about as much as was humanly possible) as that it was Bajkusa's personal conviction that anyone who screwed around with the Royal Manticoran Navy was stupid enough that he no doubt deserved his Darwinian fate. On the surface, Dunecki's plan was straightforward and reasonable, especially given the promises of backing from the imperial Andermani court. So far as logical analysis was concerned, it was very difficult to find fault with the commodore's arguments. Unfortunately, the Manty Navy had a deplorable habit of kicking the ever-living crap out of anyone foolish enough to piss it off, and Obrad Bajkusa had no particular desire to find himself a target of such a kicking.

On the other hand, orders were orders, and it wasn't as if the Manties knew his name or address. All he had to do was keep it that way.

"All right, Hugh," he told his exec. "Let's head on in and see what we can find."

"Yes, Sir," Lieutenant Wakefield replied, and the frigate PSN *Javelin* headed in-system while the star named Melchor burned steadily ahead of her.

"Well, well. What *do* we have here?"

Senior Chief Jensen Del Conte turned his head towards the soft murmur. Sensor Tech 1/c Francine Alcott was obviously unaware that she had spoken aloud. If Del Conte had harbored any doubt about that, the expression on her dark, intense face as she leaned closer to her display would have disabused him of it quickly enough.

The senior chief watched her as her fingers flickered back and forth across her panel with the unconscious precision of a concert pianist. He had no doubt whatsoever what she was doing, and he clenched his jaw and thought very loudly in her direction.

Unfortunately, she seemed remarkably insensitive to Del Conte's telepathy, and he swallowed a silent curse. Alcott was extremely good at her job. She had both a natural aptitude for it, and the sort of energy and sense of responsibility which took her that extra kilometer from merely satisfactory to outstanding, and Del Conte knew that Lieutenant Commander Hirake had already earmarked Alcott, despite her relative youth, for promotion to petty officer before this deployment was over. But for all her undoubted technical skills, Alcott was remarkably insensitive to some of the internal dynamics of *War Maiden*'s tactical department. The fact that she had been transferred to Del Conte's watch section less than two weeks earlier made the situation worse, but the senior chief felt depressingly certain that she would have been blithely blind to certain unpleasant realities even if she'd been in the same duty section since the ship left Manticore.

Del Conte glanced over his shoulder as unobtrusively as possible, then swallowed another silent expletive. Lieutenant Santino had the watch, and he sat in the command chair at the center of the bridge looking for all the world like a competent naval officer. His forearms rested squarely upon the command chair's arm rests. His squared shoulders rested firmly against the chair's upright back, his manly profile was evident as he held his head erect, and there was an almost terrifying lack of intelligence in his eyes.

Jensen Del Conte had seen more officers than he could possibly count in the course of his naval career. Some had been better than others, some had been worse; none had ever approached the abysmal depths which Elvis Santino plumbed so effortlessly. Del Conte knew Lieutenant Commander Hirake was aware of the problem, but there was very little that she could do about it, and one thing she absolutely could *not* do was to violate the ironclad etiquette and traditions of the Service by admitting to a noncommissioned officer, be he ever so senior, that his immediate superior was a complete and utter ass. The senior chief rather hoped that the lieutenant commander and the Skipper were giving Santino rope in hopes that he would manage to hang himself with it. But even if they were, that didn't offer much comfort to those unfortunate souls who found themselves serving under his immediate command—like one Senior Chief Del Conte.

Alcott continued her silent communion with her instruments, and Del Conte wished fervently that Santino's command chair were even a few meters further away from him than it was. Given its proximity, however, the lieutenant was entirely too likely to hear anything Del Conte might say to Alcott. In fact, the sensor tech was extremely fortunate that Santino hadn't already noticed her preoccupation. The lieutenant's pose of attentiveness fooled no one on the bridge, but it would have been just like him to emerge from his normal state of internal oblivion at precisely the wrong moment for Alcott. So far, he hadn't, however, and that posed a most uncomfortable dilemma for Del Conte.

The senior chief reached out and made a small adjustment on his panel, and his brow furrowed as his own display showed him a duplicate of the imagery on Alcott's. He saw immediately what had drawn her attention, although he wasn't at all certain that he would have spotted it himself without the enhancement she had already applied. Even now, the impeller signature was little more than a ghost, and the computers apparently did not share Alcott's own confidence that what she was seeing was really there. They insisted on marking the icon with the rapidly strobing amber circle which indicated a merely possible contact, and that was usually a bad sign. But Alcott possessed the trained instinct which the computers lacked, and Del Conte was privately certain that what she had was a genuine contact.

Part of the problem was the unknown's angle of approach. Whatever it was, it was overtaking from astern and very high—so high, in fact, that the upper band of *War Maiden*'s impeller wedge was between the contact and

Alcott's gravitic sensors. In theory, CIC's computers knew the exact strength of the heavy cruiser's wedge and, equipped with that knowledge, could compensate for the wedge's distorting effect. In theory. In real life, however, the wedge injected a high degree of uncertainty into any direct observation through it, which was why warships tended to rely so much more heavily on the sensor arrays mounted on their fore and aft hammerheads and on their broadsides, where their wedges did not interfere. They also carried ventral and dorsal arrays, of course, but those systems were universally regarded—with reason—as little more than precautionary afterthoughts under most circumstances. In this case, however, the dorsal arrays were the only ones that could possibly see Alcott's possible contact. The known unreliability of those arrays, coupled with the extreme faintness of the signature that had leaked through the wedge, meant that the contact (if that was what it actually was) had not yet crossed the threshold of CIC's automatic filters, so no one in CIC was so far even aware of it.

But Alcott was, and now—for his sins—Del Conte was, as well. Standing orders for such a contingency were clear, and Alcott, unfortunately, had followed them . . . mostly. She had, in fact, done precisely what she would have been expected to do if she had still been part of Lieutenant Commander Hirake's watch section, for the lieutenant commander trusted her people's abilities and expected them to routinely route their observations directly to her own plot if they picked up anything they thought she should know about. Standard operating procedure required a verbal announcement, as well, but Hirake preferred for her sensor techs to get on with refining questionable data rather than waste time reporting that they didn't yet know what it was they didn't know.

Del Conte's problem was that the lieutenant commander's attitude was that of a confident, competent officer who respected her people and their own skills. Which would have been fine, had anyone but Elvis Santino had the watch.

Because what Alcott had done was exactly what Lieutenant Commander Hirake would have wanted; she had thrown her own imagery directly onto Santino's Number Two Plot . . . and the self-absorbed jackass hadn't even noticed!

Had the contact been strong enough for CIC to consider it reliable, *they* would already have reported it, and Santino would have known it was there. Had Alcott made a verbal report, he would have known. Had he bothered to spend just a little more effort on watching his own displays and a little less effort on projecting the proper HD-image of the Complete Naval Officer, he would have known. But none of those things had happened, and so he didn't have a clue. But when CIC did get around to upgrading their classification from sensor ghost to possible real contact, even Santino was likely to notice from the time chop on the imagery blinking unnoticed (at the moment) on his plot that Alcott had identified it as such several minutes earlier. More to the point, he would realize that when Captain Bachfisch and Commander Layson got around to reviewing the bridge log, *they* would realize that he ought to have been aware of the contact long before he actually got around to reporting it to *them.* Given Santino's nature, the consequences for Alcott would be totally predictable, and wasn't it a hell of a note that a senior chief in His Majesty's Navy found himself sitting here sweating bullets trying to figure out how to protect a highly talented and capable rating from the spiteful retaliation of a completely untalented and remarkably stupid officer?

None of which did anything to lessen Del Conte's dilemma. Whatever else happened, he couldn't let the delay drag out any further without making things still worse, and so he drew a deep breath.

"Sir," he announced in his most respectful voice, "we have a possible unidentified impeller contact closing from one-six-five by one-one-five."

"What?" Santino shook himself. For an instant, he looked completely blank, and then his eyes dropped to the repeater plot deployed from the base of his command chair and he stiffened.

"Why didn't CIC report this?" he snapped, and Del Conte suppressed an almost overwhelming urge to answer in terms which would leave even Santino in no doubt of the senior chief's opinion of him.

"It's still very faint, Sir," he said instead. "If not for Alcott's enhancement, we'd never have noticed it. I'm sure it's just lost in CIC's filters until it gains a little more signal strength."

He made his voice as crisp and professional as possible, praying all the while that Santino would be too preoccupied with the potential contact to notice the time chop on his plot and realize how long had passed before its existence had been drawn to his attention.

For the moment, at least, God appeared to be listening. Santino was too busy glaring at the strobing contact to worry about anything else, and Del Conte breathed a sigh of relief.

Of premature relief, as it turned out.

Elvis Santino looked down at the plot icon in something very like panic. He was only too well aware that the Captain and that asshole Layson were both out to get him. Had he been even a little less well connected within the aristocratic cliques of the Navy, Layson's no doubt scathing endorsement of his personnel file which had almost certainly accompanied the notation that he had been relieved as OCTO for cause would have been the kiss of death. As it was, he and his family were owed sufficient favors that his career would probably survive without serious damage. But there were limits even to the powers of patronage, and he dared not give the bastards any additional ammunition.

As it happened, he *had* noticed the plot time chop. Which meant that he knew that he—or at least his bridge crew, and for that matter, his own tactical personnel—had picked up the possible contact almost six full minutes before anyone had drawn it to his attention. He could already imagine the coldly formal, impeccably correct, and brutally blistering fashion in which Bachfisch (or, even worse, that ass-kisser Layson) would ream him out for not reacting sooner. The mental picture of that . . . discussion was the only thing which prevented him from ripping out Alcott's and Del Conte's lungs for having deliberately withheld the information. But Layson had already demonstrated his taste for using noncoms and ratings as spies and informants, and Santino had no doubt that the Exec would take gleeful pleasure in adding Del Conte's ass-covering version of what had happened to his own report. So instead of kicking their insolent and disloyal asses as they so richly deserved, he forced himself to remain outwardly oblivious to what they had conspired to do to him. The time would come eventually for the debt to be paid, yet for now it was one more thing he dared not attend to.

In the meantime, he had to decide how to handle the situation, and he gnawed on his lower lip while he thought hard. Del Conte—the disloyal bastard—was undoubtedly correct about the reason for CIC's silence. But if Alcott's enhancement was solid (and it looked as if it were) then the contact was bound to burn through CIC's filters in no more than another five to ten minutes, even with only the dorsal gravitics. When that happened, he would have no option but to report it to the Captain . . . at which point the fact that Alcott and Del Conte had officially fed him the data so much earlier would also become part of the official record. And the fact that they had deliberately concealed the report by failing to announce it verbally would be completely ignored while Bachfisch and Layson concentrated on the way in which he had "wasted" so much "valuable time" before reporting it to them. And Layson, in particular, was too vindictive for Santino to doubt for a moment that he would point out the fashion in which Santino had squandered the potential advantage which his own brilliantly competent Tactical Department subordinates had won him by making such an early identification of the contact.

Frustration, fury, resentment, and fear boiled back and forth behind his eyes while he tried to decide what to do, and every second that ticked away with no decision added its own weight to the chaos rippling within him. It was such a *little* thing! So what if Alcott and Del Conte had picked up the contact six minutes, or even fifteen minutes—hell, half an hour!—before CIC did? The contact was over two and a half light-minutes behind *War Maiden*. That was a good fifty million klicks, and Alcott's best guess on its acceleration was only around five hundred gravities. With an initial overtake velocity of less than a thousand kilometers per second, it would take whatever it was over five hours to overtake *War Maiden*, so how could the "lost time" possibly matter? But it would. He knew it would, because Bachfisch and Layson would never pass up the opportunity to hammer his efficiency report all over again and—

His churning thoughts suddenly paused. Of course! Why hadn't he thought of it sooner? He felt his lips twitch and managed somehow to suppress the need to grin triumphantly as he realized the solution to his dilemma. His "brilliant" subordinates had reported the contact even before CIC, had they? Well, good for them! And as the officer of the watch, wasn't it his job to confirm whether or not the contact was valid as quickly as possible—even before the computers and the highly trained plotting crews in CIC could do so? Of course it was! And *that* was the sole reason he had delayed in reporting to the Captain: to confirm that the *possible* contact was a real one.

He caught himself just before he actually rubbed his hands together in satisfaction and then turned to the helmsman.

"Prepare to roll ship seventy degrees to port and come to new heading of two-two-three," he said crisply.

Del Conte spun his chair to face the center of the bridge before he could stop himself. He knew exactly what the lieutenant intended to do, but he couldn't quite believe that even Elvis Santino could be *that* stupid. The preparatory order he'd just given was a classic maneuver. Naval officers called it "clearing the wedge," because that was exactly what it did as the simultaneous roll and turn swept the more sensitive broadside sensor arrays across the zone which had been obstructed by the wedge before the maneuver. But it was the sort of maneuver which only warships made, and *War Maiden* had gone to enormous lengths to masquerade as a fat, helpless, *unarmed* freighter expressly to lure raiders into engagement range. If this asshole—

"Sir, I'm not sure that's a good idea," the senior chief said.

"Fortunately, *I* am," Santino said sharply, unable to refrain from smacking down the disloyal noncom.

"But, Sir, we're supposed to be a merchie, and if—"

"I'm quite aware of what we're supposed to be, Senior Chief! But if in fact this is a genuine contact and not simply a figment of someone's overheated imagination, clearing the wedge should confirm it, don't you think?"

"Yes, Sir, but—"

"They're only pirates, Senior Chief," Santino said scathingly. "We can turn to clear the wedge, lock them in for CIC, and be back on our original heading before they even notice!"

Del Conte opened his mouth to continue the argument, and then shut it with a click. There was obviously no point, and it was even remotely possible that Santino was right and that the contact would never notice such a brief course change. But if the contact had them on a gravitic sensor which wasn't obstructed by a wedge, then *War Maiden* was at least nine or ten light-minutes inside its sensor range. At that range, even a brief change in heading would be glaringly obvious to any regular warship's tactical crew. Of course, if these were your typical run-of-the-mill pirates, then Santino could just possibly get away with it without anyone's noticing. It was unlikely, but it *was* possible.

And if the asshole blows it, at least my hands will be clean. I did my level best to keep him from screwing up by the numbers, and the voice logs will show it. So screw you, Lieutenant!

The senior chief gazed into the lieutenant's eyes for five more endless seconds while he fought with himself. His stubborn sense of duty pulled one way, urging him to make one more try to salvage the situation, but everything else pushed him the other way, and in the end, he turned his chair back to face his own panel without another word.

Santino grunted in satisfaction, and returned his own attention to the helmsman.

"Execute the helm order, Coxswain!" he said crisply.

The helmsman acknowledged the order, *War Maiden* rolled up on her side and swung ever so briefly off her original track, and her broadside sensor arrays nailed the contact instantly.

Just in time to see it execute a sharp course change of its own and accelerate madly away from the "freighter" which had just cleared its wedge.

"I cannot *believe* this . . . this . . . this . . ."

Commander Abner Layson shook his head, uncertain whether he was more stunned or furious, and Captain Bachfisch grunted in irate agreement. The two of them sat in the captain's day cabin, the hatch firmly closed behind them, and the display on the captain's desk held a duplicate of Francine Alcott's plot imagery, frozen at the moment the pirate which the entire ship's company had worked so long and so hard to lure into a trap went streaking away.

"I knew he was an idiot," the commander went on after a moment in a marginally less disgusted voice, "but I figured he had to at least be able to carry out standing orders that had been explained in detail to every officer aboard."

"I agree," Bachfisch said, but then he sighed and leaned back in his chair. "I agree," he repeated more wearily, "but I can also see exactly what happened."

"Excuse me, Sir, but what *happened* was that the officer

of the watch completely failed to obey your standing order to inform you immediately upon the detection of a potential hostile unit. Worse, on his own authority, he undertook to execute a maneuver which was a dead give-away of the fact that we're a warship, with predictable results!"

"Agreed, but you know as well as I do that he did it because he knows both of us are just waiting for him to step far enough out of line that we can cut him right off at the knees."

"Well, he just gave us all the ammunition we need to do just that," Layson pointed out grimly.

"I suppose he did," Bachfisch said, massaging his eyelids with the tips of his fingers. "Of course, I also suppose it's possible his career will survive even this, depending on who his patrons are back home. And I hate to admit it, but if I were one of those patrons, I might just argue to BuPers that his actions, however regrettable, were the predictable result of the climate of hostility which you and I created for Lieutenant Santino when we arbitrarily relieved him of his duties as OCTO."

"With all due respect, Sir, that's bullshit, and you know it."

"Of course I know it. At the same time, there's a tiny element of truth in it, since you and I certainly are hostile to him. You *are* hostile towards him, aren't you, Abner?"

"Damn right I am," Layson said, then snorted as the captain grinned at him. "All right, all right, Sir. I take your point. All we can do is write it up the way we saw it and hope that The Powers That Be back home agree with us. But in the meantime, we have to decide what we're going to do about him. I certainly don't want him standing any more watches unsupervised!"

"Neither do I. For that matter, I don't want him at Tactical, even if he's just backing up Janice. Bad enough that the man is a fool, but now his own people are helping him cut his own throat!"

"Noticed that, did you, Sir?"

"Please, Abner! I'm still a few years shy of senile. Del Conte knew exactly what would happen."

"I think that may be putting it just a bit strongly, Sir," Layson said cautiously. He'd hoped without much confidence that the captain might not have noticed the senior chief's obvious decision to shut his mouth and stop arguing with his superior. "I mean," the exec went on, "Santino specifically ordered him to—"

"Oh, come on, Abner! Del Conte is an experienced man, and he damned well shouldn't have let the fact that his superior officer is an unmitigated ass push him into letting that officer blow the tactical situation all to hell, no matter how pissed off he might've been or how justified he was to be that way. You know it, I know it, and I expect you to make very certain that Senior Chief Del Conte knows that we do and that if he *ever* lets something like this happen again I will personally tear him a new asshole. I trust that I've made my feelings on this matter clear?"

"I think you might say that, Sir."

"Good," Bachfisch grunted, but then he waved a hand in a dismissive gesture. "But once you've made that clear to him—and once you're sure that you have—that's the end of it." He pretended not to notice the very slight relaxation of Layson's shoulders. "He shouldn't have let it happen, but you're right; he did exactly what his superior officer ordered him to do. Which is the problem. When a noncom of Del Conte's seniority deliberately lets his officer shoot his own foot off that spectacularly, that officer's usefulness is exactly nil. And it's also the most damning condemnation possible. Even if I weren't afraid that something like this might happen again, I don't want any King's officer who can drive his own personnel to a reaction like that in my ship or anywhere near her."

"I don't blame you, Sir. And I don't want him in *War Maiden*, either. But we're stuck with him."

"Oh, no, we're not," Bachfisch said grimly. "We still haven't sent *Gryphon's Pride* home. I believe that Lieutenant Santino has just earned himself a berth as her prize master."

Layson's eyes widened, and he started to open his mouth, then stopped. There were two reasons for a captain to assign one of his officers to command a prize ship. One was to reward that officer by giving him a shot at the sort of independent command which might bring him to the notice of the Lords of Admiralty. The other was for the captain to rid himself of someone whose competence he distrusted. Layson doubted that anyone could possibly fail to understand which reason was operating in this case, and he certainly couldn't fault Bachfisch's obvious determination to rid himself of Santino. But as *War Maiden*'s executive officer, the possibility presented him with a definite problem.

"Excuse me, Sir," the exec said after a moment, "but however weak he may be as a tac officer, he's the only assistant Janice has. If we send him away . . ."

He let his voice trail off, and Bachfisch nodded. Ideally, *War Maiden* should have carried two assistant tactical officers. Under normal circumstances, Hirake would have had both Santino and a junior-grade lieutenant or an ensign to back him up. The chronic shorthandedness of the expanding Manticoran Navy had caught the captain's ship short this time, and he drummed his fingers on his desktop while he considered his options. None of them were especially palatable, but—

"I don't care about shorthandedness," he said. "Not if it means keeping Santino aboard. Janice will just have to manage without him."

"But, Sir—" Layson began almost desperately, only to break off as Bachfisch raised a hand.

"He's gone, Abner," he said, and he spoke in the captain's voice that cut off all debate. "That part of the decision is already made."

"Yes, Sir," Layson said, and Bachfisch relented sufficiently to show him a small smile of sympathy.

"I know this is going to be a pain in the ass for you in some ways, Abner, and I'm sorry for that. But what you need to do is concentrate on how nice it will be to have Elvis Santino a hundred light-years away from us and then figure out a way to work around the hole."

"I'll try to bear that in mind, Sir. Ah, would the Captain care to suggest a way in which that particular hole might be worked around?"

"Actually, and bearing in mind an earlier conversation of ours, I believe I do," Bachfisch told him. "I would suggest that we seriously consider promoting Ms. Midshipwoman Harrington to the position of acting assistant tactical officer."

"Are you sure about that, Sir?" Layson asked. The captain raised an eyebrow at him, and the exec shrugged. "She's worked out very well so far, Sir. But she *is* a snotty."

"I agree that she's short on experience," Bachfisch replied. "That's why we send middies on their snotty cruises in the first place, after all. But I believe she's clearly demonstrated that she has the raw ability to handle the assistant tac officer's slot, and she's certainly a lot brighter and more reliable than Santino ever was."

"I can't argue with any of that, Sir. But since you've mentioned our conversation, remember what you said then about North Hollow and his clique. If they really did pull strings to put Santino aboard as OCTO and you not only relieve him of that duty, but then heave him completely off your bridge, and then take the midshipwoman they probably put him here specifically to get and put her into *his* slot—" He shook his head.

"You're right. That *will* piss them off, won't it?" Bachfisch murmured cheerfully.

"What it may do," Layson said in an exasperated tone, "is put *you* right beside her on their enemies list, Sir."

"Well, if it does, I could be in a lot worse company, couldn't I? And whether that happens or not doesn't really have any bearing on the specific problem which you and I have to solve right here and right now. So putting aside all other considerations, is there anyone in the ship's company who you think would be better qualified as an acting assistant tactical officer than Harrington would?"

"Of course there isn't. I'm not sure that putting her into

the slot will be easy to justify if BuPers decides to get nasty about it—or not on paper, at least—but there's no question in my mind that she's the best choice, taken strictly on the basis of her merits. Which, I hasten to add, doesn't mean that I won't make sure that Janice rides very close herd on her. Or that I won't be doing exactly the same thing myself, for that matter."

"Excellent!" This time there was nothing small about Bachfisch's huge grin. "And while you're thinking about all the extra work this is going to make for you and Janice, think about how Harrington is going to feel when she finds out what sort of responsibility we're dumping on her! I think it will be rather informative to see just how panicked she gets when you break the word to her. And just to be sure that she doesn't get a swelled head about her temporary elevation over her fellow snotties, you might point out to her that while the exigencies of the King's service require that she assume those additional responsibilities, we can hardly excuse her from her training duties."

"You mean—?" Layson's eyes began to dance, and Bachfisch nodded cheerfully.

"Exactly, Commander. You and Janice will have to keep a close eye on her, but I feel that we should regard that not as an additional onerous responsibility, but rather as an *opportunity*. Consider it a chance to give her a personal tutorial in the fine art of ship-to-ship tactics and all the thousand and one ways in which devious enemies can surprise, bedevil, and defeat even the finest tactical officer. Really throw yourself into designing the very best possible training simulations for her. And be sure you tell her about all the extra effort you and Janice will be making on her behalf."

"That's evil, Sir," Layson said admiringly.

"I am shocked—*shocked*—that you could even think such a thing, Commander Layson!"

"Of course you are, Sir."

"Well, I suppose 'shocked' might be putting it just a tiny bit strongly," Bachfisch conceded. "But, seriously, Abner,

I do want to take the opportunity to see how hard and how far we can push her. I think Raoul might just have been right when he told me how good he thought she could become, so let's see if we can't get her started on the right foot."

"Certainly, Sir. And I do believe that I'd like to see how far and how fast she can go, too. Not, of course," he smiled at his captain, "that I expect her to appreciate all of the effort and sacrifices Janice and I will be making when we devote our time to designing special sims just for her."

"Of course she won't. She *is* on her snotty cruise, Abner! But if she begins to exhaust your and Janice's inventiveness, let me know. I'd be happy to put together one or two modest little simulations for her myself."

"Oh, I'm sure she'll appreciate *that*, Sir."

"It looks like you're right, Sir," Commander Basil Amami said. His dark-complexioned face was alight with enthusiasm, and Obrad Bajkusa forced himself to bite his tongue firmly. Amami was a more than competent officer. He also happened to be senior to Bajkusa, but only by a few months. Under other circumstances, Bajkusa would have been more than willing to debate Amami's conclusions, and especially to have tried to abate the other officer's obvious enthusiasm. Unfortunately, Amami was also Commodore Dunecki's executive officer. It was Bajkusa's personal opinion that one major reason for Amami's present position was that he idolized Dunecki. Bajkusa didn't think Dunecki had set out to find himself a sycophant—or not deliberately and knowingly, at any rate—but Amami's very competence tended to keep people, Dunecki included, from wondering whether there was any other reason for his assignment. Perhaps the fact that his XO *always* seemed to agree with him should have sounded a warning signal for an officer as experienced as Dunecki, but it hadn't, and over the long months that Dunecki and Amami had served together, the commodore had developed an almost paternal attitude towards the younger man.

Whatever the internal dynamics of their relationship, Bajkusa had long since noticed that they had a tendency to double-team anyone who disagreed with or opposed them. Again, that was scarcely something which anyone could legitimately object to, since the two of them were supposed to be a mutually supporting command team, but it was clear to Bajkusa in this case that Amami's statement of agreement with Dunecki only reinforced the conclusion which the commodore had already reached on his own. Which meant that no mere commander in his right mind was going to argue with them both, however tenuous he might think the evidence for their conclusion was.

"Perhaps I was right, and perhaps I wasn't," Dunecki told Amami, but his cautionary note seemed more pro forma than genuine, Bajkusa thought. The commodore nodded in Bajkusa's direction. "*Javelin* did well, Captain," he said. "I appreciate your effort, and I'd like you to tell your entire ship's company that, as well."

"Thank you, Sir," Bajkusa replied. Then he decided to see if he couldn't interject a small note of caution of his own into the discussion. Indirectly, of course. "It was a closer thing than the raw log chips might indicate, though, Sir. Their EW was very good. We'd closed to just a little over two light-minutes, and I didn't even have a clue that they were a warship until they cleared their wedge. I was holding my overtake down mainly because I didn't want to attract anyone else's attention, but it never even occurred to me that the 'merchie' I was closing in on was a damned cruiser!"

"I can certainly understand why that would have been a shock," Dunecki agreed wryly.

"Especially in a system the damned Manties are hanging on to so tightly," Amami put in, and Bajkusa nodded sharply.

"That was my own thought," he said. "It's not like the Manties to invite a Confed cruiser in to keep an eye on their interests. It's usually the other way around," he added, watching the commodore carefully out of the corner of one

eye. Dunecki frowned, and for just a moment the commander hoped that his superior was considering the thing
that worried him, but then Dunecki shrugged.

"No, it's not," he acknowledged. "But your sensor read-
ings make it fairly clear that it was either an awfully big
light cruiser or decidedly on the small size for a heavy. God
knows the Confeds have such a collection of odds and sods
that they could have sent just about anything in to watch
Melchor, but the Manties don't have any light cruisers that
come close to the tonnage range your tac people suggest,
and they've been retiring their older heavy cruisers steadily
since they started their buildup. They can't have very many
this small left in their inventory. Besides, no Manty would
be as clumsy—or as stupid—as this fellow was! Clearing his
wedge at barely two light-minutes after all the trouble they'd
gone to convince you that they were a freighter in the first
place?" The commodore shook his head. "I've encountered
a lot of Manty officers, Commander, and none of them was
dumb enough to do that against something as small and fast
as a frigate."

Bajkusa wanted to continue the debate, if that was really
what it was, but he had to admit that Dunecki had a point.
A rather sizable one, in fact. Much as he loved *Javelin*,
Bajkusa was perfectly well aware why no major naval power
was still building frigates and why those navies which had
them were retiring them steadily. They were the smallest
class of hyper-capable warship, with a tonnage which fell
about midway between a dispatch boat and a destroyer,
and that gave them precious little room to pack in weapons. Indeed, *Javelin* was only a very little more heavily
armed than a light attack craft, although her missiles had
somewhat more range and she did have *some* magazine
capacity, and she and her ilk no longer had any true viable
purpose except to serve as remote reconnaissance platforms.
Even that was being taken away from them by improve-
ments in the remote sensor drones most navies regularly
employed, and Bajkusa strongly suspected that the frigates'
last stand would be as cheap, very light escorts to run

down even lighter pirates . . . or as commerce raiders (or pirates) in their own right.

So, yes, Commodore Dunecki had a point. What Manticoran cruiser captain in his right mind would have let *anything* get that close without detection. And if he had detected *Javelin* on her way in, then why in Heaven's name clear his wedge before he had her into engagement range? It certainly couldn't have been because he was afraid of the outcome!

"No," Dunecki said with another shake of his head. "Whoever this joker is, he's no Manty, and we know for a fact that no Andermani ships would be in Melchor under present conditions, so that really only leaves one thing he could be, doesn't it? Which means that he's in exactly the right place for our purposes. And as small as he is, there's no way he can match *Annika*'s weight of metal."

"Absolutely, Sir!" Amami enthused.

"But he may not be there for long," Dunecki mused aloud, "and I'd hate to let him get away—or, even worse—find out that Wegener is worried enough about keeping an eye on his investment that he doubles up on his picket there and comes up with something that could give us a real fight. That means we have to move quickly, but we also need to be sure we coordinate properly, Commander Bajkusa. So I think that while I take *Annika* to Melchor to check on the situation, I'm going to send you and *Javelin* off to Lutrell. If my brother's kept to the schedule he sent me in his last dispatch, you should find *Astrid* there. He'll probably send you on to Prism with his own dispatches, but emphasize to him that by the time he hears from you our good friend the Governor is about to find himself short one cruiser."

He smiled thinly, and Bajkusa smiled back, because on that point at least, he had complete and total faith in Dunecki's judgment.

Honor dragged herself wearily through the hatch and collapsed facedown on her bunk with a heartfelt groan. Nimitz leapt from her shoulder at the last moment and landed on the pillow where he turned to regard her with a reproving flirt of his tail. She paid him no attention at all, and he bleeked a quiet laugh and curled down beside her to rest his nose gently in the short-cropped, silky fuzz of her hair.

"Keeping us out late, I see, Ma'am," a voice observed brightly, and Honor turned her head without ever lifting it completely off the pillow. She lay with it under her right cheek and turned a slightly bloodshot and profoundly disapproving eye upon Audrey Bradlaugh.

"I'm pleased to see that *someone* finds the situation amusing," she observed, and Audrey chuckled.

"Oh, no, Honor! It's not that someone finds it amusing— it's that the entire ship's *company* does! And it's such an appropriate . . . resolution, too. I mean, after all, it was you and Del Conte between you who got rid of that asshole Santino in the first place, so it's only appropriate that the two of you should wind up on the same watch doing his job. Much better than he did, I might add. Of course, it is kind of entertaining to watch the Captain and Commander Layson—not to mention Commander Hirake—kicking your poor, innocent butt in the simulator every day. Not, of course, that I would for one moment allow the fact that you systematically annihilated Nassios and me in that sim last week—or me and Basanta last Tuesday, now that I think about it—to affect my judgment in any way."

"You are a vile and disgusting person," Honor informed her, "and God will punish you for abusing me in this fashion when I am too weak and exhausted to properly defend myself."

"Sure He will," Audrey replied. "As soon as He stops laughing, anyway!"

Honor made a rude sound and then closed her eyes and buried her face in the pillow once more. She was relieved that Audrey and the other middies had decided to take her acting promotion without jealousy, but there was an unfortunate edge of accuracy to Audrey's teasing. More than one edge, in fact.

Honor had been more than a little appalled when Commander Layson called her into his day cabin to inform her that the Captain had decided to elevate her to the position of acting assistant tactical officer. However good a tactician she might consider herself as a midshipwoman, and however exciting the notion of such a promotion might be, there was no way in the universe that she could consider herself ready to assume the duties of such a position. Nor had the Exec's blunt explanation of the situation which had impelled Captain Bachfisch to elevate her to such heights done much for her ego. It wasn't so much that Commander Layson had said anything at all unreasonable, as it was that his analysis had made it perfectly plain that the Captain had had no one else at all to put into the slot. If they *had* had anyone else, the Exec had made clear enough, then that someone else would undoubtedly have been chosen. But since Ms. Midshipwoman Harrington was all they had, she would have to do.

And just to see to it that she did, Commander Layson had informed her with an air of bland generosity, he, Commander Hirake, and the Captain himself would be only too happy to help her master her new duties.

She'd thanked him, of course. There was very little else that she could have done, whatever she'd sensed waiting in her future. Nor had her trepidation proved ill founded. None of them was quite as naturally fiendish as Captain Courvoisier, but Captain Courvoisier had been the head of the entire Saganami Island Tactical Department. He hadn't begun to have the amount of time that Honor's trio of new instructors had, and he'd certainly never been able to devote his entire attention to a single unfortunate victim at a time.

As Audrey had just suggested, Honor wasn't used to losing in tactical exercises. In fact, she admitted to herself, she had become somewhat smugly accustomed to beating the stuffing out of other people, and the string of salutary drubbings the tactical trinity of HMS *War Maiden* had administered to her had been a chastening experience. Just as they had been intended to be. Nor had her lordly new elevation altered the fact that this remained her snotty cruise. When she took her tac watch on the bridge (although, thank God, no one was prepared to even suggest that she be given the *bridge* watch itself!) she was indeed the ship's duty tactical officer. But when she was off watch, she was still Ms. Midshipwoman Harrington, and no one had seen fit to excuse her from all of the other "learning experiences" which had been the lot of RMN snotties since time out of mind.

All of which meant that she was running even harder now than she had during her final form at Saganami Island. Which seemed dreadfully unfair, given how much smaller a campus *War Maiden* was!

"You really are bushed, aren't you?" Audrey asked after a moment, and the amusement in her voice had eased back a notch.

"No," Honor said judiciously. " 'Bushed' is far too pale and anemic a word for what I am."

She was only half-joking, and it showed.

"Well, in that case, why don't you just kick off your boots and stay where you are for a while?"

"No way," Honor said, opening her eyes once more. "We've got quarters inspection in less than four hours!"

"So we do," Audrey agreed. "But you and Nassios covered my posterior with Lieutenant Saunders on that charting problem yesterday, so I guess the three of us could let you get a few hours of shut-eye while we tidy up. It's not like your locker's a disaster area, you know."

"But—" Honor began.

"Shut up and take your nap," Audrey told her firmly, and Nimitz bleeked in soft but equally firm agreement from beside her head. Honor considered protesting further, but not for very long. She'd already argued long enough to satisfy the requirements of honor, and she was too darned exhausted to be any more noble than she absolutely had to.

"Thanks," she said sleepily, and she was already asleep before Audrey could reply.

✧   ✧   ✧

"There she is, Sir," Commander Amami said. "Just as you expected."

"There we *think* she is," Anders Dunecki corrected meticulously. Whatever Bajkusa might have thought, the commodore was far from blind to Amami's tendency to accept his own theories uncritically, and he made a conscious effort to keep that in mind at times like this. "She could still be a legitimate merchantman," he added, and Amami rubbed gently at his lower lip in thought.

"She is on the right course for one of the Dillingham supply ships, Sir," he conceded after a moment. "But according to our intelligence packet, there shouldn't be another Dillingham ship in here for at least another month, and there really isn't a lot of other shipping to the system these days."

"True," Dunecki agreed. "But the flip side of that argument is that if there isn't much other shipping in the first place, then the odds are greater that any additional merchies that come calling are going to slip through without our intelligence people warning us they're on their way."

"Point taken, Sir," Amami acknowledged. "So how do you want to handle this?"

"Exactly as we planned from the beginning," Dunecki said. "I pointed out that this *could* be a merchantman, not that I really believed that it was one. And it doesn't matter if it is, after all. If we treat it as a Confed cruiser from the outset, then all we'll really do if it turns out to be a merchie is to waste a little caution on it. But if it turns out to be a cruiser and we assume otherwise, the surprise would be on the other foot. So we'll just close in on the contact all fat and happy—and dumb. We won't suspect a thing until it's got us exactly where it wants us."

He looked up from his plot to meet Amami's eyes, and their thin, shark-like smiles were in perfect agreement.

"The contact is still closing, Sir," Lieutenant Commander Hirake reported from the com screen at Captain Bachfisch's elbow.

War Maiden's senior tactical officer was once again in Auxiliary Control with Commander Layson, but Honor was on the command deck. She would have liked to think that she was there while the lieutenant commander was in AuxCon because the Captain had so much faith in her abilities. Unfortunately, she knew it was exactly the other way around. He wanted her under his own eye, and if something happened to the bridge, he wanted to be sure that Layson would have the more experienced tactical officer to back him up.

"I noticed that myself," Bachfisch replied to Hirake with a small smile. "May I assume that your latest report is a tactful effort to draw to my attention the fact that the contact seems to be an awfully large and powerful 'pirate'?"

"Something of the sort, Sir," Hirake said with an answering smile, but there was a hint of genuine concern in her expression. "According to CIC, she outmasses us by at least sixty thousand tons."

"So she does," Bachfisch agreed. "But she obviously doesn't know that we aren't just another freighter waiting for her to snap us up. Besides, if she were a Peep or an Andy, I'd be worried by her tonnage advantage. But no regular man-of-war would be closing in on a merchie this way, so that means whoever we have out there is a raider. That makes her either a straight pirate or a privateer, and neither of them is likely to have a crew that can match our people. Don't worry, Janice. I won't get cocky or take anything for granted, but I'm not scared of anything short of an Andy that size—certainly not of anything armed with the kind of crap available from the tech base here in the Confederacy! Anyway, pirates and privateers are what we're out here to deal with, so let's be about it."

"As you say, Sir," Hirake replied, and Honor hid a smile as she gazed down at her own plot. The lieutenant commander had done her job by reminding her captain (however tactfully) of the enemy's size and potential firepower, but the confidence in her voice matched that of the Captain perfectly. And rightly so, Honor concluded. The contact closing so confidently upon them obviously didn't have a clue of what it was actually pursuing, or it would have come in far more cautiously.

"Captain, I have a hail from the contact," Lieutenant Sauchuk reported suddenly.

"Oh?" Bachfisch arched one eyebrow. "Put it on the main screen and let's hear what he has to say, Yuri."

"Aye, aye, Sir."

All eyes on *War Maiden*'s bridge flipped to the main com screen as a man in the uniform of the Silesian Confederacy's navy appeared on it.

"*Sylvan Grove*," he said, addressing them by the name of the Hauptman Cartel freighter whose transponder ID codes they had borrowed for their deception, "this is Captain Denby of the Confederate Navy. Please maintain your present course and attitude while my ship makes rendezvous with you."

"Oh, of *course* you are," Honor heard Senior Chief Del Conte murmur all but inaudibly behind her.

"I think we owe the good captain a reply, Yuri," Bachfisch said after a moment. "Double-check your filters, and then give me a live pickup."

"Aye, aye, Sir," Sauchuk replied. He checked the settings on his panel carefully, then nodded. "You're live, Skipper," he said.

"Captain Denby, I'm Captain Bullard," Bachfisch said, and Honor knew that *War Maiden*'s computers were altering his image to put him into a merchant officer's uniform, rather than the black and gold of the RMN, just as the raider's computers had put *him* into Confed naval uniform. "I hope you won't take this the wrong way," Bachfisch went on, "but this isn't exactly the safest neighborhood around. It's not that I don't believe you're who you say you are, but could I ask just why it is that you want to rendez-vous with us?"

"Of course, Captain Bullard," the face on his com screen replied in the slightly stiff tone of an officer who didn't particularly like to be reminded by a mere merchant skipper of how pathetic his navy's record for maintaining order within its own borders was. "I have aboard seventeen of your nationals, the survivors from the crews of two Manticoran freighters. We took out the 'privateer' who captured their ships last week, and it seemed to me that the fastest way to repatriate them would be to turn them over to the Dillingham manager here in Melchor."

"I see," Bachfisch replied in a much warmer and less wary voice. He felt a brief flicker of something almost like admiration for "Captain Denby's" smoothness, for the other man had come up with what was actually a plausible reason for a merchantman here in Silesia to allow a warship to close with it. And "Denby" had delivered his lines perfectly, with just the right note of offended dignity coupled with a "see there" sort of flourish. "In that case, Captain," he went on, "of course we'll maintain heading and deceleration for rendezvous."

"Thank you, Captain Bullard," the man on his com screen said. "Denby out."

"Considerate of them to let us maintain course," Janice Hirake observed to Abner Layson.

"He doesn't have much choice if he's going to keep us dumb and happy," Layson pointed out, and Hirake nodded. Warships could pull far higher accelerations than any huge whale of a merchantman, and it was traditional for them to be the ones who maneuvered to match heading and velocity in the case of a deep space rendezvous.

"Still, it's handy that he came in so far above the plane of the ecliptic. Keeps him well above us and on the wrong side of our wedge."

"Somehow I doubt that they arranged things that way just to oblige us," Layson said dryly. "On the other hand, sneaking up on somebody *can* sometimes put you in a less than optimal position yourself, can't it?"

"Indeed it can," Hirake said with a small, wicked smile.

✧   ✧   ✧

"I wish we had a little better sensor angle on them, Sir," Lieutenant Quinn muttered from one side of his mouth, and Lieutenant Commander Acedo glanced at him. Acedo was *Annika*'s tactical officer, and Quinn was the most junior commissioned member of his department. But the younger man had a nose for trouble which Acedo had learned to trust, or at least listen very carefully to.

"I'd like to have a better look at them myself," the lieutenant commander replied. "But thanks to *Javelin*, we've already got a pretty good notion of what we're up against. At this point, I have to agree with the Commodore—it's more important to keep him guessing about us by avoiding the deeper parts of his sensor well. Besides, the fact that he's got his wedge between him and *our* sensors should help keep him confident that we don't know that he's a warship, too."

"I can't argue with that, Sir," Quinn acknowledged. "I guess I just want the best of both worlds, and sometimes you just can't have that."

"No, you can't," Acedo agreed. "But sometimes you can come pretty close, and the way the Old Man's set this one up qualifies for that."

Two cruisers slid inexorably together, each convinced that she knew precisely what the other one was and that the other one didn't know what *she* was . . . and both of them wrong. The distance between them fell steadily, and *Annika*'s deceleration reduced the velocity differential with matching steadiness.

"Zero-zero interception in five minutes, Sir," Honor announced. Her soprano sounded much calmer in her own ears than it felt from behind her eyes, and she raised her head to look across the bridge at the Captain. "Current range is two-one-six k-klicks and present overtake is one-three-three-one KPS squared. Deceleration is holding steady at four-five-zero gravities."

"Thank you, Tactical," Bachfisch replied, and his calm,

composed tone did more than she would have believed possible to still the excitement jittering down her nerves. The fact that their sensors still had not had a single clear look at the contact made her nervous, but she took herself firmly to task. This, too, she thought was a part of the art of command. For all of his calm, the Captain actually *knew* no more about the contact than Honor herself, but it was his job to exude the sort of confidence his people needed from him at this moment. Captain Courvoisier had stressed more than once that even if she was wrong—or perhaps *especially* if she was wrong—a commanding officer must never forget her "command face." Nothing could destroy a crew's cohesion faster than panic, and nothing produced panic better than the suggestion that the CO had lost her own confidence. But it had to be harder than usual, this time. The raider was well within effective energy range already, and just as *War Maiden*'s own crew, her people must be ready to open fire in a heartbeat. At such short range, an energy weapon duel would be deadly, which would be good . . . for whoever fired first.

Of course, the raider was expecting only an unarmed merchantship. However prepared they thought they were, the sheer surprise of finding themselves suddenly broadside-to-broadside with a King's ship was bound to shock and confuse them at least momentarily. And it was entirely possible that they wouldn't even have closed up all of their weapons crews simply to deal with a "merchantman."

"Stand ready, Mr. Saunders," the Captain said calmly. "Prepare to alter course zero-nine-zero degrees to starboard and roll port at one hundred ten thousand kilometers."

"Aye, aye, Sir," Lieutenant Saunders acknowledged. "Standing by to alter course zero-nine-zero degrees to starboard and roll port at range of one hundred ten thousand kilometers."

"Stand by to fire on my command, Ms. Harrington," Bachfisch added.

"Aye, aye, Sir. Standing by to fire on your command."

✧   ✧   ✧

"Get ready, Commander Acedo," Anders Dunecki said quietly. "At this range he won't risk challenging us or screwing around demanding we surrender, so neither will we. The instant he rolls ship to clear his wedge, blow his ass out of space."

"Yes, Sir!" Acedo agreed with a ferocious grin, and he felt just as confident as he looked. The other ship would have the advantage of knowing when she intended to alter course, but *Annika* had an even greater advantage. The commander of the enemy cruiser had to be completely confident that he had *Annika* fooled, or he would never have allowed her to come this close, and the only thing more devastating than the surprise of an ambush was the surprise of an ambusher when his intended victim turned out not to have been surprised at all.

"Coming up on one hundred ten thousand kilometers, Sir!"

"Execute your helm order, Mr. Saunders!" Thomas Bachfisch snapped.

"Aye, aye, Sir!"

War Maiden responded instantly to her helm, pivoting sharply to her right and rolling up on her left side to swing her starboard broadside up towards the raider, and Honor leaned forward, pulse hammering, mouth dry, as the icons on her plot flashed before her. It almost seemed as if it were the raider who had suddenly altered course and position as the strobing amber circle of target acquisition reached out to engulf its blood-red bead.

"Stand by, Ms. Harrington!"

"Standing by, aye, Sir."

The amber circle reached the glowing bead of the contact and flashed over to sudden crimson, and Honor's hand hovered above the firing key.

"*Fire!*"

Both ships fired in the same instant across barely a third of a light-second.

At such a short range, their grasers and lasers blasted straight through any sidewall any cruiser could have generated, and alarms screamed as deadly, focused energy ripped huge, shattered wounds through battle steel and alloy. Surprise was effectively total on both sides. Commodore Dunecki had completely deceived Captain Bachfisch into expecting *Annika* to be fatally unprepared, but despite his discussion with Commander Bajkusa, Dunecki had never seriously considered for a moment that *War Maiden* might be anything except a Silesian warship. He was totally unprepared to find himself suddenly face to face with a *Manticoran* heavy cruiser. *War Maiden*'s tautly trained crew were head and shoulders above any SN ship's company in training and efficiency. They got off their first broadside two full seconds before Dunecki had anticipated that they could. Worse, Silesian ships tended to be missile-heavy, optimized for long-range combat and with only relatively light energy batteries, and the sheer weight of fire smashing into his ship was a stunning surprise.

But even though Dunecki was unprepared for *War Maiden*'s furious fire, the Manticoran ship was still smaller and more lightly armed than his own. Worse, Captain Bachfisch had assumed that *Annika* was a typical pirate and anticipated at least a moment or two in which to act while "Captain Denby" adjusted to the fact that the "freighter" he was stalking had suddenly transformed itself from a house tabby to a hexapuma, and he didn't get it. It was the equivalent of a duel with submachine guns at ten paces, and both ships staggered as the deadly tide of energy sleeted into them.

Honor Harrington's universe went mad.

She'd felt herself tightening internally during the long approach phase, felt the dryness of her mouth and the way her nerves seemed to quiver individually, dancing within her flesh as if they were naked harp strings plucked by an icy wind. She had been more afraid than she had ever been in her life, and not just for herself. She had won friendships aboard *War Maiden* during the long weeks of their deployment, and those friends were at risk as much as she was. And then there was Nimitz, alone in his life-support module down in Snotty Row. Her mind had shied away from the thought of what would happen to him if his module suffered battle damage . . . or if she herself died. 'Cats who had adopted humans almost invariably suicided if their humans died. She'd known that before she ever applied for Saganami Island, and it had almost made her abandon her dream of Navy service, for if she put herself in harm's way, she put *him* there, as well, and only Nimitz's fierce, obvious insistence that she pursue her dream had carried her to the Academy. Now the reality of what had been only an intellectual awareness was upon them both, and a dark and terrible fear—not of death or wounds, but of loss—was a cold iron lump at the core of her.

Those fears had flowed through her on the crest of a sudden visceral awareness that she was not immortal. That the bloody carnage of combat could claim her just as easily as any other member of *War Maiden*'s company. Despite all of her training, all of her studies, all of her lifelong interest in naval and military history, that awareness had never truly been hers until this instant. Now it was, and she had spent the slow, dragging hours as the contact gradually closed with *War Maiden* trying to prepare herself and wondering how she would respond when she knew it was no longer a simulation. That there were real human beings on the other side of that icon on her plot. People who would be doing their very best to kill her ship—and her—with real weapons . . . and whom she would be trying to kill in turn. She'd made herself face and accept that, despite her fear, and she had thought—hoped—that she was ready for whatever might happen.

She'd been wrong.

HMS *War Maiden* lurched like a galleon in a gale as the transfer energy of PSN *Annika*'s fire bled into her. The big privateer carried fewer missiles and far heavier energy weapons than her counterparts in the Silesian navy, and her grasers smashed through *War Maiden*'s sidewall like brimstone sledgehammers come straight from Hell. The sidewall generators did their best to bend and divert that hurricane of energy from its intended target, but four of the heavy beams struck home with demonic fury. Graser Two, Missiles Two and Four, Gravitic Two, Radar Two and Lidar Three, Missile Eight and Magazine Four, Boat Bay One and Life Support Two . . . Entire clusters of compartments and weapons bays turned venomous, bloody crimson on the damage control panel as enemy fire ripped and clawed its way towards *War Maiden*'s heart. Frantic damage control reports crashed over Honor like a Sphinxian tidal bore while the ship jerked and shuddered. Damage alarms wailed and screamed, adding their voices to the cacophony raging through the heavy cruiser's compartments, and clouds of air and water vapor erupted from the gaping wounds torn suddenly through her armored skin.

"Heavy casualties in Missile Two!" Senior Chief Del Conte barked while secondary explosions still rolled through the hull. "Graser Six reports loss of central control, and Magazine Four is open to space! We—"

He never finished his report, and Honor's entire body recoiled as a savage explosion tore through the bridge bulkhead. It reached out to the senior chief, snatching him up as casually as some cruel child would have, and tore him to pieces before her eyes. Blood and pieces of what had been a human being seemed to be *everywhere*, and a small, calm corner of her brain realized that that was because they *were* everywhere. The explosion killed at least five people outright, through blast or with deadly splinters from ruptured bulkheads, and Honor rocked back in her padded, armored chair as the wall of devastation marched through *War Maiden*'s bridge . . . and directly over the captain's chair at its center.

Captain Bachfisch just had time to bend forward and raise an arm in an instinctive effort to protect his face when the blast front struck. It hit from slightly behind into his right, and that was all that saved his life, because even as his arm rose, he whipped the chair to his left and took the main force across the armored shell of its back. But not even that was enough to fully protect him, and the force of the explosion snatched him up and hurled him against the opposite bulkhead. He bounced back with the limp, total bonelessness of unconsciousness and hit the decksole without ever having made a sound.

He was far from the only injured person on the bridge. The same explosion which blew him out of his chair threw a meter-long splinter of battle steel across the com section. It decapitated Lieutenant Sauchuk as neatly as an executioner, then hurtled onward and drove itself through Lieutenant Saunders' chest like an ax, and Honor's mind tried to retreat into some safe, sane cave as the chaos and confusion and terror for which no simulation, no lecture, could possibly have prepared her enveloped her. She heard the whistling rush of air racing for the rents in the bulkhead even through the screams and moans of the wounded, and instinct cried out for her to race across the bridge to help the hurt and unconscious helmet up in time. Yet she didn't. The trained responses her instructors at Saganami Island had hammered mercilessly into her for four long T-years overrode even her horror and the compulsion to help. She slammed her own helmet into place, but her eyes never left the panel before her, for she dared not leave her station even to help the Captain before she knew that AuxCon and Lieutenant Commander Hirake had taken over from the mangled bridge.

War Maiden's energy mounts lashed out again, with a second broadside, even as the raider fired again, as well. More death and destruction punched their way through the hull, rending and tearing, and the heavy cruiser shuddered as one hit blew straight through her after impeller ring. Half the beta nodes and two of the alphas went down instantly, and fresh alarms shrilled as a fifth of *War Maiden*'s personnel became casualties. Lieutenant Commander LaVacher was one of them, and a simultaneous hit smashed home on Damage Control Central, killing a dozen ratings and petty officers and critically wounding Lieutenant Tergesen.

War Maiden's grasers continued to hammer at her larger, more powerful—and far younger—foe, but Honor felt a fresh and even more paralyzing spike of terror as she realized that they were still firing under the preliminary fire plan which *she* had locked in under Captain Bachfisch's orders. AuxCon should have overridden and assumed command virtually instantly . . . and it hadn't.

She turned her head, peering at what had been Senior Chief Del Conte's station through the banners of smoke riding the howling gale through the shattered bulkhead, and her heart froze as her eyes picked out AuxCon on the schematic displayed there. The compartment itself appeared to be intact, but it was circled by the jagged red and white band which indicated total loss of communications. AuxCon was cut off, not only from the bridge, but from access to the ship's computers, as well.

In the time it had taken to breathe three times, *War Maiden* had been savagely maimed, and tactical command had devolved onto a twenty-year-old midshipwoman on her snotty cruise.

The bridge about her was like the vestibule of Hell. Half the command stations had been wrecked or at least blown off-line, a quarter of the bridge crew was dead or wounded, and at least three men and women who should have been at their stations were crawling frantically through the wreckage slapping helmets and skinsuit seals on unconscious crewmates. She felt the ship's wounds as if they had been inflicted upon her own body, and all in the world she wanted in that moment was to hear someone—*anyone*—tell her what to do.

But there was no one else. She was all *War Maiden* had, and she jerked her eyes back to her own plot and drew a deep breath.

"Helm, roll ninety degrees port!"

No one on that wounded, half-broken bridge, and Honor least of all, perhaps, recognized the cool, sharp soprano which cut cleanly through the chaos, but the helmsman clinging to his own sanity with his fingernails recognized the incisive bite of command.

"Rolling ninety degrees port, aye!" he barked, and HMS *War Maiden* rolled frantically, snatching her shattered starboard broadside away from the ferocity of her enemy's fire.

Something happened inside Honor Harrington in the moment that her ship rolled. The panic vanished. The fear remained, but it was suddenly a distant, unimportant thing—something which could no longer touch her, would no longer be permitted to affect her. She looked full into the face of Death, not just for her but for her entire ship and everyone aboard it, and there was no doubt in her mind that he had come for them all. Yet her fear had transmuted into something else entirely. A cold, focused purpose that sang in her blood and bone. Her almond eyes stared into Death's empty sockets, and her soul bared its teeth and snarled defiance.

"Port broadside stand by for Fire Plan Delta Seven," that soprano rapier commanded, and confirmations raced back from *War Maiden*'s undamaged broadside even as *Annika*'s fire continued to hammer harmlessly at the impenetrable belly of her wedge.

Honor's mind raced with cold, icy precision. Her first instinct was to break off, for she knew only too well how brutally wounded her ship was. Worse, she already knew that their opponent was far more powerful—and better crewed—than anyone aboard *War Maiden* had believed she could be. Yet those very factors were what made flight impossible. The velocity differential between the two ships was less than six hundred kilometers per second, and with half her after impeller ring down, *War Maiden* could never hope to pull away from her unlamed foe. Even had her drive been unimpaired, the effort to break off would undoubtedly have proved suicidal as it exposed the after aspect of her impeller wedge to the enemy's raking fire.

No, she thought coldly. Flight was not an option, and her gloved fingers raced across the tactical panel, locking in new commands as she reached out for her ship's—*her* ship's—only hope of survival.

"Helm, stand by to alter course one-three-five degrees to starboard, forty degree nose-down skew, and roll starboard on my command!"

"Aye, aye, Ma'am!"

"All weapons crews," that voice she could not quite recognize even now went on, carrying a calm and a confidence that stilled incipient panic like a magic wand, "stand by to engage as programmed. Transmitting manual firing commands now."

She punched a button, and the targeting parameters she had locked into the main computers spilled into the secondary on-mount computers of her waiting weapons crews. If fresh damage cut her command links to them, at least they would know what she intended for them to do.

Then it was done, and she sat back in her command chair, watching the enemy's icon as it continued to angle sharply in to intercept *War Maiden*'s base track. The range was down to fifty-two thousand kilometers, falling at five hundred and six kilometers per second, and she waited tautly while the blood-red icon of her enemy closed upon her ship.

Commodore Anders Dunecki cursed vilely as the other cruiser snapped up on its side. He'd hurt that ship—hurt it badly—and he knew it. But it had also hurt him far more badly than he had ever allowed for. He'd gotten slack, a cold thought told him in his own viciously calm voice. He'd been fighting the Confeds too long, let his guard down and become accustomed to being able to take liberties with them. But his present opponent was no Silesian naval unit, and he cursed again, even more vilely, as he realized what that other ship truly was.

A Manty. He'd attacked a *Manty* warship, committed the one unforgivable blunder no pirate or privateer was ever allowed to commit more than once. That was why the other cruiser had managed to get off even a single shot of her own, because she was a Manty and she'd been just as ready, just as prepared to fire as he was.

And it was also why his entire strategy to win Andermani support for the Council for an Independent Prism had suddenly come crashing down in ruins. However badly the People's Republic might have distracted the Manticoran government, the RMN's response to what had happened here was as certain as the energy death of the universe.

But only if they know who did it, his racing brain told him coldly. *Only if they know which system government to send the battle squadrons after. But that ship has got to have detailed sensor records of* Annika's *energy signatures. If they compare those records with the Confed database, they're bound to ID us. Even if they don't get a clean hit, Wegener will know who it must have been and send them right after us. But even he won't be able to talk the Manties into hitting us without at least some supporting evidence, and the only evidence there is in the computers of that ship.*

There was only one way to prevent that data from getting out.

He turned his head to look at Commander Amami. The exec was still listening to damage reports, but Dunecki didn't really need them. A glance at the master schematic showed that *Annika*'s entire port broadside must be a mass of tangled ruin. Less than a third of her energy mounts and missile tubes remained intact, and her sidewall generators were at barely forty percent efficiency. But the Manty had to be hurt at least as badly, and she was smaller, less able to absorb damage. Better yet, he had the overtake advantage and her impeller strength had dropped drastically. He was bigger, newer, better armed, and more maneuverable, and that meant the engagement could have only one outcome.

"Roll one-eight-zero degrees to starboard and maintain heading," he told his helmsmen harshly. "Starboard broadside, stand by to fire as you bear!"

✧   ✧   ✧

Honor watched the other ship roll. Like *War Maiden*, the bigger ship was rotating her crippled broadside away from her opponent's fire. But she wasn't stopping there, and Honor let herself feel a tiny spark of hope as the raider continued to roll, and then the weapons of her undamaged broadside lashed out afresh and poured a hurricane of fire upon *War Maiden*. The belly of the Manticoran ship's impeller wedge absorbed that fire harmlessly, but that wasn't the point, and Honor knew it. The enemy was sequencing her fire carefully, so that *something* pounded the wedge continuously. If *War Maiden* rolled back for a broadside duel, that constant pounding was almost certain to catch her as she rolled, inflicting damage and destroying at least some of her remaining weapons before they ever got a chance to bear upon their foe. It was a smart, merciless tactic, one which eschewed finesse in favor of brutal practicality.

But unlike whoever was in command over there, Honor could not afford a weapon-to-weapon battering match. Not against someone that big who had already demonstrated her capabilities so convincingly. And so she had no choice but to oppose overwhelming firepower with cunning.

Every fiber of her being was concentrated on the imagery of her plot, and her lips drew back in a feral snarl as the other ship maintained her acceleration. Seconds ticked slowly and agonizingly past. Sixty of them. Then seventy. Ninety.

"Helm! On my mark, give me maximum emergency power—redline everything—and execute my previous order!" She heard the helmsman's response, but her eyes never flickered from her plot, and her nostrils flared.

"*Now!*"

Anders Dunecki had a handful of fleeting seconds to realize that he had made one more error. The Manty had held her course, hiding behind the shield of her wedge, and he'd thought that it hadn't mattered whether that arose out of panic or out of a rational realization that she couldn't have gone toe-to-toe with *Annika* even if she hadn't been so badly damaged.

Yet it did matter. The other captain hadn't panicked, but he *had* realized he couldn't fight *Annika* in a broadside duel . . . and he had no intention of doing so.

Perhaps it wasn't really Dunecki's fault. The range was insanely short for modern warships, dropping towards one which could be measured in hundreds of kilometers and not thousands, and no sane naval officer would even have contemplated engaging at such close quarters. Nor had either Dunecki or Bachfisch planned on doing any such thing, for each had expected to begin and end the battle with a single broadside which would take his enemy completely by surprise. But whatever they'd planned, their ships were here now, and no one in any navy trained its officers for combat maneuvers in such close proximity to an enemy warship. And because of that, Anders Dunecki, for all of his experience, was completely unprepared for what *War Maiden* actually did.

Strident alarms jangled as HMS *War Maiden*'s inertial compensator protested its savage abuse. More alarms howled as the load on the heavy cruiser's impeller nodes peaked forty percent beyond their "Never Exceed" levels. Despite her mangled after impeller ring, *War Maiden* slammed suddenly forward at almost five hundred and fifty gravities. Her bow swung sharply towards *Annika*, but it also dipped sharply "below" the other ship, denying the big privateer the deadly down-the-throat shot which would have spelled *War Maiden*'s inevitable doom.

Annika began a desperate turn of her own, but she had been taken too much by surprise. There wasn't enough time for her to answer her helm before *War Maiden*'s wounded charge carried her across her enemy's wake.

It wasn't the perfect up-the-kilt stern rake that was every tactical officer's dream. No neat ninety-degree crossing with every weapon firing in perfect sequence. Instead, it was a desperate, scrambling lunge—the ugly do-or-die grapple of a wounded hexapuma facing a peak bear. Honor's weapons couldn't begin to fire down the long axis of the enemy ship in a "proper" rake . . . but what they could do was enough.

Six grasers scored direct hits on the aftermost quarter of PSN *Annika*. They came in through the open after aspect of her wedge, with no sidewall to interdict or degrade them. They smashed into her armored after hammerhead, and armor shattered at their ferocious touch. They blew deep into the bigger ship's hull, maiming and smashing, crippling her after chase armament, and the entire after third of her sidewall flickered and died.

Annika fought to answer her helm, clawing around in a desperate attempt to reacquire *War Maiden* for her broadside weapons, but Honor Harrington had just discovered that she could be just as merciless a killer as Anders Dunecki. Her flying fingers stabbed a minor correction into her tactical panel, and *War Maiden* fired once more. Every graser in her surviving broadside poured a deadly torrent of energy into the gap in *Annika*'s sidewall, and the big privateer vanished in a hell-bright boil of fury.

Nimitz sat very straight and still on Honor Harrington's shoulder as she came to a halt before the Marine sentry outside the Captain's day cabin. The private gazed at her for a long, steady moment, then reached back to key the admittance signal.

"Yes?" The voice belonged to Abner Layson, not Thomas Bachfisch.

"Ms. Harrington to see the Captain, Sir!" the Marine replied crisply.

"Enter," another voice said, and the Marine stepped aside as the hatch opened. Honor nodded her thanks as she stepped past him, and for just a moment he allowed his professional nonexpression to vanish into a wink of encouragement before the hatch closed behind her once more.

Honor crossed the cabin and came to attention. Commander Layson sat behind the captain's desk, but Captain

Bachfisch was also present. *War Maiden*'s CO was propped as comfortably as possible on an out-sized couch along the cabin's longest bulkhead. He looked awful, battered and bruised and with his left arm and right leg both immobilized. Under almost any other circumstances, he would still have been locked up in sickbay while Lieutenant Chiem stood over him with a pulser to keep him there if necessary. But there was no room in sickbay for anyone with non-life-threatening injuries. Basanta Lakhia was in sickbay. Nassios Makira wasn't; he'd been in After Engineering when the hit came in, and the damage control parties hadn't even found his body.

Honor stood there, facing the executive officer and her captain, and the eighteen percent of *War Maiden*'s company who had died stood silently at her shoulder, waiting.

"Stand easy, Ms. Harrington," the captain said quietly, and she let her spine relax ever so slightly. Bachfisch gazed at her for a long, quiet moment, and she returned his gaze as calmly as she could.

"I've reviewed the bridge tapes of the engagement," Bachfisch said at last, and nodded sideways at Layson. "So have the Exec and Commander Hirake. Is there anything you'd like to add to them, Ms. Harrington?"

"No, Sir," she said, and in that moment she looked more absurdly youthful even than usual as a faint flush of embarrassment stained her cheekbones, and the treecat on her shoulder cocked his head as he studied her two superiors intently.

"Nothing at all?" Bachfisch cocked his head in a gesture that was almost a mirror image of Nimitz's, then shrugged. "Well, I don't suppose anything else is really needed. The tapes caught it all, I believe."

He fell silent for another moment, then gestured at Commander Layson with his good hand.

"Commander Layson and I asked you to come see us because of what's on those tapes, Ms. Harrington," the captain said quietly. "Obviously, *War Maiden* has no choice but to cut her deployment short and return to the Star

Kingdom for repairs. Normally, that would require you to transfer to another ship for the completion of your middy cruise, which would unfortunately put you at least six T-months or even a T-year behind your classmates for seniority purposes. In this instance, however, Commander Layson and I have decided to endorse your Form S-One-Sixty to indicate successful completion of your cruise. The same endorsement will appear in the records of Midshipwoman Bradlaugh and Midshipman Lakhia. We will also so endorse Midshipman Makira's file and recommend his posthumous promotion to lieutenant (junior-grade)."

He paused once more, and Honor cleared her throat.

"Thank you, Sir. Especially for Nassios. I think I can speak for all of us in that."

"I'm sure you can," Bachfisch said. He rubbed his nose for just a moment, then surprised her with a crooked grin.

"I have no idea what's going to happen to my own career when we return to Manticore," he told her. "A lot will no doubt depend on the findings of the Board of Inquiry, but I think we can safely assume that at least a few critics are bound to emerge. And not without some justification."

It was all Honor could do not to blink in surprise at the unexpected frankness of that admission, but he went on calmly.

"I got too confident, Ms. Harrington," he said. "Too sure that what I was looking at was a typical Silesian pirate. Oh," he waved his good hand in a small, brushing-away gesture, "it's fair enough to say that we very seldom run into anyone out here, pirate or privateer, with that much firepower and that well-trained a crew. But it's a captain's job to expect the unexpected, and I didn't. I trust that you will remember that lesson when you someday command a King's ship yourself."

He paused once more, his expression clearly inviting a response, and Honor managed not to clear her throat again.

"I'll certainly try to remember, Sir," she said.

"I'm sure you will. And from your performance here in

Melchor, I have every confidence that you'll succeed," Bachfisch said quietly. Then he gave himself a small shake.

"In the meantime, however, we have some practical housekeeping details to take care of. As you know, our casualties were heavy. Lieutenant Livanos will take over in Engineering, and Ensign Masters will take over Communications. We're fortunate that everyone in Auxiliary Control survived, but we're going to be very short of watch-standing qualified officers for the return to Manticore. In light of our situation, I have decided to confirm you as Assistant Tac Officer, with the acting rank of lieutenant (junior-grade) and the promotion on my own authority to the permanent rank of ensign." Honor's eyes widened, and he smiled more naturally. "Under the circumstances, I believe I can safely predict that regardless of the outcome of my own Board, this is one promotion which BuPers will definitely confirm."

"Sir, I—I don't know what to say, except, thank you," she said after a moment, and he chuckled.

"It's the very least I can do to thank you for saving my ship—and my people—Ms. Harrington. I wish I had the authority to promote you all the way to J. G., but I doubt that BuPers would sign off on that even under these circumstances. So all you'll really get is a five or six-month seniority advantage over your classmates."

"And," Commander Layson put in quietly, "I feel sure that the Service will take note of how and why you were promoted. No one who doesn't know you could have expected you to perform as you did, Ms. Harrington. Those of us who have come to know you, however, would have expected no less."

Honor's face blazed like a forest fire, and she sensed Nimitz's approval of the emotions of her superiors in the treecat's body language and the proprietary way his true hand rested on her beret.

"I expect that we've embarrassed you enough for one afternoon, Ms. Harrington." Bachfisch's voice mingled amusement, approval, and sympathy, and Honor felt her eyes snap back to him. "I will expect you and Commander Hirake to join me for dinner tonight, however, so that we can discuss the reorganization of your department. I trust that will be convenient?"

"Of course, Sir!" Honor blurted.

"Good. And I'll have Chief Stennis be sure we have a fresh supply of celery on hand."

Nimitz bleeked in amused enthusiasm from her shoulder, and she felt her own mouth curve in her first genuine smile since *Annika*'s explosion. Bachfisch saw it, and nodded in approval.

"Much better, Ensign Harrington! But now, shorthanded as we are, I'm sure that there's something you ought to be doing, isn't there?"

"Yes, Sir. I'm sure there is."

"In that case, I think you should go attend to it. Let's be about it, Ensign."

"Aye, aye, Sir!" Ensign Honor Harrington replied, then snapped back to attention, turned sharply, and marched out of the Captain's day cabin to face the future.

ISLANDS

A Belisarius Story

Eric Flint

Bukkur Island

He dreamed mostly of islands, oddly enough.

He was sailing, now, in one of his father's pleasure crafts. Not the luxurious barge-in-all-but-name-and-glitter which his father himself preferred for the family's outings into the Golden Horn, but in the phaselos which was suited for sailing in the open sea. Unlike his father, for whom sailing expeditions were merely excuses for political or commercial transactions, Calopodius had always loved sailing for its own sake.

Besides, it gave him and his new wife something to do besides sit together in stiff silence.

Calopodius' half-sleeping reverie was interrupted. Wakefulness came with the sound of his aide-de-camp Luke moving through the tent. The heaviness with which Luke clumped about was deliberate, designed to allow his master to recognize who had entered his domicile. Luke was quite capable of moving easily and lightly, as he had proved many times in the course of the savage fighting on the island. But the man, in this as so many things, had proven to be far more subtle than his rough and muscular appearance might suggest.

"It's morning, young Calopodius," Luke announced. "Time to clean your wounds. And you're not eating enough."

Calopodius sighed. The process of tending the wounds would be painful, despite all of Luke's care. As for the other—

"Have new provisions arrived?"

There was a moment's silence. Then, reluctantly: "No."

Calopodius let the silence lengthen. After a few seconds, he heard Luke's own heavy sigh. "We're getting very low, truth to tell. Ashot hasn't much himself, until the supply ships arrive."

Calopodius levered himself up on his elbows. "Then I will eat my share, no more." He chuckled, perhaps a bit harshly. "And don't try to cheat, Luke. I have other sources of information, you know."

"As if my hardest job of the day won't be to keep half the army from parading through this tent," snorted Luke. Calopodius felt the weight of Luke's knees pressing into the pallet next to him, and, a moment later, winced as the bandages over his head began to be removed. "You're quite the soldiers' favorite, lad," added Luke softly. "Don't think otherwise."

In the painful time that followed, as Luke scoured and cleaned and rebandaged the sockets that had once been eyes, Calopodius tried to take refuge in that knowledge. It helped. Some.

"Are there any signs of another Malwa attack coming?" he asked. Calopodius was perched in one of the bastions his men had rebuilt after the last enemy assault had overrun it—before, eventually, the Malwa had been driven off the island altogether. That had required bitter and ferocious fighting, however, which had inflicted many casualties upon the Roman defenders. His eyes had been among those casualties, ripped out by shrapnel from a mortar shell.

"After the bloody beating we gave 'em the last time?" chortled one of the soldiers who shared the bastion. "Not likely, sir!"

Calopodius tried to match the voice to a remembered face. As usual, the effort failed of its purpose. But he took the time to engage in small talk with the soldier, so as to fix the voice itself in his memory. Not for the first time, Calopodius reflected wryly on the way in which possession of vision seemed to dull all other human faculties. Since his blinding, he had found his memory growing more acute along with his hearing. A simple instinct for self-preservation, he imagined. A blind man *had* to remember better than a seeing man, since he no longer had vision to constantly jog his lazy memory.

After his chat with the soldier had gone on for a few minutes, the man cleared his throat and said diffidently: "You'd best leave here, sir, if you'll pardon me for saying so. The Malwa'll likely be starting another barrage soon." For a moment, fierce good cheer filled the man's voice: "They seem to have a particular grudge against this part of our line, seeing's how their own blood and guts make up a good part of it."

The remark produced a ripple of harsh chuckling from the other soldiers crouched in the fortifications. That bastion had been one of the most hotly contested areas when the Malwa launched their major attack the week before. Calopodius didn't doubt for a moment that when his soldiers repaired the damage to the earthen walls they had not been too fastidious about removing all the traces of the carnage.

He sniffed tentatively, detecting those traces. His olfactory sense, like his hearing, had grown more acute also.

"Must have stunk, right afterward," he commented.

The same soldier issued another harsh chuckle. "That it did, sir, that it did. Why God invented flies, the way I look at it."

Calopodius felt Luke's heavy hand on his shoulder. "Time to go, sir. There'll be a barrage coming, sure enough."

In times past, Calopodius would have resisted. But he no longer felt any need to prove his courage, and a part of him—a still wondering, eighteen-year-old part—understood that his safety had become something his own men cared about. Alive, somewhere in the rear but still on the island, Calopodius would be a source of strength for his soldiers in the event of another Malwa onslaught. Spiritual strength, if not physical; a symbol, if nothing else. But men—fighting men, perhaps, more than any others—live by such symbols.

So he allowed Luke to guide him out of the bastion and down the rough staircase which led to the trenches below. On the way, Calopodius gauged the steps with his feet.

"One of those logs is too big," he said, speaking firmly, but trying to keep any critical edge out of the words. "It's a waste, there. Better to use it for another fake cannon."

He heard Luke suppress a sigh. *And will you stop fussing like a hen?* was the content of that small sound. Calopodius suppressed a laugh. Luke, in truth, made a poor "servant."

"We've got enough," replied Luke curtly. "Twenty-odd. Do any more and the Malwa will get suspicious. We've only got three real ones left to keep up the pretense."

As they moved slowly through the trench, Calopodius considered the problem and decided that Luke was right. The pretense was probably threadbare by now, anyway. When the Malwa finally launched a full-scale amphibious assault on the island that was the centerpiece of Calopodius' diversion, they had overrun half of it before being beaten back. When the survivors returned to the main Malwa army besieging the city of Sukkur across the Indus, they would have reported to their own top commanders that several of the "cannons" with which the Romans had apparently festooned their fortified island were nothing but painted logs.

But how many? That question would still be unclear in the minds of the enemy.

Not all of them, for a certainty. When Belisarius took his main force to outflank the Malwa in the Punjab, leaving behind Calopodius and fewer than two thousand men to serve as a diversion, he had also left some of the field guns and mortars. Those pieces had wreaked havoc on the Malwa attackers, when they finally grew suspicious enough to test the real strength of Calopodius' position.

"The truth is," said Luke gruffly, "it probably doesn't really matter anyway. By now, the general's reached the Punjab." Again, the heavy hand settled on Calopodius' slender shoulder, this time giving it a little squeeze of approval. "You've already done what the general asked you to, lad. Kept the Malwa confused, thinking Belisarius was still here, while he marched in secret to the northeast. Did it as well as he could have possibly hoped."

They had reached one of the covered portions of the trench, Calopodius sensed. He couldn't see the earth-covered logs which gave some protection from enemy fire, of course. But the quality of sound was a bit different within a shelter than in an open trench. That was just one of the many little auditory subtleties which Calopodius had begun noticing in the past few days.

He had not noticed it in days past, before he lost his eyes. In the first days after Belisarius and the main army left Sukkur on their secret, forced march to outflank the Malwa in the Punjab, Calopodius had noticed very little, in truth. He had had neither the time nor the inclination to ponder the subtleties of sense perception. He had been far too excited by his new and unexpected command and by the challenge it posed.

Martial glory. The blind young man in the covered

trench stopped for a moment, staring through sightless eyes at a wall of earth and timber bracing. Remembering, and wondering.

The martial glory Calopodius had sought, when he left a new wife in Constantinople, had certainly come to him. Of that, he had no doubt at all. His own soldiers thought so, and said so often enough—those who had survived— and Calopodius was quite certain that his praises would soon be spoken in the Senate.

Precious few of the Roman Empire's most illustrious families had achieved any notable feats of arms in the great war against the Malwa. Beginning with the great commander Belisarius himself, born into the lower Thracian nobility, it had been largely a war fought by men from low stations in life. Commoners, in the main. Agathius— the great hero of Anatha and the Dam—had even been born into a *baker's* family, about as menial a position as any short of outright slavery.

Other than Sittas, who was now leading Belisarius' cataphracts in the Punjab, almost no Greek noblemen had fought in the Malwa war. And even Sittas, before the Indus campaign, had spent the war commanding the garrison in Constantinople which overawed the hostile aristocracy and kept the dynasty on the throne.

Had it been worth it?

Reaching up and touching gently the emptiness which had once been his eyes, Calopodius was still not sure. Like many other young members of the nobility, he had been swept up with enthusiasm after the news came that Belisarius had shattered the Malwa in Mesopotamia. Let the adult members of the aristocracy whine and complain in their salons. The youth were burning to serve.

And serve they had . . . but only as couriers, in the beginning. It hadn't taken Calopodius long to realize that Belisarius intended to use him and his high-born fellows mainly for liaison with the haughty Persians, who were even more obsessed with nobility of blood-line than Greeks. The posts carried prestige—the couriers rode just behind Belisarius himself in formation—but little in the way of actual responsibility.

Standing in the bunker, the blind young man chuckled harshly. "He used us, you know. As cold-blooded as a reptile."

Silence, for a moment. Then, Calopodius heard Luke take a deep breath.

"Aye, lad. He did. The general will use anyone, if he feels it necessary."

Calopodius nodded. He felt no anger at the thought. He simply wanted it acknowledged.

He reached out his hand and felt the rough wall of the bunker with fingertips grown sensitive with blindness. Texture of soil, which he would never have noticed before, came like a flood of dark light. He wondered, for a moment, how his wife's breasts would feel to him, or her belly, or her thighs. Now.

He didn't imagine he would ever know, and dropped the hand. Calopodius did not expect to survive the war, now that he was blind. Not unless he used the blindness as a reason to return to Constantinople, and spent the rest of his life resting on his laurels.

The thought was unbearable. *I am only eighteen! My life should still be ahead of me!*

That thought brought a final decision. Given that his life was now forfeit, Calopodius intended to give it the full measure while it lasted.

"Menander should be arriving soon, with the supply ships."

"Yes," said Luke.

"When he arrives, I wish to speak with him."

"Yes," said Luke. The "servant" hesitated. Then: "What about?"

Again, Calopodius chuckled harshly. "Another forlorn hope." He began moving slowly through the bunker to the tunnel which led back to his headquarters. "Having lost my eyes on this island, it seems only right I should lose my life on another. Belisarius' island, this time—not the one he left behind to fool the enemy. The *real* island, not the false one."

"There was nothing *false* about this island, young man," growled Luke. "Never say it. Malwa was broken here, as surely as it was on any battlefield of Belisarius. There is the blood of Roman soldiers to prove it—along with your own eyes. Most of all—"

By some means he could not specify, Calopodius understood that Luke was gesturing angrily to the north. "Most of all, by the fact that we kept an entire Malwa army pinned here for two weeks—by your cunning and our sweat and blood—while Belisarius slipped unseen to the north. *Two weeks.* The time he needed to slide a lance into Malwa's unprotected flank—we gave him that time. *We did. You did.*"

He heard Luke's almost shuddering intake of breath. "So never speak of a 'false' island again, boy. Is a shield 'false,' and only a sword 'true'? Stupid. The general did what he needed to do—and so did you. Take pride in it, for there was nothing false in that doing."

Calopodius could not help lowering his head. "No," he whispered.

But was it worth the doing?

"I know I shouldn't have come, General, but—"

Calopodius groped for words to explain. He could not find any. It was impossible to explain to someone else the urgency he felt, since it would only sound . . . suicidal. Which, in truth, it almost was, at least in part.

But . . .

"May—maybe I could help you with supplies or—or something."

"No matter," stated Belisarius firmly, giving Calopodius' shoulder a squeeze. The general's large hand was very powerful. Calopodius was a little surprised by that. His admiration for Belisarius bordered on idolization, but he had never really given any thought to the general's physical characteristics. He had just been dazzled, first, by the man's reputation; then, after finally meeting him in Mesopotamia, by the relaxed humor and confidence with which he ran his staff meetings.

The large hand on his shoulder began gently leading Calopodius off the dock where Menander's ship had tied up.

"I can still count, even if—"

"Forget that," growled Belisarius. "I've got enough clerks." With a chuckle: "The quartermasters don't have that much to count, anyway. We're on very short rations here."

Again, the hand squeezed his shoulder; not with sympathy, this time, so much as assurance. "The truth is, lad, I'm delighted to see you. We're relying on telegraph up here, in this new little fortified half-island we've created, to concentrate our forces quickly enough when the Malwa launch another attack. But the telegraph's a new thing for everyone, and keeping the communications straight and orderly has turned into a mess. My command bunker is full of people shouting at cross-purposes. I need a good officer who can take charge and *organize* the damn thing."

Cheerfully: "That's *you*, lad! Being blind won't be a handicap at all for that work. Probably be a blessing."

Calopodius wasn't certain if the general's cheer was real, or simply assumed for the purpose of improving the morale of a badly maimed subordinate. Even as young as he was, Calopodius knew that the commander he admired was quite capable of being as calculating as he was cordial.

But . . .

Almost despite himself, he began feeling more cheerful.

"Well, there's this much," he said, trying to match the general's enthusiasm. "My tutors thought highly of my grammar and rhetoric, as I believed I mentioned once. If nothing else, I'm sure I can improve the quality of the messages."

The general laughed. The gaiety of the sound cheered up Calopodius even more than the general's earlier words. It was harder to feign laughter than words. Calopodius was not guessing about that. A blind man aged quickly, in some ways, and Calopodius had become an expert on the subject of false laughter, in the weeks since he lost his eyes.

This was real. This was—

Something he could *do.*

A future which had seemed empty began to fill with color again. Only the colors of his own imagination, of course. But Calopodius, remembering discussions on philosophy with learned scholars in far away and long ago Constantinople, wondered if reality was anything *but* images in the mind. If so, perhaps blindness was simply a matter of custom.

"Yes," he said, with reborn confidence. "I can do that."

For the first two days, the command bunker was a madhouse for Calopodius. But by the end of that time, he had managed to bring some semblance of order and procedure to the way in which telegraph messages were received and transmitted. Within a week, he had the system functioning smoothly and efficiently.

The general praised him for his work. So, too, in subtle little ways, did the twelve men under his command. Calopodius found the latter more reassuring than the former. He was still a bit uncertain whether Belisarius' approval was due, at least in part, to the general's obvious feeling of guilt that he was responsible for the young officer's blindness. Whereas the men who worked for him, veterans all, had seen enough mutilation in their lives not to care about yet another cripple. Had the young nobleman not been a blessing to them instead of a curse, they would not have let sympathy stand in the way of criticism. And the general, Calopodius was well aware, kept an ear open to the sentiments of his soldiers.

Throughout that first week, Calopodius paid little attention to the ferocious battle which was raging beyond the heavily timbered and fortified command bunker. He traveled nowhere, beyond the short distance between that bunker and the small one—not much more than a covered hole in the ground—where he and Luke had set up what passed for "living quarters." Even that route was sheltered by soil-covered timber, so the continual sound of cannon fire was muffled.

The only time Calopodius emerged into the open was for the needs of the toilet. As always in a Belisarius camp, the sanitation arrangements were strict and rigorous. The latrines were located some distance from the areas where the troops slept and ate, and no exceptions were made even for the blind and crippled. A man who could not reach the latrines under his own power would either be taken there, or, if too badly injured, would have his bedpan emptied for him.

For the first three days, Luke guided him to the latrines. Thereafter, he could make the journey himself. Slowly, true, but he used the time to ponder and crystallize his new ambition. It was the only time his mind was not preoccupied with the immediate demands of the command bunker.

Being blind, he had come to realize, did not mean the end of life. Although it did transform his dreams of fame and glory into much softer and more muted colors. But finding dreams in the course of dealing with the crude realities of a latrine, he decided, was perhaps appropriate. Life was a crude thing, after all. A project begun in confusion, fumbling with unfamiliar tools, the end never really certain until it came—and then, far more often than not, coming as awkwardly as a blind man attends to his toilet.

Shit is also manure, he came to understand. A man does what he can. If he was blind . . . he was also educated, and rich, and had every other advantage. The rough soldiers who helped him on his way had their own dreams, did they not? And their own glory, come to it. If he could not share in that glory directly, he could save it for the world.

When he explained it to the general—awkwardly, of course, and not at a time of his own choosing—Belisarius gave the project his blessing. That day, Calopodius began his history of the war against the Malwa. The next day, almost as an afterthought, he wrote the first of the *Dispatches to the Army* which would, centuries after his death, make him as famous as Livy or Polybius.

They had approached Elafonisos from the south, because Calopodius had thought Anna might enjoy the sight of the great ridge which overlooked the harbor, with its tower perched atop it like a hawk. And she had seemed to enjoy it well enough, although, as he was coming to recognize, she took most of her pleasure from the sea itself. As did he, for that matter.

She even smiled, once or twice.

The trip across to the island, however, was the high point of the expedition. Their overnight stay in the small tavern in the port had been . . . almost unpleasant. Anna had not objected to the dinginess of the provincial tavern, nor had she complained about the poor fare offered for their evening meal. But she had retreated into an even more distant silence—almost sullen and hostile—as soon as they set foot on land.

That night, as always since the night of their wedding, she performed her duties without resistance. But also with as much energy and enthusiasm as she might have given to reading a particularly dull piece of hagiography. Calopodius found it all quite frustrating, the more so since his wife's naked body was something which aroused him greatly. As he had suspected in the days before the marriage, his wife was quite lovely once she could be seen. And felt.

So he performed his own duty in a perfunctory manner. Afterward, in another time, he might have spent the occasion idly considering the qualities he would look for in a courtesan—now that he had a wife against whose tedium he could measure the problem. But he had already decided to join Belisarius' expedition to the Indus. So, before falling asleep, his thoughts were entirely given over to matters of martial glory. And, of course, the fears and uncertainties which any man his age would feel on the eve of plunging into the maelstrom of war.

The Euphrates

When trouble finally arrived, it was Anna's husband who saved her. The knowledge only increased her fury.

Stupid, really, and some part of her mind understood it perfectly well. But she still couldn't stop hating him.

Stupid. The men on the barge who were clambering eagerly onto the small pier where her own little river craft was tied up were making no attempt to hide their leers. Eight of them there were, their half-clad bodies sweaty from the toil of working their clumsy vessel up the Euphrates.

A little desperately, Anna looked about. She saw nothing beyond the Euphrates itself; reed marshes on the other bank, and a desert on her own. There was not a town or a village in sight. She had stopped at this little pier simply because the two sailors she had hired to carry her down to Charax had insisted they needed to take on fresh water. There was a well here, which was the only reason for the pier's existence. After taking a taste of the muddy water of the Euphrates, Anna couldn't find herself in disagreement.

She wished, now, that she'd insisted on continuing. Not that her insistence would have probably done much good. The sailors had been civil enough, since she employed them at a small town in the headwaters of the Euphrates. But they were obviously not overawed by a nineteen-year-old girl, even if she did come from the famous family of the Melisseni.

She glanced appealingly at the sailors, still working the well. They avoided her gaze, acting as if they hadn't even noticed the men climbing out of the barge. Both sailors were rather elderly, and it was clear enough they had no intention of getting into a fracas with eight rivermen much younger than themselves—all of whom were carrying knives, to boot.

The men from the barge were close to her, and beginning to spread out. One of them was fingering the knife in a scabbard attached to his waist. All of them were smiling in a manner which even a sheltered young noblewoman understood was predatory.

Now in sheer desperation, her eyes moved to the only other men on the pier. Three soldiers, judging from their weapons and gear. They had already been on the pier when Anna's boat drew up, and their presence had almost been enough to cause the sailors to pass by entirely. A rather vicious-looking trio, they were. Two Isaurians and a third one whom Anna thought was probably an Arab. Isaurians were not much better than barbarians; Arabs might or might not be, depending on where they came from. Anna suspected this one was an outright bedouin.

The soldiers were lounging in the shade of a small pavilion they had erected. For a moment, as she had when she first caught sight of them, Anna found herself wondering how they had gotten there in the first place. They had no boat, nor any horses or camels—yet they possessed too much in the way of goods in sacks to have lugged them on their own shoulders. Not through this arid country, with their armor and weapons. She decided they had probably traveled with a caravan, and then parted company for some reason.

But this was no time for idle speculation. The rivermen were very close now. The soldiers returned Anna's beseeching eyes with nothing more than indifference. It was clear enough they had no more intention of intervening than her own sailors.

Still—they *could*, in a way which two elderly sailors couldn't.

Pay them.

Moving as quickly as she could in her elaborate clothing—and cursing herself silently, again, for having been so stupid as to make this insane journey without giving a thought to her apparel—Anna walked over to them. She could only hope they understood Greek. She knew no other language.

"I need help," she hissed.

The soldier in the center of the little group, one of the Isaurians, glanced at the eight rivermen and chuckled.

"I'd say so. You'll be lucky if they don't kill you after they rob and rape you."

His Greek was fluent, if heavily accented. As he proceeded to demonstrate further. "Stupid noblewoman. Brains like a chicken. Are you some kind of idiot, traveling alone down this part of Mesopotamia? The difference between a riverman here and a pirate—" He turned his head and spit casually over the leg of the other Isaurian. His brother, judging from the close resemblance.

"I'll pay you," she said.

The two brothers exchanged glances. The one on the side, who seemed to be the younger one, shrugged. "We can use her boat to take us out of Mesopotamia. Beats walking, and the chance of another caravan . . . But nothing fancy," he muttered. "We're almost home."

His older brother grunted agreement and turned his head to look at the Arab. The Arab's shrug expressed the same tepid enthusiasm. "Nothing fancy," he echoed. "It's too hot."

The Isaurian in the middle lazed to his feet. He wasn't much taller than Anna, but his stocky and muscular build made him seem to loom over her.

"All right. Here's the way it is. You give us half your money and whatever other valuables you've got." He tapped the jeweled necklace around her throat. "The rivermen can take the rest of it. They'll settle for that, just to avoid a brawl."

She almost wailed. Not quite. "I *can't*. I need the money to get to—"

The soldier scowled. "Idiot! We'll keep them from taking your boat, we'll leave you enough—just enough—to get back to your family, and we'll escort you into Anatolia."

He glanced again at the rivermen. They were standing some few yards away, hesitant now. "You've no business here, girl," he growled quietly. "Just be thankful you'll get out of this with your life."

His brother had gotten to his feet also. He snorted sarcastically. "Not to mention keeping your precious hymen intact. That ought to be worth a lot, once you get back to your family."

The fury which had filled Anna for months boiled to the surface. "I don't *have* a hymen," she snarled. "My husband did for that, the bastard, before he went off to war."

Now the Arab was on his feet. Hearing her words, he laughed aloud. "God save us! An abandoned little wife, no less."

The rivermen were beginning to get surly, judging from the scowls which had replaced the previous leers. One of them barked something in a language which Anna didn't recognize. One of the Aramaic dialects, probably. The Isaurian who seemed to be the leader of the three soldiers gave them another glance and an idle little wave of his hand. The gesture more or less indicated: *relax, relax— you'll get a cut.*

That done, his eyes came back to Anna. "Idiot," he repeated. The word was spoken with no heat, just lazy derision. "Think you're the first woman got abandoned by a husband looking to make his fortune in war?"

"He already *has* a fortune," hissed Anna. "He went looking for fame. Found it too, damn him."

The Arab laughed again. "Fame, is it? Maybe in your circles! And what is the name of this paragon of martial virtue? Anthony the Illustrious Courier?"

The other three soldiers shared in the little laugh. For a moment, Anna was distracted by the oddity of such flowery phrases coming out of the mouth of a common soldier. She remembered, vaguely, that her husband had once told her of the poetic prowess of Arabs. But she had paid little attention, at the time, and the memory simply heightened her anger.

"He *is* famous," Anna insisted. A certain innate honesty forced her to add: "At least in Constantinople, after Belisarius' letter was read to the Senate. And his own dispatches."

The name *Belisarius* brought a sudden little stillness to the group of soldiers. The Isaurian leader's eyes narrowed.

"Belisarius? What's the general got to do with your husband?"

"And what's his name?" added the Arab.

Anna tightened her jaws. "Calopodius. Calopodius Saronites."

The stillness turned into frozen rigidity. All three soldiers' eyes were now almost slits.

The Isaurian leader drew a deep breath. "Are you trying to tell us that you are the wife of *Calopodius the Blind*?"

For a moment, a spike of anguish drove through the anger. She didn't really understand where it came from. Calopodius had always seemed blind to her, in his own way. But . . .

Her own deep breath was a shaky thing. "They say he is blind now, yes. Belisarius' letter to the Senate said so. *He* says it himself, in fact, in his letters. I—I guess it's true. I haven't seen him in many months. When he left . . ."

One of the rivermen began to say something, in a surly tone of voice. The gaze which the Isaurian now turned on him was nothing casual. It was a flat, flat gaze. As cold as a snake's and just as deadly. Even a girl as sheltered as Anna had been all her life understood the sheer physical menace in it. The rivermen all seemed to shuffle back a step or two.

He turned his eyes back to Anna. The same cold and flat gleam was in them. "If you are lying . . ."

"Why would I lie?" she demanded angrily. "And how do you expect me to prove it, anyway?"

Belatedly, a thought came to her. "Unless . . ." She glanced at the little sailing craft which had brought her here, still piled high with her belongings. "If you can *read* Greek, I have several of his letters to me."

The Arab sighed softly. "As you say, 'why would you lie?'" His dark eyes examined her face carefully. "God help us. You really don't even understand, do you?"

She shook her head, confused. "Understand what? Do you know him yourself?"

The Isaurian leader's sigh was a more heartfelt thing. "No, lass, we didn't. We were so rich, after Charax, that we left the general's service. We"—he gestured at his brother—"I'm Illus, by the way, and he's Cottomenes—had more than enough to buy us a big farm back home. And Abdul decided to go in with us."

"I'm sick of the desert," muttered the Arab. "Sick of camels, too. Never did like the damn beasts."

The Arab was of the same height as the two Isaurian brothers—about average—but much less stocky in his frame. Still, in his light half-armor and with a spatha scabbarded to his waist, he seemed no less deadly.

"Come to think of it," he added, almost idly, "I'm sick of thieves too."

The violence which erupted shocked Anna more than anything in her life. She collapsed in a squat, gripping her knees with shaking hands, almost moaning with fear.

There had been no sign; nothing, at least, which she had seen. The Isaurian leader simply drew his spatha— so quick, so quick!—took three peculiar little half steps and cleaved the skull of one of the rivermen before the man even had time to do more than widen his eyes. A second or two later, the same spatha tore open another's throat. In the same amount of time, his brother and the Arab gutted two other rivermen.

Then—

She closed her eyes. The four surviving rivermen were desperately trying to reach their barge. From the sounds—

clear enough, even to a young woman who had never seen a man killed before—they weren't going to make it. Not even close. The sounds, wetly horrid, were those of a pack of wolves in a sheep pen.

Some time later, she heard the Isaurian's voice. "Open your eyes, girl. It's over."

She opened her eyes. Catching sight of the pool of blood soaking into the planks of the pier, she averted her gaze. Her eyes fell on the two sailors, cowering behind the well. She almost giggled, the sight was so ridiculous.

The Isaurian must have followed her gaze, because he began chuckling himself. "Silly looking, aren't they? As if they could hide behind that little well."

He raised his voice. "Don't be stupid! If nothing else, we need you to sail the boat. Besides—" He gestured at the barge. "You'll want to loot it, if there's anything in that tub worth looting. We'll burn whatever's left."

He reached down a hand. Anna took it and came shakily to her feet.

Bodies everywhere. She started to close her eyes again.

"Get used to it, girl," the Isaurian said harshly. "You'll see plenty more of that where you're going. Especially if you make it to the island."

Her head felt muzzy. "Island? What island?"

"*The* island, idiot. 'The Iron Triangle,' they call it. Where your husband is, along with the general. Right in the mouth of the Malwa."

"I didn't know it was an island," she said softly. Again, honesty surfaced. "I'm not really even sure where it is, except somewhere in India."

The Arab had come up in time to hear her last words. He was wiping his blade clean with a piece of cloth. "God save us," he half-chuckled. "It's not really an island. Not exactly. But it'll do, seeing as how the general's facing about a hundred thousand Malwa."

He studied her for a moment, while he finished wiping the blood off the sword. Then, sighed again. "Let's hope you learn *something,* by the time we get to Charax. After that, you'll be on your own again. At least—"

He gave the Isaurian an odd little look. The Isaurian shrugged. "We were just telling ourselves yesterday how stupid we'd been, missing out on the loot of Malwa itself. What the hell, we may as well take her the whole way."

His brother was now there. "Hell, yes!" he boomed. He bestowed on Anna a very cheerful grin. "I assume you'll recommend us to the general? Not that we deserted or anything, but I'd *really* prefer a better assignment this time than being on the front lines. A bit dicey, that, when the general's running the show. Not that he isn't the shrewdest bastard in the world, mind you, but he *does* insist on fighting."

The other two soldiers seemed to share in the humor. Anna didn't really understand it, but for the first time since she'd heard the name of Calopodius—spoken by her father, when he announced to her an unwanted and unforeseen marriage—she didn't find it hateful.

Rather the opposite, in fact. She didn't know much about the military—nothing, really—but she suspected . . .

"I imagine my husband needs a bodyguard," she said hesitantly. "A bigger one than whatever he has," she added hastily. "And he's certainly rich enough to pay for it."

"Done," said the Isaurian leader instantly. "Done!"

Not long afterward, as their ship sailed down the river, Anna looked back. The barge was burning fiercely now. By the time the fire burned out, there would be nothing left but a hulk carrying what was left of a not-very-valuable cargo and eight charred skeletons.

The Isaurian leader—Illus—misunderstood her frown. "Don't worry about it, girl. In this part of Mesopotamia, no one will care what happened to the bastards."

She shook her head. "I'm not worrying about *that.* It's just—"

She fell silent. There was no way to explain, and one glance at Illus' face was enough to tell her that he'd never understand.

Calopodius hadn't, after all.

"So why the frown?"

She shrugged. "Never mind. I'm not used to violence, I guess."

That seemed to satisfy him, to Anna's relief. Under the circumstances, she could hardly explain to her rescuers how much she hated her husband. Much less why, since she didn't really understand it that well herself.

Still, she wondered. Something important had happened on that pier, something unforeseen, and she was not too consumed by her own anger not to understand that much. For the first time in her life, a husband had done something other than crush her like an insect.

She studied the surrounding countryside. So bleak and dangerous, compared to the luxurious surroundings in which she had spent her entire life. She found herself wondering what Calopodius had thought when he first saw it. Wondered what he had thought, and felt, the first time he saw blood spreading like a pool. Wondered if he had been terrified, when he first went into a battle.

Wondered what he thought now, and felt, with his face a mangled ruin.

Another odd pang of anguish came to her, then. Calopodius had been a *handsome* boy, even if she had taken no pleasure in the fact.

The Isaurian's voice came again, interrupting her musings. "Weird world, it is. What a woman will go through to find her husband."

She felt another flare of anger. But there was no way to explain; in truth, she could not have found the words herself. So all she said was: "Yes."

The Iron Triangle

The next day, as they sailed back to the mainland, he informed Anna of his decision. And for the first time since he met the girl, she came to life. All distance and ennui vanished, replaced by a cold and spiteful fury which completely astonished him. She did not say much, but what she said was as venomous as a serpent's bite.

Why? he wondered. He would have thought, coming from a family whose fame derived from ancient exploits more than modern wealth, she would have been pleased.

He tried to discover the source of her anger. But after her initial spate of hostile words, Anna fell silent and refused to answer any of his questions. Soon enough, he gave up the attempt. It was not as if, after all, he had ever really expected any intimacy in his marriage. For that, if he survived the war, he would find a courtesan.

As always, the sound of Luke's footsteps awakened him. This time, though, as he emerged from sleep, Calopodius sensed that other men were shuffling their feet in the background.

He was puzzled, a bit. Few visitors came to the bunker where he and Luke had set up their quarters. Calopodius suspected that was because men felt uncomfortable in the presence of a blind man, especially one as young as himself. It was certainly not due to lack of space. The general had provided him with a very roomy bunker, connected by a short tunnel to the great command bunker buried beneath the small city which had emerged over the past months toward the southern tip of the Iron Triangle. The Roman army called that city "the Anvil," taking the name from the Punjabi civilians who made up most of its inhabitants.

"Who's there, Luke?" he asked.

His aide-de-camp barked a laugh. "A bunch of boys seeking fame and glory, lad. The general sent them."

The shuffling feet came nearer. "Begging your pardon,

sir, but we were wondering—as he says, the general sent us to talk to you—" The man, whoever he was, lapsed into an awkward silence.

Calopodius sat up on his pallet. "Speak up, then. And who are you?"

The man cleared his throat. "Name's Abelard, sir. Abelard of Antioch. I'm the hecatontarch in charge of the westernmost bastion at the fortress of—"

"You had hot fighting yesterday," interrupted Calopodius. "I heard about it. The general told me the Malwa probe was much fiercer than usual."

"Came at us like demons, sir," said another voice. Proudly: "But we bloodied 'em good."

Calopodius understood at once. The hecatontarch cleared his throat, but Calopodius spoke before the man was forced into embarrassment.

"I'll want to hear all the details!" he exclaimed forcefully. "Just give me a moment to get dressed and summon my scribe. We can do it all right here, at the table there. I'll make sure it goes into the next dispatch."

"Thank you, sir," said Abelard. His voice took on a slightly aggrieved tone. "T'isn't true, what Luke says. It's neither the fame nor the glory of it. It's just . . . your *Dispatches* get read to the Senate, sir. Each and every one, by the Emperor himself. And then the Emperor—by express command—has them printed and posted all over the Empire."

Calopodius was moving around, feeling for his clothing. "True enough," he said cheerfully. "Ever since the old Emperor set up the new printing press in the Great Palace, everybody—every village, anyway—can get a copy of something."

"It's our families, sir," said the other voice. "They'll see our names and know we're all right. Except for those who died in the fighting. But at least . . ."

Calopodius understood. Perfectly. "Their names will exist somewhere, on something other than a tombstone."

Charax

"I *can't*," said Dryopus firmly. Anna glared at him, but the Roman official in charge of the great port city of Charax was quite impervious to her anger. His next words were spoken in the patient tone of one addressing an unruly child.

"Lady Saronites, if I allowed you to continue on this—" he paused, obviously groping for a term less impolite than *insane* "—headstrong project of yours, it'd be worth my career." He picked up a letter lying on the great desk in his headquarters. "This is from your father, demanding that you be returned to Constantinople under guard."

"My father has no authority over me!"

"No, he doesn't." Dryopus shook his head. "But your husband *does*. Without his authorization, I simply can't allow you to continue. I certainly can't detail a ship to take you to Barbaricum."

Anna clenched her jaws. Her eyes went to the nearby window. She couldn't see the harbor from here, but she could visualize it easily enough. The Roman soldiers who had all-but-formally arrested her when she and her small party arrived in the great port city of Charax on the Persian Gulf had marched her past it on their way to Dryopus' palace.

For a moment, wildly, she thought of appealing to the Persians who were now in official control of Charax. But the notion died as soon as it came. The Aryans were even more strict than Romans when it came to the independence of women. Besides—

Dryopus seemed to read her thoughts. "I should note that *all* shipping in Charax is under Roman military law. So there's no point in your trying to go around me. No ship captain will take your money, anyway. Not without a permit issued by my office."

He dropped her father's letter back onto the desk. "I'm sorry, but there's nothing else for it. If you wish to continue, you will have to get your husband's permission."

"He's all the way up the Indus," she snapped angrily. "And there's no telegraph communication between here and there."

Dryopus shrugged. "There is between Barbaricum and the Iron Triangle. And by now the new line connecting Barbaricum and the harbor at Chabahari may be completed. But you'll still have to wait until I can get a ship there— and another to bring back the answer."

Anna's mind raced through the problem. On their way down the Euphrates, Illus had explained to her the logic of travel between Mesopotamia and India. During the winter monsoon season, it was impossible for sailing craft to make it to Barbaricum. Taking advantage of the relatively sheltered waters of the Gulf, on the other hand, they could make it as far as Chabahari—which was the reason the Roman forces in India had been working so hard to get a telegraph line connecting Chabahari and the Indus.

So if *she* could get as far as Chabahari . . . She'd still have to wait, but if Calopodius' permission came she wouldn't be wasting weeks here in Mesopotamia.

"Allow me to go as far as Chabahari then," she insisted.

Dryopus started to frown. Anna had to fight to keep from screaming in frustration.

"Put me under guard, if you will!"

Dryopus sighed, lowered his head, and ran his fingers through thinning hair. "He's not likely to agree, you know," he said softly.

"He's my husband, not yours," pointed out Anna. "You don't know how he thinks." She didn't see any reason to add: *no more than I do.*

His head still lowered, Dryopus chuckled. "True enough. With that young man, it's always hard to tell."

He raised his head and studied her carefully. "Are you *that* besotted with him? That you insist on going into the jaws of the greatest war in history?"

"He's my *husband,*" she replied, not knowing what else to say.

Again, he chuckled. "You remind me of Antonina, a bit. Or Irene."

Anna was confused for a moment, until she realized he was referring to Belisarius' wife and the Roman Empire's former head of espionage, Irene Macrembolitissa. Famous women, now, the both of them. One of them had even become a queen herself.

"I don't know either one," she said quietly. Which was true enough, even though she'd read everything ever written by Macrembolitissa. "So I couldn't say."

Dryopus studied her a bit longer. Then his eyes moved to her bodyguards, who had been standing as far back in a corner as possible.

"You heard?"

Illus nodded.

"Can I trust you?" he asked.

Illus' shoulders heaved a bit, as if he were suppressing a laugh. "No offense, sir—but if it's worth *your* career, just imagine the price *we'd* pay." His tone grew serious: "We'll see to it that she doesn't, ah, escape on her own."

Dryopus nodded and looked back at Anna. "All right, then. As far as Chabahari."

On their way to the inn where Anna had secured lodgings, Illus shook his head. "If Calopodius says 'no,' you realize you'll have wasted a lot of time and money."

"He's my *husband*," replied Anna firmly. Not knowing what else to say.

The Iron Triangle

After the general finished reading Anna's message, and the accompanying one from Dryopus, he invited Calopodius to sit down at the table in the command bunker.

"I knew you were married," said Belisarius, "but I know none of the details. So tell me."

Calopodius hesitated. He was deeply reluctant to involve the general in the petty minutia of his own life. In the little silence that fell over them, within the bunker, Calopodius could hear the artillery barrages. As was true day and night, and had been for many weeks, the Malwa besiegers of the Iron Triangle were shelling the Roman fortifications—and the Roman gunners were responding with counter-battery fire. The fate of the world would be decided here in the Punjab, some time over the next few months. That, and the whole future of the human race. It seemed absurd—grotesque, even—to waste the Roman commander's time . . .

"Tell me," commanded Belisarius. For all their softness, Calopodius could easily detect the tone of command in the words.

Still, he hesitated.

Belisarius chuckled. "Be at ease, young man. I can spare the time for this. In truth—" Calopodius could sense, if not see, the little gesture by which the general expressed a certain ironic weariness. "I would enjoy it, Calopodius. War is a means, not an end. It would do my soul good to talk about ends, for a change."

That was enough to break Calopodius' resistance.

"I really don't know her very well, sir. We'd only been married for a short time before I left to join your army. It was—"

He fumbled for the words. Belisarius provided them.

"A marriage of convenience. Your wife's from the Melisseni family."

Calopodius nodded. With his acute hearing, he could detect the slight sound of the general scratching his chin, as he was prone to do when thinking.

"An illustrious family," stated Belisarius. "One of the handful of senatorial families which can actually claim an ancient pedigree without paying scribes to fiddle with the historical records. But a family which has fallen on hard times financially."

"My father said they wouldn't even have a pot to piss in if their creditors ever really descended on them." Calopodius sighed. "Yes, General. An illustrious family, but now short of means. Whereas my family, as you know . . ."

"The Saronites. Immensely wealthy, but with a pedigree that needs a *lot* of fiddling."

Calopodius grinned. "Go back not more than three generations, and you're looking at nothing but commoners. Not in the official records, of course. My father can afford a *lot* of scribes."

"That explains your incredible education," mused Belisarius. "I had wondered, a bit. Not many young noblemen have your command of language and the arts." Calopodius heard the scrape of a chair as the general stood up. Then, heard him begin to pace about. That was another of Belisarius' habits when he was deep in thought. Calopodius had heard him do it many times, over the past weeks. But he was a bit astonished that the general was giving the same attention to this problem as he would to a matter of strategy or tactics.

"Makes sense, though," continued Belisarius. "For all the surface glitter—and don't think the Persians don't make plenty of sarcastic remarks about it—the Roman aristocracy will overlook a low pedigree as long as the 'nobleman' is wealthy *and* well educated. Especially—as you are—in grammar and rhetoric."

"I can drop three Homeric and biblical allusions into any sentence," chuckled Calopodius.

"I've noticed!" laughed the general. "That official history you're writing of my campaigns would serve as a Homeric and biblical commentary as well." He paused a moment. "Yet I notice that you don't do it in your *Dispatches to the Army.*"

"It'd be a waste," said Calopodius, shrugging. "Worse than that, really. I write those for the morale of the soldiers, most of whom would just find the allusions confusing. Besides, those are really *your* dispatches, not mine. And you don't talk that way, certainly not to your soldiers."

"They're *not* my dispatches, young man. They're yours. I approve them, true, but you write them. And when they're read aloud by my son to the Senate, Photius presents them as *Calopodius'* dispatches, not mine."

Calopodius was startled into silence.

"You didn't know? My son is almost eleven years old, and quite literate. And since he *is* the Emperor of Rome, even if Theodora still wields the actual power, he insists on reading them to the Senate. He's very fond of your dispatches. Told me in his most recent letter that they're the only things he reads which don't bore him to tears. His tutors, of course, don't approve."

Calopodius was still speechless. Again, Belisarius laughed. "You're quite famous, lad." Then, more softly; almost sadly: "I can't give you back your eyes, Calopodius. But I *can* give you the fame you wanted when you came to me. I promised you I would."

The sound of his pacing resumed. "In fact, unless I miss my guess, those *Dispatches* of yours will someday—centuries from now—be more highly regarded than your official history of the war." Calopodius heard a very faint noise, and guessed the general was stroking his chest, where the jewel from the future named Aide lay nestled in his pouch. "I have it on good authority," chuckled Belisarius, "that historians of the future will prefer straight narrative to flowery rhetoric. And—in my opinion, at least—you write straightforward narrative even better than you toss off classical allusions."

The chair scraped as the general resumed his seat. "But let's get back to the problem at hand. In essence, your marriage was arranged to lever your family into greater respectability, and to provide the Melisseni—discreetly, of course—a financial rescue. How did you handle the dowry, by the way?"

Calopodius shrugged. "I'm not certain. My family's so wealthy that a dowry's not important. For the sake of appearances, the Melisseni provided a large one. But I suspect my father *loaned* them the dowry—and then made arrangements to improve the Melisseni's economic situation by linking their own fortunes to those of our family." He cleared his throat. "All very discreetly, of course."

Belisarius chuckled drily. "Very discreetly. And how did the Melisseni react to it all?"

Calopodius shifted uncomfortably in his chair. "Not well, as you'd expect. I met Anna for the first time three days after my father informed me of the prospective marriage. It was one of those carefully rehearsed 'casual visits.' She and her mother arrived at my family's villa near Nicodemia."

"Accompanied by a small army of servants and retainers, I've no doubt."

Calopodius smiled. "Not such a small army. A veritable host, it was." He cleared his throat. "They stayed for three days, that first time. It was very awkward for me. Anna's mother—her name's Athenais—barely even tried to disguise her contempt for me and my family. I think she was deeply bitter that their economic misfortunes were forcing them to seek a husband for their oldest daughter among less illustrious but much wealthier layers of the nobility."

"And Anna herself?"

"Who knows? During those three days, Anna said little. In the course of the various promenades which we took through the grounds of the Saronites estate—God, talk about chaperones!—she seemed distracted to the point of being almost rude. I couldn't really get much of a sense of her, General. She seemed distressed by something. Whether that was her pending marriage to me, or something else, I couldn't say."

"And you didn't much care. Be honest."

"True. I'd known for years that any marriage I entered would be purely one of convenience." He shrugged. "At least my bride-to-be was neither unmannerly not uncomely. In fact, from what I could determine at the time—which wasn't much, given the heavy scaramangium and headdress and the elaborate cosmetics under which Anna labored—she seemed quite attractive."

He shrugged again. "So be it. I was seventeen, General." For a moment, he hesitated, realizing how silly that sounded. He was only a year older than that now, after all, even if . . .

"You were a boy then; a man, now," filled in Belisarius. "The world looks very different after a year spent in the carnage. I know. But then—"

Calopodius heard the general's soft sigh. "Seventeen years old. With the war against Malwa looming ever larger in the life of the Roman Empire, the thoughts of a vigorous boy like yourself were fixed on feats of martial prowess, not domestic bliss."

"Yes. I'd already made up my mind. As soon as the wedding was done—well, and the marriage consummated— I'd be joining your army. I didn't even see any reason to wait to make sure that I'd provided an heir. I've got three younger brothers, after all, every one of them in good health."

Again, silence filled the bunker and Calopodius could hear the muffled sounds of the artillery exchange. "Do you think that's why she was so angry at me when I told her I was leaving? I didn't really think she'd care."

"Actually, no. I think . . ." Calopodius heard another faint noise, as if the general were picking up the letters lying on the table. "There's this to consider. A wife outraged by abandonment—or glad to see an unwanted husband's back—would hardly be taking these risks to find him again."

"Then why is she doing it?"

"I doubt if she knows. Which is really what this is all about, I suspect." He paused; then: "She's only a year older than you, I believe."

Calopodius nodded. The general continued. "Did you ever wonder what an eighteen-year-old girl wants from life? Assuming she's high-spirited, of course—but judging from the evidence, your Anna is certainly that. Timid girls, after all, don't race off on their own to find a husband in the middle of a war zone."

Calopodius said nothing. After a moment, Belisarius chuckled. "Never gave it a moment's thought, did you? Well, young man, I suggest the time has come to do so. And not just for your own sake."

The chair scraped again as the general rose. "When I said I knew nothing about the details of your marriage, I was fudging a bit. I *didn't* know anything about what you might call the 'inside' of the thing. But I knew quite a bit about the 'outside' of it. This marriage is important to the Empire, Calopodius."

"Why?"

The general clucked his tongue reprovingly. "There's more to winning a war than tactics on the battlefield, lad. You've also got to keep an eye—always—on what a future day will call the 'home front.'" Calopodius heard him resume his pacing. "You can't be *that* naïve. You must know that the Roman aristocracy is not very fond of the dynasty."

"*My* family is," protested Calopodius.

"Yes. Yours—and most of the newer rich families. That's because their wealth comes mainly from trade and commerce. The war—all the new technology Aide's given us—has been a blessing to you. But it looks very different from the standpoint of the old landed families. You know as well as I do—you *must* know—that it was those families which supported the Nika insurrection a few years ago. Fortunately, most of them had enough sense to do it at a distance."

Calopodius couldn't help wincing. And what he wasn't willing to say, the general was. Chuckling, oddly enough.

"The Melisseni came *that* close to being arrested, Calopodius. Arrested—the whole family—and all their property seized. If Anna's father Nicephorus had been even slightly less discreet . . . the truth? His head would have been on a spike on the wall of the Hippodrome, right next to that of John of Cappadocia's. The only thing that saved him was that he *was* discreet enough—barely—and the Melisseni are one of the half-dozen most illustrious families of the Empire."

"I didn't know they were that closely tied . . ."

Calopodius sensed Belisarius' shrug. "We were able to keep it quiet. And since then, the Melisseni seem to have retreated from any open opposition. But we were delighted—

I'm speaking of Theodora and Justinian and myself, and Antonina for that matter—when we heard about your marriage. Being tied closely to the Saronites will inevitably pull the Melisseni into the orbit of the dynasty. Especially since—as canny as your father is—they'll start getting rich themselves from the new trade and manufacture."

"Don't tell them that!" barked Calopodius. "Such work is for plebeians."

"They'll change their tune, soon enough. And the Melisseni are very influential among the older layers of the aristocracy."

"I understand your point, General." Calopodius gestured toward the unseen table, and the letters atop it. "So what do you want me to do? Tell Anna to come to the Iron Triangle?"

Calopodius was startled by the sound of Belisarius' hand slapping the table. "Damn fool! It's time you put that splendid mind of yours to work on *this*, Calopodius. A marriage—if it's to work—needs grammar and rhetoric also."

"I don't understand," said Calopodius timidly.

"I know you don't. So will you follow my advice?"

"Always, General."

Belisarius chuckled. "You're more confident than I am! But . . ." After a moment's pause: "Don't *tell* her to do anything, Calopodius. Send Dryopus a letter explaining that your wife has your permission to make her own decision. And send Anna a letter saying the same thing. I'd suggest . . ."

Another pause. Then: "Never mind. That's for you to decide."

In the silence that followed, the sound of artillery came to fill the bunker again. It seemed louder, perhaps. "And that's enough for the moment, young man. I'd better get in touch with Maurice. From the sound of things, I'd say the Malwa are getting ready for another probe."

Calopodius wrote the letters immediately thereafter. The letter to Dryopus took no time at all. Neither did the one to Anna, at first. But Calopodius, for reasons he could not determine, found it difficult to find the right words to conclude. Grammar and rhetoric seemed of no use at all.

In the end, moved by an impulse which confused him, he simply wrote:

Do as you will, Anna. For myself, I would like to see you again.

Chabahari

Chabahari seemed like a nightmare to Anna. When she first arrived in the town—city, now—she was mainly struck by the chaos in the place. Not so long ago, Chabahari had been a sleepy fishing village. Since the great Roman-Persian expedition led by Belisarius to invade the Malwa homeland through the Indus valley had begun, Chabahari had been transformed almost overnight into a great military staging depot. The original fishing village was now buried somewhere within a sprawling and disorganized mass of tents, pavilions, jury-rigged shacks—and, of course, the beginnings of the inevitable grandiose palaces which Persians insisted on putting anywhere that their grandees resided.

Her first day was spent entirely in a search for the authorities in charge of the town. She had promised Dryopus she would report to those authorities as soon as she arrived.

But the search was futile. She found the official headquarters easily enough—one of the half-built palaces being erected by the Persians. But the interior of the edifice was nothing but confusion, a mass of workmen swarming all over, being overseen by a handful of harassed-looking supervisors. Not an official was to be found anywhere, neither Persian nor Roman.

"Try the docks," suggested the one foreman who spoke Greek and was prepared to give her a few minutes of his time. "The noble sirs complain about the noise here, and the smell everywhere else."

The smell *was* atrocious. Except in the immediate vicinity of the docks—which had their own none-too-savory aroma—the entire city seemed to be immersed in a miasma made up of the combined stench of excrement, urine, sweat, food—half of it seemingly rotten—and, perhaps most of all, blood and corrupting flesh. In addition to being a staging area for the invasion, Chabahari was also a depot where badly injured soldiers were being evacuated back to their homelands.

Those of them who survive this horrid place, Anna thought angrily, as she stalked out of the "headquarters." Illus and Cottomenes trailed behind her. Once she passed through the aivan onto the street beyond—insofar as the term "street" could be used at all for a simple space between buildings and shacks, teeming with people—she spent a moment or so looking south toward the docks.

"What's the point?" asked Illus, echoing her thoughts. "We didn't find anyone there when we disembarked." He cast a glance at the small mound of Anna's luggage piled up next to the building. The wharf boys whom Anna had hired to carry her belongings were lounging nearby, under Abdul's watchful eye.

"Besides," Illus continued, "it'll be almost impossible to keep your stuff from being stolen, in that madhouse down there."

Anna sighed. She looked down at her long dress, grimacing ruefully. The lowest few inches of the once-fine fabric, already ill-used by her journey from Constantinople, was now completely ruined. And the rest of it was well on its way—as much from her own sweat as anything else. The elaborate garments of a Greek noblewoman, designed for salons in the Roman Empire's capital, were torture in this climate.

A glimpse of passing color caught her eye. For a moment, she studied the figure of a young woman moving down the street. Some sort of Indian girl, apparently. Since the war had erupted into the Indian subcontinent, the inevitable human turbulence had thrown people of different lands into the new cauldrons of such cities as Chabahari. Mixing them up like grain caught in a thresher. Anna had noticed several Indians even in Charax.

Mainly, she just envied the woman's clothing, which was infinitely better suited for the climate than her own. By her senatorial family standards, of course, it was shockingly immodest. But she spent a few seconds just *imagining* what her bare midriff would feel like, if it didn't feel like a mass of spongy, sweaty flesh.

Illus chuckled. "You'd peel like a grape, girl. With your fair skin?"

Anna had long since stopped taking offense at her "servant's" familiarity with her. That, too, would have outraged her family. But Anna herself took an odd little comfort in it. Much to her surprise, she had discovered over the weeks of travel that she was at ease in the company of Illus and his companions.

"Damn you, too," she muttered, not without some humor of her own. "I'd toughen up soon enough. And I wouldn't mind shedding some skin, anyway. What I've got right now feels like it's gangrenous."

It was Illus' turn to grimace. "Don't even think it, girl. Until you've seen real gangrene . . ."

A stray waft of breeze from the northwest illustrated his point. That was the direction of the great military "hospital" which the Roman army had set up on the outskirts of the city. The smell almost made Anna gag.

The gag brought up a reflex of anger, and, with it, a sudden decision.

"Let's go there," she said.

"*Why?*" demanded Illus.

Anna shrugged. "Maybe there'll be an official there. If nothing else, I need to find where the telegraph office is located."

Illus' face made his disagreement clear enough. Still— for all that she allowed familiarity, Anna had also established over the past weeks that she *was* his master.

"Let's go," she repeated firmly. "If nothing else, that's

probably the only part of this city where we'd find some empty lodgings."

"True enough," said Illus, sighing. "They'll be dying like flies, over there." He hesitated, then began to speak. But Anna cut him off before he got out more than three words.

"I'm not insane, damn you. If there's an epidemic, we'll leave. But I doubt it. Not in this climate, this time of year. At least . . . not if they've been following the sanitary regulations."

Illus' face creased in a puzzled frown. "What's that got to do with anything? What regulations?"

Anna snorted and began to stalk off to the northwest. "Don't you read *anything* besides those damned *Dispatches*?"

Cottomenes spoke up. "No one does," he said. Cheerfully, as usual. "No soldier, anyway. Your husband's got a way with words, he does. Have you ever tried to *read* official regulations?"

Those words, too, brought a reflex of anger. But, as she forced her way through the mob toward the military hospital, Anna found herself thinking about them. And eventually came to realize two things.

One. Although she was a voracious reader, she *hadn't* ever read any official regulations. Not those of the army, at any rate. But she suspected they were every bit as turgid as the regulations which officials in Constantinople spun out like spiders spinning webs.

Two. Calopodius *did* have a way with words. On their way down the Euphrates—and then again, as they sailed from Charax to Chabahari—the latest *Dispatches* and the newest chapters from his *History of Belisarius and the War* had been available constantly. Belisarius, Anna had noted, seemed to be as adamant about strewing printing presses behind his army's passage as he was about arms depots.

The chapters of the *History* had been merely perused on occasion by her soldier companions. Anna could appreciate the literary skill involved, but the constant allusions in those pages were meaningless to Illus and his brother, much less the illiterate Abdul. Yet they pored over each and every *Dispatch*, often enough in the company of a dozen other soldiers. One of them reading it aloud, while the others listened with rapt attention.

As always, her husband's fame caused some part of Anna to seethe with fury. But, this time, she also *thought* about it. And if, at the end, her thoughts caused her anger to swell, it was a much cleaner kind of anger. One which did not coil in her stomach like a worm, but simply filled her with determination.

The hospital was even worse than she'd imagined. But she did, not surprisingly, find an unused tent in which she and her companions could make their quarters. And she did discover the location of the telegraph office—which, as it happened, was situated right next to the sprawling grounds of the "hospital."

The second discovery, however, did her little good. The official in charge, once she awakened him from his afternoon nap, yawned and explained that the telegraph line from Barbaricum to Chabahari was still at least a month away from completion.

"That'll mean a few weeks here," muttered Illus. "It'll take at least that long for couriers to bring your husband's reply."

Instead of the pure rage those words would have brought to her once, the Isaurian's sour remark simply caused Anna's angry determination to harden into something like iron.

"Good," she pronounced. "We'll put the time to good use."

"How?" he demanded.

"Give me tonight to figure it out."

It didn't take her all night. Just four hours. The first hour she spent sitting in her screened-off portion of the tent, with her knees hugged closely to her chest, listening to the moans and shrieks of the maimed and dying soldiers who surrounded it. The remaining three, studying the books she had brought with her—especially her favorite, Irene Macrembolitissa's *Commentaries on the Talisman of God*, which had been published just a few months before Anna's precipitous decision to leave Constantinople in search of her husband.

Irene Macrembolitissa was Anna's private idol. Not that the sheltered daughter of the Melisseni had ever thought to emulate the woman's adventurous life, except intellectually. The admiration had simply been an emotional thing, the heroine-worship of a frustrated girl for a woman who had done so many things she could only dream about. But now, carefully studying those pages in which Macrembolitissa explained certain features of natural philosophy as given to mankind through Belisarius by the Talisman of God, she came to understand the hard practical core which lay beneath the great woman's flowery prose and ease with classical and biblical allusions. And, with that understanding, came a hardening of her own soul.

Fate, against her will and her wishes, had condemned her to be a wife. So be it. She would begin with that practical core; with concrete truth, not abstraction. She would steel the bitterness of *a* wife into the driving will of *the* wife. The wife of Calopodius the Blind, Calopodius of the Saronites.

The next morning, very early, she presented her proposition.

"Do any of you have a problem with working in trade?"

The three soldiers stared at her, stared at each other, broke into soft laughter.

"We're not senators, girl," chuckled Illus.

Anna nodded. "Fine. You'll have to work on speculation, though. I'll need the money I have left to pay the others."

"What 'others'?"

Anna smiled grimly. "I think you call it 'the muscle.' "

Cottomenes frowned. "I thought *we* were 'the muscle.' "

"Not any more," said Anna, shaking her head firmly.

"You're promoted. All three of you are now officers in the hospital service."

"*What* 'hospital service'?"

Anna realized she hadn't considered the name of the thing. For a moment, the old anger flared. But she suppressed it easily enough. This was no time for pettiness, after all, and besides—it was now a *clean* sort of anger.

"We'll call it Calopodius' Wife's Service. How's that?"

The three soldiers shook their heads. Clearly enough, they had no understanding of what she was talking about.

"You'll see," she predicted.

It didn't take them long. Illus' glare was enough to cow the official "commander" of the hospital—who was as sorry-looking a specimen of "officer" as Anna could imagine. And if the man might have wondered at the oddness of such glorious ranks being borne by such as Illus and his two companions—Abdul looked as far removed from a *tribune* as could be imagined—he was wise enough to keep his doubts to himself.

The dozen or so soldiers whom Anna recruited into the Service in the next hour—"the muscle"—had no trouble at all believing that Illus and Cottomenes and Abdul were, respectively, the *chiliarch* and two *tribunes* of a new army "service" they'd never heard of. First, because they were all veterans of the war and could recognize others—and knew, as well, that Belisarius promoted with no regard for personal origin. Second—more importantly—because they were wounded soldiers cast adrift in a chaotic "military hospital" in the middle of nowhere. Anna—Illus, actually, following her directions—selected only those soldiers whose wounds were healing well. Men who could move around and exert themselves. Still, even for such men, the prospect of regular pay meant a much increased chance at survival.

Anna wondered, a bit, whether walking-wounded "muscle" would serve the purpose. But her reservations were settled within the next hour, after four of the new "muscle"—at Illus' command—beat the first surgeon into a bloody pulp when the man responded to Anna's command to start boiling his instruments with a sneer and a derogatory remark about meddling women.

By the end of the first day, eight other surgeons were sporting cuts and bruises. But, at least when it came to the medical staff, there were no longer any doubts—none at all, in point of fact—as to whether this bizarre new "Calopodius' Wife's Service" had any actual authority.

Two of the surgeons complained to the hospital's commandant, but that worthy chose to remain inside his headquarters' tent. That night, Illus and three of his new "muscle" beat the two complaining surgeons into a still bloodier pulp, and all complaints to the commandant ceased thereafter.

Complaints from the medical staff, at least. A body of perhaps twenty soldiers complained to the hospital commandant the next day, hobbling to the HQ as best they could. But, again, the commandant chose to remain inside; and, again, Illus—this time using his entire corps of "muscle," which had now swollen to thirty men—thrashed the complainers senseless afterward.

Thereafter, whatever they might have muttered under their breath, none of the soldiers in the hospital protested openly when they were instructed to dig real latrines, *away* from the tents—and use them. Nor did they complain when they were ordered to help completely immobilized soldiers use them as well.

By the end of the fifth day, Anna was confident that her authority in the hospital was well enough established. She spent a goodly portion of those days daydreaming about the pleasures of wearing more suitable apparel, as she made her slow way through the ranks of wounded men in the swarm of tents. But she knew full well that the sweat which seemed to saturate her was one of the prices she would have to pay. Lady Saronites, wife of Calopodius the Blind, daughter of the illustrious family of the Melisseni, was a figure of power and majesty and authority—and had the noble gowns to prove it, even if they were soiled and frayed. Young Anna, all of nineteen years old, wearing a sari, would have had none at all.

By the sixth day, as she had feared, what was left of the money she had brought with her from Constantinople was almost gone. So, gathering her now-filthy robes in two small but determined hands, she marched her way back into the city of Chabahari. By now, at least, she had learned the name of the city's commander.

It took her half the day to find the man, in the *taberna* where he was reputed to spend most of his time. By the time she did, as she had been told, he was already half-drunk.

"Garrison troops," muttered Illus as they entered the tent which served the city's officers for their entertainment. The tent was filthy, as well as crowded with officers and their whores.

Anna found the commandant of the garrison in a corner, with a young half-naked girl perched on his lap. After taking half the day to find the man, it only took her a few minutes to reason with him and obtain the money she needed to keep the Service in operation.

Most of those few minutes were spent explaining, in considerable detail, exactly what she needed. Most of that, in specifying tools and artifacts—*more shovels to dig more latrines; pots for boiling water; more fabric for making more tents, because the ones they had were too crowded.* And so forth.

She spent a bit of time, at the end, specifying the sums of money she would need.

"Twenty solidi—a day." She nodded at an elderly wounded soldier whom she had brought with her along with Illus. "That's Zeno. He's literate. He's the Service's accountant in Chabahari. You can make all the arrangements through him."

The garrison's commandant then spent a minute explaining

to Anna, also in considerable detail—mostly anatomical—what she could do with the tools, artifacts and money she needed.

Illus' face was very strained, by the end. Half with fury, half with apprehension—this man was no petty officer to be pounded with fists. But Anna herself sat through the garrison commander's tirade quite calmly. When he was done, she did not need more than a few seconds to reason with him further and bring him to see the error of his position.

"My husband is Calopodius the Blind. I will tell him what you have said to me, and he will place the words in his next *Dispatch*. You will be a lucky man if all that happens to you is that General Belisarius has you executed."

She left the tent without waiting to hear his response. By the time she reached the tent's entrance, the garrison commander's face was much whiter than the tent fabric and he was gasping for breath.

The next morning, a chest containing 100 solidi was brought to the hospital and placed in Zeno's care. The day after that, the first of the tools and artifacts began arriving.

Four weeks later, when Calopodius' note finally arrived, the mortality rate in the hospital was less than half what it had been when Anna arrived. She was almost sorry to leave.

In truth, she might not have left at all, except by then she was confident that Zeno was quite capable of managing the entire service as well as its finances.

"Don't steal anything," she warned him as she prepared to leave.

Zeno's face quirked with a rueful smile. "I wouldn't dare risk the Wife's anger."

She laughed, then; and found herself wondering through all the days of their slow oar-driven travel to Barbaricum why those words had brought her no anger at all.

And, each night, she took out Calopodius' letter and

wondered at it also. Anna had lived with anger and bitterness for so long—"so long," at least, to a nineteen-year-
old girl—that she was confused by its absence. She was
even more confused by the little glow of warmth which
the last words in the letter gave her, each time she read
them.

"You're a strange woman," Illus told her, as the great
battlements and cannons of Barbaricum loomed on the
horizon.

There was no way to explain. "Yes," was all she said.

The first thing she did upon arriving at Barbaricum was
march into the telegraph office. If the officers in command
thought there was anything peculiar about a young Greek
noblewoman dressed in the finest and filthiest garments
they had ever seen, they kept it to themselves. Perhaps
rumors of "the Wife" had preceded her.

"Send a telegram immediately," she commanded. "To my
husband, Calopodius the Blind."

They hastened to comply. The message was brief:

IDIOT. ADDRESS MEDICAL CARE AND SANITATION IN
NEXT DISPATCH. FIRMLY.

The Iron Triangle

When Calopodius received the telegram—and he received
it immediately, because his post was in the Iron Triangle's
command and communication center—the first words he
said as soon as the telegraph operator finished reading it
to him were:

"God, I'm an idiot!"

Belisarius had heard the telegram also. In fact, all the
officers in the command center had heard, because they
had been waiting with an ear cocked. By now, the peculiar journey of Calopodius' wife was a source of feverish
gossip in the ranks of the entire army fighting off the Malwa

siege in the Punjab. *What the hell is that girl doing, anyway?* being only the most polite of the speculations.

The general sighed and rolled his eyes. Then, closed them. It was obvious to everyone that he was reviewing all of Calopodius' now-famous *Dispatches* in his mind.

"We're both idiots," he muttered. "We've maintained proper medical and sanitation procedures *here,* sure enough. But . . ."

His words trailed off. His second-in-command, Maurice, filled in the rest.

"She must have passed through half the invasion staging posts along the way. Garrison troops, garrison officers— with the local butchers as the so-called 'surgeons.' God help us, I don't even want to think . . ."

"I'll write it immediately," said Calopodius.

Belisarius nodded. "Do so. And I'll give you some choice words to include." He cocked his head at Maurice, smiling crookedly. "What do you think? Should we resurrect crucifixion as a punishment?"

Maurice shook his head, scowling. "Don't be so damned flamboyant. Make the punishment fit the crime. Surgeons who do not boil their instruments will be boiled alive. Officers who do not see to it that proper latrines are maintained will be buried alive in them. That sort of thing."

Calopodius was already seated at the desk where he dictated his *Dispatches* and the chapters of the *History.* So was his scribe, pen in hand.

"I'll add a few nice little flourishes," his young voice said confidently. "This strikes me as a good place for grammar and rhetoric."

Barbaricum

Anna and her companions spent their first night in India crowded into the corner of a tavern packed full with Roman soldiers and all the other typical denizens of a great port city—longshoremen, sailors, petty merchants and their womenfolk, pimps and prostitutes, gamblers, and the usual sprinkling of thieves and other criminals.

Like almost all the buildings in Barbaricum, the tavern was a mudbrick edifice which had been badly burned in the great fires which swept the city during the Roman conquest. The arson had not been committed by Belisarius' men, but by the fanatic Mahaveda priests who led the Malwa defenders. Despite the still-obvious reminders of that destruction, the tavern was in use for the simple reason that, unlike so many buildings in the city, the walls were still standing and there was even a functional roof.

When they first entered, Anna and her party had been assessed by the mob of people packed in the tavern. The assessment had not been as quick as the one which that experienced crowd would have normally made. Anna and her party were . . . odd.

The hesitation worked entirely to her advantage, however. The tough-looking Isaurian brothers and Abdul were enough to give would-be cutpurses pause, and in the little space and time cleared for them, the magical rumor had time to begin and spread throughout the tavern. Watching it spread—so obvious, from the curious stares and glances sent her way—Anna was simultaneously appalled, amused, angry, and thankful.

It's her. Calopodius the Blind's wife. Got to be.

"Who started this damned rumor, anyway?" she asked peevishly, after Illus cleared a reasonably clean spot for her in a corner and she was finally able to sit down. She leaned against the shelter of the walls with relief. She was well-nigh exhausted.

Abdul grunted with amusement. The Arab was frequently amused, Anna noted with exasperation. But it was an old and well-worn exasperation, by now, almost pleasant in its predictability.

Cottomenes, whose amusement at life's quirks was not much less than Abdul's, chuckled his own agreement. "You're hot news, Lady Saronites. Everybody on the docks was talking about it, too. And the soldiers outside the telegraph office." Cottomenes, unlike his older brother, never allowed himself the familiarity of calling her "girl." In all other respects, however, he showed her a lack of fawning respect which would have outraged her family.

After the dockboys whom Anna had hired finished stacking her luggage next to her, they crowded themselves against a wall nearby, ignoring the glares directed their way by the tavern's usual habitués. Clearly enough, having found this source of incredible largesse, the dockboys had no intention of relinquishing it.

Anna shook her head. The vehement motion finished the last work of disarranging her long dark hair. The elaborate coiffure under which she had departed Constantinople, so many weeks before, was now entirely a thing of the past. Her hair was every bit as tangled and filthy as her clothing. She wondered if she would ever feel clean again.

"*Why?*" she whispered.

Squatting next to her, Illus studied her for a moment. His eyes were knowing, as if the weeks of close companionship and travel had finally enabled a half-barbarian mercenary soldier to understand the weird torments of a young noblewoman's soul.

Which, indeed, perhaps they had.

"You're different, girl. What you do is *different*. You have no idea how important that can be, to a man who does nothing, day after day, but toil under a sun. Or to a woman who does nothing, day after day, but wash clothes and carry water."

She stared up at him. Seeing the warmth lurking somewhere deep in Illus' eyes, in that hard tight face, Anna was stunned to realize how great a place the man had carved for himself in her heart. *Friendship* was a stranger to Anna of the Melisseni.

"And what is an angel, in the end," said the Isaurian softly, "but something *different*?"

Anna stared down at her grimy garments, noting all the little tears and frays in the fabric.

"In *this*?"

✧   ✧   ✧

The epiphany finally came to her, then. And she wondered, in the hour or so that she spent leaning against the walls of the noisy tavern before she finally drifted into sleep, whether Calopodius had also known such an epiphany. Not on the day he chose to leave her behind, all her dreams crushed, in order to gain his own; but on the day he first awoke, a blind man, and realized that sight is its own curse.

And for the first time since she'd heard Calopodius' name, she no longer regretted the life which had been denied to her. No longer thought with bitterness of the years she would never spend in the shelter of the cloister, allowing her mind to range through the world's accumulated wisdom like a hawk finally soaring free.

When she awoke the next morning, the first thought which came to her was that she finally understood her own faith—and never had before, not truly. There was some regret in the thought, of course. Understanding, for all except God, is also limitation. But with that limitation came clarity and sharpness, so different from the froth and fuzz of a girl's fancies and dreams.

In the gray light of an alien land's morning, filtering into a tavern more noisome than any she would ever have imagined, Anna studied her soiled and ragged clothing. Seeing, this time, not filth and ruin but simply the carpet of her life opening up before her. A life she had thought closeted forever.

"Practicality first," she announced firmly. "It is not a sin."

The words woke up Illus. He gazed at her through slitted, puzzled eyes.

"Get up," she commanded. "We need uniforms."

A few minutes later, leading the way out the door with her three-soldier escort and five dock urchins toting her luggage trailing behind, Anna issued the first of that day's rulings and commandments.

"It'll be expensive, but my husband will pay for it. He's rich."

"He's not here," grunted Illus.

"His name is. He's also famous. Find me a banker."

It took a bit of time before she was able to make the concept of "banker" clear to Illus. Or, more precisely, differentiate it from the concepts of "pawnbroker," "usurer" and "loan shark." But, eventually, he agreed to seek out and capture this mythological creature—with as much confidence as he would have announced plans to trap a griffin or a minotaur.

"Never mind," grumbled Anna, seeing the nervous little way in which Illus was fingering his sword. "I'll do it myself. Where's the army headquarters in this city? *They'll* know what a 'banker' is, be sure of it."

That task *was* within Illus' scheme of things. And since Barbaricum was in the actual theater of Belisarius' operations, the officers in command of the garrison were several cuts of competence above those at Chabahari. By midmorning, Anna had been steered to the largest of the many new moneylenders who had fixed themselves upon Belisarius' army.

An Indian himself, ironically enough, named Pulinda. Anna wondered, as she negotiated the terms, what secrets—and what dreams, realized or stultified—lay behind the life of the small and elderly man sitting across from her. How had a man from the teeming Ganges valley eventually found himself, awash with wealth obtained in whatever mysterious manner, a paymaster to the alien army which was hammering at the gates of his own homeland?

Did he regret the life which had brought him to this place? Savor it?

Most likely both, she concluded. And was then amused, when she realized how astonished Pulinda would have been had he realized that the woman with whom he was quarreling over terms was actually awash in good feeling toward him.

Perhaps, in some unknown way, he sensed that warmth. In any event, the negotiations came to an end sooner than Anna had expected. They certainly left her with better terms than she had expected.

Or, perhaps, it was simply that magic name of Calopodius again, clearing the waters before her. Pulinda's last words to her were: "Mention me to your husband, if you would."

By midafternoon, she had tracked down the tailor reputed to be the best in Barbaricum. By sundown, she had completed her business with him. Most of that time had been spent keeping the dockboys from fidgeting as the tailor measured them.

"You also!" Anna commanded, slapping the most obstreperous urchin on top of his head. "In the Service, cleanliness is essential."

The next day, however, when they donned their new uniforms, the dockboys were almost beside themselves with joy. The plain and utilitarian garments were, by a great margin, the finest clothing they had ever possessed.

The Isaurian brothers and Abdul were not quite as demonstrative. Not quite.

"We look like princes," gurgled Cottomenes happily.

"And so you are," pronounced Anna. "The highest officers of the Wife's Service. A rank which will someday"—she spoke with a confidence far beyond her years—"be envied by princes the world over."

The Iron Triangle

"Relax, Calopodius," said Menander cheerfully, giving the blind young officer a friendly pat on the shoulder. "I'll see to it she arrives safely."

"She's already left Barbaricum," muttered Calopodius. "Damnation, why didn't she *wait?*"

Despite his agitation, Calopodius couldn't help smiling when he heard the little round of laughter which echoed around him. As usual, whenever the subject of Calopodius' wife arose, every officer and orderly in the command had listened. In her own way, Anna was becoming as famous as anyone in the great Roman army fighting its way into India.

Most husbands, to say the least, do not like to discover that their wives are the subject of endless army gossip. But since, in his case, the cause of the gossip was not the usual sexual peccadilloes, Calopodius was not certain how he felt about it. Some part of him, ingrained with custom, still felt a certain dull outrage. But, for the most part—perhaps oddly—his main reaction was one of quiet pride.

"I suppose that's a ridiculous question," he admitted ruefully. "She hasn't waited for anything else."

When Menander spoke again, the tone in his voice was much less jovial. As if he, too, shared in the concern which—much to his surprise—Calopodius had found engulfing him since he learned of Anna's journey. Strange, really, that he should care so much about the well-being of a wife who was little but a vague image to him.

But . . . Even before his blinding, the world of literature had often seemed as real to Calopodius as any other. Since he lost his sight, all the more so—despite the fact that he could no longer read or write himself, but depended on others to do it for him.

Anna Melisseni, the distant girl he had married and had known for a short time in Constantinople, meant practically nothing to him. But *the Wife of Calopodius the Blind,* the unknown woman who had been advancing toward him for weeks now, she was a different thing altogether. Still mysterious, but not a stranger. How could she be, any longer?

Had he not, after all, written about her often enough in his own *Dispatches*? In the third person, of course, as he always spoke of himself in his writings. No subjective mood was ever inserted into his *Dispatches*, any more than into the chapters of his massive *History of the War*. But, detached or not, whenever he received news of Anna he included at least a few sentences detailing for the army her latest adventures. Just as he did for those officers and men who had distinguished themselves. And he was no longer surprised to discover that most of the army found a young wife's exploits more interesting than their own.

She's *different*.

"Difference," however, was no shield against life's misfortunes—misfortunes which are multiplied several times over in the middle of a war zone. So, within seconds, Calopodius was back to fretting.

"Why didn't she *wait*, damn it all?"

Again, Menander clapped his shoulder. "I'm leaving with the *Victrix* this afternoon, Calopodius. Steaming with the riverflow, I'll be in Sukkur long before Anna gets there coming upstream in an oared river craft. So I'll be her escort on the last leg of her journey, coming into the Punjab."

"The Sind's not *that* safe," grumbled Calopodius, still fretting. The Sind was the lower half of the Indus river valley, and while it had now been cleared of Malwa troops and was under the jurisdiction of Rome's Persian allies, the province was still greatly unsettled. "Dacoits everywhere."

"Dacoits aren't going to attack a military convoy," interrupted Belisarius. "I'll make sure she gets a Persian escort of some kind as far as Sukkur."

One of the telegraphs in the command center began to chatter. When the message was read aloud, a short time later, even Calopodius began to relax.

"Guess not," he mumbled—more than a little abashed. "With *that* escort."

The Lower Indus

"I don't believe this," mumbled Illus—more than a little abashed. He glanced down at his uniform. For all the finery of the fabric and the cut, the garment seemed utterly drab matched against the glittering costumes which seemed to fill the wharf against which their river barge was just now being tied.

Standing next to him, Anna said nothing. Her face was stiff, showing none of the uneasiness she felt herself. Her own costume was even more severe and plainly cut than those of her officers, even if the fabric itself was expensive. And she found herself wishing desperately that her cosmetics had survived the journey from Constantinople. For a woman of her class, being seen with a face unadorned by anything except nature was well-nigh unthinkable. In *any* company, much less . . .

The tying-up was finished and the gangplank laid. Anna was able to guess at the identity of the first man to stride across it.

She was not even surprised. Anna had read everything ever written by Irene Macrembolitissa—several times over—including the last book the woman wrote just before she left for the Hindu Kush on her great expedition of conquest. *The Deeds of Khusrau,* she thought, described the man quite well. The Emperor of Persia was not particularly large, but so full of life and energy that he seemed like a giant as he strode toward her across the gangplank.

What am I doing here? she wondered. *I never planned on such as this!*

"So! You are the one!" were the first words he boomed. "To live in such days, when legends walk among us!"

In the confused time which followed, as Anna was introduced to a not-so-little mob of Persian officers and officials—most of them obviously struggling not to frown with disapproval at such a disreputable woman—she pondered on those words.

They seemed meaningless to her. Khusrau Anushirvan— "Khusrau of the Immortal Soul"—was a legend, not she. So why had he said that?

By the end of that evening, after spending hours sitting stiffly in a chair while Iran's royalty and nobility wined and dined her, she had mustered enough courage to lean over to the emperor—sitting next to her!—and whisper the question into his ear.

Khusrau's response astonished her even more than the question had. He grinned broadly, white teeth gleaming in a square-cut Persian beard. Then, he leaned over and whispered in return:

"I am an expert on legends, wife of Calopodius. Truth be told, I often think the art of kingship is mainly knowing how to make the things."

He glanced slyly at his assembled nobility, who had not stopped frowning at Anna throughout the royal feast—but always, she noticed, under lowered brows.

"But keep it a secret," he whispered. "It wouldn't do for my noble *vurzurgan* to discover that their emperor is really a common manufacturer. I don't need another rebellion this year."

She *did* manage to choke down a laugh, fortunately. The effort, however, caused her hand to shake just enough to spill some wine onto her long dress.

"No matter," whispered the emperor. "Don't even try to remove the stain. By next week, it'll be the blood of a dying man brought back to life by the touch of your hand. Ask anyone."

She tightened her lips to keep from smiling. It was nonsense, of course, but there was no denying the emperor was a charming man.

But, royal decree or no, it was still nonsense. Bloodstains aplenty there had been on the garments she'd brought from

Constantinople, true enough. Blood and pus and urine and excrement and every manner of fluid produced by human suffering. She'd gained them in Chabahari, and again at Barbaricum. Nor did she doubt there *would* be bloodstains on this garment also, soon enough, to match the wine stain she had just put there.

Indeed, she had designed the uniforms of the Wife's Service with that in mind. That was why the fabric had been dyed a purple so dark it was almost black.

But it was still nonsense. Her touch had no more magic power than anyone's. Her *knowledge*—or rather, the knowledge which she had obtained by reading everything Macrembolitissa or anyone else had ever written transmitting the Talisman of God's wisdom—now, *that* was powerful. But it had nothing to do with her, except insofar as she was another vessel of those truths.

Something of her skepticism must have shown, despite her effort to remain impassive-faced. She was only nineteen, after all, and hardly an experienced diplomat.

Khusrau's lips quirked. "You'll see."

The next day she resumed her journey up the river toward Sukkur. The emperor himself, due to the pressing business of completing his incorporation of the Sind into the swelling empire of Iran, apologized for not being able to accompany her personally. But he detailed no fewer than four Persian war galleys to serve as her escort.

"No fear of dacoits," said Illus, with great satisfaction. "Or deserters turned robbers."

His satisfaction turned a bit sour at Anna's response.

"Good. We'll be able to stop at every hospital along the way then. No matter how small."

And stop they did. Only briefly, in the Roman ones. By now, to Anna's satisfaction, Belisarius' blood-curdling threats had resulted in a marked improvement in medical procedures and sanitary practices.

But most of the small military hospitals along the way

were Persian. The "hospitals" were nothing more than tents pitched along the riverbank—mere staging posts for disabled Persian soldiers being evacuated back to their homeland. The conditions within them had Anna seething, with a fury that was all the greater because neither she nor either of the Isaurian officers could speak a word of the Iranian language. Abdul could make himself understood, but his pidgin was quite inadequate to the task of convincing skeptical—even hostile—Persian officials that Anna's opinion was anything more than female twaddle.

Anna spent another futile hour trying to convince the officers in command of her escort to send a message to Khusrau himself. Clearly enough, however, none of them were prepared to annoy the emperor at the behest of a Roman woman who was probably half-insane to begin with.

Fortunately, at the town of Dadu, there was a telegraph station. Anna marched into it and fired off a message to her husband.

WHY TALISMAN MEDICAL PRECEPTS NOT TRANSLATED INTO PERSIAN? INSTRUCT EMPEROR IRAN DISCIPLINE HIS IDIOTS.

"Do it," said Belisarius, after Calopodius read him the message.

The general paused. "Well, the first part, anyway. The Persian translation. I'll have to figure out a somewhat more diplomatic way to pass the rest of it on to Khusrau."

Maurice snorted. "How about hitting him on the head with a club? That'd be 'somewhat' more diplomatic."

By the time the convoy reached Sukkur, it was moving very slowly.

There were no military hospitals along the final stretch of the river, because wounded soldiers were kept either in Sukkur itself or had already passed through the evacuation routes. The slow pace was now due entirely to the native population.

By whatever mysterious means, word of the Wife's passage had spread up and down the Indus. The convoy was constantly approached by small river boats bearing sick and injured villagers, begging for what was apparently being called "the healing touch."

Anna tried to reason, to argue, to convince. But it was hopeless. The language barrier was well-nigh impassible. Even the officers of her Persian escort could do no more than roughly translate the phrase "healing touch."

In the end, not being able to bear the looks of anguish on their faces, Anna laid her hands on every villager brought alongside her barge for the purpose. Muttering curses under her breath all the while—curses which were all the more bitter since she was quite certain the villagers of the Sind took them for powerful incantations.

At Sukkur, she was met by Menander and the entire crew of the *Victrix*. Beaming from ear to ear.

The grins faded soon enough. After waiting impatiently for the introductions to be completed, Anna's next words were: "Where's the telegraph station?"

URGENT. MUST TRANSLATE TALISMAN PRECEPTS INTO NATIVE TONGUES ALSO.

Menander fidgeted while she waited for the reply.

"I've got a critical military cargo to haul to the island," he muttered. "Calopodius may not even send an answer."

"He's my husband," came her curt response. "Of course he'll answer me."

Sure enough, the answer came very soon.

CANNOT. IS NO WRITTEN NATIVE LANGUAGE. NOT EVEN ALPHABET.

After reading it, Anna snorted. "We'll see about that."

❖   ❖   ❖

YOU SUPPOSEDLY EXPERT GRAMMAR AND RHETORIC.
INVENT ONE.

"You'd best get started on it," mused Belisarius. The
general's head turned to the south. "She'll be coming soon."
"Like a tidal bore," added Maurice.

The Iron Triangle

That night, he dreamed of islands again.

*First, of Rhodes, where he spent an idle day on his
journey to join Belisarius' army while his ship took on
supplies.*

*Some of that time he spent visiting the place where, years
before, John of Rhodes had constructed an armaments
center. Calopodius' own skills and interests were not
inclined in a mechanical direction, but he was still curious enough to want to see the mysterious facility.*

*But, in truth, there was no longer much there of inter-
est. Just a handful of buildings, vacant now except for
livestock. So, after wandering about for a bit, he spent the
rest of the day perched on a headland staring at the sea.*

*It was a peaceful, calm, and solitary day. The last one
he would enjoy in his life, thus far.*

*Then, his dreams took him to the island in the Strait
of Hormuz where Belisarius was having a naval base constructed. The general had sent Calopodius over from the
mainland where the army was marching its way toward
the Indus, in order to help resolve one of the many minor
disputes which had erupted between the Romans and Persians who were constructing the facility. Among the members of the small corps of noble couriers who served Belisarius*

for liaison with the Persians, Calopodius had displayed a great deal of tact as well as verbal aptitude.

It was something of a private joke between him and the general. "I need you to take care of another obstreperous aunt," was the way Belisarius put it.

The task of mediating between the quarrelsome Romans and Persians had been stressful. But Calopodius had enjoyed the boat ride well enough; and, in the end, he had managed to translate Belisarius' blunt words into language flowery enough to slide the command through—like a knife between unguarded ribs.

Toward the end, his dreams slid into a flashing nightmare image of Bukkur Island. A log, painted to look like a field gun, sent flying by a lucky cannon ball fired by one of the Malwa gunships whose bombardment accompanied that last frenzied assault. The Romans drove off that attack also, in the end. But not before a mortar shell had ripped Calopodius' eyes out of his head.

The last sight he would ever have in his life was of that log, whirling through the air and crushing the skull of a Roman soldier standing in its way. What made the thing a nightmare was that Calopodius could not remember the soldier's name, if he had ever known it. So it all seemed very incomplete, in a way which was too horrible for Calopodius to be able to express clearly to anyone, even himself. Grammar and rhetoric simply collapsed under the coarse reality, just as fragile human bone and brain had collapsed under hurtling wood.

The sound of his aide-de-camp clumping about in the bunker awoke him. The warm little courtesy banished the nightmare, and Calopodius returned to life with a smile.

"How does the place look?" he asked.

Luke snorted. "It's hardly fit for a Melisseni girl. But I imagine it'll do for *your* wife."

"Soon, now."

"Yes." Calopodius heard Luke lay something on the small

table next to the cot. From the slight rustle, he understood that it was another stack of telegrams. Private ones, addressed to him, not army business.

"Any from Anna?"

"No. Just more bills."

Calopodius laughed. "Well, whatever else, she still spends money like a Melisseni. Before she's done, that banker will be the richest man in India."

Beyond a snort, Luke said nothing in response. After a moment, Calopodius' humor faded away, replaced by simple wonder.

"Soon, now. I wonder what she'll be like?"

The Indus

The attack came as a complete surprise. Not to Anna, who simply didn't know enough about war to understand what could be expected and what not, but to her military escort.

"What in the name of God do they think they're *doing?*" demanded Menander angrily.

He studied the fleet of small boats—skiffs, really—pushing out from the southern shore. The skiffs were loaded with Malwa soldiers, along with more than the usual complement of Mahaveda priests and their mahamimamsa "enforcers." The presence of the latter was a sure sign that the Malwa considered this project so near-suicidal that the soldiers needed to be held in a tight rein.

"It's an ambush," explained his pilot, saying aloud the conclusion Menander had already reached. The man pointed to the thick reeds. "The Malwa must have hauled those boats across the desert, hidden them in the reeds, waited for us. We don't keep regular patrols on the south bank, since there's really nothing there to watch for."

Menander's face was tight with exasperation. "But what's the *point* of it?" For a moment, his eyes moved forward, toward the heavily-shielded bow of the ship where the

Victrix's fire-cannon was situated. "We'll burn them up like so many piles of kindling."

But even before he finished the last words, even before he saw the target of the oncoming boats, Menander understood the truth. The fact of it, at least, if not the reasoning.

"*Why?* They're all dead men, no matter what happens. In the name of God, she's just a woman!"

He didn't wait for an answer, however, before starting to issue his commands. The *Victrix* began shuddering to a halt. The skiffs were coming swiftly, driven by almost frenzied rowing. It would take the *Victrix* time to come to a halt and turn around; time to make its way back to protect the barge it was towing.

Time, Menander feared, that he might not have.

"What should we do?" asked Anna. For all the strain in her voice, she was relieved that her words came without stammering. A Melisseni girl could afford to scream with terror; she couldn't. Not any longer.

Grim-faced, Illus glanced around the barge. Other than he and Cottomenes and Abdul, there were only five Roman soldiers on the barge—and only two of those were armed with muskets. Since Belisarius and Khusrau had driven the Malwa out of the Sind, and established Roman naval supremacy on the Indus with the new steam-powered gunboats, there had been no Malwa attempt to threaten shipping south of the Iron Triangle.

Then his eyes came to rest on the vessel's new feature, and his tight lips creased into something like a smile.

"God bless good officers," he muttered.

He pointed to the top of the cabin amidships, where a shell of thin iron was perched. It was a turret, of sorts, for the odd and ungainly looking "Puckle gun" which Menander had insisted on adding to the barge. The helmeted face and upper body of the gunner was visible, and Illus could see the man beginning to train the weapon on the oncoming canoes.

"Get up there—*now*. There's enough room in there for you, and it's the best armored place on the barge." He gave the oncoming Malwa a quick glance. "They've got a few muskets of their own. Won't be able to hit much, not shooting from skiffs moving that quickly—but keep your head *down* once you get there."

It took Anna a great deal of effort, encumbered as she was by her heavy and severe gown, to clamber atop the cabin. She couldn't have made it at all, if Abdul hadn't boosted her. Climbing over the iron wall of the turret was a bit easier, but not much. Fortunately, the gunner lent her a hand.

After she sprawled into the open interior of the turret, the hard edges of some kind of ammunition containers bruising her back, Anna had to struggle fiercely not to burst into shrill cursing.

I have got *to design a new costume. Propriety be damned!*

For a moment, her thoughts veered aside. She remembered that Irene Macrembolitissa, in her *Observations of India,* had mentioned—with some amusement—that Empress Shakuntala often wore pantaloons in public. Outrageous behavior, really, but . . . when *you're* the one who owns the executioners, you can afford to outrage public opinion.

The thought made her smile, and it was with that cheerful expression on her lips that she turned her face up to the gunner frowning down at her.

"Is there anything I can do to help?"

The man's face suddenly lightened, and he smiled himself.

"Damn if you aren't a prize!" he chuckled. Then, nodding his head. "Yes, ma'am. As a matter of fact, there is."

He pointed to the odd-looking objects lying on the floor of the turret, which had bruised Anna when she landed on them. "Those are called cylinders." He patted the strange looking weapon behind which he was half-crouched. "This thing'll wreak havoc, sure enough, as long as I can keep it loaded. I'm supposed to have a loader, but since we added this just as an afterthought . . ."

He turned his head, studying the enemy vessels. "Better do it quick, ma'am. If those skiffs get alongside, your men and the other soldiers won't be enough to beat them back. And they'll have grenades anyway, they're bound to. If I can't keep them off, we're all dead."

Anna scrambled around until she was on her knees. Then seized one of the weird-looking metal contraptions. It was not as heavy as it looked. "What do you need me to do? Be precise!"

"Just hand them to me, ma'am, that's all. I'll do the rest. And keep your head down—it's *you* they're after."

Anna froze for a moment, dumbfounded. "Me? *Why?*"

"Damned if I know. Doesn't make sense."

But, in truth, the gunner did understand. Some part of it, at least, even if he lacked the sophistication to follow all of the reasoning of the inhuman monster who commanded the Malwa empire. The gunner had never heard—and never would—of a man named Napoleon. But he was an experienced soldier, and not stupid even if his formal education was rudimentary. *The moral is to the material in war as three-to-one* was not a phrase the man would have ever uttered himself, but he would have had no difficulty understanding it.

Link, the emissary from the new gods of the future who ruled the Malwa in all but name and commanded its great army in the Punjab, had ordered this ambush. The "why" was self-evident to its superhuman intelligence. Spending the lives of a few soldiers and Mahaveda priests was well worth the price, if it would enable the monster to destroy *the Wife* whose exploits its spies reported. Exploits which, in their own peculiar way, had become important to Roman morale.

Cheap at the price, in fact. Dirt cheap.

The Iron Triangle

The battle on the river was observed from the north bank by a patrol of light Arab cavalry in Roman service. Being

Beni Ghassan, the cavalrymen were far more sophisticated in the uses of new technology than most Arabs. Their commander immediately dispatched three riders to bring news of the Malwa ambush to the nearest telegraph station, which was but a few miles distant.

By the time Belisarius got the news, of course, the outcome of the battle had already been decided, one way or the other. So he could do nothing more than curse himself for a fool, and try not to let the ashen face of a blind young man sway his cold-blooded reasoning.

"I'm a damned fool not to have foreseen the possibility. It just didn't occur to me that the Malwa might carry *boats* across the desert. But it should have."

"Not your fault, sir," said Calopodius quietly.

Belisarius tightened his jaws. "Like hell it isn't."

Maurice, standing nearby, ran fingers through his bristly iron-gray hair. "We all screwed up. I should have thought of it, too. We've been so busy just being entertained by the episode that we didn't think about it. Not seriously."

Belisarius sighed and nodded. "There's still no point in me sending the *Justinian*. By the time it got there, it will all have been long settled—and there's always the chance Link might be trying for a diversion."

"You *can't* send the *Justinian*," said Calopodius, half-whispering. "With the *Victrix* gone—and the *Photius* down at Sukkur—the Malwa might try an amphibious attack on the Triangle."

He spoke the cold truth, and every officer in the command center knew it. So nothing further was said. They simply waited for another telegraph report to inform them whether Calopodius was a husband or a widower.

The Indus

Before the battle was over, Anna had reason to be thankful for her heavy gown.

As cheerfully profligate as he was, the gunner soon used up the preloaded cylinders for the Puckle gun. Thereafter, Anna had to reload the cylinders manually with the cartridges she found in a metal case against the shell of the turret. Placing the new shells *into* a cylinder was easy enough, with a little experience. The trick was taking out the spent ones. The brass cartridges were hot enough to hurt her fingers, the first time she tried prying them out.

Thereafter, following the gunner's hastily shouted instructions, she started using the little ramrod provided in the ammunition case. Kneeling in the shelter of the turret, she just upended the cylinders—carefully holding them with the hem of her dress, because they were hot also—and smacked the cartridges loose.

The cartridges came out easily enough, that way—right onto her lap and knees. In a lighter gown, a less severe and formal garment, her thighs would soon enough have been scorched by the little pile of hot metal.

As it was, the heat was endurable, and Anna didn't care in the least that the expensive fabric was being ruined in the process. She just went about her business, brushing the cartridges onto the floor of the turret, loading and reloading with the thunderous racket of the Puckle gun in her ears, ignoring everything else around her.

Throughout, her mind only strayed once. After the work became something of a routine, she found herself wondering if her husband's mind had been so detached in battles. Not whether he had ignored pain—of course he had; Anna had learned that much since leaving Constantinople—but whether he had been able to ignore his continued existence as well.

She suspected he had, and found herself quite warmed by the thought. She even handed up the next loaded cylinder with a smile.

The gunner noticed the smile, and that too would become part of the legend. He would survive the war, as it happened; and, in later years, in taverns in his native Anatolia, whenever he heard the tale of how the Wife smote down Malwa boarders with a sword and a laugh, saw no reason to set the matter straight. By then, he had come to half-believe it himself.

Anna sensed a shadow passing, but she paid it very little attention. By now, her hands and fingers were throbbing enough to block out most sensation beyond what was necessary to keep reloading the cylinders. She barely even noticed the sudden burst of fiery light and the screams which announced that the *Victrix* had arrived and was wreaking its delayed vengeance on what was left of the Malwa ambush.

Which was not much, in truth. The gunner was a very capable man, and Anna had kept him well-supplied. Most of the skiffs now drifting near the barge had bodies draped over their sides and sprawled lifelessly within. At that close range, the Puckle gun had been murderous.

"Enough, ma'am," said the gunner gently. "It's over."

Anna finished reloading the cylinder in her hands. Then, when the meaning of the words finally registered, she set the thing down on the floor of the turret. Perhaps oddly, the relief of finally not having to handle hot metal only made the pain in her hands—and legs, too, she noticed finally—all the worse.

She stared down at the fabric of her gown. There were little stains all over it, where cartridges had rested before she brushed them onto the floor. There was a time, she could vaguely remember, when the destruction of an expensive garment would have been a cause of great concern. But it seemed a very long time ago.

"How is Illus?" she asked softly. "And the others? The boys?"

The gunner sighed. "One of the boys got killed, ma'am. Just bad luck—Illus kept the youngsters back, but that one grenade . . ."

Vaguely, Anna remembered hearing an explosion. She began to ask which boy it was, whose death she had caused, of the five urchins she had found on the docks of Barbaricum and conscripted into her Service. But she could not bear that pain yet.

"Illus?"

"He's fine. So's Abdul. Cottomenes got cut pretty bad."

Something to do again. The thought came as a relief. Within seconds, she was clambering awkwardly over the side of the turret again—and, again, silently cursing the impractical garment she wore.

Cottomenes was badly gashed, true enough. But the leg wound was not even close to the great femoral artery, and by now Anna had learned to sew other things than cloth. Besides, the *Victrix*'s boiler was an excellent mechanism for boiling water.

The ship's engineer was a bit outraged, of course. But, wisely, he kept his mouth shut.

The Iron Triangle

"It's not much," said Calopodius apologetically.

Anna's eyes moved over the interior of the little bunker where Calopodius lived. Where she would now live also. She did not fail to notice all the little touches here and there—the bright, cheery little cloths; the crucifix; even a few native handcrafts—as well as the relative cleanliness of the place. But . . .

No, it was not much. Just a big pit in the ground, when all was said and done, covered over with logs and soil.

"It's fine," she said. "Not a problem."

She turned and stared at him. Her husband, once a handsome boy, was now a hideously ugly man. She had expected the empty eye sockets, true enough. But even after all the carnage she had witnessed since she left Constantinople, she had not once considered what a mortar shell would do to the *rest* of his face.

Stupid, really. As if shrapnel would obey the rules of

poetry, and pierce eyes as neatly as a goddess at a loom.
The upper half of his face was a complete ruin. The
lower half was relatively unmarked, except for one scar
along his right jaw and another puckerlike mark on his
left cheek.

His mouth and lips, on the other hand, were still as she
vaguely remembered them. A nice mouth, she decided,
noticing for the first time.

"It's fine," she repeated. "Not a problem."

A moment later, two soldiers came into the bunker haul-
ing her luggage. What was left of it. Until they were gone,
Anna and Calopodius were silent. Then he said, very softly:

"I don't understand why you came."

Anna tried to remember the answer. It was difficult. And
probably impossible to explain, in any event. *I wanted a
divorce, maybe . . .* seemed . . . strange. Even stranger, though
closer to the truth, would be: *or at least to drag you back
so you could share the ruins of my own life.*

"It doesn't matter now. I'm here. I'm staying."

For the first time since she'd rejoined her husband, he
smiled. Anna realized she'd never really seen him smile
before. Not, at least, with an expression that was anything
more than politeness.

He reached out his hand, tentatively, and she moved
toward him. The hand, fumbling, stroked her ribs.

"God in Heaven, Anna!" he choked. "How can you *stand*
something like that—in this climate? You'll drown in sweat."

Anna tried to keep from laughing; and then, realizing
finally where she was, stopped trying. Even in the haugh-
tiest aristocratic circles of Constantinople, a woman was
allowed to laugh in the presence of her husband.

When she was done—the laughter was perhaps a bit
hysterical—Calopodius shook his head. "We've got to get
you a sari, first thing. I can't have my wife dying on me
from heat prostration."

Calopodius matched deed to word immediately. A few
words to his aide-to-camp Luke, and, much sooner than

Anna would have expected, a veritable horde of Punjabis from the adjacent town were packed into the bunker.

Some of them were actually there on business, bringing piles of clothing for her to try on. Most of them, she finally understood, just wanted to get a look at her.

Of course, they were all expelled from the bunker while she changed her clothing—except for two native women whose expert assistance she required until she mastered the secrets of the foreign garments. But once the women announced that she was suitably attired, the mob of admirers was allowed back in.

In fact, after a while Anna found it necessary to leave the bunker altogether and model her new clothing on the ground outside, where everyone could get a good look at her new appearance. Her husband insisted, to her surprise.

"You're beautiful," he said to her, "and I want everyone to know it."

She almost asked how a blind man could tell, but he forestalled the question with a little smile. "Did you think I'd forget?"

But later, that night, he admitted the truth. They were lying side by side, stiffly, still fully clothed, on the pallet in a corner of the bunker where Calopodius slept. "To be honest, I can't remember very well what you look like."

Anna thought about it, for a moment. Then:

"I can't really remember myself."

"I wish I could see you," he murmured.

"It doesn't matter." She took his hand and laid it on her bare belly. The flesh reveled in its new coolness. She herself, on the other hand, reveled in the touch. And did not find it strange that she should do so.

"Feel."

His hand was gentle, at first. And never really stopped being so, for all the passion that followed. When it was all over, Anna was covered in sweat again. But she didn't mind at all. Without heavy and proper fabric to cover her—with nothing covering her now except Calopodius' hand—the sweat dried soon enough. That, too, was a great pleasure.

"I warn you," she murmured into his ear. "We're not in Constantinople any more. Won't be for a long time, if ever. So if I catch you with a courtesan, I'll boil you alive."

"The thought never crossed my mind!" he insisted. And even believed it was true.

CHOOSING SIDES
A Hammer's Slammers Story

David Drake

The driver of the lead combat car revved his fans to lift the bow when he reached the bottom of the starship's steep boarding ramp. The gale whirling from under the car's skirts rocked Lieutenant Arne Huber forward into the second vehicle—his own *Fencing Master*, still locked to the deck because a turnbuckle had kinked when the ship unexpectedly tilted on the soft ground.

Huber was twenty-five standard years old, shorter than average and fit without being impressively muscular. He wore a commo helmet now, but the short-cropped hair beneath it was as black as the pupils of his eyes.

Sighing, he pushed himself up from *Fencing Master*'s bow slope. His head hurt the way it always did just after star-travel—which meant worse than it did any other time in his life. Even without the howling fans of *Foghorn*, the lead car, his ears would be roaring in time with his pulse.

None of the troopers in Huber's platoon were in much better shape, and he didn't guess the starship's crew were more than nominal themselves. The disorientation from star travel, like a hangover, didn't stop hurting just because it'd become familiar.

"Look!" said Sergeant Deseau, shouting so that the three starship crewmen could hear him over the fans' screaming. "If you don't have us free in a minute flat, starting *now*, I'm going to shoot the cursed thing off and you can worry about the damage to your cursed deck without me to watch you. Do you understand?"

Two more spacers were squeezing through the maze of vehicles and equipment in the hold, carrying a power tool between them. This sort of problem can't have been unique to *Fencing Master*.

Huber put his hand on Deseau's shoulder. "Let's get out of the way and let them fix this, Sarge," he said, speaking through the helmet intercom so that he didn't have to raise his voice. Shouting put people's backs up, even if you didn't mean anything by it except that it was hard to hear. "Let's take a look at Plattner's World."

They turned together and walked to the open hatch. Deseau was glad enough to step away from the problem.

The freighter which had brought Platoon F-3, Arne Huber's command, to Plattner's World had a number rather than a name: KPZ 9719. It was much smaller than the vessels which usually carried the men and vehicles of Hammer's Regiment, but even so it virtually overwhelmed the facilities here at Rhodesville. The ship had set down normally, but one of the outriggers then sank an additional meter into the soil. The lurch had flung everybody who'd already unstrapped against the bulkheads and jammed *Fencing Master* in place, blocking two additional combat cars behind it in the hold.

Huber chuckled. That made his head throb, but it throbbed already. Deseau gave him a sour look.

"It's a good thing we hadn't freed the cars before the outrigger gave," Huber explained. "Bad enough people bouncing off the walls; at least we didn't have thirty-tonne combat cars doing it too."

"I don't see why we're landing in a cow pasture anyway," Deseau muttered. "Isn't there a real spaceport somewhere on this bloody tree-farm of a planet?"

"Yeah, there is," Huber said dryly. "The trouble is, it's in Solace. The people the United Cities are hiring us to fight."

The briefing cubes were available to everybody in the Slammers, but Sergeant Deseau was like most of the enlisted personnel—and no few of the officers—in spending the time between deployments finding other ways to entertain himself. It was a reasonable enough attitude. Mercenaries tended to be pragmatists. Knowledge of the local culture wasn't a factor when a planet hired mercenary soldiers, nor did it increase the gunmen's chances of survival.

Deseau spit toward the ground, either a comment or just a way of clearing phlegm from his throat. Huber's mouth felt like somebody'd scrubbed a rusty pot, then used the same wad of steel wool to scour his mouth and tongue.

"Let's hope we capture Solace fast so we don't lose half our supplies in the mud," Deseau said. "This place'll be a swamp the first time it rains."

KPZ 9719 had come down on the field serving the dirigibles which connected Rhodesville with the other communities on Plattner's World—and particularly with the spaceport at Solace in the central highlands. The field's surface was graveled, but there were more soft spots than the one the starship's outrigger had stabbed down through. Deseau was right about what wet weather would bring.

The starship sat on the southern edge of the kilometer-square field. On the north side opposite them were a one-story brick terminal with an attached control tower, and a dozen warehouses with walls and trusses of plastic extrusion. Those few buildings comprised the entire port facilities.

Tractors were positioning lowboys under the corrugated metal shipping containers slung beneath the 300-meter-long dirigible now unloading at the east end of the field. A second dirigible had dropped its incoming cargo and was easing westward against a mild breeze, heading for the mooring mast where it would tether. The rank of outbound shipping containers there waited to be slung in place of the food and merchandise the United Cities imported. The containers had been painted a variety of colors, but rust now provided the most uniform livery.

A third dirigible was in the center of the field, its props turning just fast enough to hold it steady. The four shipping containers hanging from its belly occasionally kicked up dust as they touched the ground. A port official stood in an open-topped jitney with a flashing red light. He was screaming through a bullhorn at the dirigible's forward cockpit, but the crew there seemed to be ignoring him.

Trooper Learoyd, *Fencing Master*'s right wing gunner—Huber chose to ride at the left gun, with Deseau in the vehicle commander's post in the center—joined them at the hatch. He was stocky, pale, and almost bald even though he was younger than Huber by several years. He looked out and said, "What's worth having a war about this place?"

"There's people on it," Deseau said with a sharp laugh. "That's all the reason you need for a war, snake. You ought to know that by now."

According to the briefing cubes, Rhodesville had a permanent population of 50,000; the residents provided light manufacturing and services for the moss-hunters coursing thousands of square kilometers of the surrounding forest. Only a few houses were visible from the port. The community wound through the forest, constructed under the trees instead of clearing them for construction. The forest was the wealth of Plattner's World, and the settlers acted as though they understood that fact.

"There's a fungus that's a parasite on the trees here," Huber explained. "They call it moss because it grows in patches of gray tendrils from the trunks. It's the source of an anti-aging drug. The processing's done offworld, but there's enough money in the business that even the rangers who gather the moss have aircars and better holodecks than you'd find in most homes on Friesland."

"Well I'll be," Learoyd said, though he didn't sound excited. He rubbed his temples, as if trying to squeeze the pain out through his eyesockets.

Deseau spat again. "So long as they've got enough set by to pay our wages," he said. "I'd like a good, long war this time, because if I never board a ship again it'll be too soon."

The third dirigible was drifting sideways. Huber wouldn't have been sure except for the official in the jitney; he suddenly dropped back into his seat and drove forward to keep from being crushed by the underslung cargo containers. The official stopped again and got out of his vehicle, running back toward the dirigible with his fists raised overhead in fury.

Huber looked over his shoulder to see how the spacers were making out with the turnbuckle. The tool they'd brought, a cart with chucks on extensible arms, wasn't working. Well, that was par for the course.

Trooper Kolbe sat in the driver's compartment, his chin bar resting on the hatch coaming. His faceshield was down, presenting an opaque surface to the outside world. Kolbe could have been using the helmet's infrared, light-amplification, or sonic imaging to improve his view of the dimly lit hold, but Huber suspected the driver was simply hiding the fact that his eyes were closed.

Kolbe needn't have been so discreet. If Huber hadn't thought he ought to set an example, he'd have been leaning his forehead against *Fencing Master*'s cool iridium bow slope and wishing he didn't hurt so much.

Platoon Sergeant Jellicoe was at the arms locker, issuing troopers their personal weapons. Jellicoe seemed as dispassionate as the hull of her combat car, but Trooper Coblentz, handing out the weapons as the sergeant checked them off, looked like he'd died several weeks ago.

Unless and until Colonel Hammer ordered otherwise, troopers on a contract world were required to go armed at all times. Revised orders were generally issued within hours of landing; troopers barhopping in rear areas with sub-machine guns and 2-cm shoulder weapons made the Regiment's local employers nervous, and rightly so.

On Plattner's World the Slammers had to land at six sites scattered across the United Cities, a nation that was mostly forest. None of the available landing fields was large enough to take the monster starships on which the Regiment preferred to travel, and only the administrative capital, Benjamin, could handle more than one twenty-vehicle company at a time. Chances were that even off-duty troopers would be operating in full combat gear for longer than usual.

"What's that gas-bag doing?" Deseau asked. "What do they fill 'em with here, anyway? If it's hydrogen and it usually is . . ."

Foghorn had shut down, well clear of the starship's ramp. Her four crewmen were shifting their gear out of the open-topped fighting compartment and onto the splinter shield of beryllium net overhead. A Slammers' vehicle on combat deployment looked like a bag lady's cart; the crew knew that the only things they could count on having were what they carried with them. Tanks and combat cars could shift position by over 500 klicks in a day, smashing the flank or rear of an enemy who didn't even know he was threatened; but logistics support couldn't follow the fighting vehicles as they stabbed through hostile territory.

"Aide, unit," Huber said, cueing his commo helmet's AI to the band all F-3 used in common. "Tatzig, pull around where that dirigible isn't going to hit you. Something's wrong with the bloody thing and the locals aren't doing much of a job of sorting it out."

Sergeant Tatzig looked up. He grunted an order to his driver, then replied over the unit push, "*Roger, will do.*"

There was a clang from the hold. A spacer had just hit the turnbuckle with a heavy hammer.

A huge, hollow metallic racket sounded from the field; the dirigible had dropped its four shipping containers. The instant the big metal boxes hit the ground, the sides facing the starship fell open. Three of them did, anyway: the fourth container opened halfway, then stuck.

The containers were full of armed men wearing uniforms of chameleon cloth that mimicked the hue of whatever it was close to. The troops looked like pools of shadow from which slug-throwers and anti-armor missiles protruded.

"Incoming!" Huber screamed. "We're under attack!"

One of the attacking soldiers had a buzzbomb, a shoulder-launched missile, already aimed at Huber's face. He fired. Huber reacted by instinct, grabbing his two companions and throwing himself down the ramp instead of back into the open hold.

The missile howled overhead and detonated on *Fencing Master*'s bow. White fire filled the universe for an instant. The blast made the ramp jump, flipping Huber from his belly to his right side. He got up. He was seeing double, but he could see; details didn't matter at times like this.

The attack had obviously been carefully planned, but things went wrong for the hostiles as sure as they had for Huber and his troopers. The buzzbomber had launched early instead of stepping away from the shipping container as he should've done. The steel box caught the missile's backblast and reflected it onto the shooter and those of his fellows who hadn't jumped clear. They spun out of the container, screaming as flames licked from their tattered uniforms.

A dozen automatic weapons raked *Foghorn*, killing Tatzig and his crewmen instantly. The attackers' weapons used electromagnets to accelerate heavy-metal slugs down the bore at hypersonic velocity. When slugs hit the car's iridium armor, they ricocheted as neon streaks that were brilliant even in sunlight.

Slugs that hit troopers chewed their bodies into a mist of blood and bone.

The starship's hold was full of roiling white smoke, harsh as a wood rasp on the back of Huber's throat in the instant before his helmet slapped filters down over his nostrils. The buzzbomb had hit *Fencing Master*'s bow slope at an angle. Its shaped-charge warhead had gouged a long trough across the armor instead of punching through into the car's vitals. There was no sign of Kolbe.

The tie-down, jammed turnbuckle and all, had vanished in the explosion. Two pairs of legs lay beside the vehicle. They'd probably belonged to spacers rather than Huber's troopers, but the blast had blown the victims' clothing off at the same time it pureed their heads and torsos.

Slugs snapped through the starship's hatchway, clanging and howling as they ricocheted deeper into the hold. Huber mounted *Fencing Master*'s bow slope with a jump and a quick step. He dabbed a hand down and the blast-heated armor burned him. He'd have blisters in the morning, if he lived that long.

Huber thought the driver's compartment was empty, but Kolbe's body from the shoulders on down had slumped onto the floor. Huber bent through the hatch and grabbed him. The driver's right arm came off when Huber tugged.

Huber screamed in frustration and threw the limb out of the vehicle, then got a double grip on Kolbe's equipment belt and hauled him up by it. Bracing his elbows for leverage, Huber pulled the driver's torso and thighs over the coaming and let gravity do the rest. The body slithered down the bow, making room for Huber inside. The compartment was too tight to share with a corpse and still be able to drive.

Kolbe had raised the seat so that he could sit with his head out of the vehicle. Huber dropped it because he wanted the compartment's full-sized displays instead of the miniature versions his faceshield would provide. The slugs whipping around the hold would've been a consideration if he'd had time to think about it, but right now he had more important things on his mind than whether he was going to be alive in the next millisecond.

"All Fox elements!" he shouted, his helmet still cued to the unit push. Half a dozen troopers were talking at the same time; Huber didn't know if anybody would hear the order, but they were mostly veterans and ought to react the right way without a lieutenant telling them what that was. "Bring your cars on line and engage the enemy!"

Arne Huber was F-3's platoon leader, not a driver, but right now the most critical task the platoon faced was getting the damaged, crewless, combat car out of the way of the two vehicles behind it. With *Fencing Master* blocking the hatch, the attackers would wipe out the platoon like so many bugs in a killing bottle. Huber was the closest trooper to the job, so he was doing it.

The fusion bottle that powered the vehicle was on line. Eight powerful fans in nacelles under *Fencing Master*'s hull sucked in outside air and filled the steel-skirted plenum chamber at pressure sufficient to lift the car's thirty tonnes. Kolbe had switched the fans on but left them spinning at idle, their blades set at zero incidence, while the spacers freed the turnbuckle.

Huber palmed the combined throttles forward while his thumb adjusted blade incidence in concert. As the fusion bottle fed more power to the nacelles, the blades tilted on their axes so that they drove the air rather than merely cutting it. Fan speed remained roughly constant, but *Fencing Master* shifted greasily as her skirts began to lift from the freighter's deck.

A second buzzbomb hit the bow.

For an instant, Huber's mind went as blank as the white glare of the blast. The shock curtains in the driver's compartment expanded, and his helmet did as much as physics allowed to save his head. Despite that, his brain sloshed in his skull.

He came around as the shock curtains shrank back to their ready state. He didn't know who or where he was. The display screen before him was a gray, roiling mass. He switched the control to thermal imaging by trained reflex and saw armed figures rising from the ground to rush the open hatch.

I'm Arne Huber. We're being attacked.

His right hand was on the throttles; the fans were howling. He twisted the grip, angling the nacelles back so that their thrust pushed the combat car instead of just lifting it. *Fencing Master*'s bow skirt screeched on the deck, braking the vehicle's forward motion beyond the ability of the fans to drive it.

The second warhead had opened the plenum chamber like a ration packet. The fan-driven air rushed out through the hole instead of raising the vehicle as it was meant to do.

The attackers had thrown themselves flat so that the missile wouldn't scythe them down also. Three of them reached the base of the ramp, then paused and opened fire. Dazzling streaks crisscrossed the hold, and the *whang* of slugs hitting the *Fencing Master*'s iridium armor was loud even over the roar of the fans.

Huber decoupled the front four nacelles and tilted them vertical again. He shoved the throttle through the gate, feeding full emergency power to the fans. The windings would burn out in a few minutes under this overload, but right now Huber wouldn't bet he or anybody in his platoon would be alive then to know.

Fencing Master's ruined bow lifted on thrust alone. Not high, not even a finger's breadth, but enough to free the skirt from the decking and allow the rear nacelles to shove her forward. Staggering like a drunken ox, the car lurched from the hold and onto the ramp. Her bow dragged again, but this time the fans had gravity to aid them. She accelerated toward the field, scraping up a fountain of red sparks from either side of her hull.

The attackers tried to jump out of the way. Huber didn't know and didn't much care what happened to them when they disappeared below the level of the sensor pickups feeding *Fencing Master*'s main screen. A few gunmen more or less didn't matter; Huber's problem was to get this car clear of the ramp so that *Flame Farter* and *Floosie*, still aboard the freighter, could deploy and deal with the enemy.

Fencing Master reached the bottom of the ramp and drove a trench through the gravel before shuddering to a halt. The shock curtains swathed Huber again; he'd have disengaged the system if he'd had time for nonessentials after the machine's well-meant swaddling clothes freed him. Skewing the stern nacelles slightly to port, he pivoted *Fencing Master* around her bow and rocked free of the rut.

The air above him sizzled with ozone and cyan light: two of the tribarrels in the car's fighting compartment had opened up on the enemy. Somebody'd managed to board while Huber was putting the vehicle in motion. *Fencing Master* was a combat unit again.

There must've been about forty of the attackers all told, ten to each of the shipping containers. Half were now bunched near *Foghorn* or between that car and the starship's ramp. Huber switched *Fencing Master*'s Automatic Defense System live, then used the manual override to trigger three segments.

The ADS was a groove around the car's hull, just above the skirts. It was packed with plastic explosive and faced with barrel-shaped osmium pellets. When the system was engaged, sensors triggered segments of the explosive to send blasts of pellets out to meet and disrupt an incoming missile.

Fired manually, each segment acted as a huge shotgun. The clanging explosions chopped into cat food everyone who stood within ten meters of *Fencing Master*. Huber got a whiff of sweetly-poisonous explosive residues as his nose filters closed again. The screaming fans sucked away the smoke before he could switch back to thermal imaging.

An attacker aboard *Foghorn* had seen the danger in time to duck into the fighting compartment; the pellets scarred the car's armor but didn't penetrate it. The attacker rose, pointing his slug thrower down at the hatch Huber hadn't had time to close. A tribarrel from *Fencing Master* decapitated the hostile.

A powergun converted a few precisely aligned copper atoms into energy which it directed down the weapon's mirror-polished iridium bore. Each light-swift bolt continued in a straight line to its target, however distant, and released its energy as heat in a cyan flash. A 2-cm round like those the tribarrels fired could turn a man's torso into steam and fire; the 20-cm bolt from a tank's main gun could split a mountain.

One of the shipping containers was still jammed halfway open. Soldiers were climbing out like worms squirming up the sides of a bait can. Two raised their weapons when they saw a tribarrel slewing in their direction. Ravening light slashed across them, flinging their maimed bodies into the air. The steel container flashed into white fireballs every time a bolt hit it.

Huber's ears were numb. It looked like the fighting was over, but he was afraid to shut down *Fencing Master*'s fans just in case he was wrong; it was easier to keep the car up than it'd be to raise her again from a dead halt. He did back off the throttles slightly to bring the fans down out of the red zone, though. The bow skirt tapped and rose repeatedly, like a chicken drinking.

Flame Farter pulled into the freighter's hatchway and dipped to slide down the ramp under full control. Platoon Sergeant Jellicoe was behind the central tribarrel. She'd commandeered the leading car when the shooting started rather than wait for her own *Floosie* to follow out of the hold.

Jellicoe fired at something out of sight beyond the shipping containers. Huber touched the menu, importing the view from Jellicoe's gunsight and expanding it to a quarter of his screen.

Three attackers stood with their hands in the air; their weapons were on the gravel behind them. Jellicoe had plowed up the ground alongside to make sure they weren't going to change their minds.

Mercenaries fought for money, not principle. The Slammers and their peers took prisoners as a matter of policy, encouraging their opponents toward the same professional ideal.

Enemies who killed captured Slammers could expect to be slaughtered man, woman and child; down to the last kitten that mewled in their burning homes.

"Bloody Hell . . ." Huber muttered. He raised the seat to look out at the shattered landscape with his own eyes, though the filters still muffled his nostrils.

Haze blurred the landing field. It was a mix of ozone from powergun bolts and the coils of the slug-throwers, burning paint and burning uniforms, and gases from superheated disks that had held the copper atoms in alignment: empties ejected from the tribarrels. Some of the victims were fat enough that their flesh burned also.

The dirigible that'd carried the attackers into position now fled north as fast as the dozen engines podded on outriggers could push it. That wasn't very fast, even with the help of the breeze to swing the big vessel's bow; they couldn't possibly escape.

Huber wondered for a moment how he could contact the dirigible's crew and order them to set down or be destroyed. Plattner's World probably had emergency frequencies, but the data hadn't been downloaded to F-3's data banks yet.

Sergeant Jellicoe raked the dirigible's cabin with her tribarrel. The light-metal structure went up like fireworks in the cyan bolts. An instant later all eight gunners in the platoon were firing, and the driver of *Floosie* was shooting a pistol with one hand as he steered his car down the ramp with the other.

"Cease fire!" Huber shouted, not that it was going to make the Devil's bit of difference. "Unit, cease fire *now!*"

The dirigible was too big for the powerguns to destroy instantly, but the bolts had stripped away swathes of the outer shell and ruptured the ballonets within. Deseau had guessed right: the dirigible got its lift from hydrogen, the lightest gas and cheap enough to dump and replace after every voyage so that the ballonets didn't fill with condensed water over time.

The downside was the way it burned.

Flames as pale and blue as a drowned woman's flesh licked from the ballonets, engulfing the middle of the great vessel. The motors continued to drive forward, but the stern started to swing down as fire sawed the airship in half.

The skeleton of open girders showed momentarily, then burned away.

"Oh bloody buggering Hell!" Huber said. He idled *Fencing Master's* fans and stood up on the seat. *"Hell!"*

"What's the matter, sir?" Learoyd asked. He'd lost his helmet, but he and Sergeant Deseau both were at their combat stations. The tribarrels spun in use, rotating a fresh bore up to fire while the other two cooled. Even so the barrels still glowed yellow from their long bursts. "They were hostiles too, the good Lord knows."

"They were," Huber said grimly. "But the folks living around here are the ones who've hired us."

The remaining ballonets in the dirigible's bow exploded simultaneously, flinging blobs of burning metal hundreds of meters away. Fires sprang up from the treetops, crackling and spewing further showers of sparks.

Huber heard a siren wind from somewhere deep in the forest community. It wasn't going to do a lot of good.

The dirigible's stern, roaring like a blast furnace, struck the terminal building. Some of those inside ran out; they were probably screaming, but Huber couldn't hear them over the sound of the inferno. One fellow had actually gotten twenty meters from the door when the mass of airship and building exploded, engulfing him in flames. He was a carbonized husk when they sucked back an instant later.

Huber sighed. That pretty well put a cap on the day, he figured.

Base Alpha—regimental headquarters on every world that hired the Slammers was Base Alpha—was a raw wasteland bulldozed from several hectares of forest. The clay was deep red when freshly turned, russet when it dried by itself to a form of porous rock, and oddly purple when mixed with plasticizer to form the roadways and building foundations of the camp.

The aircar and driver that'd brought Huber from Rhodesville to Base Alpha were both local, though the woman driving had a cap with a red ball insignia and the words

LOGISTICS SECTION
HAMMER'S REGIMENT

marking her as a Slammers' contract employee. Colonel Hammer brought his own combat personnel and equipment to each deployment, but much of the Regiment's logistics tail was procured for the operation. Supplies and the infrastructure to transport them usually came from what the hiring state had available.

Huber stopped in front of the building marked PROVOST MARSHAL and straightened his equipment belt. The guards, one of them in a gun jeep mounting a tribarrel, watched him in the anonymity of mirrored faceshields. The tribarrel remained centered on Huber's midriff as he approached.

The orders recalling Lieutenant Arne Huber from F-3 directed him to report to the Provost Marshal's office on arrival at Base Alpha. Huber had left his gear with the clerk at the Transient Barracks—he wasn't going to report to the Regiment's hatchetman with a dufflebag and two footlockers—but he hadn't taken time to be assigned a billet. There was a good chance—fifty-fifty, Huber guessed— that he wouldn't be a member of the Slammers when the present interview concluded.

He felt cold inside. He'd known the possibilities the instant he saw the first bolts rake the dirigible, but the terse recall message that followed his report had still made his guts churn.

Nothing to be done about it now. Nothing to be done about it since Sergeant Jellicoe shifted her aim to the dirigible and thumbed her butterfly trigger.

"Lieutenant Huber reporting to the Provost Marshal, as ordered," he said to the sergeant commanding the squad of guards.

"You're on the list," the sergeant said without inflexion. He and the rest of his squad were from A Company; they were the Regiment's police, wearing a stylized gorget as their collar flash. In some mercenary outfits the field police were called Chain Dogs from the gorget; in the Slammers they were the White Mice. "You can leave your weapons with me and go on in."

"Right," said Huber, though the order surprised him. He unslung his belt with the holstered pistol, then handed over the powerknife clipped to a trouser pocket as well.

"He's clean," said a guard standing at the read-out from a detection frame. The sergeant nodded Huber forward.

The Slammers were used to people wanting to kill them. Major Joachim Steuben, the Regiment's Provost Marshal, was obviously used to the Slammers themselves wanting to kill *him*.

Huber opened the door and entered. The building was a standard one-story new-build with walls of stabilized earth and a roof of plastic extrusion. It was a temporary structure so far as the Slammers were concerned, but it'd still be here generations later unless the locals chose to knock it down.

It was crude, ugly, and as solid as bedrock. You could use it as an analogy for the Slammers' methods, if you wanted to.

The door facing the end of the hallway was open. A trim, boyishly handsome man sat at a console there; he was looking toward Huber through his holographic display. If it weren't for the eyes, you might have guessed the fellow was a clerk. . . .

Huber strode down the hall, staring straight ahead. Some of the side doors were open also, but he didn't look into them. He wondered if this was how it felt to be a rabbit facing a snake.

I'm not a rabbit. But if half the stories told about him were true, Joachim Steuben was a snake for sure.

Before Huber could raise his hand to knock on the door jamb, the man behind the desk said, "Come in, Lieutenant; and close it behind you."

A holographic landscape covered the walls of Joachim Steuben's office; flowers poked through brightly lit snow, with rugged slopes in the background. The illusion was seamless and probably very expensive.

"You know why you're here, Huber?" Steuben asked. Everything about the little man was expensive: his manicure, his tailored uniform of natural silk, and the richly chased pistol in a cut-away holster high on his right hip.

The only chair in the office was the one behind Steuben's console.

"I'm here because of the ratfuck at Rhodesville, sir," Huber said. He held himself at attention, though the major's attitude wasn't so much formal as playfully catlike.

Instead of staring at the wall over Steuben's shoulder, Huber met the major's eyes directly. If he hadn't, he'd have been giving in to fear. Because Major Joachim Steuben scared the crap out of him.

"Close enough," Steuben said as though he didn't much care. "What's your excuse?"

"Sir!" Huber said, truly shocked this time. "No excuse, *sir.*"

It was the Nieuw Friesland Military Academy answer, and it was the right answer this time beyond question. Platoon F-3's commander had started to disembark his unit without waiting to issue sidearms and to cycle ammunition for the vehicles' tribarrels up from their storage magazines. Five troopers had died, a sixth had lost her left arm to a ricocheting slug, and it was the Lord's mercy alone that kept the damage from being worse.

Steuben raised an eyebrow and smiled faintly. His console's holographic display was only a shimmer of light from the back side, so Huber didn't know whether the major was really viewing something—Huber's file? A stress read-out?—or if he just left it up to make the interviewee more uncomfortable.

Which would be a pretty good trick, as uncomfortable as Huber felt even before he entered the office.

"A fair number of people in the United Cities think it'd be a mistake to go to war with Solace, Huber," Steuben said calmly. "They want to use the way you gutted Rhodesville as an excuse to cancel the Regiment's contract and go back to peaceful negotiation with Solace over port fees. Do you have any comment about that?"

Huber licked his lips. "Sir," he said, "everything my platoon did at Rhodesville was by my direct order. No blame whatever should attach to any of my troopers."

Steuben laughed. It was a horrible sound, a madman's titter. "Goodness," he said. "An officer who has complete control of his troops while he's driving a damaged combat car? You're quite a paragon, Lieutenant."

Huber licked his lips again. He had to pull his eyes back to meet Steuben's. *Like looking at a cobra. . . .*

"For the time being," the major continued, suddenly businesslike and almost bored, "you've been transferred to command of Logistics Section, Lieutenant Huber. Your office is in Benjamin proper, not Base Alpha here, because most of your personnel are locals. You have a cadre of six or so troopers, all of them deadlined for one reason or another."

He laughed again. "None of the others have burned down a friendly community, however," he added.

"Yes sir," Huber said. He felt dizzy with relief. He'd thought he was out. He'd been pretending he didn't, but he'd walked into this office believing he'd suddenly become a civilian again, with no friends and no future.

Major Steuben shut down his display and stood. He was a small man with broad shoulders for his size and a wasp waist. From any distance, the word "pretty" was the one you'd pick to describe him. Only if you were close enough to see Steuben's eyes did you think of snakes and death walking on two legs. . . .

"I don't have any problem with what you did in Rhodesville, Lieutenant," Steuben said quietly. "But I don't have a problem with a lot of things that seem to bother other people. If the Colonel told me to, I'd shoot you down where you stand instead of transferring you to Log Section. And it wouldn't bother me at all."

He smiled. "Do you understand?"

"Yes sir," Huber said. "I understand."

"Lieutenant Basime was a friend of yours at the Academy, I believe," Steuben said with another of his changes of direction. "She's acting head of our signals liaison with the UC now. Drop in and see her before you report to Log Section. She can fill you in on the background you'll need to operate here in the rear."

He waved a negligent hand. "You're dismissed, Lieutenant," he said. "Close the door behind you."

Huber swung the panel hard—too hard. It slipped out of his hands and slammed.

Major Steuben's terrible laugh followed him back down the hallway.

The ten-place aircar that ferried Huber into Benjamin had six other passengers aboard when it left Base Alpha: three troopers going into town on leave, and three local citizens returning from business dealings with the Regiment. Each trio kept to itself, which was fine with Arne Huber. He wasn't sure what'd happened in Joachim Steuben's office, whether it had all been playacting or if Steuben had really been testing him.

A test Huber'd passed, in that case; seeing as he was not only alive, he'd been transferred into a slot that normally went to a captain. But he wasn't sure, of that or anything else.

He was the only passenger remaining when the car reached its depot, what had been a public school with a sports arena in back. The freshly painted sign out front read

BENJAMIN LIAISON OFFICE
HAMMER'S REGIMENT

with a red lion rampant on a gold field. The driver set the car down by the sign, then lifted away to the arena to shut down as soon as Huber had gotten his luggage off the seat beside him.

Would the local have been more helpfully polite if he'd known Huber was his new boss? Huber smiled faintly. He was too wrung out, from the firefight and now from the interview with Major Steuben, to really care that a direct subordinate had just dumped him out on the pavement.

He bent to shoulder the dufflebag's strap. "We'll watch it for you, sir!" called one of the guards on the front steps. They were alert and fully armed, but they seemed relaxed compared to the White Mice guarding the Provost Marshal's office at Base Alpha.

The troopers of F-3 had been relaxed when they started to disembark, too. Huber winced, wondering how long he was going to remember the feel of Kolbe's body slipping through his fingers like a half-filled waterbed. For the rest of his life, he supposed.

Gratefully he left his gear behind as he mounted the stone steps to the front doors. The four troopers were from G Company, wearing their dismounted kit and carrying 2-cm shoulder weapons. Their two combat cars and the remaining crew members were parked at opposite ends of the arena with their tribarrels elevated on air-defense duty. They'd track anything that came over the horizon, whether aircraft or artillery shell, and blast it if required.

"Where's the signals office, Sergeant?" Huber asked the trooper who'd offered to watch his gear.

"All the way down and to the left, ground floor," the fellow said. "Ah, sir? You're Lieutenant Huber?"

"Yeah, I am," Huber said, suddenly cold. The name tape above his left breast pocket was too faded to read; the fellow must have recognized his face.

"It's an honor to meet you, sir," the sergeant said. "You saved everybody's ass at Rhodesville. We all watched the imagery."

For a moment Huber frowned, thinking that the man was being sarcastic. But he wasn't, and the other troopers were nodding agreement.

"Thank you, Sergeant," he said. His voice wanted to tremble, but he didn't let it. "That isn't the way it looked from where I was sitting, but I appreciate your viewpoint on the business."

Huber went inside quickly, before anybody else could speak. He was as shocked as if the guards had suddenly stripped off their uniforms and started dancing around him. Their words didn't belong in the world of Arne Huber's mind.

Dungaree-clad locals under the direction of a Slammers sergeant were bringing cartloads of files up the back stairs, two on each cart. When they got inside, they rolled them down the hallway to the big room on the right marked CAFETERIA. It was a clerical office now; the tables were arranged back to back and held data consoles manned by locals.

Huber moved to the left to let the carts get past. The sergeant turned from shouting at somebody in the six-wheeled truck outside and saw him. He looked like he was going to speak, but Huber ducked into the door with the recent SIGNALS LIAISON sign before he could.

Huber could have understood it if troopers turned their backs on him and whispered: five dead in a matter of seconds was a heavy loss for a single platoon. That wasn't what was happening.

Lieutenant Adria Basime—Doll to her friends—was bent over the desk of a warrant leader by the door, pointing out something on his console. She saw Huber and brightened. "Arne!" she said. "Come back to my office! My broom closet, more like, but it's got a door. Tory, have me those numbers when I come out, right?"

"Right, El-Tee," agreed the warrant leader. Even Huber, who'd never seen the fellow before, could read the relief in his expression. "Just a couple minutes, that's all I need."

There were a dozen consoles in the outer office, only half of them occupied. Three of the personnel present were Slammers, the others locals.

"I've got ten more people under me," Doll explained as she closed the door of the inner office behind her. "They're out trying to set up nets that we can at least pretend are secure. Plattner's World has a curst good commo network—they'd just about have to, as spread out as the population is. The trouble is, it *all* goes through Solace."

Doll's office wasn't huge, but it compared favorably with the enclosed box of a command car, let alone the amount of space there was in the fighting compartment of a combat car like *Fencing Master*. All a matter of what you've gotten used to, Huber supposed. Doll gestured him to a chair and took the one beside it instead of seating herself behind the console.

"What're you here for, Arne?" she asked. "Did you debrief to the Colonel in person?"

"I thought they were pulling me back to cashier me," Huber said carefully. "I didn't need Major Steuben to tell me how much damage we did to Rhodesville in the firefight. Apparently the locals want to void our contract for that."

Doll frowned. She was petite and strikingly pretty, even in a service uniform. She wore her hair short, but it fluffed like a dazzle of blonde sunlight when she wasn't wearing a commo helmet.

"Some of them maybe do," she said. "The government's in it all the way now, though. They can't back down unless they want to risk not only losing their places but likely being tried for treason if the peace party gets into power."

"Well, I'm transferred to run local transport," Huber said. He felt better already for talking to Doll. She came from a powerful family on Nieuw Friesland and had a keen political sense. If she said Huber hadn't jeopardized the Regiment's contract, that was the gospel truth. "They had to get me out of the field after the way I screwed up, after all."

"Screwed up?" Doll said in surprise. "You guys got ambushed by a company of Harris's Commando while you were still aboard the ship that brought you. You not only saved your platoon, you wiped out the kill team pretty much single-handedly, the way *I* heard it."

"That's not—" Huber said; and as he spoke, his mind flashed him a shard of memory, his finger selecting three segments of the Automatic Defense System and the *Whang!* as they fired simultaneously. He hadn't been thinking of the bunched infantry as human beings, just as a problem to be solved like the jammed turnbuckle. They were figures on his display; and after he'd fired the ADS, they were no longer a problem.

"Via," he whispered. "There must've been twenty of them. . . ."

Huber had killed before, but he hadn't thought of what he'd done in Rhodesville as killing until Doll stated the obvious. He'd been thinking of other things.

"Yeah, well . . ." he said, looking toward the window. "Given the way they caught us with our pants down, things went as well as they could. But we *were* caught. I was caught."

Huber shrugged, forced a smile, and looked at his friend. "Major Steuben said you could give me a rundown on my new section, Doll. The people, I mean. I called up the roster on my helmet on the way here, but they were mostly locals and there's nothing beyond date of hire."

"I can tell you about Hera Graciano," Doll said with a grin. "She's your deputy, and she put the section together before the Regiment's combat assets started to arrive. For what it's worth, it seemed to me she was running things by herself even on the days Captain Cassutt was in the office."

The grin grew broader. She went on, "That wasn't many days, from what I saw. And he's on administrative leave right now."

"I'm glad there'll be one of us who knows the job, then," Huber said, feeling a rush of relief that surprised him. Apparently while his conscious mind was telling him how lucky he was to be alive and still a member of the Regiment, his guts were worried about handling a rear echelon job in which his only background was a three-month rotation in the Academy four years earlier.

"Her father's Agis Graciano," Doll said. "He's Minister of Trade for the UC at the moment, but the ruling party shifts ministries around without changing anything important. He was Chief Lawgiver when the motion to hire the Slammers passed, and he's very much the head of the war party."

Huber frowned as he ran through the possibilities. It was good to have a competent deputy, but a deputy who'd gotten in the habit of running things herself *and* who had political connections could be a problem in herself. And there was one more thing. . . .

"Does the lady get along with her father?" he asked. "Because I know sometimes that can be a worse problem than strangers ever thought of having."

Doll laughed cheerfully. "Hera lives with her father," she said. "They're very close. It's the elder brother, Patroklos, who's the problem. He's in the Senate too, and he'd say it was midnight if his father claimed it was noon."

Her face hardened as she added, "Patroklos is somebody I'd be looking at if I wanted to know how Harris's Commando learned exactly when a single platoon was going to land at Rhodesville, but that's not my job. You shouldn't have any trouble with him now that you're in Log Section."

"Thanks, Doll," Huber said as he rose to his feet. "I guess I'd better check the section out myself now. They're on the second floor?"

"Right," Doll said as she stood up also. "Two things more, though. Your senior non-com, Sergeant Tranter? He's a technical specialist and he's curst good at it. He's helped me a couple times here, finding equipment and getting it to work. The only reason he's not still in field maintenance is he lost a leg when a jack slipped and the new one spasms anytime the temperature gets below minus five."

"That's good to know," Huber said. "And the other thing?"

Doll's grin was back, broader than ever before. "Mistress Graciano is a real stunner, trooper," she said. "And she wasn't a bit interested when *I* tried to chat her up, so I figure that means a handsome young hero like you is in with a chance."

Huber gave his buddy a hug. They were both laughing as they walked back into the outer office.

✧   ✧   ✧

Instead of a stenciled legend, the words LOGISTICS SEC-
TION over the doorway were of brass letters on a background
of bleached hardwood. Huber heard shuffling within the
room as he reached the top of the stairs, then silence. He
frowned and had to resist the impulse to fold back the
flap of his pistol holster before he opened the door.

"All rise for Lieutenant Huber!" bellowed the non-com
standing in front of the console nearest the doorway. He
had curly red hair and a fluffy moustache the full width
of his face. There wasn't a boot on his mechanical left
leg, so Huber didn't need the name tape over the man's
left breast to identify him as Sergeant Tranter.

There were ten consoles in the main room but almost a
score of people, and they'd been standing before Tranter gave
his order. Beside Tranter stood a wispy Slammers trooper;
his left arm below the sleeve of his khakis was covered with
a rash which Huber hoped to the good Lord's mercy wasn't
contagious. The others were local civilians, and the black-
haired young woman who stepped forward offering her hand
was just as impressive as Adria said she was.

"I'm glad you made it, Lieutenant Huber," she said in
a voice as pleasantly sexy as the rest of her. "I'm your
deputy, Hera Graciano."

"Ma'am," Huber said, shaking the woman's hand gingerly.
Was he supposed to have kissed it? There might be something in the briefing cubes that he'd missed, but he doubted
they went into local culture at this social level. It wasn't the
sort of thing the commander of a line platoon was likely to
need.

"Sergeant Tranter, sir," said the non-com. He didn't salute;
saluting wasn't part of the Slammers' protocol, where all
deployments were to combat zones and the main thing a
salute did was target the recipient for any snipers in the
vicinity. "This is Trooper Bayes, he's helping me go over
the vehicles we're offered for hire."

Hera looked ready to step in and introduce her staff too.
Huber raised his hand to forestall her.

"Please?" he said to get attention. "Before I try to

memorize names, Deputy Graciano, could you give me a quick rundown of where the section is and where it's supposed to be?"

He flashed the roomful of people an embarrassed smile. "I intend to carry my weight, but an hour ago I couldn't have told you anything about Log Section beyond that there probably was one."

"Of course," Hera said. "We can use your office—" she nodded to a connecting door "—or mine," this time indicating a cubicle set off from the rest of the room by waist-high paneling.

"We'll use yours," Huber said, because he was pretty sure from what he'd heard about Captain Cassutt that useful information was going to be in the deputy's office instead. "Oh—and I don't have quarters, yet. Is there a billeting officer here or—?"

"I'll take care of it, sir," Tranter said. "Do we need to go pick up your baggage too?"

"It's out in front of the building," Huber said. "I—"

"Right," said Tranter. "Come on, Bayes. Sir, you'll be in Building Five in back of the vehicle park. They're temporaries but they're pretty nice, and engineering threw us up a nice bulletproof wall around the whole compound. Just in case—which I guess I *don't* have to explain to you."

Chuckling at the reference to Rhodesville, the two troopers left the room. Huber smiled too. It was gallows humor, sure; but if you couldn't laugh at grim jokes, you weren't going to laugh very much on service with the Slammers.

And it wasn't that Tranter didn't have personal experience with disaster. The nonskid sole of his mechanical foot thumped the floor with a note distinct from that of the boot on his right foot.

"I'm impressed by Sergeant Tranter," Hera said in a low voice as she stepped into her alcove after Huber. Though it seemed open to the rest of the room, a sonic distorter kept conversations within the cubicle private by canceling any sounds that crossed the invisible barrier. "As a matter of fact, I'm impressed by all the, ah, soldiers assigned to this section. I'd assumed that because they weren't fit for regular duties. . . ."

"Ma'am," Huber said, hearing the unmeant chill in his voice. "We're the Slammers. It's not just that everybody in the Regiment's a volunteer—that's true of a lot of merc outfits. We're the best. We've got the best equipment, we get the best pay, and we've got our pick of recruits. People who don't do the job they're assigned to because they don't feel like it, they go someplace else. By their choice or by the Colonel's."

"I'm sorry," the woman said. "I didn't mean . . ."

Her voice trailed off. She *had* meant she expected people on medical profile to slack off while they were on temporary assignment to ash and trash jobs.

Huber gave an embarrassed chuckle. He felt like an idiot to've come on like a regimental recruiter to somebody who was trying to offer praise.

"Ma'am," he said, "I was out of line. I just mean the folks who stay in the Slammers are professionals. Sergeant Tranter, now—he could retire on full pay. If he didn't, it's because he wants to stay with the Regiment. And I'd venture a guess—"

Made more vivid by Huber's own sudden vision of being cast out of the Slammers.

"—that it's because he's grown to like being around other professionals, other people who do their job *because* it's their job. You don't find a lot of that in the outside world."

She looked at him without expression. "No," she said, "you don't. Well, Lieutenant Huber, again I'm glad for your arrival. And if it's agreeable to you, I prefer 'Hera' to 'ma'am' or 'Deputy Graciano.' But of course it's up to you as section head to decide on the etiquette."

"Hera's fine and so's Arne," Huber said in relief. "And ah—Hera? About Captain Cassutt?"

She gestured to affect disinterest.

"No, you deserve to hear," Huber said, "after the way I got up on my haunches. Cassutt had a bad time the deployment before this one. It wasn't his fault, mostly at any rate, but he got pulled out of the line."

The same way I did, but Huber didn't say that.

"He's off on leave, now," he continued. "He'll either dry out or he'll *be* out. If he's forcibly retired, his pension will keep him in booze as long as his liver lasts—but he won't be anywhere he's going to screw up the business of the Regiment."

"I . . ." Hera said. There was no way of telling what the thought she'd smothered unspoken was. "I see that. Ah, here's the transport that I've either purchased or contracted for, based on volume requirements sent me by the regimental prep section. If you'd like to go over them . . . ?"

She'd set her holographic projector on a 360-degree display so that they both could read the data from their different angles. Huber checked the list of tonnage per unit per day, in combat and in reserve, then the parallel columns giving vehicles and payloads. Those last figures floored him.

"Ma'am?" he said, careting the anomaly with his light wand. "Hera, I mean, these numbers—oh! They're dirigibles?"

She nodded warily. "Yes, we use dirigibles for most heavy lifting," she explained. "They're as fast as ground vehicles even on good roads, and we don't have many good surface roads on Plattner's World."

She frowned and corrected herself, "In the Outer States, that is. Solace has roads and a monorail system for collecting farm produce."

"I don't have anything against dirigibles in general," Huber said, then said with the emphasis of having remembered, "*Hera*. But in a war zone they're—"

He kept his voice steady with effort as his mind replayed a vision of the dirigible crashing into Rhodesville's brick-faced terminal building and erupting like a volcano.

"—too vulnerable. We'll need ground transport, or—how about surface effect cargo carriers? Do you have them here? They look like airplanes, but their wings just compress the air between them and the ground instead of really flying."

"I don't see how that could work over a forest," Hera said tartly—and neither did Huber, when he thought about it. "And as for vulnerable, trucks are vulnerable too if they're attacked, aren't they?"

"A truck isn't carrying five hundred tonnes for a single powergun bolt to light up," Huber said, careful to keep his voice neutral. "And it's not chugging along fifty or a hundred meters in the air where it's a target for a gunner clear in the next state if he knows what he's doing."

He shook his head in memory. "Which some of them will," he added. "If Solace hired Harris's Commando, they'll get a good outfit for air defense too."

Hera didn't move for a moment. Her hands on the display controller in her lap could've been carved from a grainless wood. Then she said, "Yes, if we . . ."

Her fingers caressed the controller. The display shifted like a waterfall; Huber could watch the data, but they meant nothing to him at the speed they cascaded across the air-projected holograms.

"Yes . . ." Hera repeated, then looked up beaming. "There isn't anything like enough ground transport available in the UC alone, but if the other Outer States send us what *they* have, we should be able to meet your needs. Though roads . . ."

"We can use dirigibles to stage supplies to forward depots," Huber said, leaning forward reflexively though the data still didn't mean a cursed thing to him. "We'll need a topo display and for that matter a battle plan to know where, but—"

"Can you do that?" Hera said, also excited by breaking through a barrier she hadn't known of a few moments before. "The map and the battle plan?"

Huber laughed out loud—for the first time since Rhodesville, he guessed. "The topo display's easy," he said, "but lieutenants don't plan regimental operations by themselves. I'll forward what we have to the S-3, the Operations Officer, and his shop'll fill us in when they know more."

He locked his faceshield down and used the helmet's internal processor to sort for the address of the Log Section Deputy's console, then transfer the Regiment's full topographic file on Plattner's World to it. The commo helmet had both the storage and processing power to handle the task alone, but given where they were and the size of the file, Huber let Central in Base Alpha do the job.

He raised his faceshield and saw Hera disconnecting from a voice call. "Oh!" he said. "I'm sorry, I didn't explain—"

"I assumed you were doing your job," she said with a smile that exalted a face already beautiful. "And I can't tell you how reassuring it is to, ah, work for someone who can do that."

She gestured to the phone. "That's what I've been doing too," she said. "I just talked to my father. He's . . ."

She waved a hand in a small circle as if churning a pile of words.

"I've been told who he is," Huber said, saving Hera the embarrassment of explaining that Agis Graciano was the most important single person in the state which had employed the Slammers.

"Good," Hera said with a grateful nod. "When I said we can get ground transport from the other Outer States, I didn't mean that I could commandeer it myself. Father has connections; he'll use them. It'll have to be made to look like a business transaction, even though the other states are helping to fund the UC's stand against the tyranny of Solace."

Huber nodded acknowledgment. He knew better than to discuss politics with anybody, especially a local like Hera Graciano. It wasn't that he didn't understand political science and history: the Academy had an extensive mandatory curriculum in both subjects.

The problem was that the locals always wanted to talk about the rightness of their position. By the time they'd hired Hammer's Slammers, the only right that mattered rode behind iridium armor.

"Ah, Arne?" Hera said. "It's going to be two hours, maybe

three, before father gets back to me. We've certainly got enough work to occupy us till then—"

Their wry grins mirrored one another.

"—but do you have dinner plans for tonight?"

"Ma'am," Huber said in surprise, "I don't know any more about rations than I did about billeting."

The thought made him turn his head. Sergeant Tranter was back; he gave Huber the high sign. The locals still in the office buried their expressions quickly in their consoles; they'd obviously been covertly watching Hera and their new chief the instant before.

"As a matter of fact, I haven't eaten anything yet today," Huber continued to his deputy. "Hera. I didn't have an appetite before my meeting with Major Steuben."

Hera's face changed. "I've met Major Steuben," she said without expression.

Huber nodded understandingly. "I told you we were the best the UC could hire," he said. "Joachim Steuben is better at his job than anybody else I've heard of. But because of what his job is, he's an uncomfortable person to be around for most people."

For everybody who wasn't a conscienceless killer; but Huber didn't say that aloud.

"Yes," Hera said, agreeing with more than the spoken words. "Well, what I was saying—can I take you out to dinner tonight, Lieutenant? You've kept me from making a terrible mistake with the dirigibles, and I'd like to thank you."

"I'd be honored," Huber said, perfectly truthful and for a wonder suppressing his urge to explain he was just doing his job. She knew that, and if she wanted to go to dinner with him, that was fine. He didn't guess it much mattered who paid, not judging from the off-planet dress suit she was wearing even here at work.

"When you say 'trucks,'" he resumed, "what're we talking about? Five-tonners or little utility haulers?"

Hera Graciano was *very* attractive. And if Arne Huber didn't keep his mind on his business, he was going to start blushing.

❖   ❖   ❖

The restaurant was quite obviously expensive. Huber could afford to eat here on his salary, but he probably wouldn't have chosen to.

"Well, I suppose you could say there was significant opposition to confronting Solace," Hera said, frowning toward a point beyond Huber's shoulder as she concentrated on the past. "Some people are always afraid to stand up for their rights, that's inevitable. But the vote in our Senate to hire your Regiment was overwhelming as soon as we determined that the other Outer States would contribute to the charges. My brother's faction only mustered nineteen votes out of the hundred, with seven abstentions."

Wooden beams supported the restaurant's domed ceiling. Their curves were natural, and the polished branches which carried the light fixtures seemed to grow from the wall paneling. The food was excellent—boned rabbit in a bed of pungent leaves, Huber thought, but he'd learned on his first deployment never to ask what went into a dish he found tasty.

His only quibble was with the music: to him it sounded like the wind blowing over a roof missing a number of tiles. The muted keening didn't get in the way of him talking with Hera, and her voice was just as pleasant as the rest of the package.

"And all your income, the income of the Outer States," Huber said, "comes from gathering the raw moss? There's no diversification?"

"The factories refining the *Pseudofistus thalopsis* extract into Thalderol base are in Solace," she said, gesturing with her left hand as she held her glass poised in her right. "That isn't the problem, though: we could build refineries in the Outer States quite easily. We'd have to import technicians for the first few years, but there'd be plenty of other planets ready to help us."

"But . . . ?" said Huber, sipping his own wine. It was pale yellow, though that might have been a product of the beads of light on the branch tips which illuminated the room.

They pulsed slowly and were color-balanced to mimic candleflames.

"But we couldn't build a spaceport capable of handling starships the size of those that now land at Solace," Hera explained. "It's not just the expense, though that's bad enough. The port at Solace is built on a sandstone plate. There's no comparable expanse of bedrock anywhere in the Outer States. An artificial substrate that could support three-hundred kilotonne freighters is beyond possibility."

"I've seen the problems of bringing even small ships down in the UC," Huber said with studied calm. "Though I suppose there's better ports than Rhodesville's."

Hera sniffed. "Better," she said, "but not much better. And of course even the refined base is a high-volume cargo, so transportation costs go up steeply on small hulls."

The dining room had about twenty tables, most of them occupied by expensively dressed locals. The aircar Hera'd brought him here in was built on Nonesuch; it had an agate-faced dashboard and showed a number of other luxury details. She'd parked adjacent to the restaurant, in a tree-shaded lot where the other vehicles were of comparable quality.

Huber wore his newest service uniform, one of three he'd brought on the deployment. The Regiment had a dress uniform, but he'd never bothered to invest in one. Even if he *had* owned such a thing it'd be back in his permanent billet on Nieuw Friesland, since a platoon leader in the field had less space for personal effects than he had formal dinner occasions.

Huber's commo helmet was in his quarters, but his holstered pistol knocked against the arm of the chair he sat in. The Colonel hadn't issued a revised weapons policy for Plattner's World yet; and even if he had, Huber would probably have stuck his 1-cm powergun in a cargo pocket even if he couldn't carry it openly. He'd felt naked in Rhodesville when he saw the buzzbomb swing in his direction and he couldn't do anything but duck.

"Ten months ago . . ." Hera went on. "Ah, that's seven months standard. Ten months ago, Solace raised landing fees five percent. The buyers, Nonesuch and the other planets buying our base and processing it to Thalderol, refused to raise the price they'd pay. We in the Outer States, the people who actually do the work, were left to make up the difference out of our pockets!"

It didn't look like Hera had spent much of her life ranging the forest and gathering moss, but Huber wouldn't have needed his history courses to know that politicians generally said "we" when they meant "you." The funny thing was, they generally didn't see there was a difference.

That wasn't a point a Slammers officer raised with a well-placed member of the state which had hired the Regiment. Aloud he said, "But you do have multiple markets for your drugs? For your base, I mean?"

"Nonesuch takes about half the total," Hera said, nodding agreement. "The rest goes to about a dozen other planets, some more than others. The final processing takes temperature and vibration control beyond anything we could do on Plattner's World. Building a second spaceport would be easier."

She paused, looking at her wine, then across at Huber again. "The government of Nonesuch has been very supportive," she said carefully. "They couldn't get directly involved, but they helped to make the arrangements that led to our hiring Hammer's Regiment."

"But they wouldn't simply raise their payments for Thalderol base?" Huber said, keeping his tone empty of everything but mild curiosity.

"Where would it stop?" Hera blazed. "If those vultures on Solace learn that they can get away with extortion, they'll keep turning the screws!"

Based on what Huber knew about the price of anti-aging drugs, he didn't think a five-percent boost in the cost of raw materials was going to make a lot of difference, but he didn't need to get into that. There was more going on than he saw; more going on than Hera was willing to tell him, that was obvious; and probably a lot more going on than even she knew.

None of that mattered. The result of all those unseen wheels whirling was that Colonel Hammer had a lucrative contract, and Lieutenant Arne Huber was spending the evening with a very attractive woman.

"My brother claims that even with other states defraying the costs, the UC is taking all the military risk itself," Hera continued. "But somebody has to have the courage to take a stand! When the other states see Solace back down, they'll be quick enough to step up beside us and claim credit!"

"It didn't seem when I arrived . . ." Huber said, the chill in his guts cooling his tone more than he'd intended. "That backing down was the way Solace was planning to play it."

He smiled, hoping that would make his words sound less like the flat disagreement that he felt. Hera was smart and competent, but she was turning her face from the reality the ambush at Rhodesville would've proved to a half-wit. It wasn't what she wanted to believe, so she was using her fine intellect to prove a lie.

"Well then, if they persist—" she said, but broke off as the waiter approached the table.

"More wine, sir and madam?" he asked. "Or perhaps you've changed your mind about dessert?"

The outside door opened, drawing Huber's eyes and those of the waiter. It was late for customers, though the restaurant hadn't started dimming the lights.

"Patroklos!" Hera said, her head turning because Huber's had. "What are you doing here?"

Not coming for dinner, that was for sure. Senator Patroklos Graciano was a good twenty years older than his sister. He was a beefy man, not fat but heavier than he'd have been if he were a manual laborer. His features were regular, handsome even, but they showed no resemblance whatever to Hera's.

Huber wondered if the two children had different mothers,

but that wasn't the question at the top of his mind just this instant. He got to his feet; smoothly, he thought, but he heard the chair go over behind him with a crash on the hardwood floor and he didn't care about *that* either.

"What am I doing here?" Patroklos said. He had a trained voice; he used its volume to fill the domed restaurant. "I'm not entertaining the butcher who destroyed Rhodesville, that's one thing! Are you part of the mercenaries' price, dear sister? Your body as an earnest for the bodies of all the women of the United Cities?"

Chairs were scuffling all over the room; a pair of diners edged toward the service area since Patroklos stood in front of the outside door. There were two waiters and the female manager looking on, but they'd obviously decided to leave the business to the principals involved for now.

Huber was as sure as he could be that there wasn't going to be trouble—worse trouble—here unless something went badly wrong. Patroklos wasn't nearly as angry as he sounded, and he'd come into the restaurant by himself. If his bodyguards had been with him—Patroklos was the sort who had bodyguards—it would've been a different matter.

"Patroklos, you're drunk!" Hera said. He wasn't drunk, but maybe Hera didn't see her brother's real plan. "Get out of here and stop degrading the family name!"

She hadn't gotten up at the first shouting. Now that Patroklos was only arm's length away, she was trapped between the table and her brother's presence.

Huber thought of walking around to join her, but that might start things moving in the wrong direction. From the corners of his eyes he could see that others of the remaining customers were eyeing him with hard faces. The "butcher of Rhodesville" line had probably struck a chord even with people who didn't support Patroklos' position on the Regiment as a whole.

"Degrade the family name?" Patroklos shouted. "A fine concern for a camp follower!"

Huber scraped the table back and toward his left side, spilling a wine glass and some flatware onto the floor. Freed from its presence, Hera jumped to her feet and retreated to where Huber stood. He swung her behind him with his left arm.

That wasn't entirely chivalry. Huber wasn't worried about her brother, but the chance of somebody throwing a bottle at him from behind was another matter.

If I'd known there was going to be a brawl, I'd have asked for a table by the wall. He grinned at the thought; and that was probably the right thing to do, because Patroklos' mouth—open for another bellow—closed abruptly.

The Slammers didn't spend a lot of training time on unarmed combat: people didn't hire the Regiment for special operations, they wanted an armored spearhead that could punch through any shield the other guy raised. Huber wasn't sure that barehanded he could put this older, less fit man away since the fellow outweighed him by double, but he wasn't going to try. Huber would use a chair with the four legs out like spearpoints and then finish the job with his boots. . . .

"Fine, hide behind your murderer for now, you whore!" Patroklos said, but his voice wasn't as forceful as before. He eased his body backward though as yet without shifting his feet. "You'll have nowhere to hide when the citizens of our glorious state realize the madness into which you and our father have thrown them!"

Patroklos backed quickly, then jerked the door open and stomped out into the night. The last glance he threw over his shoulder seemed more speculative than angry or afraid.

"Ma'am!" Huber said, turning his head a few degrees to face the manager without ever letting his eyes leave the empty doorway. "Get our bill ready ASAP, will you?"

"Maria, put it on my account!" Hera said. She swept the room with her gaze. In the same clear, cold voice she went on, "I won't bother apologizing for my brother, but I hope his display won't encourage others into drunken boorishness!"

She's noticed the temper of the onlookers too, Huber thought. Stepping quickly, he led the girl between tables Patroklos had emptied with his advance. They went out the front door.

The night air was warm and full of unfamiliar scents. A track of dust along the street and the howl of an aircar accelerating—though by now out of sight—indicated how and where Patroklos had departed. There were no pedestrians or other vehicles; the buildings across the street were offices over stores, closed and dark at this hour.

Huber sneezed. Hera whirled with a stark expression.

"Just dust," he explained. He rubbed the back of his hand over his eyes. "Or maybe the tree pollen, that's all. Nothing important."

He felt like a puppeteer pulling the strings of a body that'd once been his but was now an empty shell. The thing that walked and talked like Arne Huber didn't have a soul for the moment; that'd been burned out by the adrenaline flooding him in the restaurant a few moments ago. The emotionless intellect floating over Huber's quivering body was bemused by the world it observed.

"I can't explain my brother's behavior!" Hera said. She walked with her head down, snarling the words to her feet. "He's angry because father remarried—there's no other reason for what he does!"

Huber didn't speak. He didn't care about the internal politics of the Graciano clan, and the girl was only vaguely aware of his presence anyway. She was working out her emotions while he dealt with his. They were different people, so their methods were different.

It hadn't been a lucky night, but things could've been worse. Just as at Rhodesville . . .

They stepped around the corner of the building into the parking lot. Things got worse.

There were at least a dozen of them, maybe more, waiting among the cars. They started forward when Huber and the girl appeared. They had clubs; maybe some of them had guns besides. The light on the pole overhead concealed features instead of revealing them.

"Who are you?" Hera called in a voice of clear command. "Attendant! Where's the lot attendant?"

"Get back into the restaurant," Huber said. *"Now!"*

He grabbed the girl's shoulder with his left hand and swung her behind him, a more brutal repetition of what he'd done with her earlier. Patroklos had been posturing in the restaurant. These thugs of his, though—this was meant for real.

Huber thumbed open his holster flap and drew his pistol. He held it muzzle-down by his thigh for the moment.

"He's got a gun!" said one of the shadowy figures in a rising whisper. That was a good sign; it meant they hadn't figured on their victim being armed.

"Shut up, Lefty!" another voice snarled.

The pistol had a ten-round magazine. Huber knew how to use the weapon, but if these guys were really serious he wouldn't be able to put down more than two or three of them before it turned into work for clubs and knives. . . .

Huber backed a step, hoping Hera had done as he ordered; hoping also that there wasn't another gang of them waiting at the restaurant door to close the escape route. If Huber got around the corner again, he could either wait and shoot every face that appeared or he could run like Hell was on his heels. Running was the better choice, but he didn't think—

"Easy now," said the second voice. "Now, all to—"

A big aircar—it might've been the one that ferried Huber from Base Alpha to Benjamin—came down the street in a scream of fans. It hit hard, lifting a doughnut of dust from the unpaved surface. That wasn't a bad landing, it was a combat insertion where speed counted and grace just got you killed.

Half the score of men filling the back of the vehicle wore khaki uniforms; they unassed the bouncing aircar with the ease of training and experience. The civilians were clumsier, but they were only a step or two behind when the

Slammers tore into the local thugs with pipes, wrenches, and lengths of reinforcing rod.

"Run for it!" shouted the voice that'd given the orders before. He was preaching to the converted; none of his gang had stayed around to argue with the rescue party. Huber stood where he was, now holding the pistol beside his ear.

"Arne!" Doll Basime called. "This way, fast!"

She stood in the vehicle's open cab, her sub-machine gun ready but not pointed. Sergeant Tranter was at the rear of the aircar; he had a 2-cm shoulder weapon. Both wore their faceshields down, probably using light-enhanced viewing. If a thug had decided to turn it into a gunfight, he and his buddies were going to learn what a *real* gunfight was like.

Huber ran for the truck. He heard screams from the parking lot; thumps followed by crackling meant that some of the expensive aircars were going to have body damage from being used as trampolines by troops in combat boots.

That didn't even begin to bother Huber. He remembered the eyes on him in the restaurant.

"Recall! Recall! Recall!" bellowed the loudspeaker built into Tranter's commo helmet. The other troopers had helmet intercoms, but the civilians didn't.

"How'd you get the word, Doll?" Huber said as he jumped into the back of the vehicle, just behind Basime. Another of the party had been driving; the cab would be crowded even with two.

Doll was too busy doing her job to answer him. Her throat worked as she snarled an order over the intercom, though with the faceshield down her helmet muted the words to a shadow.

Sirens sounded from several directions. They were coming closer.

The rescue party piled into the back of the truck. Two Slammers and a civilian remained in the parking lot, putting the boot in with methodical savagery. Their victim was out of sight behind the parked cars. One of the thugs must've tried to make a fight out of it—that, or he'd hit some-body while flailing about in panic.

"Move it, Bayes!" Tranter called.

Huber pointed his pistol skyward and fired. The *thump*! and blue flash both reflected from overhanging foliage. For a moment the bolt was as striking as the blast from a tank's main gun. The three stragglers looked up in palpable shock, then ran to join their fellows.

Huber hung over the truck's sidewall to make sure Hera was all right. She wasn't in sight, so she'd probably gotten back into the restaurant. If she hadn't, well, better the local cops look into it than that the cops spend their energy discussing matters with the rescue party. *That* was a situation that could go really wrong fast.

The fans roared. Kelso, a civilian clerk from Log Section, was in the driver's seat. From the way the vehicle'd nosed in, Huber'd guessed a trooper was at the controls.

The aircar slid forward, gathering speed but staying within a centimeter of the gravel. Faces staring from the restaurant's front windows vanished as the car roared by in cascades of dust and pebbles.

Only when the vehicle had reached 90 kph and the end of the block did Kelso lift it out of ground effect. He banked *hard* through a stand of towering trees.

Huber could still hear sirens, but they didn't seem to be approaching nearly as fast as a moment before. Witnesses being what they were, Huber's single pistol shot had probably been described as a tank battle.

Doll put her hand on Huber's shoulder. Raising her faceshield she shouted over the windrush, "That was a little too close on the timing, Arne. Sorry about that."

"It was perfect, Doll," he shouted back. The aircar was racketing along at the best speed it could manage with the present overload. That was too fast for comfort in an open vehicle, but torn metal showed where the folding top had been ripped off in a hurry to lower the gross weight. "Perfect execution, too. What brought you?"

They were heading in the direction of the Liaison Office,

staying just over the treetops. Kelso had his running lights off. Red strobes high in the sky marked the emergency vehicles easing gingerly toward the summons.

"That's a funny thing," Doll said, her pretty face scrunched into a frown. "Every trooper billeted at Base Benjamin got an alert, saying a trooper needed help—and if there was shooting, the best result would be courts martial for everybody involved. It gave coordinates that turned out to be you. We hauled ass till we got here."

She shrugged. "Sergeant Tranter invited some civilian drivers from Log Section, too. I guess there was a card game going when the call came."

"But who gave the alert?" Huber said. "Did the—"

He'd started to ask if the restaurant manager had called it in; that was dumb, so he swallowed the final words. There hadn't been time for a civilian to get an alarm through the regimental net.

"There was no attribution," Basime said. She lifted her helmet and ran a hand through her short hair; it was gleaming with sweat. "That means it had to come from Base Alpha; and it had to be a secure sector besides, not the regular Signals Office."

"The White Mice?" Huber said. That was the only possible source, but . . . "But if it was them, why didn't they respond themselves?"

"You're asking me?" Doll said. She grinned, but the released strain had aged her by years. She'd known she was risking her career—and life—to respond to the call.

"I will say, though," she added quietly, "that whoever put out the alarm seems to be a friend of yours. And that's better than having him for an enemy."

"Yeah," said Huber. Through the windscreen he could see the converted school and the temporary buildings behind it. Kelso throttled back.

Much better to have him for a friend; because the people whom Joachim Steuben considered enemies usually didn't live long enough to worry about it.

✧　　　✧　　　✧

This time Huber had his equipment belt unbuckled and his knife in his hand before he stepped out of the four-place aircar in which Sergeant Tranter had brought him to the Provost Marshal's office. The sky of Plattner's World had an omnipresent high overcast; it muted what would otherwise be an unpleasantly brilliant sun and was turning the present dawn above Base Alpha into gorgeous pastels.

Tranter had shut down the car in the street. He sat with his arms crossed, staring into the mirrored faceshields of the White Mice on guard.

The guards didn't care, but the trivial defiance made Tranter feel better; and Huber felt a little better also. He wasn't completely alone this time as he reported as ordered to Major Steuben.

"Go on through, Lieutenant," said the faceless guard who took Huber's weapons. "He's waiting for you."

Huber walked down the hall to the office at the end. The door was open again, but this time Steuben dimmed his holographic display as Huber approached. The major even smiled, though that was one of those things that you didn't necessarily want to take as a good omen.

"Close the door behind you, Lieutenant," Steuben said as Huber raised his hand to knock. "I want to discuss what happened last night. How would you—"

He waited till the panel closed behind Huber's weight; it was a much sturdier door than it looked from the thin plastic sheathing on the outside.

"—describe the event?"

"Sir," Huber said. He didn't know what Steuben expected him to say. The truth might get some good people into difficulties, so in a flat voice he lied, "I was eating with my deputy in a restaurant she'd chosen. When we went out to get into her aircar, we were set on by thugs who'd been breaking into cars. Fortunately some off-duty troopers were passing nearby and came to our aid. My deputy went home in her own vehicle—"

He sure hoped she had. He didn't have a home number

to call Hera at, and the summons waiting at Huber's billets to see the Provost Marshal at 0600 precluded Huber
from waiting to meet Hera when she arrived at office.

"—and I returned to my quarters with the fellows who'd
rescued us."

"Want to comment on the shooting?" Steuben asked with
a raised eyebrow. "The use of powerguns in the middle
of Benjamin?"

"Sir," Huber said, looking straight into the hard brown
eyes of Colonel Hammer's hatchetman, "I didn't notice any
shooting. I believe the business was handled with fists
alone, though some of the thugs may have had clubs."

Steuben reached into his shirt pocket and came out with
a thin plastic disk. He flipped it to Huber, who snatched
it out of the air. It was the pitted gray matrix which had
held copper atoms in place in a powergun's bore; a 1-cm
empty, fired by a pistol or sub-machine gun.

Specifically, fired from Huber's pistol.

"Sir, I don't have anything useful to say about this,"
Huber said. The bastard across the desk could only kill
him once, so there wasn't any point in going back now.
"If it came from the scene of the fight, it must have been
fired after we left there."

"It's old news, Lieutenant," Steuben said, "and we won't
worry about it. If there had been a shooting incident . . . let's
say, if you'd shot one or more citizens of the UC, you'd
have been dismissed from the Regiment. It's very possible
that you'd have been turned over to the local authorities
for trial. Our contract with the UC really *is* in the balance
as a result of what happened at Rhodesville."

"Then I'm glad there wasn't any shooting, sir," Huber
said. "I intend to stay inside the Liaison Office for the foreseeable future so that there won't be a repetition."

The holographic scenes on the major's wall weren't still
images as Huber had thought the first time he'd seen them.
What had initially been a tiny dot above the horizon had
grown during the interview to a creature flying at a great
height above the snowfields.

Steuben giggled. Huber felt his face freeze in a rictus of horror.

"Aren't you going to tell me it isn't fair, Lieutenant?" the major said. "Or perhaps you'd like to tell me that you're an innocent victim whom I'm making the scapegoat for political reasons?"

For the first time since the the ambush at Rhodesville, Huber felt angry instead of being frightened or sick to his stomach. "Sir, you know it's not fair," he said, much louder than he'd allowed his voice to range before in this room. "Why should I waste my breath or your time? And why should you waste *my* time?"

"I take your point, Lieutenant," the major said. He rose to his feet; gracefully as everything he did was graceful. He was a small man, almost childlike; he was smiling now with the same curved lips as a serpent's. "You're dismissed to your duties—unless perhaps there's something you'd like to ask me?"

Huber started to turn to the door, then paused with a frown. "Sir?" he said. "How many people could have given Harris's Commando—given Solace—accurate information as to when a single platoon was landing at Rhodesville?"

"Besides members of the Regiment itself?" Steuben said, his reptilian smile a trifle wider. Huber nodded tersely. He wasn't sure if the question was serious, so he treated it as though it was.

"A handful of people within the UC government certainly knew," the major said. "A larger number, also people within the government or with connections to it, could probably have gotten the information unattributably. But it wasn't something that was being discussed on the streets of Rhodesville, if that's what you meant."

"Yes sir," said Huber. "That's what I meant."

He went out the door, closing it behind him as he'd been told to do the first time he'd left Major Steuben's presence. It was good to have the heavy panel between him and the man in that room.

He walked quickly. There was a lot of work waiting in

Log Section; and there was another job as well, a task for the officer who'd been commanding platoon F-3 when it landed at Rhodesville.

Huber hadn't forgotten Kolbe or the crew of *Foghorn*; and he hadn't forgotten what he owed their memory.

Hera Graciano arrived at Log Section half an hour after Huber and the sergeant got back from Base Alpha, well before the staff was expected to show up for work. She stepped in, looking surprised to find the Slammers at their consoles.

"I rearranged things a bit." Huber said with a grin. "I moved my desk into the main office here; I figure we can use Captain Cassutt's office for a break room or something, hey?"

"Well, if you like . . ." Hera said. "But I don't think . . ."

"If they see me . . ." Huber explained quietly. Sergeant Tranter watched with the care of an enlisted man who knows that the whims of his superiors may mean his job or his life. "Then it's easier for them to believe we're all part of the same team. Given the number of factions in the UC right at the moment, I'd like there to be a core of locals who figure I'm on whatever their side is."

"I'm very sorry about last night!" Hera said, bowing her head in the first real confusion Huber had noticed in her demeanor. She crossed the room quickly without glancing at Tranter by the door. "That isn't normal, even for my brother. I think something's gone wrong with him, badly wrong."

"Any one you walk away from," Huber said brightly. He was immensely relieved to learn that Hera was all right, but he *really* didn't want to discuss either last night or the wider situation with her. "I'm paid to take risks, after all. Let's let it drop, shall we?"

"Yes," she said, settling herself behind her desk. Her expression was a mixture of relief and puzzlement. "Yes, of course."

Hera hadn't powered up the privacy shield as yet, so Huber could add smilingly, "By the way—does the UC have a central population registry? An office that tracks everybody?"

"What?" Hera said in amazement. "No, of course not! I mean, do other planets have that sort of thing? We have a voter's list, is that what you mean?"

"Some places are more centralized, yeah," Huber said, thinking of the cradle to grave oversight that the Frisian government kept on its citizens. Those who stayed on the planet, at least; which was maybe a reason to join a mercenary company, though the Colonel kept a pretty close eye on his troopers as well.

Through the White Mice . . .

"No matter," he continued. "Would you download a list of all the Regiment's local employees and their home addresses to me before you get onto your own work, Hera? It may be in this console I inherited from the good captain, but I sure haven't been able to locate it."

"Yes, of course . . ." she said, bringing her console live. She seemed grateful for an excuse to look away from Huber. Last night had been a real embarrassment to her.

One more thing to thank her brother for. It was pretty minor compared to the rest of what Huber suspected Patroklos was involved in, though.

Other clerks were coming in to the office; perhaps merely to make a good impression on the new director, but maybe they'd heard about the business last night and hoped to get more gossip. Huber grinned blandly and set to work with the file that appeared in his transfer box.

The business of the day proceeded. Log Section had been running perfectly well without Huber for the past three weeks, but as more starships landed—three in one mad hour at the relatively large field here in Benjamin, and four more during the day at other members of the United Cities—there were frequent calls to the Officer in Command of Log Section. None of the Slammers calling wanted to talk to a wog: they wanted a *real* officer wearing the lion rampant of the Regiment. They were fresh out of stardrive, with headaches and tempers to match.

Huber fielded the calls. He almost never knew the answer to the angry questions himself, but he dumped quick summaries to Hera through his console while holding the speaker on the line. As a general rule she had the answer for him—a vehicle dispatched, a storage warehouse located, or a staff member on the way to the scene—in a minute or less. When it was going to take longer, that warning appeared on Huber's console and he calmed the caller down as best he could.

Not everybody wanted to calm down. An artillery lieutenant shouted, "Look, are you going to stop being a dickheaded pissant and get my bloody hog out of the marsh you had us land in?"

Huber shouted back, "Look, redleg, when my platoon drove out of the ship there was a kill-team from Harris's Commando waiting for us. We managed. If you fools can't avoid a hole in the ground, then don't expect a lot of sympathy here! Now, I say again—there's a maintenance and recovery platoon due in Youngblood's Vale tomorrow and I'll vector the recovery vehicle to you people in Henessey ASAP. If you'd prefer to keep saying you want me to drag heavy equipment out of my ass because your driver's blind, you can talk to an open line!"

There was a pause, then, "Roger, we'll wait. Two-Ay-Six out."

One thing a soldier learns by surviving any length of time in a war zone is that you use whatever you've got available. Huber smiled grimly.

In between the work of the Log Section, he played with the data he was gathering on his other job. Huber didn't have the sort of mind that leaped instantly to the right answer to complex questions. He worked things over mentally, turning the bits and fitting them first this way, then another. It was a lot like doing jigsaw puzzles. At the end of the process there was an answer, and he guessed he'd be working on it till he found what the answer was.

Hera left for lunch. She invited Huber but didn't argue when he turned her down, and she didn't argue either when he insisted she go on as she'd planned instead of staying in the office because he was staying. Huber knew as well as the next guy how important it was to get some time away from the place you were working; otherwise you could lock yourself down tighter than happened to most prisoners.

It didn't apply to him, of course. He was too busy to worry about where his butt happened to be located at the moment.

The Regiment already employed more than three hundred UC citizens. There'd be over a thousand by the time the deployment was complete, and that was without counting the number of recreation personnel hired to deal with the off-duty requirements of the combat troopers. On a place like Plattner's World most of that last group would be freelance, but the Colonel would set up and staff official brothels if the free market didn't appear to him to be up to the job.

Central Repair was one of the larger employers of local personnel. CR was where heavily damaged vehicles were brought: for repair if possible, for stripping and scrapping if it weren't. Line maintenance was mostly done at company level, but at battalion in the case of major drive-train components; Central Repair dealt with more serious or complex problems.

Fencing Master was thus far the Regiment's only serious battle damage on Plattner's World, but there were plenty of things that could go wrong with complex vehicles transiting between star systems. Furthermore, there were a dozen blowers deadlined from the previous contract. They'd been shipped to Plattner's World for repair instead of being held behind and repaired in place.

Late in the day, Huber got around to checking addresses. There were many groupings of employees who gave the same home address. That didn't concern him. Besides members of the same family all working in the booming new industry, war, many of the personnel came into Benjamin from outlying locations. Those transients lived in apartments or rooming houses here in the city.

Three of the mechanics in Central Repair lived at what the voter registration records—forwarded to Huber by Doll Basime; he didn't go through Hera to get them—listed as the address of Senator Patroklos Graciano. *That* was a matter for concern.

Huber looked around the office. Hera was out of the room; off to the latrine, he supposed. That made things a little simpler. Kelso, the local who'd driven the rescue vehicle the night before, looked up and caught his eye. Huber gestured him over, into the area of the privacy screen.

"Sir?" Kelso said brightly. His thin blond hair made him look younger than he probably was; close up Huber guessed the fellow was thirty standard years old. Kelso dressed a little more formally than most of the staff and he seemed to want very much to please. *Looking for a permanent billet with the Regiment,* Huber guessed; which was all right with Huber, and just might work out.

"I've got three names and lists of former employers here," Huber said, running hardcopy of the employment applications as he spoke. "I want you to check these out—just go around to the listed employers and ask about the people. I'm not looking for anything formal. If the boss isn't in—"

He handed the three flimsies to Kelso.

"—but the desk clerk remembers them, that's fine. Take one of the section jeeps, and I'd rather have the information sooner than later."

"Sir, it's pretty late . . ." Kelso said with a concerned expression. "Should I chase people down at their homes if the business is closed, or—"

Huber thought for a moment, then laughed. "No, nothing like that," he said. "But if you can get me the data before tomorrow midday, I'd appreciate it."

"You can count on me, sir!" the fellow said. Holding

the hardcopy in his hand, he trotted past the consoles—
some of them empty; it *was* getting late—and out the door
just as Hera returned.

They passed; she glanced questioningly from the disap-
pearing local and then to Huber. Huber waved cheerfully
and immediately bent to his console, calling up information on the Officer in Charge of Central Repair. Hera might
have asked what was going on with Kelso if Huber hadn't
made it pointedly clear that he was busy.

Which he was, of course, but it bothered him to treat
her this way. Well, it'd bother her worse if he told her
what he was doing; and there was also the risk that . . .

Say it: the risk that this bright, competent, woman,
attractive in all respects—would be loyal to her brother if
push came to shove, instead of being loyal to the regiment of off-planet killers she happened to be working for
at the moment. Surviving in a combat environment meant
taking as few risks as possible, because the ones you
couldn't avoid were plenty bad enough.

CR was at present under the command of Senior Warrant Leader Edlinger; Buck Edlinger to his friends, and
Huber knew him well enough from previous deployments
to be in that number. Instead of doing a data transmission through the console, Huber made a voice call. It took
a moment for Edlinger to answer; he didn't sound pleased
as he snarled, "Edlinger, and who couldn't bloody wait
for me to call back, tell me!"

"Arne Huber, Buck," Huber replied calmly. He'd been
shouted at before—and worse. Edlinger'd been squeezed
into a place too tight for him to wear his commo helmet,
and he wasn't best pleased to be dragged out of there to
take a voice call slugged URGENT. "I've got a problem that
may turn out to be your problem too. Are your people
working round the clock right now?"

"Via!" Edlinger said. "No, not by a long ways. You're
in Log Section now, Huber? What're you about to drop
on us? Did a shipload of blowers come down hard?"

"Nothing like that, Buck," Huber said. Edlinger must have

checked Huber's status when *Fencing Master* came in for repair. "I want to check what three of your locals've been working on, and I want to check it when the locals and their friends aren't around."

"What d'ye know about maintenance oversight, Huber?" Edlinger said; not exactly hostile, but not as friendly as he'd have been if it hadn't seemed an outsider was moving in on his territory.

"I know squat," Huber said, "but I've got a tech here, Sergeant Tranter, who you gave curst good fitness reports to back when when he worked for you. And you can help, Buck—I'd just as soon you did. But this isn't a joke."

That was the Lord's truth. This could be much worse than a company of armored vehicles getting bent in a starship crash.

"You got Tranter?" Edlinger said. "Oh, that's okay, then. Look, Huber, I can have everybody out of here by twenty hundred hours if that suits you. Okay?"

"That's great, Buck," Huber said, nodding in an enthusiasm that Edlinger couldn't see over a standard regimental voice-only transmission. "We'll be there at twenty hundred hours."

"Hey Huber?" Edlinger added as he started to break the connection.

"Right?"

"Can you tell me who you're worried about, or do I have to guess?"

That was a fair question. "Their names are Galieni, Osorio, and Triulski," Huber said, reading them off the display in front of him. "Do they ring a bell?"

Edlinger snorted something between disgust and real concern. "Ring a bell?" he said. "You bet they do. They're the best wrenches I've been able to find. I'd recommend them all for permanent status in the Regiment if they wanted to join."

Huber grimaced. "Yeah, I thought it might be like that," he said.

"And Huber?" Edlinger added. "One more thing. You

wanted to know what they're working on? That's easy. They're putting your old blower, *Fencing Master,* back together. She'll go out late tomorrow the way things are getting on."

When Tranter came in with Bayes, the sergeant laughing as the trooper gestured in the air, Huber cued his helmet intercom and said, "Sarge? Come talk to me in my little garden of silence, will you?"

A console with regimental programming like Hera Graciano's could eavesdrop on intercom transmissions unless Huber went to more effort on encryption than he wanted to. It was simpler and less obtrusive to use voice and the privacy screen that was already in place around his area of the office.

Tranter patted Bayes on the shoulder and sauntered over to the lieutenant as though the idea was his alone rather than a response to a summons. Huber was becoming more and more impressed with the way Tranter picked up on things without need for them to be said. Sometimes Huber wasn't sure exactly what he'd say if he did have to explain.

"Do we have a problem, El-Tee?" Tranter asked as he bent over the console, resting his knuckles on the flat surface beside the holographic display.

Huber noticed the "we." He grinned. "We're going maybe to solve one before it crops up, Sarge," he said. "Are you up to poking around in a combat car tonight?"

"I guess," Tranter said, unexpectedly guarded. "Ah—what would it be we're looking for, El-Tee? Booze? Drugs?"

Huber burst out laughing when he understood Tranter's concern. "Via, Sarge!" he said. "You've been on field deployments, haven't you? All that stuff belongs, and so does anything else that helps a trooper get through the nights he's not going to get through any other way. No, I'm looking for stuff that our people didn't put there. I don't know what it'll be; but I do know that if something's there, I want to know what it is. Okay?"

Tranter beamed as he straightened up. "Hey, a chance

to be a wrench again instead of pushing electrons? You got it, boss!"

"Pick me up at the front of the building at a quarter of eight, then," Huber said. "We need to be at Central Repair on the hour—I've cleared it with the chief. Oh, and Tranter?"

"Sir?" The sergeant looked . . . not worried exactly, but wary. He wasn't going to ask what was going on; but something was and though he seemed to trust Huber, a veteran non-com knows just how disastrously wrong officers' bright ideas are capable of going.

"Don't talk about it," Huber said. "And you know that gun you were holding last night? Think you could look one up for me?"

"Roger that, sir!" Tranter said, perfectly cheerful again. "Or if you'd rather have a sub-machine gun?"

Huber shook his head. "I want something with authority," he explained. "I don't think there's a chance in a million we'll have somebody try to pull something while we're flying between here and Central Repair tonight . . . but I do think that if it happens, I'm going to make sure we're the car still in the air at the end of it."

Chuckling in bright good humor, the sergeant returned to his console. The other clerks looked at him, but Hera was watching Huber instead.

Huber cued his intercom and said, "What's the latest on the ground transport situation, Hera? Did your father come through?"

The best way to conceal the rest of what was going on was to bury it in the work of Log Section; and the fact that quite a lot of work was getting done that way was a nice bonus.

Central Repair was a block of six warehouses in the north-central district of Benjamin. Engineer Section had thrown up a wall of plasticized earth around the complex as a basic precaution, but the location was neither secure nor really defensible despite the infantry company and platoon of combat cars stationed there.

Tranter brought the four-place aircar down at CR's entrance gate. They were tracked all the way by a tribarrel of the combat car there—*Flesh Hook*, another F Company vehicle—and, for as long as the aircar was above the horizon, by the guns of two more cars within the compound. Huber would've been just as happy to ride to Repair in a Regimental-standard air-cushion jeep, but Tranter was proud of being able to drive an aircar. There were plenty of them in Log Section's inventory since they were the normal means of civilian transportation on Plattner's World.

Tranter wasn't a good aircar driver—he was too heavy-handed, trying to outguess the AI—and there was always the chance that a trooper on guard would decide the car wobbling toward the compound was hostile despite Huber's extreme care to check in with detachment control. Still, Tranter was investing his time and maybe more to satisfy his section leader's whim; the least the section leader could do was let him show off what he fondly imagined were his talents.

The car bumped hard on the gravel apron in front of Central Repair. The gate was open, but *Flesh Hook* had parked to block the entrance. Huber raised his faceshield and said, "Lieutenant Huber, Log Section, to see Chief Edlinger. He's expecting me."

"Good to see you, El-Tee," called the trooper behind the front tribarrel. The driver watched from his hatch, but the two wing guns were unmanned; they continued to search the sky in air defense mode under detachment control. "You guys earned your pay at Rhodesville, didn't you? Curst glad it was you and not us in F-2."

"I don't know that I feel the same way," Huber said; but even if he'd shouted, he couldn't have been heard over the rising howl of drive fans as the combat car shifted sideways to open the passage. Tranter drove through the gate in surface effect.

Central Repair would've been much safer against external attack if it had been located within Base Alpha. It remained separate because of the greater risk of having so

many local personnel—well over a hundred if combat operations persisted for any length of time—inside the Regimental HQ. Losing Central Repair would be a serious blow
to the Regiment; the sort of damage a saboteur could do
within Base Alpha wouldn't be survivable.

The warehouses had been placed following the curve of
the land instead of being aligned on a grid pattern. Tranter
followed the access road meandering past the front of the
buildings. Three of them were empty, held against future
need. The sliding doors of the fourth from the gate were
closed, but light streamed out of the pedestrian entrance
set beside them.

Three troopers looked down from the warehouse roof
as Tranter pulled the aircar over. Huber waved at them
with his left hand; he held the 2-cm powergun in his right.

Chief Edlinger met them at the door. "Good to see you
again, Huber," he said. "Tranter, you need a hand?"

"I haven't forgotten how to carry a toolchest, Chief,"
the sergeant said, lifting his equipment out of the back
of the car with a grunt. And of course he hadn't, but his
mechanical leg didn't bend the way the one he'd been born
with had; balance was tricky with such a heavy weight.

Huber had offered help when they got into the car. If
Tranter wanted to prove he could move a toolchest or do
any other curst thing he wanted without help, then more
power to him.

"I appreciate this, Buck," Huber said as he entered the
warehouse. The air within was chilly and had overtones
of lubricant and ozone; it was a place which only tolerated human beings. "I'd like there not to be a problem,
but—"

"But you think there is," Edlinger completed grimly. He
was a wiry little man whose sandy hair was more gray
than not; he'd rolled his sleeves up, showing the tattoos
covering both arms. Time and ingrained grease had blurred
their patterns. If even the chief could identify the designs,
he'd have to do it from memory.

Huber laughed wryly. "I think so enough that if we don't

find something, I'll worry more," he admitted. "I won't believe it isn't there, just that we didn't find it."

"That looks like the lady," Tranter said, striding purposefully across the cracked concrete floor. There were two other combat cars in the workshop, but *Fencing Master* wore like a flag across her bow slope the marks of the buzzbomb and the welding repairs. Iridium was named for Iris, the goddess of the rainbow, because of the range of beautiful colors that heat spread across the metal.

Tranter and the chief spent the next two hours taking off panels, running diagnostics, and sending fiber optic filaments up passages that Huber hadn't known were parts of a combat car's structure. He stayed clear, sitting mostly on an empty forty-liter lubricant container. The techs worked with the natural rhythm of men who'd worked together often in the past; they spoke in a verbal shorthand, and they never got in one another's way.

It struck Huber that the chief must really have regretted losing Tranter from his section. Huber hadn't known the sergeant very long, and *he'd* bloody well miss him if something happened.

"Hel-*lo*, what have we here?" Tranter called, his voice echoing out of the iridium cavern into which he'd crawled. He'd removed a hull access plate beneath the driver's compartment; only his feet showed outside the opening. "Chief, what d'ye make of this? I'm sending it on channel seven."

Huber locked his faceshield down and cued it to the imagery Tranter's probe was picking up. He had no context for what he was looking at: a series of chips were set in a board bracketed between iridium bulkheads. On the bottom of the board was an additional chip, attached to the circuits on the other side with hair-fine wires.

"Hang on, I've got the catalog," Edlinger replied. They were using lapel mikes because their commo helmets were too bulky for some of the spaces they were slipping into. "Can you give me more magnification? Are those two reds, a blue and a . . ."

"Purple and white, chief," Tranter said. "The fourth line's a purple and white."

"Roger that," said Edlinger. "A simple control circuit, sonny. Probably made on Sonderby, wouldn't you say?"

A dozen chips flashed up on Huber's faceshield beside the real-time image, matches that the chief's AI had found in a catalog of parts and equipment. They could've been yea many mirror images as far as Huber could tell, but the techs and their electronics apparently found minute differences among them.

"Galieni said he'd been trained on Sonderby," Edlinger added in a somber voice. "I don't doubt that he was, but I'd be willing to bet that it wasn't North Star Spacelines that hired him when he left school."

The original image blanked as Sergeant Tranter squirmed back out of the equipment bay. Huber raised his faceshield as the chief walked around from the other side of the car.

"All right," said Huber. "What does it do? Is it a bomb?"

"It isn't a bomb, El-Tee," Tranter said, squatting for a moment before he got to his feet. "It's a control circuit, and it's been added to the air defense board. It's got an antenna wire out through the channel for the running lights—that's how I noticed it."

"They could've set it to switch off the guns when somebody sent a coded radio signal, Huber," Edlinger added. "That's the most likely plan, though it depends on exactly where on the board they were plugged in. I'm not sure we can tell with just the maintenance manuals I've got here."

"I've got a better guess than that, Buck," Huber said, standing and feeling his gut contract. "Shutting the guns off wouldn't be a disaster if it just affected one car in a platoon. What if that chip locked all three tribarrels on full automatic fire in the middle of Benjamin? What do you suppose would happen to the houses for a klick in every direction?"

"Bloody hell," Tranter muttered.

Huber nodded. "Yeah, that's exactly what would happen:

bloody hell. And coming on top of Rhodesville, the UC government'd cancel the Regiment's contract so fast we'd be off-planet with our heads swimming before we knew what happened."

The technicians looked at one another, then back to Huber. "What do we do now, El-Tee?" Tranter asked.

"Have you disconnected the chip?" Huber asked.

"You bet!" Tranter said with a frown of amazement. "I cut both leads as soon as I saw them. Whatever the thing was, I knew it didn't belong."

"Then we shut things up and I go talk to Major Steuben in the morning," Huber said. "I'd do it now, but—"

He grinned with wry honesty.

"—not only do I think it'll keep, I *don't* think I'm in any shape to talk to the major before I've had a good night's sleep."

Sergeant Tranter rubbed the back of his neck with his knuckles. "And maybe a stiff drink or two, hey El-Tee?" he said. "Which I'm going to share with you, if you don't mind."

"I'm buying for both of you for what you've done tonight," Huber said, thinking of the coming interview. "And I just wish you could carry it the rest of the way with the major, but that's my job. . . ."

Major Steuben wasn't available through the regimental net at dawn plus thirty, at noon, or at any of the other times Huber checked for him into mid afternoon. Huber didn't leave a message—he was sure Steuben would learn about the calls as soon as he wanted to know—and it didn't even cross his mind to talk to some other member of the White Mice. Little as Huber liked the major, this was no time to bring a subordinate up to speed on the problem. He began to wonder if he was going to reach Steuben before 1800 hours, close of business for the regular staff.

Huber smiled at his own presumption; he'd gotten to think that Steuben would be there any time he wanted him—because the major had been in his office the times

he summoned Huber. Why his mind should've reversed the
pattern was just one of those mysteries of human arrogance, Huber supposed.

It wasn't like Log Section didn't have work to do, after
all.

Now that more crews and vehicles were on the ground,
the Regiment was setting up a second operations base
outside Arbor Palisades, the second-largest of the United
Cities and located on the northeast border with Solace. Two
platoons from L Troop plus support vehicles would be
leaving Base Alpha tonight for the new location. Huber
with the approval of the S-3 shop had decided to send a
column of thirty wheeled vehicles along with them. The
civilian trucks could've moved on their own—the UC and
Solace weren't at war despite the level of tension—but it
gave both the troopers and the civilian drivers practice in
convoy techniques.

"Via, El-Tee," Sergeant Tranter said, shaking his head
in amusement. "You better not let anybody in L Troop catch
you in a dark alley. The trip'll take 'em four times as long
and be about that much rougher per hour besides."

"Right," said Huber. "And nobody's shooting at them.
Which won't be the case if we have to do it for real,
as we bloody well will when those trucks start supply-
ing forward bases inside Solace territory as soon as the
balloon goes up."

Huber didn't take lunch, though he gnawed ration bars
at his desk. Most people claimed the bars tasted like compressed sawdust, but Huber found them to have a series
of subtle flavors. They were bland, sure, but bland wasn't
such a bad thing. The commander of a line platoon had
enough excitement in his life without needing it in his food.

At random moments throughout the day, Huber checked
in with the Provost Marshal's office. At 1530 hours instead
of a machine voice announcing, "Unavailable," Major
Steuben himself said, "Go ahead."

"Sir!" Huber said. His brain disconnected but he'd
rehearsed his approach often enough in his head to blurt

it out now: "May I see you ASAP with some information about the Rhodesville ambush?"

"If by 'as soon as possible' you mean in fifteen minutes, Lieutenant . . ." Steuben said. He had a pleasant voice, a modulated tenor as smooth and civilized as his appearance; and as deceptive, of course. "Then you may, yes."

"Sir, on the way, sir!" Huber said, standing and breaking the connection.

"Tranter!" he shouted across the room as he rounded his console; he snatched the 2-cm powergun slung from the back of his chair. "I need to be in front of Major Steuben in fifteen minutes! That means an aircar, and I don't even pretend to drive the cursed things."

Huber waved at Hera as he followed the sergeant out the door. "I'll be back when I'm back," he said. "I don't expect to be long."

The good Lord knew he *hoped* it wouldn't be long.

He and Tranter didn't talk much on the short flight from Benjamin to Base Alpha. The sergeant turned his head toward his passenger a couple times, but he didn't speak. Huber was concentrating on the open triangle formed by his hands lying in his lap. He was aware of Tranter's regard, but he really needed to compose himself before he brought this to Major Steuben.

This time when Huber got out of the car in front of the Provost Marshal's, he reflexively scooped the 2-cm shoulder weapon from the butt-cup holding it upright beside his seat. If he'd been thinking he'd have left the heavy weapon in the vehicle, but since he was holding it anyway he passed it to the watching guard along with his pistol and knife.

"Expecting some excitement, Lieutenant?" said the man behind the mirrored faceshield as he took the weapons.

"What would a desk jockey like me know about excitement?" Huber said cheerfully as he opened the main door.

He wondered about his comment as he strode down the hallway. It struck him that it was the first interaction he'd had with the guards that wasn't strictly professional. As

with so much of his life since he'd landed on Plattner's
World, Huber had the feeling that he was running downhill in the darkness and the only thing that was going to
save him was pure dumb luck.

Major Steuben nodded him into the office. Huber closed
the door behind him and without preamble said, "Sir! Three
of the techs in Central Repair are living at Senator Graciano's
townhouse. That is, Patroklos Graciano, the—"

"I know who Patroklos Graciano is," Steuben said through
his cold smile. "Continue."

"Right," said Huber. He was blurting what he knew in
the baldest fashion possible. He understood Major Steuben
too well to want to exchange empty pleasantries with the
man. "We checked—Chief Edlinger and a former tech in
my section, that is—checked the combat car they were
working on. There's an extra control chip in the air
defense board with an antenna for external inputs. I think
it was meant to send the tribarrels berserk while the car
was in the middle of Benjamin."

"You've disconnected the chip?" Steuben said. For a
moment there was a spark from something very hard glinting
in his voice.

"Yes sir, but that's all we've done thus far," Huber said.
His muscles were tight across his rib cage and his tongue
seemed to be chipping out the words. In a firefight he
wouldn't have been this tense, because he'd have known
the rules. . . .

"Good," said the major, smoothly unconcerned again.
"You've properly reported the matter and your suspicions,
Lieutenant. Now go back to your duties in Logistics and
take no more action on the matter. Do you understand?"

Huber felt the anger rise in his throat. "No sir," he said.
He spoke in a normal voice, maybe even a little quieter
than usual. "I don't understand at all. Senator Graciano
is certainly a traitor, probably the traitor who set up me
and my platoon at Rhodesville. We can't leave him out
there, looking for another place to slide the knife into us.
One more chance may be just the one he needed!"

Steuben didn't rise, but he leaned forward very slightly in his seat. He wore his 1-cm pistol in a cutaway holster high on his right hip. Inlays of platinum, gold, and rich violet gold-uranium alloy decorated the weapon's receiver, but the pistol was still as deadly as the service weapon Huber had left with the guards outside the building.

And the dapper little man who wore it was far more deadly than Huber had ever thought of being.

"You've shown initiative, Lieutenant," Steuben said. "Because of that, I'm going to politely point something out to you instead of treating your insolence as I normally would: even if everything you believe regarding Senator Graciano is true, he remains *Senator* Graciano. He has a large following in the United Cities and is in some ways more influential in the remainder of the Outer States than any other UC politician, his father included. Probably the best way to boost his standing still further would be for off-planet mercenaries to accuse him of being a traitor."

"Sir, I lost friends at Rhodesville!" Huber said.

"Then you were lucky to have friends to begin with, Lieutenant," the major said, rising to his feet. "Friendship is an experience I've never shared. Now *get* back to Log Section and your duties. Or submit your resignation from the Regiment, which I assure you will be accepted at the moment you offer it."

Huber's lips were dry. He didn't speak.

"I asked you before if you understood," Steuben said, his left fingertips resting lightly on the desk top. "You chose to discuss the matter. Now the only thing for you to understand is this: you will go back to your duties in Log Section, or you will resign. *Do* you understand?"

"Sir!" Huber said. "May I return to my duties now?"

"Dismissed, Lieutenant," the major said. "And Lieutenant? I don't expect to see you again until I summon you."

As Huber walked down the hallway, his back to the door he'd closed behind him, he kept thinking, *It's in the hands*

*of the people who ought to be handling it. It's none of my
business any more.*

The trouble was, he knew that at the level of Steuben
and Colonel Hammer it was a political problem. Political
problems were generally best solved by compromise and
quiet neglect.

Huber didn't think he'd ever be able to chalk up the
sound of Kolbe's body squishing down *Fencing Master*'s
bow slope to political expedience, though.

"Got any plans for tonight, El-Tee?" Sergeant Tranter asked
as he followed Huber up the stairs to Log Section. "There's
a game on in the maintenance shed."

The paint on the stairwell walls had been rubbed at the
height of children's shoulders; it was a reminder of what
the building had been. Whether it'd ever be a school again
depended on how well the Slammers performed. If things
went wrong, the Outer States—at least the United Cities—
would be paying reparations to Solace that'd preclude luxu-
ries like public schooling.

"I'm thinking about throwing darts into a target," Huber
muttered. "And don't ask whose picture I'm thinking of
using for the target!"

Hera wasn't at her desk. In her absence and Huber's,
a senior clerk named Farinelli was in titular charge—and
he obviously had no idea of how to deal with the two
armed Slammers who stood before his console. Their backs
were to the door and the remainder of the staring locals.

"Can I help you gentle—" Huber began, politely but with
a sharp undertone. A stranger listening could have guessed
that he didn't much like aggrieved troopers making personal visits to Log Section when a call or data transmission would get the facts into his hands without disrupting
the office. Midway in Huber's question, the troopers turned.

"Deseau!" Huber said. "And you, Learoyd! Say, they didn't
reassign you guys too, did they?"

The troopers smiled gratefully, though Learoyd knuckled
his bald scalp in embarrassment and wouldn't meet Huber's

eyes. "Nothing like that, Lieutenant," the sergeant said. "We're here to take *Fencing Master* back to the unit as soon as they assign us a couple bodies from the Replacement Depot. I figured you wouldn't mind if we stopped in and saw how you were making out."

From the way Deseau spoke and Learoyd acted, they weren't at all sure that Huber *wouldn't* mind. They were line troopers, neither of them with any formal education; the only civilians they were comfortable with were whores and bartenders. It must have been a shock to come looking for the lieutenant who'd been one of them and find themselves in an office full of well-dressed locals who stared as if they were poisonous snakes.

Huber thought suddenly of the ropes of 2-cm bolts sending the dirigible down in fiery destruction over Rhodesville. There was never a poisonous snake as dangerous as either of these two men; or as Arne Huber, who *was* after all one of them.

"Mind?" he said. "I'm delighted! Sergeant Tranter—"

Huber took his men by either hand and raised his voice as his eyes swept the office. "Everybody? These are two of the people who kept me alive at the sharp end: my blower captain Sergeant Deseau and Trooper Learoyd, my right wing gunner. That won't mean much to you civilians, but you can understand when I say I wouldn't have survived landing on Plattner's World if it weren't for these men!"

Learoyd muttered something to his shoes, but he looked pleased. Deseau's expression didn't change, but he didn't seem to mind either.

"Do you have plans for tonight?" Huber asked. "Ah, Sergeant Tranter? Do you think we could find these men a billet here in the compound?" He switched his eyes back to Deseau and Learoyd, continuing, "There's usually a card game, and I think I can promise something to drink."

"And if he couldn't get you booze, I can," Tranter said cheerfully. "Sure, we can put you guys up. It's best the El-Tee not go wandering around, but you won't miss Benjamin."

"If I never see Warrant Leader Niscombe," Learoyd said to his boots, "it'll be too soon."

"Niscombe runs the enlisted side of Transient Depot, sir," Deseau explained. "He figures that something bad'll happen if he lets folks passing through from field duty just rest and relax. He'll find a lot of little jobs for us if we bunk there."

"Something bad'll happen to Niscombe if he ever shows his face out in the field," Learoyd muttered with a venom Huber hadn't expected to hear in that trooper's voice. "Which he won't do, you can be sure of that."

"Right," said Huber. "I'll send a temporary duty request for the two of you through channels, but for now consider yourselves at liberty."

He glanced at Hera's empty desk. "Ah, does anybody know when Deputy Graciano's due back?" he asked the room in a raised voice.

Everybody stared at him; nobody answered the question, though. It struck Huber that all this was out of the locals' previous experience with the Slammers. When Captain Cassutt was director, there hadn't been troopers with personal weapons standing in the middle of the office.

"Sir?" said Kelso from the back of the room.

"What?" said Huber. "Via, if you know something, spit it out!"

"Yessir," said Kelso, swallowing. "Ah, I don't know when the deputy's coming back, but she went out as soon as I gave her the information you requested, sir."

"Information?" Huber repeated. For a moment he didn't know what the local was talking about; nonetheless his stomach slid toward the bottom of an icy pit.

Then he remembered. "You mean the previous employment data."

"Yessir!" said Kelso, more brightly this time. "None of those techs had worked at the places they put down. Not a soul remembered any one of the three!"

Huber opened his mouth to ask another question, but he really didn't have to. He'd given Kelso the full applications including the applicants' home addresses. That's what Hera had seen, and she wouldn't have had to check to recognize the address of her brother's townhouse. The fact that the men's listed employment records were phony would be a red flag to anybody with brains enough to feed themselves.

"What's the matter, sir?" Tranter said.

"I screwed up," Huber said. His face must've gone white; he felt cold all over. "It's nobody's fault but mine."

Hera could've gone to her father with the information; she could've gone to the civil authorities—though Huber wasn't sure the United Cities had security police in the fashion that larger states generally did; or she could even have gone to Colonel Hammer. Any of those choices would have been fine. The possibility that scared Huber, though, was that instead—

His helmet pinged him with an URGENT call. Huber wasn't in a platoon and company net, so the sound was unexpected. He locked down his faceshield to mute the conversation and said, "Fox three-six, go ahead!"

In his surprise—and fear—he'd given his old call signal. Somebody else was leader of platoon F-3 nowadays.

"*Arne, this is Doll,*" said Lieutenant Basime's voice. "*We don't exactly monitor the civil police here, but we are a signals liaison section. Ah—*"

"Say it!" Huber snapped.

"*There was a police call just now,*" Doll said mildly. She was a solid lady, well able to stand up for her rights and smart enough to know when that wasn't the best choice. "*There's an aircar down west of town. The driver and sole occupant is dead. Initial report is that it's your deputy, Hera Graciano.*"

"Right," said Huber. He felt calm again, much as he'd been as he watched the stern of the blazing dirigible slide slowly into the terminal building. The past was the past; now there were only the consequences to deal with. "Can you download the coordinates of the crash site?"

"*You've got 'em,*" Doll said. There was an icon Huber

hadn't noticed in the terrain box on his faceshield. *"Any-thing more I can do, snake?"*

"Negative, Doll," Huber said. "I'll take it from here. Three-six out."

He broke the connection and raised his faceshield. "Trouble, El-Tee?" said Sergeant Tranter. Tranter had been in the field, but he didn't have a line trooper's instincts. Deseau and Learoyd stood facing outward from their former platoon leader; their feet were spread and their sub-machine guns slanted in front of them. They weren't aiming at anything, not threatening anybody; but they hadn't had to ask if there was trouble, and they were ready to deal in their own way with anything that showed itself.

The civilian clerks looked terrified, as they well should have been.

"Tranter, I need a ride," Huber said. "West of town there's been an aircar crash. I'll transfer the coordinates to the car's navigation system."

"We're coming along," Deseau said. He continued to watch half the room and the doorway, while the trooper watched the clerks on the other side. "Learoyd and me."

"You go relax," Huber said in a tight voice. "This is Log Section business, not yours."

"Fuck that," said Deseau. "You said we're at liberty. Fine, we're at liberty to come with you."

"Right," said Huber. He was still holding his big shoulder weapon; he hadn't had time to put it down since he entered the office. "You—Farinelli? You're in charge till I get back." He thought for a moment and added, "Or you hear that I've been replaced."

"But Director Huber!" the clerk said. "What if Deputy Graciano comes back?"

"She won't," Huber snarled. Then to his men he added, "Come on, troopers. Let's roll!"

"She was up about a thousand meters," said the cop. He was a young fellow in a blue jacket and red trousers with a blue stripe down the seam. For all that he was determined not to be cowed by the heavily armed mercenaries, he behaved politely instead of blustering to show his authority. "She had the top down and wasn't belted in, so she came out the first time the car tumbled."

It was probably chance then that the body and the vehicle had hit the ground within fifty meters of one another, Huber realized. Hera had gone through tree-branches face-first, hit the ground, and then bounced over to lie on her back. Her features were distorted, but he could've identified her easily if the UC policeman had been concerned about that; he wasn't.

There was almost no blood. The dent in the center of her forehead had spilled considerable gore over Hera's face, but that had been dry when the branches slashed her and wiped much of it off. Huber was no pathologist, but he'd seen death often and in a variety of forms. Hera Graciano had been dead for some length of time before her body hit the ground.

"Why did the car tumble?" Tranter said, kneeling to check the underside of the crumpled vehicle. It'd nosed in, then fallen back on its underside with its broken frame cocked up like an inverted V. "There's an air turbine that deploys when you run outa fuel. It generates enough juice to keep your control gyro spinning."

"You're friends of the lady?" the cop asked. He was expecting backup, but the Slammers had arrived almost as soon as he did himself. He seemed puzzled, which Huber was willing to grant him the right to be.

But it was a really good thing for the cop that he hadn't decided to throw his weight around. Huber wasn't in a mood for it; and while he wasn't sure how Sergeant Tranter would react, he knew that the two troopers from *Fencing Master* would obey without question if their lieutenant told them to blow the local's brains out.

"She was my deputy," Huber said. "She worked for the Regiment in a civilian capacity."

"Somebody whacked the turbine with a heavy hammer,"

Tranter said, rising from where he knelt. "That's why it's still stuck in the cradle."

He pulled at an access plate on the wreck's quarter panel. It didn't come till he took a multitool from his belt and gave the warped plastic a calculated blow.

The local policeman looked at the sky again and fingered his lapel communicator. He didn't try to prod the dispatcher, though. "There was an anonymous call that the car had been circling up here and just dropped outa the sky," he explained. "D'ye suppose it was maybe, well . . . suicide?"

"No," said Huber. "I don't think that."

"That's good," said the cop, misunderstanding completely. "Because you guys might not know it, but this lady was from a bloody important family here in the UC. I don't want to get caught in some kinda scandal, if you see what I mean."

"I see what you mean," Huber said. His eyes drifted across Tranter for a moment, then resumed scanning their surroundings. They were within ten klicks of the center of Benjamin, but the forest was unbroken. Trees on Plattner's World had enough chlorophyll in their bark to look deep green from a distance. Their branches twisted like snakes, but the leaves were individually tiny and stuck on the twigs like a child's drawing.

The cop grimaced. "I wish the Commander Miltianas would get the lead outa his pants and take over here," he went on. "Of course, he probably doesn't want to be mixed up in this either—but curse it, it's what they're paying him the big bucks for, right?"

"There's four fuel cells in this model," Tranter said, his head inside the vehicle's stern section. "The back three are disconnected and there's a puncture in the forward cell."

He straightened, looking puzzled and concerned. "El-Tee," he said. "It looks to me like—"

"Drop the subject for now, Sergeant," Huber said. He gestured to their own vehicle, a ten-place bus rather than the little runabout Tranter had used to ferry Huber alone.

Four troopers in combat gear would've been a crowd and a burden for the smaller car. "We'll talk on the way back to the office."

"But—" said Tranter.

Deseau rapped the side of Tranter's commo helmet with his knuckles. "Hey!" Deseau said. "He's the man, right? He just gave you an order!"

Tranter looked startled, then nodded in embarrassment and trotted for the bus. There were three aircars approaching fast from Benjamin. Two had red strobe lights flashing, but they weren't running their sirens.

Huber turned to the cop. "Thanks for letting us look over the site," he said. "We'll leave you to your business now. And we'll get back to our own."

"Yeah, right," said the local man with a worried frown. "I sure hope I don't wind up holding the bucket on this one. A death like this can be a lot of trouble!"

"You got that right," Huber muttered as he got into the cab with Tranter. The tech already had the fans live; now he boosted power and wobbled into the air, narrowly missing a line of trees.

Kelso would have done a better job driving, but this was no longer business for civilians. Huber locked his faceshield down.

"Unit, switch to intercom," he ordered. Nobody but the three men in the car with him could hear the discussion without a lot of decryption equipment and skill. "Tranter, I'm leaving you in the circuit, but I'm not expecting you to get involved. You'll have to keep your mouth shut, that's all. Can you handle that?"

"*Fuck not being involved,*" Tranter said. His hands were tight on the control yoke and his eyes were straight ahead; a degree of hurt sounded in his voice. "*I knew the deputy better than you did, sir. She was a good boss; and anyway, she was one of ours even if she didn't wear the uniform. Which I do.*"

"Right," said Huber. "Deseau and Learoyd, you don't know the background. I figure her brother killed her or one of his thugs did. It was probably an accident, but maybe not. She'd have gone to see him, threatening to tell the world he was an agent for Solace. She maybe even guessed he'd set up the ambush at Rhodesville."

Sergeant Deseau made a sound loud enough to trip the intercom. In something like a normal voice he went on, *"We gonna take care of him, then?"*

"He's got a lot of pull," Huber warned. "I went to Major Steuben about him and got told to mind my own business. It's going to make real waves if somebody from the Regiment takes him out. *Real* waves, about as bad as it gets."

"El-Tee?" Learoyd said, frustration so evident in his tone that Huber could visualize the trooper trying to knuckle his bald scalp through his commo helmet. *"Just tell us what to do, right? That's your job. Don't worry about me and Frenchie doing ours."*

Learoyd was correct, of course. He had a simple approach of necessity, and he cut through all the nonsense that smarter people wrapped themselves up with.

"Right," Huber repeated. "There'll be a gang of thugs at the guy's townhouse, and they'll have guns available even if they aren't going out on the street with them just yet. It could be that he'd got a squad of Harris's Commando on premises. I doubt it because of the risk to him if it comes out, but we've got to figure we're going up against people who know what they're doing."

He paused, arranging his next words. The aircar was over Benjamin now, but Tranter was taking them in a wide circuit of the suburbs where the tree cover was almost as complete as over the virgin forest beyond.

"For that reason," Huber said, "I figure to borrow *Fencing Master* for the operation. There's a detachment leaving Central Repair for Base Alpha tonight. We'll tag onto the back and trail off when we're close to the bastard's compound. If we can, we'll duck back to CR when we're done—but I *don't* expect to get away with this, troops."

"I been shot at before," Deseau said calmly. *"I can't*

see anything worse'n that that's going to happen if they catch us."

Learoyd didn't bother to speak. Huber heard the *clack* as the trooper withdrew his sub-machine gun's loading tube, then locked it back home in the receiver. Like he'd said, he was getting ready to do his part of the job.

"Sergeant Tranter," Huber said, turning to the tech beside him. "Now that you know what we're talking about, I think it'd be a good night for you to spend playing cards back at the billets. You're a curst good man, but this really isn't your line of work."

Tranter's face was red with suppressed emotion. *"Guess you'll need a driver, right?"* he snapped. *"Guess I've driven the Lord's great plenty of combat cars, shifting them around for repair. I guess it bloody well is my line of work. Sir."*

"Well in that case, troopers . . ." Huber said. "We'll leave our billets for Central Repair at twenty hundred. Start time for the draft is twenty-one hundred, but they'll be late. That'll make the timing about right."

Tranter muttered, *"Roger,"* Deseau grunted, and Learoyd said as little as he usually did. There wasn't a lot *to* say at this point.

Huber wasn't frightened; it was all over but the consequences.

Senator Patroklos Graciano was about to learn the consequences of fucking with Hammer's Slammers.

The racket of drive fans made every joint in the girder-framed warehouse rattle and sing. There were two other combat cars besides *Fencing Master*; all three thirty-tonne monsters were powered up, their fans supporting them on

the words had he not been looking into Deseau's face and watching his lips move.

"Can it!" Huber snapped. "Take care of your own end and keep your mouth shut."

Deseau grimaced agreement and faced front again. They were all nervous. Well, three of them were, at any rate; Learoyd seemed about as calm as he'd been a couple hours before, when he'd been methodically loading spare magazines for his sub-machine gun.

"*Seven Red, this is Green One,*" ordered the detachment commander—an artillery captain who happened to be the senior officer in the temporary unit. If the move had been more serious than the five kilometers between Central Repair and Base Alpha, the detachment would've been under the control of a line officer regardless of rank. "*Pull into place behind Five Blue. Eight Red, follow Seven. Unit, prepare to move out. Green One out.*"

"Tranter, slide in behind the second blower," Huber ordered. "Don't push up their ass, just keep normal interval so it looks like we belong."

Chief Edlinger had put Huber and his men on the list for admission to Central Repair, but that was easily explained if it needed to be. The chief didn't know what Huber planned—just that it wasn't something he *ought* to know more about. The detachment commander didn't know even that: he was in the self-propelled gun at the head of the column. The eight vehicles leaving for Base Alpha included two tanks, four combat cars, the detachment commander's hog, and a repair vehicle with a crane and a powered bed that could lift a combat car. The crews didn't know one another, and nobody would wonder or even notice that a fifth car had joined the procession.

The lead car jerked toward the open door. The driver, inexperienced or jumpy from the long wait, canted his nacelles too suddenly. The bow skirt dipped and scraped a shrieking line of sparks along the concrete floor until the car bounced over the threshold and into the open air.

The second car followed with greater care but the same

lack of skill, rising nearly a hand's-breadth above the ground. The skirts spilled air in a roar around their whole circuit. The car wallowed; when the driver nudged his controls forward Huber thought for a moment the vehicle was going to slide into the jamb of the sliding door.

"They've got newbie crews," Tranter said scornfully. *"Via, I could do better than that with my eyes closed!"*

"I'll settle for you keeping your eyes open and not attracting attention," Huber said tightly. "Move out, Trooper."

Fencing Master slid gracefully through the doorway and into the warm night. The skirts ticked once on the door track, but that wasn't worth mentioning.

"Let's keep him, El-Tee," Deseau said with a chuckle. *"He's as good as Kolbe was, and a curst sight better than I ever thought of being as a driver."*

"Keep your mind on the present job, didn't I tell you?" Huber snapped. "I don't think any of us need to plan for a future much beyond tonight."

Deseau laughed. Huber supposed that was as good a response as any.

Plattner's World had two moons, but neither of them was big enough to provide useful illumination. The pole lights placed for security when these were warehouses threw bright pools at the front of each building, but that just made the night darker when *Fencing Master* moved between them. Huber locked down his faceshield and switched to light enhancement, though he knew he lost depth perception that way.

The rocket howitzer at the head of the column started to negotiate the gate to the compound, then stopped. The tank immediately following very nearly drove up its stern.

The CQ kept saying the same thing. So did the captain, though he varied the words a bit.

Huber listened for a moment to make sure that what was going on didn't affect him, then switched to intercom. "They'll get it sorted out in a bit," he said to his crew. "The blowers are straight out of the shops and half the crews are newbies. Nothing to worry about."

"*Who's worried?*" Deseau said. He stretched at his central gun station, then turned and grinned at Huber.

They were all wearing body armor, even Tranter. The bulky ceramic clamshells crowded the fighting compartment even without the personal gear and extra ammo that'd pack the vehicle on a line deployment.

Learoyd could've been a statue placed at the right wing gun. He didn't fidget with the weapon or with the submachine gun slung across his chest. Though his body was motionless, his helmet would be scanning the terrain and careting movement onto his lowered faceshield. If one of the highlights was a hostile pointing a weapon in the direction of *Fencing Master*—and anybody pointing a weapon at *Fencing Master* was hostile, in Learoyd's opinion and Huber's as well—his tribarrel would light the night with cyan destruction.

"*Unit, we're moving,*" the captain announced in a disgruntled tone. As he spoke, the hog shifted forward again. Metal rang as the drivers of other vehicles in the column struggled to react to the sudden change from stasis to movement. Skirts were stuttering up and down on the roadway of stabilized earth. *You get lulled into patterns in no time at all. . . .*

Huber brought up a terrain display in the box welded to the pintle supporting his tribarrel. *Fencing Master* didn't have the sensor and communications suite of a proper command car, but it did have an additional package that allowed the platoon leader to project displays instead of taking all his information through the visor of his commo helmet.

The column got moving in fits and starts; a combat

car *did* run into the back of the tank preceding it. Huber's helmet damped the sound, but the whole fabric of *Fencing Master* shivered in sympathy to the impact of a thirty-tonne hammer hitting a hundred-and-seventy-tonne anvil.

"Via, that'll hold us up for the next three hours!" Sergeant Deseau snarled. *"We'll be lucky if we get away before bloody dawn!"*

Huber thought the same. Instead the detachment commander just growled, *"Unit, hold your intervals,"* as his vehicle proceeded down the road on the set course.

"Dumb bastard," Deseau muttered. *"Dicked around all that time for nothing, and now he's going to put the hammer down and string the column out to make up the time he lost."*

That was close enough to Huber's appreciation of what was going on that he didn't bother telling the sergeant to shut up. He grinned beneath his faceshield. Under the circumstances, a lieutenant couldn't claim to have any authority over the enlisted men with him except what they chose to give him freely.

The tank got moving again smoothly; *its* driver at least knew how to handle his massive vehicle. Tanks weren't really clumsy, and given the right terrain and enough time they were hellaciously fast; but the inertia of so many tonnes of metal required the driver to plan her maneuvers a very long way ahead.

The collision hadn't sprung the skirts of the following combat car, so it was able to proceed also. Its driver kept a good hundred and fifty meters between his vehicle's dented bow slope and the tank's stern. The rest of the

"Tranter, when we make the corner up ahead," Huber ordered, "cut your headlights and running lights. Can you drive using just your visor's enhancement?"

"*Roger,*" the driver said calmly. Behind them the guard vehicle was pulling back across the compound's gateway; ahead, the last of the cars in the detachment proper slid awkwardly around an elbow in the broad freight road leading west and eventually out of Benjamin.

Even here in the center of the administrative capital of the UC, there were more trees than houses. The locals built narrow structures three or four stories high, with parking for aircars either beneath the support pilings or on rooftop landing pads. Most of the windows were dark, but occasionally they lighted as armored vehicles howled slowly by on columns of air.

Even without lights, *Fencing Master* wasn't going to pass unnoticed in Senator Graciano's neighborhood of expensive residences. This'd have to be a quick in and out; or at least a quick in.

Tranter was keeping a rock-solid fifty meter interval between him and the stern of Red Eight. He seemed to judge what the driver ahead would do well before that fellow acted.

"Start opening the distance, Tranter," Huber said, judging their position on the terrain display against the quivering running lights of Red Eight. "We'll peel off to the right at the intersection half a kay west of our present position. As soon as Red Eight's out of sight, goose it hard. We've got eighteen hundred meters to cover, and I want to be there before they have time to react to the sound of our fans."

"*Roger,*" Tranter said. He still didn't sound nervous; maybe he was concentrating on his driving.

And maybe the technician didn't really understand what was about to happen. Well, there were a lot of cases where intellectual understanding fell well short of emotional realities.

Fencing Master slowed almost imperceptibly; the fan note didn't change, but Tranter cocked the nacelles toward the vertical so that their thrust was spent more on lifting the car than driving it forward. Red Eight ahead had gained another fifty meters by the time its lights shifted angle, then glittered randomly through the trees of a grove that the road twisted behind.

"Here we go, Tranter," Huber warned, though the driver obviously had everything under control. "Easy right turn, then get on—"

Fencing Master was already swinging; Tranter dragged the right skirt, not in error but because the direct friction of steel against gravel was hugely more effective at transferring momentum than a fluid coupling of compressed air. As the combat car straightened onto a much narrower street than the route they'd been following from Repair, the headlights of four ten-wheeled trucks flooded over them. An air cushion jeep pulled out squarely in front of the combat car.

"Blood and bleeding Martyrs!" somebody screamed over the intercom, and the voice might've been Huber's own. Tranter lifted *Fencing Master*'s bow, dumping air and dropping the skirts back onto the road. The bang jolted the teeth of everybody aboard and rattled the transoms of nearby houses.

The combat car hopped forward despite the impact. They'd have overrun the jeep sure as sunrise if its driver hadn't been a real pro as well. The lighter vehicle lifted on the gust from *Fencing Master*'s plenum chamber, surfing the bow wave and bouncing down the other side on its own flexible skirts.

A trim figure stood beside the jeep's driver, touching the top of the windscreen for balance but not locked to it in a deathgrip the way most people would've been while riding weapon skyward. "That's Major Steuben, and we won't get two mistakes!"

Tranter never quite lost control of *Fencing Master*, but it wasn't till the third jounce that he actually brought the car to rest. Each impact blasted a doughnut of dust and grit from the road; Huber's nose filters swung down and saved him from the worst of it, but his eyes watered. The jeep stayed just ahead of them, then curved back when the bigger vehicle halted.

The trucks—they had civilian markings and weren't from the Logistics Section inventory—moved up on either side of the combat car, two and two. They were stake-beds; a dozen troopers lined the back of each, their weapons ready for anybody in *Fencing Master* to make the wrong move.

That wasn't going to happen: Huber and his men were veterans; they knew what was survivable.

"*Bloody fucking hell,*" Deseau whispered. He kept his hands in sight and raised at his sides.

"*Get out, all four of you,*" Major Steuben ordered through the commo helmets. He sounded amused. "*Leave your guns behind.*"

Huber slung his 2-cm weapon over the raised tribarrel, then unbuckled his equipment belt and hung it on the big gun also. He paused and looked, really *looked*, at the White Mice watching *Fencing Master* and her crew through the sights of their weapons. They wore ordinary Slammers combat gear—helmets, body armor, and uniforms—but the only powergun in the whole platoon was the pistol on Major Steuben's hip. The rest of the unit carried electromagnetic slug-throwers and buzzbombs.

"Unit," Huber ordered, "let me do the talking."

He raised himself to the edge of the fighting compartment's armor, then swung his legs over in a practiced motion. His boots clanged down on the top of the plenum chamber. Starting with the coaming as a handhold, he let himself slide along the curve of the skirts to the ground.

Deseau and Learoyd were dismounting with similar ease, but Tranter—awkward in body armor—was having more difficulty in the bow. The technician also hadn't taken off his holstered pistol; he'd probably forgotten he was wearing it.

Huber opened his mouth to call a warning. Before he could, Steuben said, "*Sergeant Tranter, I'd appreciate it if you'd drop your equipment belt before you step to the ground. It'll save me the trouble of shooting you.*"

He tittered and added, "*Not that it would be a great deal of trouble.*"

Startled, Tranter undid the belt. He wobbled on the hatch coaming, then lost his balance. He and the belt slipped down the bow in opposite directions, though Tranter was able to keep from landing on his face by dabbing a hand to the ground.

Huber stepped briskly toward the jeep, stopping two paces away. He threw what was as close to an Academy salute as he could come after five years in the field.

"Sir!" he said. Steuben stood above him by the height of the jeep's plenum chamber. "The men with me had no idea what was going on. I ordered them to accompany me on a test drive of the repaired vehicle."

"Fuck that," Deseau said, swaggering to Huber's side. "We were going to put paid to the bastards that set us up and got our buddies killed. Somebody in the Regiment's got to show some balls, after all."

He spit into the dust beside him. Deseau had the bravado of a lot of little men; his pride was worth more to him than his life just now.

Slammers combat car killed a senior UC official and destroyed his house, Lieutenant?" Steuben asked. The anger in his tone was all the more terrible because his eyes were utterly dispassionate. "Didn't it occur to you that other officials, even those who opposed the victim, would decide that Hammer's Regiment was more dangerous to its employers than it was to the enemy?"

"I'm not a politician, sir," Huber said. He was trembling, not with fear—he was beyond fear—but with hope. "I don't know what would happen afterwards."

"Not a politician?" Steuben's voice sneered while his eyes laughed with anticipation. "You were about to carry out a political act, weren't you? You do understand that, don't you?"

"Yes sir, I do understand," Huber said. The four trucks that surrounded *Fencing Master* had turned off their lights, though their diesel engines rattled at idle. The jeep's headlights fell on Huber and his men, then reflected from the combat car's iridium armor; they stood in almost shadowless illumination.

"Is there anything you want to say before I decide what I'm going to do with you, Lieutenant?" Steuben said with a lilt like the curve of a cat's tongue.

"Sir," Huber said. His muscles were trembling and his mind hung outside his body, watching what was going on with detached interest. "I'd like to accompany you and your troops on the operation you've planned. It may not be necessary to discipline me afterward."

"You mean it won't be possible to discipline you if you get your head blown off," the major said. He laughed again with a terrible humor that had nothing human in it. "Yes, that's a point."

"El-Tee?" said Learoyd. "Where are you going? Can I come?"

Huber looked toward the trooper. "They're carrying nonissue weapons, Learoyd," he said. He didn't know if he was explaining to Deseau and Tranter at the same time. "Probably the hardware we captured at Rhodesville. They're going to take out Graciano just like we planned, but they're going to do it in a way that doesn't point straight back at the Regiment."

"I shot off my mouth when I shouldn't've, Major," Deseau said. "I do that a lot. I'm sorry."

Huber blinked. He couldn't have been more surprised if his sergeant had started chanting nursery rhymes.

Deseau cleared his throat and added, "Ah, Major? We carried an EM slug-thrower in the car for a while till we ran out of ammo for it. The penetration was handy sometimes. Anyway, we're checked out on hardware like what I see there in the back of your jeep."

"So," Steuben said very softly. "You understand the situation, *gentlemen*, but do you also understand the rules of an operation like this? There will be no prisoners, and there will be no survivors in the target location."

"I understand," Huber said; because he did.

"Works for me," said Deseau. Learoyd knuckled his skull again; he probably didn't realize he'd been asked a question.

"We're going to kill everybody in the senator's house, Learoyd," Huber said, leaning forward to catch the trooper's eyes.

"Right," said Learoyd. He put his helmet back on.

"Caxton," Major Steuben said to his driver, "issue slug-throwers to these three troopers. Sergeant Tranter?"

Tranter stiffened to attention.

"You'll drive the combat car here back to Central Repair," Steuben said. "And forget completely about what's happened tonight."

"Sir!" said Tranter. His eyes were focused into the empty

only thing any of us deserve, Sergeant, is to die; which I'm sure we all will before long."

He looked toward the cab of an idling truck and said in a whipcrack voice, "Gieseking, Sergeant Tranter here is going to drive your vehicle. Take the combat car back to Central Repair and wait there for someone to pick you up."

Huber took the weapon Steuben's driver handed him. It was a sub-machine gun, lighter than its powergun equivalent but longer as well. It'd do for the job, though.

And so would Arne Huber.

Major Steuben's jeep led two trucks down the street at the speed of a fast walk. Their lights were out, and sound of their idling engines was slight enough to be lost in the breeze to those sleeping in the houses to either side.

Huber and the men from *Fencing Master* rode in the bed of the first truck; Sergeant Tranter was driving. The only difference between the line troopers and the White Mice around them was that the latter wore no insignia; Huber, Deseau, and Learoyd had rank and branch buttons on the collars. Everyone's faceshield was down and opaque.

In this wealthy suburb, the individual structures—houses and outbuildings—were of the same tall, narrow design as those of lesser districts, but these were grouped within compounds. Road transport in Benjamin was almost completely limited to delivery vehicles, so the two-meter walls were for privacy rather than protection. Most were wooden, but the one surrounding the residence of Patroklos Graciano was brick on a stone foundation like the main house.

Huber muttered a command to the AI in his helmet, cueing the situation map in a fifty percent overlay. He could still see—or aim—through the faceshield on which terrain features and icons of the forty-six men in the combat team were projected.

The other two trucks had gone around to the back street—not really parallel, the way things were laid out in Benjamin, but still a route that permitted those squads to approach the compound from the rear. They were already in position, waiting for anybody who tried to escape in that direction. The squads in front would carry out the assault by themselves unless something went badly wrong.

Few lights were on in the houses the trucks crawled past; the Graciano compound was an exception. The whole fourth floor of the main building was bright, and the separate structure where the servants lived had many lighted windows as well.

The gate to the Graciano compound was of steel or wrought iron, three meters high and wide enough to pass even trucks the size of those carrying the assault force if the leaves were open. As they very shortly would be . . .

An alert flashed red at the upper right-hand corner of Huber's visor; the truck braked to a gentle halt. The light went green.

Huber and all but three of the troopers ducked, leaning the tops of their helmets against the side of the truck. The three still standing launched buzzbombs with snarling roars that ended with white flashes. The hollow *bang*s would've been deafening were it not for the helmets' damping. Gusts of hot exhaust buffeted the kneeling men, but they were out of the direct backblast. The second truck loosed a similar volley.

Two missiles hit the gate pillars, shattering them into clouds of mortar and pulverized brick. The leaves dangled crazily, their weight barely supported by the lowest of the three sets of hinges on either side. Tranter cramped his steering wheel and accelerated as hard as the truck's big diesel would allow.

The rest of the buzzbombs had gone through lighted windows of both structures and exploded within. The ser-

The truck's tailgate was already open. Huber was the first man out, leaping to the gravel with Deseau beside him and Learoyd following with the first of the squad of White Mice. The ground glittered with shards of glass blown from all the windows.

A buzzbomb had hit the front door; the missile must've been fired moments after the initial volley or the gate would've been in the way. The doorpanel was wood veneer over a steel core, but a shaped-charge warhead designed to punch through a tank's turret had blown it off its hinges.

Scores of fires burned in the entrance hall. White-hot metal had sprayed the big room, overwhelming the retardant which impregnated the paneling. Huber's nose filters flipped into place as he ran for the staircase; his faceshield was already on infrared, displaying his surroundings in false color. If fire raised the background temperature too high for infrared to discriminate properly, he'd switch to sonic imaging—but he wasn't coming out till he'd completed his mission. . . .

There were two bodies in the hall. Parts of two bodies, at any rate; the bigger chunks of door armor had spun through them like buzzsaws. They were wearing uniforms of some sort; guards, Huber assumed. One of them had a slug-thrower but the other's severed right arm still gripped a 2-cm powergun.

The stairs curved from both sides of the entrance to a railed mezzanine at the top. Huber's visor careted movement as he started up. Before he could swing his submachine gun onto the target, a trooper behind him with a better angle shredded it and several balustrades with a short burst.

The staircase was for show; the owner and guests used the elevator running in a filigree shaft in the center of the dwelling. It started down from the top floor when Huber reached the mezzanine, which was appointed for formal entertainments. He couldn't see anything but the solid bottom of the cage. He put a burst into it, chewing the embossed design, but he didn't think his sub-machine gun's light pellets were penetrating.

One of the White Mice standing at the outside door put seven slugs from his heavy shoulder weapon through the cage the long way. One of them hit the drive motor and ricocheted, flinging parts up through the floor at an angle complementary to that of the projectile. The elevator stopped; a woman's arm flopped out of the metal lacework.

Huber jerked open the door to the narrow stairwell leading upward from the mezzanine. A pudgy servant in garishly-patterned pajamas almost ran into him. Huber shot the fellow through the body and shoved him out of the way. The servant continued screaming for the moment until Deseau, a step behind his lieutenant, ripped a burst through the dying man's head.

Huber ran up the stairs, feeling the weight and constriction of his body armor and also the filters that kept him from breathing freely. Platoon leaders in the combat car companies didn't spend a lot of time climbing stairwells in the normal course of their business, but he'd asked for the job.

The door to the third floor was closed. Huber ignored it as he rounded the landing and started up the last flight. Teams of White Mice would clear the lower floors and the basement; the men from F-3 were tasked with the senator's suite at the top of the building.

The door at the stairhead was ajar. Huber fired through the gap while he was still below the level of the floor. As he'd expected, that drew a pistol shot—from a powergun— though it hit the inside of the panel instead of slapping the stairwell.

"Learoyd!" Huber shouted. He crouched, swapping his

The grenade blew the door shut with a bright flash that to the naked eye would've been blue. The bomb's capacitors dumped their charge through an osmium wire. Electrical grenades had very little fragmentation effect, but their sudden energy release was both physically and mentally shattering for anybody close to the blast. Huber rose to his feet, leaped the final steps to the landing, and kicked the door open again. He went in shooting.

For the first instant he didn't have a target, just the need to disconcert anybody who hadn't lost his nerve when the grenade went off. The carpet of the sitting room beyond was on fire. A man lay in the middle of it, screaming and beating the floor with the butt of his pistol. Huber's burst stitched him from the middle of one shoulderblade to the other. The man flopped like a fish on dry land, then shuddered silent.

There was a doorway ahead of Huber and another to the right, toward the back of the building. Huber went straight, into a small foyer around the elevator shaft. The top of the cage remained just above floor level.

Huber jerked open the door across the foyer. The room beyond was a mass of flame. It'd been a bedroom, and the buzzbomb had ignited all the fabric. Huber slammed the door again. His hands were singed; and only his faceshield had saved his eyes and lungs from the fire's shriveling touch.

At the back of the foyer was a window onto the grounds; concussion from the warhead going off in the bedroom had blown out the casement an instant before it slammed the connecting door. Through the empty window, Huber heard the lift fans of an aircar spin up.

He jumped to the opening. To his right a closed car with polarized windows sat on a pad cantilevered off the back of the building, trembling as its driver built up speed in the fan blades. It was a large vehicle, capable of carrying six in comfort. The front passenger door was open and a uniformed man leaned out of it, firing a heavy slug-thrower back toward the sitting room. The aluminum skirts that propelled the osmium projectiles vaporized in the dense magnetic flux, blazing as white muzzle flashes in Huber's thermal vision.

Huber aimed between the hinge side of the car door and the jamb, then shot the guard in the neck and head. The fellow sprang forward like a headless chicken, flinging his gun away with nerveless hands.

The aircar lifted, the door swinging closed from momentum. Huber fired, starring the windscreen but not penetrating it. Deseau and Learoyd were in the doorway now, pocking the car's thick plastic side-panels; their submachine guns couldn't do real damage.

The car half-pivoted as its driver prepared to dive off the edge of the platform and use gravity to speed his escape. A buzzbomb detonated on the underside of the bow, flipping the vehicle over onto its back. The instant the warhead hit, Huber saw a spear of molten metal stab through the car's roof in a white dazzle. The driver would've been in direct line with the explosion-formed hypersonic jet.

The blast rocked Huber away from the window, but the car had taken the direct impact and the building had protected him from the worst of the remainder. Deseau and Learoyd, running toward the vehicle when the warhead went off, bounced into the wall behind them and now lay sprawled on the deck. Learoyd had managed to hang onto his sub-machine gun; Deseau patted the tiles numbly, trying to find his again.

A man crawled out of the overturned car. The right side of his face was bloody, but Huber recognized Senator Patroklos Graciano.

beautiful woman tried to squirm out, hampered by the necklaces and jewel-glittering rings she clutched to her breasts with both hands. She wore a diaphanous shift that accentuated rather than hid her body, but on her a gunny-sack would've been provocative.

Huber aimed. She looked up at him, her elbows on the chest of her lover so freshly dead that his corpse still shuddered. A powergun bolt blew out her left eyesocket and lifted the top of her skull. Her arms straightened convulsively, scattering the jewelry across the landing platform.

Major Steuben stood in the doorway from the sitting room, his pistol in his delicate right hand. His faceshield was raised and he was smiling.

The girl still in the car was probably a maid. She opened her mouth to scream when she saw her mistress die. The second pistol bolt snapped between her perfect teeth and nearly decapitated her. Her body thrashed wildly in the passenger compartment.

Learoyd was getting to his feet. Steuben grabbed the collar of Deseau's clamshell armor and jerked the sergeant upright; the major must have muscles like steel cables under his trim exterior. The muzzle of the powergun in his other hand was a white-hot circle.

He turned toward Huber, looking out of the adjacent window, and shouted, "Come along, Lieutenant. We've taken care of our little problem and it's time to leave now."

Huber met them in the sitting room. Steuben waved him toward the stairwell. Sergeant Deseau still walked like a drunk, so Huber grabbed his arm in a fireman's carry and half-lifted, half-dragged the man to the trucks. Every floor of the building was burning. The major was the last man out.

In all the cacophony—the screams and the blasts and the weeping desperation—that Arne Huber had heard in the past few minutes, there was only one sound that would haunt his future nightmares. That was Joachim Steuben's laughter as he blew a girl's head off.

✧　　✧　　✧

If I buy the farm here on Plattner's World, Huber thought as he walked toward the open door of Major Steuben's office, *they're going to have to name this the Lieutenant Arne C. Huber Memorial Hallway.*

There's never a bad time for humor in a war zone. This was a better time than most.

"Come in and close the door, Lieutenant," Steuben said as Huber raised his hand to knock on the jamb. "And *don't,* if you please, attempt to salute me ever again. You're not very good at it."

Huber obeyed meekly. The major was working behind a live display, entering data on the touchpad lying on his wooden desk. It wasn't a game this time: Steuben was finishing a task before he got on to the business who'd just walked in his door.

He shut down the display and met Huber's eyes. He smiled; Huber didn't try to smile back.

"This will be brief, Lieutenant," Steuben said. "The United Cities are in a state of war with Solace, or will be when the Senate meets in a few hours. There's been a second attack within UC territory by mercenaries in Solace pay. This one was directed against Senator Patroklos Graciano here in Benjamin."

Steuben quirked a smile. "It was quite a horrific scene, according to reports of the event," he went on. "Graciano and his whole household were killed."

Huber looked at the man across the desk, remembering the same smile lighted by the flash of a powergun. "If I may ask, sir?" he said. "Why did the, ah, mercenaries attack the particular senator?"

"It's believed that the Solace authorities had made an

I wonder how many of the senators believe the official story, Huber thought, *and how many are afraid they'll go the same way as Patroklos Graciano if they continue to get in the way of the Regiment's contract?*

Well, it didn't really matter. Like he'd told Major Steuben last night, he wasn't a politician. Aloud he said, "I see, sir."

"None of that matters to you, of course," Steuben continued. "I called you here to say that a review of your actions at Rhodesville the day you landed has determined that you behaved properly and in accordance with the best traditions of the Regiment."

He giggled. "You may even get a medal out of it, Lieutenant."

Huber's mouth was dry; for a moment he didn't trust himself to speak. Then he said, "Ah, sir? Does this mean that I'm being returned to my platoon?"

Steuben looked up at Huber. He smiled. "Well, Lieutenant," he said, "that's the reason I called you here in person instead of just informing you of the investigation outcome through channels. How would you like a transfer to A Company? You'd stay at the same rank, but you probably know already that the pay in A Company is better than the same grade levels in line units."

"A Company?" Huber repeated. He couldn't have heard right. "The White Mice, you mean?"

"Yes, Lieutenant," Steuben said. His face didn't change in a definable way, but his smile was suddenly very hard. "The White Mice. The company under my personal command."

"I don't . . ." Huber said, then realized that among the things he didn't know was how to end the sentence he'd begun. He let his voice trail off.

"Recent events have demonstrated that you're smart and that you're willing to use your initiative," the major said. His fingers were tented before him, but his wrists didn't quite rest on the touchpad beneath them.

The smile became amused again. He added, "Also, you can handle a gun. You'll have ample opportunity to exercise all these abilities in A Company, I assure you."

"Sir . . ." said Huber's lips. He was watching from outside himself again. "I don't think I have enough . . ."

This time he stopped, not because he didn't know how to finish the sentence but because he thought of Steuben's hell-lit smile the night before. The words choked in his throat.

"Ruthlessness, you were perhaps going to say, Lieutenant?" the major said with his cat's-tongue lilt. "Oh, I think you'll do. I'm a good judge of that sort of thing, you know."

He giggled again. "You're dismissed for now," Steuben said. "Go back to Logistics—you'll have to break in your replacement no matter what you decide. But rest assured, you'll be hearing from me again."

Arne Huber's soul watched his body walking back down the hallway. Even his mind was numb, and despite the closed door behind him he continued to hear laughter.